A Siren by Thomas Adolphus Trollope

Thomas Adolphus Trollope was born on the April 29th, 1810 in Bloomsbury, London.

He was the eldest son to the barrister, Thomas Anthony and writer Frances Milton (middle names are crucial as there are many writers in the Trollope family) and is the older brother to Anthony Trollope.

Thomas had a fine education at Harrow and Winchester College prior to studying at Oxford University.

There followed a brief spell teaching at a Birmingham Grammar school. But for him other horizons were soon to beckon.

A great traveller and explorer his first book, A Summer in Brittany, was published in 1840, it was to be the beginning of a long and prolific career.

His mother, the well-known and highly regarded, especially for her novels that took on social injustice, Frances Milton Trollope, now offered him a writing partnership. Writing books was a profession she had taken up due to the necessity of earning money following the disintegration of a Utopian community in the United States that she had taken the family to and her husband's continual financial misfortune.

Her husband had died in 1838 and she was now intent of moving forward on new works and in a new country.

She moved with Thomas to Florence. Their partnership soon proved successful as Thomas was a historian, traveller, scholar and researcher as well as being a writer and his mother already had a reputation as a writer.

Whilst there, Thomas was introduced too, and soon married, a guest of his mother's, the English poet and writer, Theodosia Garrow, who also wrote and supported Italian Nationalism.

Theodosia's inheritance and Trollope's earnings allowed them to create a beautiful home in Florence, the Villino Trollope, where numerous British literary figures visited and stayed and became a centre for expats from George Eliot to Elizabeth and Robert Browning. The library there was said to contain 5,000 volumes.

In March 1853, a daughter, Beatrice, was born to them.

Whilst overshadowed by his brother Anthony's literary success, many noted a striking resemblance in style and physical appearance of the two as well as in their literary works. And one trait that was common to all the Trollope's was their output. Thomas alone was responsible for sixty volumes during his career. Although not of the first rank as an author he was nonetheless respected and thorough in his research and workings.

Anthony was always full of praise for his brother and the two remained close with their mother, Frances Milton, who died in 1863, the authoress of over 100 volumes.

Tragically Theodosia was to die only two years later in 1865. Personally these were times of great distress for Thomas.

Thomas did however, marry again, and to another writer, Frances Eleanor, (née Ternan) and, despite an age gap of twenty five years, they set up a similarly beautiful home and centre for literary socialising and expats but this time in Rome.

Thomas was a versatile writer whose works often featured Italy whether it be its history, locations or characters, and were strong literary accomplishments although he himself was modest about his literary talents.

In 1890 he and Frances retired to Devon where he wrote three volumes of his autobiography.

Thomas Adolphus Trollope died on November 11th, 1892 while visiting Bristol and had said to his wife: "Where I fall let me lie."

This she did and he was buried in Arnos Vale Cemetery.

Index of Contents

BOOK I

Ash Wednesday Morning

CHAPTER I

The Last Night of Carnival

It was Carnival time in the ancient and once imperial, but now provincial and remote, city of Ravenna. It was Carnival time, and the very acme and high-tide of that season of mirth and revel. For the theory of Carnival observance is, that the life of it, unlike that of most other things and beings, is intensified with a constantly crescendo movement up to the last minutes of its existence. And there now remained but an hour before midnight on the Tuesday preceding the first day of Lent, Ash Wednesday—Dies Cinerum!—that sad and sober morrow which has brought with it "sermons and soda-water" to so many generations of revellers.

Of course Carnival, according to the Calendar and Time's hour-glass, is over at twelve o'clock on the night of Shrove Tuesday. Generally, however, in the pleasure-loving cities of Italy, a few hours' law are allowed or winked at. The revellers are not supposed to become aware that it is past midnight till about three or four in the morning.

Very generally the wind-up of the season of fun and frolic consists of what is called a "Veglione," or "great making a night of it," which means a masked ball at the theatre. And the great central chandelier does not begin to descend into the body of the house, to have its lights flapped out by the handkerchiefs of the revellers amid a last frantic rondo, till some four hours after midnight. But in provincial Ravenna, a Pope's city under the rule of a Cardinal Legate, there is—or was in the days when the Pope held sway there—no Veglione. Its place was supplied, as far as "the society" of the city was concerned, by a ball at the "Circolo dei Nobili."

It was not, therefore, till four o'clock in the morning, or perhaps even a little later, that the lights would be extinguished on the night in question at the "Circolo dei Nobili," and Carnival would, in truth, be over, and the tired holiday-makers would go home to their beds.

A few hours more remained, and the revelry was at its height, and the dancers danced as knowing that their minutes were numbered.

There had been a ball on the previous night at the Palazzo of the Marchese Lamberto di Castelmare. But the scene at the Circolo was a much more brilliant, animated, and varied one than that of the night before at the Castelmare palace. The Marchese Lamberto was the wealthiest noble in Ravenna, and—putting aside his friend the Cardinal Legate—was, in many other respects, the first and foremost man of the city. He was a bachelor of some fifty years old. And bachelors' houses and bachelors' balls have the reputation of enjoying the privilege of a somewhat freer and more unreserved gaiety and jollity than those of their neighbours more heavily weighted with the cares and responsibilities of life. But such was not the case at the Palazzo Castelmare. Presided over on such occasions as that of the great annual Carnival ball by a widowed sister-in-law of the Marchese, the Castelmare palace was the most decorous and respectable house, as its master was the most decorous and respectable man, in Ravenna.

Not that it was a dull house. The Marchese Lamberto, though a grave and dignified personage in the eyes of the "jeunesse doree" of Ravenna, was looked up to as one of the best loved, as well as most respected, men in the city. And there was not a member of the "society" who would not have been sadly hurt at not being invited to the great annual Carnival ball at the Castelmare palace. But the same degree of laissez aller jollity would not have been "de mise" there as was permissible at the Circolo. The fun was not so fast and furious as it was wont to be at the club of the nobles on the last night of Carnival.

The whole society were at the latter gathering. All the nobles of Ravenna were the hosts, and everybody was there solely and entirely to amuse and enjoy themselves. Host and guests, indeed, were almost identical. There were but few persons present, and those strangers to the town, who did not belong to their own class.

To the Marchese, on the previous night, most of the company had contented themselves with going in "domino." At the Circolo ball a very large proportion of the dancers were in costume. The Conte Leandro Lombardoni, lady-killer, Don Juan, and poet, whose fortunes and misfortunes in these characters had made him the butt of the entire society, and had perhaps contributed, together with his well-known extraordinarily pronounced propensity for cramming himself with pastry, to give him the pale, puffed, pasty face, swelling around a pair of pale fish-like eyes, that distinguished him, the Conte Leandro Lombardoni; indeed, had gone to the Castelmare palace as "Apollo," in a costume which young Ludovico Castelmare, the Marchese Lamberto's nephew, would insist on mistaking for that of Aesop; and had now, according to a programme perfectly well known previously throughout the city, come to the Circolo as "Dante." The Tuscan "lucco," or long flowing gown, had at least the advantage of concealing from the public eye much that the Apollo costume had injudiciously exhibited.

Ludovico Castelmare had adopted the costume of a Venetian noble of the sixteenth century; and very strikingly handsome he looked in that most picturesque of all dresses. The Marchese Lamberto was at the ball, of course, but not in costume. Perhaps the most striking figure in the rooms, however, was one of those few persons who have been mentioned as present, but not belonging to Ravenna, or to the class of its nobles. This was a lady, well known at that day throughout Italy as Bianca Lalli—"La Lalli," or "La Bianca," in theatrical parlance—for she was one of the first singers of the day. Special circumstances—to be explained at a future page—had rendered it possible for remote little Ravenna to secure the celebrated artist for the Carnival, which was now expiring. The Marchese Lamberto, who, among many other avocations and occupations, all of them contributing in some way or other to the welfare and advantage of his native city, was a great lover and connoisseur of music, and patron of the theatre, had been mainly instrumental in bringing La Lalli to Ravenna. The engagement had been a most successful one. The "Diva Bianca" had sung through the Carnival, charming all ears and hearts in Ravenna with her voice, and all eyes with her very remarkable and fascinating beauty. And now, on this last night of the festive season, she was the cynosure of all eyes at the ball.

Bianca had, as it so happened, also chosen a Venetian costume of the same period as that of Ludovico—about the middle of the sixteenth century. In truth, it was mere chance that had led to this similarity. And neither of them, as it happened, had mentioned to the other the dress they intended to wear. Bianca, in fact, used as she was to wear costumes of all sorts, and to outshine all beauties near her in all or any of them, had thought nothing about her dress, till the evening before; and then had consulted the Marchese Lamberto on the subject: but had been so much occupied with him during nearly the whole of that evening at his ball, that she had not said a word about it to any one else.

It could not but seem, however, to everybody that the Marchese Ludovico and La Lalli had agreed together to represent a pair belonging to the most gorgeous and picturesque days of Venetian history. And a most magnificently handsome pair they made. Bianca's dress, or at least the general appearance and effect of it, will readily be imagined by those acquainted with the full-length portraits of Titian or Tintoretto. A more strictly "proper" costume no lady could wish to wear. And the jeunesse doree of Ravenna, who had thought it likely that the Diva would appear as some light-skirted Flora, or high-kirtled Diana, were altogether disappointed.

But there was much joking and raillery about the evident and notable pair-ship of Ludovico and Bianca; and it came to pass that, almost without any special intention on their own part, they were thrown much together, and danced together frequently. And this, under the circumstances, was still more the case than it would have otherwise been, in consequence of the Marchese Lamberto not dancing. It was a long time since he had done so. There were many men dancing less fitted than he, as far as appearance and capability, and even as far as years went, to join in such amusements. Nevertheless, all Ravenna would have been almost as much surprised to see the Marchese Lamberto dressed in mumming costume, and making one among Carnival revellers, as to see the Cardinal himself doing the same things. He had made for himself a social position, and a life so much apart from any such levities, that his participation in them would have seemed a monstrosity.

It may be doubted, however, whether on this occasion, at least, the dignified Marchese was satisfied with the position he had thus made for himself. It would have been too absurd and remarkable for La Bianca to have abstained from dancing and attached herself to him in the ball-room, instead of consorting with the younger folks. Of course that was entirely out of the question. But none the less for that was the evening a time of cruel suffering and martyrdom to the Marchese. Of course he believed that the adoption of so singularly similar a costume by Bianca and his nephew was the result of pre-arranged agreement. And the thought, and all that his embittered fancy built upon the thought, were making everything around him, and all the prospect of his life before him, utterly intolerable to him.

Ludovico and Bianca had been dancing together for the third time—a waltz fast and furious, which they had kept up almost incessantly till the music had ceased. Heated and breathless, he led her out of the ball-room to get some refreshment. There was a large supper-room which, on the cessation of the waltz, immediately became crowded by other couples bent on a similar errand. But there had also been established a little subsidiary buffet in a small cabinet at the furthest end of the suite of rooms, for the purpose of drawing off some of the crowd from the main supper-room. And thither Ludovico led Bianca, thinking to avoid the crush of people rushing in to the larger room.

The young Marchese—the "Marchesino," as he was often called, to distinguish him from his uncle, the Marchese Lamberto—was one of the small committee of the Circolo, who had had the management of all the arrangements for the ball; and was, accordingly, well aware of the whereabouts of this little "succursale" to the supper-room. But it is probable that the existence of it was unknown to the great majority of the company. At all events, so it happened, that when Ludovico and Bianca reached it, it was wholly untenanted, save by Dante, in his long red gown, solitarily occupied in cramming himself with pastry.

"What, Dante in exile!" cried Ludovico. "Pray, Sir Poet, which bolgia was set apart for those who are lost by the 'peccato della gola?' or is a bilious fit in the more immediate future bolgia fearful enough?"

"It is not so bad a bolgia as that appointed some other sins," said the Conte Leandro, with mouth stuffed with cake, as he moved out of room.

"What an animal it is!" said Ludovico, laughing, as he gave Bianca a glass of champagne, and filled another for himself.

"Take some of this woodcock pie, Signora Bianca? You must be starved by this time; and I can recommend it."

"How so? You have not tasted it yourself yet."

"No; but I am going to do so. And my recommendation is based on my knowledge of the qualities of our woodcocks. They are the finest in the world. The marshes in the neighbourhood of the Pineta breed them in immense quantities."

"Oh, I have heard so much of the Pineta. They say it is so lovely."

"The most beautiful forest in the world. And this is just the time when it is in its greatest beauty, the early spring, when the wild flowers are all beginning to blossom, and the birds are all singing. There is nothing like our Pineta!"

"I should so like to see it. It does seem really a shame to leave Ravenna without ever having seen the Pineta."

"Oh, you must not dream of doing so. You must make a little excursion one of these fine spring days. It is just the time for it. Some morning, the earlier the better. But I dare say your habits are not very matutinal, Signora?"

"Well, not very, for the most part. But I would willingly make them matutinal for such a purpose at any time. How far is it?"

"Oh, a mere nothing—at the city gates almost a couple of miles, perhaps. You may go out by the Porta Nuova, at the end of the Corso, and so to that part of the forest which lies to the southward of the city; or by the northern road, which very soon enters the wood on that side. Perhaps the finest part of the Pineta is that to the southwards. Of all places in the world it is the spot for a colazione al fresco."

"I should so like it. I have heard of the Pineta di Ravenna all my life."

"What do you say to going this very morning?" said Ludovico, after thinking for a minute. "There is no time like the present. It will be a charming finish to our Carnival—new and original, too! Do you feel as if you had go enough left for it?"

"Oh, as for that," said Bianca, laughing with lips and eyes, "I am up to anything. I should like it of all things. But—"

"Ah! what a terrible word that 'but' is. But what?" said Ludovico, who had no sooner conceived the idea than he became eager to put it into execution. "But what?"

"But—a great many things. Unhappily, there is no word comes oftener into one's life than that odious 'but.' But who is to go with me? I cannot go all alone by myself?"

"Oh, that's no but at all. Of course, Signora, I did not propose such an expedition to you without proposing to myself the honour of accompanying you," said Ludovico with a profound bow.

"What a scappata! I should like it of all things. But—there it comes again! 'But' the second; will not the good people say all sorts of ill-natured and absurd things?"

"Not a bit of it—in my case, Signora. Everybody knows that we have been very good friends; and that I have not been coxcomb enough to have ever hoped to be aught more to you, having been protected, as they all know, from such danger in the only way in which a man could possibly be protected from it," said Ludovico, bowing again.

"Dear me! What way is that? It might be so useful to know. Would it be equally applicable to a lady, I wonder?" said Bianca, looking at him half laughingly, half-poutingly, with her head on one side. "Oh yes! perfectly applicable in all cases, Signora. It is only to have no heart to lose, having lost it already," returned he.

"Oh, come! This is a confidence dans les regles! And in return for it, Signor Ludovico, do you know—speaking in all seriousness—that—if we really do put this wild scheme into execution—I have a confidence to give you, and may take that opportunity of making it—a confidence, not which may or may not be made, like yours, but which I ought to make to you, the necessity of making which furnishes, to say the truth, a very plausible reason for our projected tete-a-tete."

"Davvero, Signora! Better and better; I shall be charmed to receive such a mark of your friendship," said Ludovico, thinking and caring little on what subject it might be that the Diva purposed speaking to him: "and then, the fact is," he continued, "that to-morrow morning will be the best morning for the purpose of all the days of the year. For we shall be quite sure that every soul here will be in bed and asleep. On the first morning in Lent one is tolerably safe not to fall in with early risers. Our little trip, you may be very sure, will never be heard of by anybody, unless we choose to tell of it ourselves."

"And I am sure that I do not see why we should not," said Bianca.

"I see no reason against telling all the town, for my part," rejoined Ludovico; "afterwards though—you understand; and not beforehand, or our little escapade would be spoilt by some blockhead or other insisting on joining us. Our friend Leandro there, for instance; think of it!"

"The idea is a nightmare! No; we will not say a word till afterwards. 'Tis the most charming notion for a finale to a Carnival that ever was conceived. I make you my compliments on it, Signor Ludovico."

"So, then, all the 'buts' have been butted and rebutted?" said he.

"Well, I suppose so,"—by the help of a strong desire to yield to the temptation of so pleasant a scheme, the way 'buts' generally are answered. "But we cannot go on the expedition as we are, I suppose?" said she.

"I don't see why not. I dare say the old pines have seen similar figures beneath them before now. But you would not be comfortable without changing your dress, and the mornings are still sharp. This is how it must be. I will slip away before long, and make all preparation necessary. I will get a bagarino and a pony—not from the Castelmare stables, you understand, but from a man I know and can trust—and I will come with it to the door of your lodging at six o'clock. You will stay at the ball till the end. Everybody will go by four o'clock, or soon after. That will give you plenty of time to change your dress. By six o'clock every soul in Ravenna will be fast asleep. We shall drive to a little farm-house I know on the border of the forest, leave our bagarino there, and have our stroll under the trees just as long and as far as is agreeable to you. Won't that do?"

"Perfect! I shall enjoy it amazingly. I will be sure to be ready when you come at six o'clock."

"I will be there at six or thereabouts. Now we will go back to the ball-room; but don't dance till you have not a leg left to stand on. We must have a good long stroll in the Pineta."

"Lascia fare a me! I dare say I shan't dance another dance—unless, indeed, we have one more turn together before you go. Is there time?"

"Oh yes, for that plenty of time. If you are not afraid of tiring yourself, one more last dance by all means."

So giving her his arm, the Marchesino led his beautiful and fascinating companion back to the ballroom, where the music was again making the most of the time with another waltz.

CHAPTER II

Apollo Vindex

The Conte Leandro Lombardoni had not passed a pleasant Carnival. Reconciled, as he had recently professed himself to be—after some one of the frequent misfortunes that happened to his intercourse with them—with the fair sex, he had begun his Carnival by attempting to make his merit acceptable in the eyes of La Lalli; and had failed to obtain any recognition from her, even as a poet, to say nothing of his pretensions as a Don Juan. To a certain limited degree, it had been forced upon his perception, that he had been making an ass of himself; and the appreciation of that fact by the other young men among whom he lived had been indicated with that coarse brutality, as the poet said to himself, which was the outcome of minds not "softened by the study of the ingenuous arts," as his own was. He had been consistently snubbed and flouted, he and his poetry, and his love-making, and his carefully prepared Carnival costumes.

The result was, that at the ball on that last night of the Carnival, the Conte Leandro was not in charity with all men, and, indeed, hardly with any man. He was feeling very sore, and would fain have avenged his pain by making any one else feel equally sore, if he had it in his power to do so.

He was especially angry with Ludovico di Castelmare. Had he not chaffed him unmercifully about the verses he had sent to La Bianca? Was it not, to all appearance, due to him that the Diva had never condescended to cast a glance on either him or his poetry? Had he not called him Aesop, when it was plain to all the world that he represented Apollo? And now this night, again, he had taken the opportunity of turning him into ridicule in the presence of La Bianca; and he and she had spoken of the possibility of their being troubled with his company as of a nightmare. For the painful fact was that their uncomplimentary expressions had been heard by the poet; who, when he had left Ludovico and Bianca in the little supper-room together, had retreated no further than just to the other side of a curtain, which hung, Italian fashion, by the side of the open door. Finding that there was nobody there—for the little buffet was at the end of the entire suite of rooms, and all those who were not either in the ball-room, or in the card-room, were at that moment in the principal supper-room—it had seemed well to the Conte Leandro, in his dudgeon and spite against all the world, to ensconce himself quietly behind the curtain, and hear what use Ludovico and Bianca would make of their tete-a-tete.

The first advantage he obtained was to hear himself spoken of as a nightmare; and that naturally prompted him to prick up his ears to hear more. But when he had thus learned the whole secret of the projected expedition, it struck him, as well worth considering, whether there might not be found in this the means of making his tormentor pay him for some of the annoyances he had suffered at his hands.

So! the Marchese Ludovico, who ought to be paying his addresses to the Contessa Violante in the sight of all Ravenna—the Contessa Violante Marliani was great niece of the Cardinal Legate, between whom and the Marchese Ludovico their respective families had projected an alliance—was, instead of that, going off on a partie fine with the notorious Bianca Lalli! A tete-a-tete in the Pineta! Mighty fine, indeed! So sure, too, that nobody in the world would find them out on Ash Wednesday morning! And he is to be at her door at six o'clock in the morning! Very good! Capitally well arranged—were it not that Leandro Lombardoni may perhaps think fit to put a spoke in the wheel.

A little further consideration of the manner in which such spoke might be most effectually supplied, decided the angry and malicious poet—(poets, like women, will become malicious when scorned)—to seek out the Marchese Lamberto, whom he thought he should probably find in the card-room. For though the Marchese was no great card-player, and never touched a card in his own house, he was wont, at the Circolo, on such occasions as the present, to cast in his lot with those who so consoled themselves for the years that made the ball-room no longer their proper territory.

But the Conte Leandro did not find the Marchese among the card-players.

The events of the evening had already thrown him back again into a very miserable state of mind, from which the Marchese had been suffering such torments as the jealous only know, during all the latter half of the Carnival. It was strange that such a man as the Marchese Lamberto—it would have seemed passing strange to any of those his fellow-citizens who had known him, thoroughly as they supposed, all his life; very strange that such a man, so calm, so judicious, so little liable to the gusts of passion of any sort; a man, the even tenor of whose well-regulated life had ever been such as to expose him rather to the charge of almost apathetic placidity of temper, should thus suddenly, in the full meridian time of his mature years, become subject to such violent oscillations of passion; to such buffetings by storms, blowing now from one and now from the opposite quarter of the sky. But no length of prosperous navigation in the quiet waters of a land-locked harbour will give evidence of the vessel's fitness to encounter the storms and the waves of the open sea. The storm-wind of a strong passion had, all at once for the first time, blown in upon the sheltered harbour in which that placid life had been led.

And yet that storm-wind did not produce the same effect, as it would have produced, and is seen to produce every day on the strong, wide-spread canvas of some young navigator on the ocean of life, putting out into the open waters at the time when such storms are frequent. Every day we see such craft scudding with all sails spread before the blast without attempt at reefing or tacking. Right ahead they drive before the wind with no doubtful course. But it was not and could not be so in the case of the Marchese Lamberto. The whole habits of a life—the ways, notions, hopes, desires, ambitions, that time had made into a part of the nature of the man; the passions, which though calm and unviolent in their nature, had become strong, not by forcible energy, but by the deep and unconscious sinking of their roots into the depths of his character—all these things opposed a resistance to the new and suddenly-loosed passion-wind, such as that which the deep-rooted oak opposes to the tempest with no result of conquering it, only with the result of causing its own leaves and branches to be buffeted to and fro, torn, broken, and wrecked.

Thus it was that the unhappy Marchese was violently driven to and fro from hour to hour between the extremities of love and hate, till his brain reeled in the terrible conflict; and alternate attraction and repulsion bandied his soul backwards and forwards between them.

A ball-room is not a pleasant exercise-ground for a jealous man who does not dance. No "bolgia" of the hell invented by the sombre imagination of the great poet could have surpassed, in torment, the Circolo ball-room on that last Carnival night to the Marchese Lamberto.

The sight of the sorceress who had bewitched him, as he watched her in the dance, had once again scattered to the winds all resolution, all hope of the possibility of escaping from the toils. What was all else that he desired to be put in comparison with that raging, craving desire that he felt and sickened with for her? That was what he really wanted—what he must have or die. It was madness to see her, as he saw her then, in the arms of other men, laughing, sparkling, brilliant with animation and enjoyment. Worst hell of all to see her thus with his nephew, her admiration for whom she had frankly confessed; whose ways with women he knew, and whose intimacy with Bianca had already become suspicious to him.

Yet not the less did he stand and gaze, as they danced together, clearly the handsomest and best-matched couple in the room—matched so admirably evidently by design and forethought.

He had seen Ludovico and Bianca leave the ball-room, after the last dance, together with the crowd of most of those who had been joining in it, and had begun fluttering, poor moth, after the irresistible attraction, to follow them towards the supper-room. Missing sight of them in the throng for a minute, he had followed on to the principal supper-room, and not finding them there (for the reason the reader wots of) had returned on his steps, and was sitting on the end of a divan, by the door of the next room to the ball-room, through which all had to pass who wished to go thence to the supper-room. There were people passing through the centre of the room from door to door; but there was no other, save the Marchese, sitting down in it.

There the Conte Leandro found him, and came and sat down by his side; much, at first, to the Marchese's annoyance.

"What! you not in the supper-room, Signor Leandro. I thought your place was always there?" said the Marchese.

"I'm no greater a supper-eater than another; let them say what they please. But I have just been getting a glass of wine and a biscuit in the little supper-room at the further end there."

"What, are there two supper-rooms? I did not know that!"

"Only a buffet in the little room at the end, where the papers generally are. It was mainly Ludovico's doing, in order to have less crowd in the supper-room, and perhaps to have a quiet place for a tete-a-tete supper himself. Oh! I knew better than not to clear out, when he and La Diva Bianca came in; specially as there was nobody else there. Faith! I left them there alone together."

"Oh! that's where he is supping, then?" said the Marchese, in the most unconcerned tone he could manage.

"Yes; supping, or enjoying himself in some other way, quite as delightful. The fact is, Signor Marchese," continued the poet, in a lowered voice, and rapidly glancing around to see that there were no ears within such a distance as to overhear his words, "the fact is, that I am afraid Signor Ludovico is less cautious than it would be well for him to be, circumstanced as he is! I am sure I did not want to listen to what he and the Lalli were saying to each other. It is nothing to me. But they spoke with such little precaution, that I could not help overhearing what they said; and what do you think Ludovico is up to now?"

"How should I know!" said the Marchese, with the tips of his pale lips; for he was grinding his teeth together to prevent them from chattering in his head.

"He is off at six o'clock to-morrow morning tete-a-tete with La Bianca, on an excursion to the Pineta. Coming it strong, isn't it?"

"To-morrow morning!" said the Marchese under his breath, and with difficulty; for his blood seemed suddenly to rush back cold to his heart, and he was shivering all over.

"Niente meno! I heard them arrange it all. He is to slip away from the ball presently, in order to make all needful preparations, and to be at her door with a bagarino at six o'clock in the morning. Doing the thing nicely, isn't it?"

For a minute or two the Marchese was utterly unable to answer him a word. His head swam round. He felt sick. A cold perspiration broke out all over him; and he feared that he should have fallen from his seat.

"He is a great fool for his pains," he said at last, mastering himself by a great effort, sufficiently to enable himself to utter the words in an ordinary voice and manner.

"Well, it seemed to me a mad scheme, considering all things. And the truth is, that I thought your lordship would very likely think it well to put a stop to it. And that is why I have bored your lordship by mentioning it to you."

"At six o'clock, you say?" asked the Marchese.

"Yes; that was the hour they fixed. Then he is to drive her to a farm-house on the border of the forest, leave the bagarino there, and go into the wood for a stroll. Not a bad idea for a wind-up of the Carnival, upon my word!"

"I think you have done very wisely and kindly in telling me this, Signor Conte," said the Marchese, in as quiet tones as he could command; "and if you will complete your kindness by saying no word of it to anybody else, I shall esteem myself much obliged to you."

"Oh! for that you may depend on me, Signor Marchese. I should never have thought of mentioning it to you, but for thinking that it would be a real kindness to Ludovico to put a stop to it."

"Thanks, Signor Conte. A rivederla!" said the Marchese, rising.

"Felicissima notte, Signor Marchese," returned Leandro, rising also, and bowing to his companion.

CHAPTER III

St. Apollinare in Classe

The Marchese remained at the ball to see one more dance between Ludovico and Bianca after their supper; and then left the rooms. There was nothing at all to cause remark in his thus retiring before the evening. He never danced;—he happened not to be playing cards on that evening. It was quite natural that such a man should prefer going home to bed to remaining with the jeunes gens till the break-up of the ball.

How he enjoyed that last dance, which he stayed to see, the reader may perhaps imagine. Standing by a chimney-piece, on one corner of which he rested his elbow, he in great measure shaded his face with his hand, yet not so as to prevent him from seeing every movement of the persons, and every expression of the faces of the couple he was watching. There was a raging hell in his heart. And yet he stood there, and gazed eagerly, greedily one would have said. And every minute, and every movement blasted his eyes and stabbed his heart, and poured poison into his veins.

When the dance was over he did not move for some time; for he doubted his power to hold himself upright and walk steadily. Presently, however, when Ludovico and Bianca had again quitted the ball-room together, he gathered himself up, and moved slowly away, shaking in every limb, pale, fever-lipped, and haggard.

The man who gave him his cloak in the ante-room remarked to another servant, as soon as he was gone, that he would bet that the Marchese Lamberto would not be at the next Carnival ball.

At six o'clock, with wonderful punctuality for an Italian, Ludovico, with a neat little bagarino and fast-trotting pony, was at the door of the Diva's lodging. But Bianca was not ready. Her maid came down to the door with all sorts of apologies, and assurances that her mistress would be ready in a few minutes. The few minutes, however, became half an hour, as minutes will under such circumstances. And the result of this delay was that Ludovico and his companion were not the first travellers out of the Porta Nuova that morning.

During the whole of the past Carnival and the latter months of the previous year there had been living in Ravenna a young girl, an artist from Venice, who had come to Ravenna with a commission given her by a travelling Englishman to make copies of some of the more remarkable of the very extraordinary and unique series of mosaics which exist in the old imperial city. She had brought with her a letter of introduction from her employer to the Marchese Lamberto, a circumstance which had led to a degree of intimacy between the Marchesino Ludovico and the extremely attractive young artist, which threatened to stand more or less in the way of the match which had been arranged by the high-contracting parties between Ludovico and the Lady Violante, the great niece of the Cardinal. The girl's name was Paolina Foscarelli.

It is probable that in due time and season the reader may become better acquainted with Paolina. But at present there is no need of troubling him with more particulars respecting her than the above, save to mention that, having industriously and successfully completed the greater portion of her task in the churches within the city, she had determined to make her first visit to the strange old Basilica of St. Apollinare in Classe, on that same Ash Wednesday morning. She did not purpose beginning her task there on that day; but intended merely to reconnoitre the ground, look to the needful preparations that had been made for her work, and ascertain how far the spot was within her powers of walking.

Paolina, too, had felt that the morning of Ash Wednesday was a favourable time for the first experiment of an undertaking that a little alarmed her. For she also had calculated that on such a morning she should be little likely to meet anybody. It was just about six o'clock when Paolina started on her proposed walk; and she passed through the Porta Nuova, therefore, a little more than half-an-hour before Ludovico and his companion passed, travelling in the same direction.

The road, which it was necessary for her to follow in order to reach St. Apollinare in Classe, is the same for the whole of the distance between the city and the ancient church as that which Ludovico and Bianca would follow to reach the celebrated pine forest. The soil on which the forest stands is composed of the accumulation of sand which the rivers—mainly the Po—have brought from distant mountains, and deposited in the bed of the Adriatic since the old church was built "in Classe,"—where the fleet once used to be moored. The building thus stands nearly at the edge of the forest, hardly more than a stone's throw from the furthest advanced sentinels of the wood. The road coming out from the city by the Porta Nuova, on its way to the little town of Cervia, a few miles to the southward, traverses ground once thickly covered with palaces, streets, and churches, now open fields, and passes by the western front and doorway of the almost deserted old Basilica, a little before it reaches the turning off towards the left, which enters the forest.

The walk before Paolina, when she had passed the city gate, was about two miles or rather more. So that had La Bianca taken a few less minutes to put the finishing touches to the charming morning toilette which replaced the gorgeous Venetian costume she had taken off, the bagarino which carried her and Ludovico would infallibly have overtaken the young artist. As it was, however, having more than half-an-hour's start of it, she reached the church before they came within sight of it.

Little Paolina had felt rather nervous when first stepping into the cool fresh morning air from the door of the lodging she occupied. But the street was utterly empty, and she took courage. The first human beings she saw on her way were the octroi officers at the gate. They sat apparently half asleep at the doorway of their den, by the side of the city gate, wrapped in huge cloaks; and took not even so much heed of her as to say "Good morning."

The long bit of straight flat road outside the gate was equally deserted; and Paolina, braced by the morning air, stepped out vigorously, and began to enjoy her walk.

There is little enough, however, in the country through which she was passing to delight the eye. The fields in the immediate neighbourhood of the city are cultivated, and not devoid of trees. But the cheerfulness thence arising does not last long. Very soon the trees cease, and there are no more hedge-rows. Large flat fields, imperfectly covered with coarse rank grass, and divided by the numerous branches of streams, all more or less diked to save the land from complete inundation, succeed. The road is a causeway raised above the level of the surrounding district; and presently a huge lofty bank is seen traversing the desolate scene for miles, and stretching away towards the shore of the neighbouring Adriatic. This is the dike which contains the sulkily torpid but yet dangerous Montone.

Gradually, as the traveller proceeds, the scene grows worse and worse. Soon the only kind of cultivation to be seen from the road consists of rice-grounds, looking like—what in truth they are—poisonous swamps. Then come swamps pure and simple, too bad even to be turned into rice grounds, or rather simply swamps impure; for a stench at most times of the year comes from them, like a warning of their pestilential nature, and their unfitness for the sojourn of man. A few shaggy, wild-looking cattle may be seen wandering over the flat waste, muddy to the shoulders from wading in the soft swamps. A scene of more utter desolation it is hardly possible to meet with in such close neighbourhood to a living city.

Paolina shivered, and drew her little grey cloak more closely around her shoulders; not from cold, though a bleak wind was blowing across the marshes. She was warmed by walking; but the aspect of the scene before her almost frightened the Venetian girl by the savagery of its desolation.

The raised causeway, however, keeps on its course amid the low-lying marshes on either side of it; and presently the peculiar form of outline belonging to a forest composed entirely of the maritime pine is distinguishable on the horizon to the left. The road quickly draws nearer to it; and the large, heavy, velvet-like masses of dark verdure become visible. In a forest such as the famous Pineta, consisting of the maritime pine only, the lines, especially when seen at a distance, have more of horizontal and less of perpendicular direction than in any other assemblage of trees. And the effect produced by the continuity of spreading umbrella-like tops is peculiar.

Then, soon after the forest has become visible, the road brings the wayfarer within sight of a vast lonely structure heaving its huge long back against the low horizon, like some monster antidiluvian saurian, the fit denizen of this marsh world. It is the venerable Basilica of St. Apollinare in Classe.

Through all this dismal scene Paolina tripped lightly along with a quick step through the crisp morning air, no little awed by the dreary, voiceless desolation of it, but yet encouraged and not unpleased by the solitude of it.

The walk she found to be quite within her powers, at all events at that hour of the morning and in that season of the year; and when she stood before the western door of the ancient church, in front of which the road passes, Ludovico and Bianca were only then on the point of starting from the quarters of the latter, in the Strada di Porta Sisi.

Though knowing but little of the long and strangely diversified story which presses on the mind of a stranger read in history as he stands before the door of that desolate old church, Paolina could not but be much struck by the appearance of the building and of the scene around it. If ever a spot was expressive in every way by which a locality can speak to the imagination of the abomination of desolation, the view which spreads before the eye at the huge doorway of the Basilica of St. Apollinare in Classe is so. The general character of the country around it has been described. But the church itself is the most dreary and melancholy feature in the landscape. No desolation resulting solely from the operations of Nature, even in her least kindly mood, can ever suffice to speak to the imagination as the change and decay of the works of man's hand speak. To produce the effect of desolation in its highest degree man must have at some former period been present on the scene, and the remains of his work must be there to show that activity, life, energy, has once existed where it exists no more. Nature is always and everywhere progressive, and no sentiment of sadness belongs to progress. Man's ruined work alone imparts the suggestion—(a delusive one, indeed, but most forcible)—of falling back from the better to the worse.

Wonderfully eloquent after this fashion are the temples of Paestum, far away there to the south beyond Naples, on the flat strip of miserably cultivated soil between the Apennines and the Mediterranean. But they are too far gone in ruin and decay to speak with so living a voice of sadness as does this old Byzantine church. The human element is at Paestum too far away, too utterly dead and forgotten. In St. Apollinare life still lingers. Life, flickering in its last spark, like the twinkling of a lamp which the next moment will extinguish, is still there. Life more suggestive of death, than any utter absence of life could be.

There are some dilapidated remains of conventual buildings on the southern side of the church, mean, and of a date some thousand years subsequent to that of the Basilica. They are nearly ruinous, but are still—or were till within a few years—inhabited by one Capucin friar, and one lay brother of the order, whose duty it was to mutter a mass, with ague-chattering jaws, at the high altar, and act as guardians of the building.

Small guardianship is needed. The huge ancient doors—made of planks from vine trunks which grew fifteen hundred years ago on the Bosphorus—are never closed; probably because their weight would defy the efforts of the two poor old friars, to whom the keeping of the building is committed, to move them. But a poor and mean low gate of iron rails has been fitted to the colossal marble door-posts, which suffices to prevent the wandering cattle of the waste from straying into the church, but does not prevent the fever-laden mists from the marshes from drifting into the huge nave, and depositing their unwholesome moisture in great trickling drops upon the green-stained walls.

But not even the low iron gateway was closed when Paolina reached the church. It stood partially open. After having stood a minute or two before the building to look round upon the scene, Paolina stepped up to the gate and looked into the church, but could see no human being. Within, as without, all was utter death-like silence. She shivered, and drew her cloak more closely round her, as she stood at the gate; for the healthy blood was running rapidly through her veins after her brisk walk, and the deadly cold damp air from the church struck her with a shudder, which was but the physical complement of the moral impression produced by the aspect of the place.

After a minute, however, wondering at the stillness, half frightened at the utter solitude, and awed by the vast gloomy grandeur of the naked but venerable building, she pushed the gate, and entered.

CHAPTER IV

Father Fabiano

Paolina entered hesitatingly, and starting at the echoes of her footsteps on the flagstones, wet and green, and slimy from the water, which often in every year lies many inches deep on the floor of the church. She advanced towards a small marble altar which stands quite isolated in the middle of the huge nave. And as she neared it she perceived, with a violent start, that there was a living figure kneeling at it. So still, so utterly motionless had this solitary worshipper been, so little visible in the dim light was the hue of the Franciscan's frock that entirely covered him, that Paolina had not imagined that there had been any living creature in the church. She saw, however, in the same instant that she became aware of his presence, that the figure was that of a Capucin friar, and doubted not that he must be the guardian of the church, whom she had been told she would find there.

The little low altar, of an antiquity coeval with that of the church, which stands in the centre of the nave, is the sole exception to the entire and utter emptiness of the place. There are, indeed, ranged along the walls of the side aisles, several ancient marble coffins, curiously carved, and with semi-circular covers, which contain the bodies of the earliest Bishops of the See. But the little altar is the sole object that breaks the continuity of the open floor. The body of St. Apollinare was originally laid beneath it, but was in a subsequent age removed to a more specially honourable position under the high altar at the eastern end of the church. There is still, however, the slab deeply carved with letters of ancient form, which tells how St. Romuald, the founder of the order of Camaldoli, praying by night at that altar, saw in a vision St. Apollinare, who bade him leave the world, and become the founder of an order of hermits.

It was on the same stones that the knees of St. Romuald had pressed, that the Capucin was kneeling, as Paolina walked up the nave of the church. The peaked hood of his brown frock was drawn over his head, for the air of the church was deadly cold, and the fever and ague of many a successive autumn had done their work upon him. He was called Padre Fabiano, and was said to be, and looked to be, upwards of eighty years old. Probably, however, his age was much short of that. For the nature of his dwelling-place was such as to stand in the place of time, in its power to do worse than time's work on the human frame.

Of course, it can be no matter of question, why a monk is here or is there, does this or does that. Obedience to the will of his superiors is the only reason for all that, in the case of other human beings, depends on their own volition. The monk has no volition.

No human being who had, it might be supposed, would consent to live at St. Apollinare in Classe, with one lay brother for a companion, and discharge the duties assigned to the Padre Fabiano. But the question why his superiors sent him there, was still one that might suggest itself, though it was little likely ever to be answered. And the absence of all answer to such question was supplied by the gossips of Ravenna, by tales of some terrible crime against ecclesiastical discipline of which the Padre Fabiano had been guilty some sixty years or so ago. Certain it was that he had occupied his dreary position for many years; and it was wonderful that fever and ague and the marsh pestilence had not long since dismissed him to the reward of his long penitence on earth.

He rose from his knees as Paolina approached him, and gravely bent his cowled head to her in salutation.

"You are early, Signora," he said. "I suppose you are the person for whom yonder scaffold has been prepared."

"Yes, father, I am the artist for whom leave has been obtained to copy some of your mosaics."

"You will find it cold work, daughter. The church is damp somewhat. You would do better, methinks, not to begin your day's work till the sun has had time to warm the air a little."

"I had no thought, father, of beginning to-day. I have brought nothing with me. I only thought that I would walk out and have a look at the job before me. It is not so far from the city as I thought."

"It is far enough to be as lonely and as deserted as if it were a thousand miles from a human habitation," said the monk, looking into the girl's face with a grave smile.

"Yet you live here, from year's end to year's end all alone, Padre mio," said Paolina, timidly.

"Not quite so, daughter," replied he. "Brother Barnaba, a lay brother of our order, is my companion. But he is ill with a touch of ague at present."

"And how early would it be not inconvenient to you, Padre mio, to open the church for me?" asked Paolina.

"I spoke not of your being early on my account, daughter. If you come here at sunrise, you will find the gate open, and me where you found me this morning; and if you come at midnight you will find the same."

"At midnight, father!" said Paolina, with a glance of surprise and pity.

"Last October I was down with the fever," returned the monk; "but since that time I have not failed one night to be on my knees where the blessed St. Romauld knelt at the stroke of midnight. But I have not had his reward;—doubtless because I am not worthy of it."

"What was the reward of St. Romauld, father?" demanded Paolina.

"His midnight prayers were rewarded by the vision of St. Apollinare in glory, who spoke to him, and gave him the counsel he sought. Night after night, and hour after hour, have I knelt and prayed. And I have heard the moaning of the wind from the Adriatic among the pines of the forest yonder, and I have seen the great crucifix above the high altar sway and move in the moonlight when it comes streaming through the southern windows; and sometimes I have hoped—and prayed—and hoped—but no vision came!"

The old monk sighed, and dropped his head upon his bosom; and Paolina gazed at him with a feeling of awe, mingled with a suddenly rising fear, that the tall and emaciated old man, whose light-blue eyes gleamed out from beneath his cowl, was not wholly right in his mind. She would have been more alarmed had she been aware that the old Padre Fabiano of St. Apollinare was generally considered in Ravenna to be crazed by all those who did not, instead of that, deem him a saint.

Before she had gained courage to answer him, however, he lifted his head, with another deep sigh, and said, in a very quiet and ordinary tone and manner,

"Your scaffold is all prepared for you there, Signora, according to the directions of the Signor Marchese Ludovico di Castelmare, who brought with him an order from the Archbishop's Chancellor. Will you look at it, and see if it is as you wish, and say where you wish to have it placed."

The mosaics in the apse of the centre nave are the most remarkable of those that remain at St. Apollinare, though many of the series of medallion portraits of the Bishops of the See from the foundation of it, which circle the entire nave, are very curious. Paolina had engaged to copy two or three of the most remarkable of these; but she intended to begin her work by attacking the larger figures in the apse. And the scaffolding had been placed there on the southern side.

"I think that is just where I should wish to have it," said Paolina, looking up at the vault. "If I may, I will go up and see whether it is near enough to the figure I have to copy."

"Do so, my daughter. It looks a great height, but I have no doubt that it is quite safe. The Signor Marchese was very particular in seeing to it himself. See, I will go up first to give you courage."

And so saying, the old man with a slow but firm step began to ascend the ladder of the scaffolding. And when he had reached the platform at the top, Paolina, more used to such climbing than he, and who in truth had felt no alarm whatever, followed him with a lighter step.

"Yes, this will do nicely, Padre mio!" she said, when she had reached the top; "it is placed just where it should be, and this large window gives just all the light I want. It is a much better light than I had to work by in San Vitale."

"I never was in San Vitale," replied the monk. "I have been here fourteen years next Easter, and I have never once been in Ravenna in all that time, nor, indeed, further away from this church than just a stroll within the edge of the Pineta."

"That is the Pineta we see from this window, of course, Padre mio. What a lovely view of it! And how beautiful it is! Where does that road go to, Padre? To Venice?"

"No, figliuola mia. It goes in exactly the opposite direction, southwards, to Cervia. The Venice road lies away to the northward, through the wood that you can see on the furthest horizon. It was by that road I came to Ravenna. I shall never travel it again."

"From Venice, father? Did you come from Venice?" asked Paolina, eagerly.

"From La bella Venezia I came, daughter—fourteen years ago. And once in every month I indulge myself by going to the top of our tower—you can't see it from this window, it is on the northern side of the church—and looking out over the north Pineta as far as I can see towards it. May God and St. Mark grant that no tempter ever offer me the sight of Venice again at the price of my soul's salvation! I shall never, never see Venice more!"

"You must be a Venetian, father, surely, to love it so well?" said Paolina, after a minute or two of silence.

"A Venetian I am—or was, daughter; as I well knew you were when you first spoke. Might I ask your name?"

"Paolina Foscarelli, father. I am an orphan," said she, softly.

"No!" said the monk, shaking his head, with a deep sigh, and looking earnestly into the girl's face, but without any appearance of surprise, "No; you are not Paolina Foscarelli."

"Indeed, father, that is my name," said Paolina, again recurring to her doubt whether the monk was altogether of sound mind, and speaking very quietly and gently; "my father's name was Foscarelli, and the baptismal name of my mother was the same as mine—Paolina."

"Jacopo and Paolina Foscarelli, who lived in the little house at the corner of the Campo di San Pietro and Paolo," rejoined the monk, speaking in a dreamy far-away kind of manner.

"I have truly heard that they lived there," said she; "but I was only four years old when they died, one very soon after the other, and since that I have lived with a friend of my mother's, Signora Steno."

"The child of Jacopo and Paolina Foscarelli," said the monk, in the same dreamy tone, and pressing his thin emaciated hands before his eyes as he spoke; "and you have come here to find me?"

"Nay, father, not to find you. I knew not that the padre guardiano of St. Apollinare was a Venetian. I came only to copy these pictures for my employer."

"Wonderful, wonderful, wonderful are the ways of God! Paolina Foscarelli, daughter of Jacopo and Paolina, I Fabiano—"

"Look, padre min!" cried Paolina, suddenly and sharply, turning very pale, and grasping the parapet rung of the scaffolding as she spoke, "look! in the bagarino there on the road, just passing the church; certainly that must be the Signor Marchese Ludovico!—And with him—that lady?—yes, it is—it certainly is La Lalli—the prima donna, who has been singing at the theatre this Carnival."

She pointed as she spoke to a bagarino that had just passed the western front of the church, and was now moving along the bit of road visible from the high window at which the monk and Paolina were standing.

The tone in which she spoke caused the friar to look at her first, before turning his glance in the direction to which she pointed. She was pale, and evidently much moved, after a fashion that, taken together with the nature of the objects to which she drew his attention, and the fact that it was the Marchese Ludovico who had come to St. Apollinare to make the arrangements needed for the artist's work there, left but little doubt in the old man's mind as to the nature of her emotion.

He looked shrewdly and earnestly into her face for a moment; and then turning his eyes to the stretch of road below, answered her:

"Certainly, my daughter, that is the Marchese Ludovico. The lady I never saw before as far as I am aware. They are going towards Cervia."

"No! See, father! They are turning off from the road to the left. Where does that turning to the left go?"

"Only into the forest, daughter, or to that little farm-house you see there just at the edge of it. You may get as far as the sea-shore through the Pineta; but the road is very bad for a carriage."

"To the sea-shorn!" said Paolina, dreamily.

"Yes, by keeping the track due east. The shore is not above a couple of miles away. But there is no port, or even landing-place there. And there are many tracks through the forest. You may get to Cervia, too, that way. But it is hardly likely that any one would leave the road to find a longer way by worse ways through the forest. More likely the object of the Signor Marchese is only to show the lady the famous Pineta."

Paolina, while the monk was thus speaking, had kept her eyes fixed upon the little carriage, which was making its way along a by-road constructed on the top of a dike by the side of one of the numerous streams that intersect all the district; and she continued to watch it till she saw it stop at the entrance to the yard of the little farmhouse, to which the monk had called her attention. She then saw Ludovico and his companion descend from the carriage, and leave it apparently in the charge of a man, who came out from the farm-yard. And they then left the spot where they had alighted on foot, and in another minute were no longer visible from the window at which Paolina and the monk stood.

"How long a walk is it, father, from here into the wood?" asked Paolina, musingly.

"It is a very short distance, daughter. There is a footpath practicable in dry weather like this, a good deal nearer than the road we saw the bagarino follow. You might get to the edge of the Pineta in that way in less than ten minutes."

"And would it be possible to return to the city that way, instead of coming back to the road?" enquired Paolina.

"Yes; for a part of the way there is a path along the border of the wood. Then you must fall back into the road. The way lies by the gate of the farm-house."

"I think I will go back to the city now, father. This scaffold is just where it will suit me. And to-morrow, a little later perhaps than this, I hope to come and begin my work. I shall have to come in a carriage, at all events, the first time, because of bringing my things. I am so much obliged to you, father, for your kindness. And I am so glad that you are a Venetian. I little thought to find a fellow-countryman here."

"Or I to see this morning a Venetian—much less—but we will speak more of that another time—if you will permit an old man sometimes to speak to you when you are at your work?"

"Ma come—I can talk while I work. It will be a real pleasure to me to hear the dear home tongue. I will go down the ladder first. I am not the least afraid."

So Paolina left the church, and the monk stood at the yawning ever-open western door, looking after her as she took the path he had indicated to her towards the forest.

CHAPTER V

"The Hours Passed, and Still She Came Not"

There was misgiving in the heart of the old man as he stood at the door of the Basilica looking after the light little form of Paolina as she moved along the path, raised above the swamp on either side, that led towards the edge of the forest.

The rays of the sun slanting from the eastward lighted up all the path on which she was walking; and though the western front of the church was still in shade, had begun to suck up the mists, and to make the air feel at least somewhat more genial and wholesome. The monk pushed back the cowl of his frock, which had hitherto been drawn over his head, the better to watch the receding figure of the girl as she moved slowly along the path; and still, as he gazed after her, he shook his head from time to time with an uneasy sense of misgiving.

It was not that the mere fact of the girl's entering the Pineta alone seemed to him, accustomed as he was to the place and its surroundings, to involve any danger to her of any sort, beyond, indeed, the possibility of losing herself for a few hours in the forest. The whole extent of it is very frequently traversed by the men in the employment of the farmers to whom the Papal government was in the practice of letting out the right of pasturage and management of the wood. And these people were all known. There were, it is true, encroachers on these rights, who might well be less known, and less responsible persons; and possibly the forest paths might sometimes be traversed by people bound on some errand of smuggling. But nothing had ever happened of late years in the forest to suggest the probability of any danger.

It was rather the nature of Paolina's own motives for her expedition, as they were patent to the old monk, that disquieted him on her behalf. He had marked the expression of her face when she had seen the bagarino with Ludovico and his companion pass along the road towards the forest, and the change in her whole manner after that. And monk, and octogenarian as he was, he had been at no loss to comprehend the nature of the emotions which had been aroused in her mind by the sight. And he feared that evil might arise from the collision of passions, which it seemed likely were about to be brought into the presence of each other.

Perhaps, monk and aged as he was, the apprehensions with which his mind was busy seemed more big with possible evil than they might to another. Perhaps it was so long since he had had aught to do with stormy passions that the contemplation of them affrighted his stagnant mind all the more by reason of the long years of passionless placidity to which it was accustomed. Perhaps he had known passions stormy enough in the long long past, and had experience of the harvest of evils which might be expected to be produced by them.

Report said, that when Father Fabiano had been sent by his superiors to occupy the miserable and forlorn sentinel's post at the church-door of St. Apollinare, amid inundations in winter, and fever and ague in summer, his appointment to the dreary office had been of the nature of a penance and an exile. It was said, too, that the sentence of exile, which placed him in his present position, had been an alleviation of a more rigorous punishment; that he had been allowed, after a period of many years of imprisonment in a monastery of his order at Venice, to change that punishment for the duty to which he had been appointed, and which would scarcely have seemed an amelioration of destiny to any one save a man who had for years been deprived of the light of the sun and the scent of the free air. Some deed there had been in that life which had called for such monastic discipline; some outcome of human passion when the blood, that now crept slowly, while the aged monk passed the hours in waiting for visions before the altar of St. Apollinare, was running in his veins too rapidly for monastic requirements.

It was evident from the few words that he had let drop, when he became aware who the young Venetian visitor to the church under his care was, that some special circumstances caused him to feel a more than ordinary interest in her. Some connection there must have been between some portion of his life and that of some member or members of her family. Of what nature was it? Monkish tribunals, however else they may treat those subjected to them, at least keep their secrets. Frailties must be expiated; but they need not be exposed. And the true story of the fault which condemned Father Fabiano to end his days amid the swamps of St. Apollinare, as well as the precise nature of the connection which had existed between him and Paolina's parents, can be only matter of conjecture.

Paolina, as has been said, pursued her path slowly. She had tripped along much more lightly on her way from the city to St. Apollinare. And yet she was urged on by a burning anxiety to know whither Ludovico and Bianca had gone, and for what purpose they had come thither. But, despite this nervous anxiety, she stepped slowly, because her heart disapproved of the course she was taking. It seemed as if she was drawn on towards the forest by some mysterious mechanical force, which she had not the strength to resist. Again and again she had well nigh made up her mind to turn aside from the path she was following. She would go only a few steps further towards the edge of the forest. She looked out eagerly before her, standing on tip-toe on every little bit of vantage ground which the path afforded. She would only go as far as that next bend in the path. But the bend in the path disclosed a stile a little further on, from which surely a view of all the ground between the path she was on and the farmhouse at which Ludovico and his companion had descended, might be had. She would go so far and no further. And thus, poor child, she went on and on, long and long after the monk had lost sight of her, and with a deep sigh, had turned to go back again into the church.

It had been six o'clock when Paolina started on her walk to the church, and nothing had been settled with any accuracy between her and the old friend and protectress, with whom she had come to Ravenna, and lived during her stay there, as to the exact time at which she might be expected to return. The name of the protectress in question was Signora Orsola Steno, an old friend of her mother's, who, when Paolina Foscarelli had been left an orphan, had, for pure charity and friendship's sake, taken the child, and brought her up. Latterly, by the exercise of the talent inherited from her father, Paolina had been able to do something, not only towards meeting her own expenses, but towards making some return for all that the good Orsola had done for her out of her own poverty. And now this commission of the Englishman who had sent her to Ravenna would go far towards improving the prospects of both Paolina and her old friend.

Old Orsola did not know exactly at what time to expect Paolina back; but she knew that Paolina's purpose on that Ash Wednesday morning was merely to walk to the church, and, having seen the preparations that had been made for her work, to return, without on that occasion remaining to begin her task. So that when the hour of the midday meal arrived, and her young friend had not returned, old Orsola began to be a little uneasy about her.

Nor was her uneasiness lessened by her entire ignorance as to there being little or much, or no cause at all for it. Never having left Venice before in her life, old Orsola was as much a stranger in Ravenna, and felt herself to be in an unknown world, as completely as an Englishman would in Japan. Since she had been in Ravenna she had frequently heard the Pineta spoken of, and the old church out there in which her young friend was to do a portion of her task. But she had heard them both mentioned as strange and wild places, not exactly like all the rest of the world. And the old woman felt, that, for aught she knew, this Pineta, and the old church in the wilderness on the borders of it, might be a place full of dangers for a young girl all by herself.

And as the hours crept on, and no Paolina came, her uneasiness increased till she felt it impossible to sit quietly at home waiting for her any longer. She must go out, and—do what? The poor old woman did not in the least know what to do; or of whom to make any inquiry. The only person with whom the two Venetian strangers had become at all intimate in Ravenna was the Marchese Ludovico. And the only step in her difficulty which old Orsola could think of taking, after much doubt and hesitation, was to go to the Palazzo Castelmare, and endeavour to speak with the Marchesino. The letter of introduction, which they had brought from the English patron, was addressed to the Marchese Lamberto. But the acquaintance of the Venetians with him had remained very slight; and Orsola felt so much awe of so grand and reverend a Signor, that it was to the nephew only that she thought of applying.

So, not without much doubt and misgiving, the old woman put on her bonnet and cloak and made the best of her way to the Castelmare palace. There she found a porter lounging before the door, to whom she made her petition to be allowed to speak to the Signor Marchese Ludovico.

"My name is Orsola Steno," said the old woman humbly, a little in awe of the majestic porter, chosen for that situation for his size; "and the Signor Marchesino knows me very well. I am sure he would not refuse to see me."

Insolent servants in a great house are generally a sure symptom of something amiss in the moral nature of their masters. Good and kindly masters have and make civil and kindly servants; and the big porter of the palazzo Castelmare was accordingly by no means a terrible personage.

"Signora Orsola Steno! To be sure. I remember you very well, Signora, when you called on the padrone last summer. I am sure the Signor Marchesino would have pleasure in seeing you, if he were at home. But he is not here. And to tell you the truth, we have no idea where he is. He came home early this morning after the ball, and instead of going to bed, changed his dress, and went out again at once; and has not been back since. Some devilry or other! Che vuole! We were all young once upon a time, eh, Signora Orsola? And as for the Marchesino, he is as good a gentleman as any in Ravenna or out of it, for that matter. But he is young, Signora, he is young! And that's all the fault he has. Can I give him any message for you, Signora?"

"The fact is," said old Orsola, after a few moments of rapid reflection as to the expediency of telling her trouble to the porter, and a decision prompted by the good-natured manner of the man, and by the poor woman's extreme need of some one to tell her trouble to, "the fact is, that I wanted to ask the advice of the Signor Marchesino about a young friend of mine, the Signora Paolina Foscarelli, who went out of the city early this morning to go to St. Apollinare in Classe, and ought to have been back hours ago. And I am quite uneasy about her."

"Why, your trouble, Signora, is of a piece with our own," said the porter, with a burly laugh; "and it seems to me like enough we can help each other. You miss a young lady; and we miss a young gentleman. When I used to go out into the marshes a-shooting with the Marchese, we used to be sure, when we had put up the cock bird, that the hen was not far off; or, if we got the hen, we knew we had not far to look for the cock. Do you see, Signora? Two to one the pair of runaways are together; and they'll come home safe enough when they've had their fun out. I dare say the Signor Marchesino and the Signorina you speak of are old friends?"

"Why, yes, Signore. For that matter they are old friends!" replied Orsola, adopting the porter's phrase for want of one which could express the meaning she had in her mind more desirably.

"To be sure—to be sure. And if you will take my advice, Signora, you will go home, and give yourself no trouble at all about the young lady. Lord bless us! what though 'tis Lenten-tide? Young folks will be young, Signora Orsola. They'll come home safe enough. And maybe I might as well say nothing to the Signor Marchesino about your coming here, you know. When folks have come to that time of life, Signora, as brings sense with it, they mostly learn that least said is soonest mended," said the old porter, with a nod of deep meaning.

And Signora Orsola was fain to take the porter's advice, so far as returning to her home went. But it was not equally easy to give herself no further trouble about Paolina. It might be as the porter said; and if she could have been sure that it was so the old lady would have been perfectly easy. But it was not at all like Paolina to have planned such an escapade without telling her old friend anything about it. She felt sure that when Paolina said she was going to St. Apollinare to look after the preparations for her copying there, she had no other or further intention in her thoughts. To be sure there was the possibility that Ludovico might have known her purpose of going thither, and might have planned to accompany her on her expedition, without having apprized her of any such scheme. And it might not be unlikely that in such a case they had been tempted to spend a few hours in the Pineta. And with these possibilities Signora Steno was obliged to tranquillize herself as she best might.

She returned home not without some hope that she might find that Paolina had returned during her absence; but such was not the case—Paolina was still absent. And though it was now some eight or nine hours from the time she had left home, old Orsola had nothing for it but to wait for tidings of her as patiently as she could.

CHAPTER VI

Gigia's Opinion

The aged monk of St. Apollinare, after watching Paolina as she departed from the Basilica, and took the path towards the forest, returned into the church to his devotions at the altar of the saint, as has been said. But he found himself unable to concentrate his attention as usual, not on the meaning of the words of the litanies he uttered, that, it may be imagined, few such worshippers do, or even attempt to do, but on such devotional thoughts as, on other occasions, constituted his mental attitude during the hours he spent before the altar.

He could not prevent his mind from straying to thoughts of the girl who had just left him; of certain long-sleeping recollections of his own past, which her name had recalled to him; of her very manifest emotion at the sight of the couple in the bagarino, and the too easy interpretation of the meaning of that emotion; and specially of her implied intention of taking the same route that they had taken.

He thought of these things, and a certain sense of uneasiness and misgiving came over him. The young artist had spoken kindly and sweetly to him. She had seemed to him wonderfully pretty, and that is not without its influence even on eyes over which the cowl had been drawn for more than three-score years; she was a fellow-Venetian too, and that with Italians, who find themselves in a stranger city, is a stronger tie of fellowship than the people of less divided nations can readily appreciate; and, above all, there were motives connected with those awakened remembrances of the old man which made her an object of interest to him. And the result of all this was, that he was uneasy at seeing her depart on the errand on which he suspected that she had gone.

After awhile he arose from his knees, and, returning to the great open door of the church, stood awhile irresolutely gazing out towards the forest to the southward. He could not see the farmhouse, which has been so frequently mentioned, from where he stood, because it is to the eastward of the church. After awhile he strolled out and along the road, till he came in sight of the house on the border of the forest. But there was no human being to be seen. Then, apparently having taken a resolution, he went into the dilapidated remains of the old convent, and ascended a stair to the room where his sole companion, the lay brother, was ill in bed. He gave the sick man a potion, placed a cup with drink by his side, smoothed his pillow, and replaced a crucifix at the bed-foot before the patient's eyes; and then, with a word of consolation, descended again to the road, and after a long look towards the forest, slowly moved off the nearest border of it.

It was between eight and nine when Father Fabiano, moving slowly and irresolutely, thus sauntered off in the direction of the forest; but it was nearly time for him to sound the "Angelus" at midday before he returned.

Perhaps it was the fear that he might be late for this duty, a task which devolved on him, the lay brother being ill, that made his steps, as he returned, very different from those with which he had set forth. He came back hurrying, with a haggard, wild terror in his eyes, shaking in every limb, and with great drops of perspiration standing on his brow. One would have said that all this evident perturbation could not be caused only by the fear of being late to ring the "Angelus." His first care, however, was to pay another visit to his patient.

"Ah! Padre, you are going to have your turn again. It is early this year. All this wet weather. Why, your hand is shaking worse than mine!" said the sick man, as the old monk handed him his draught. And it was true enough that not only Father Fabiano's hands were shaking, but he was, indeed, trembling all over; and any one but a sick man, lying as the fevered lay-brother was lying, could not have failed to see that it was from mental agitation, rather than from the shivering of incipient ague, that he was suffering.

"You think of getting well yourself, brother Simone. I have not got the fever yet," said the monk, making an effort to control himself and speak in his ordinary manner.

"May the saints grant that your reverence do not fall ill before I am able to get up, or I don't know what we should do."

"It is years, brother Simone, that make my hand shake, more than ague this time, years, and many a former touch of the fever. I am not ill this time yet. And now I must go and ring the 'Angelus.'"

And the old monk did go, and the "Angelus" was duly rung. But Brother Simone, as he lay upon his fevered bed, was very well able to tell that the rope was pulled by a very uncertain and unsteady hand. "Poor old fellow! he's going fast! I wonder whether there's any chance of their moving me when he's gone?" thought Brother Simone to himself.

But Father Fabiano, for his own part, judged that prayer and penance were more needed for the healing of his present disorder, than either bark or quinine. And when he had rung the bell, he betook himself again to the altar of St. Apollinare, and with cowl drawn over his head, and frequent prostrations till his forehead touched the marble flags of the altar-step, spent before it most of the remaining hours of that day. Nevertheless, it was true that, be the cause what it might, the aged friar was ill, not in mind only, but also in the body. And before the hour of evensong came, his coadjutor, Fra Simone, the lay-brother, being by that time so much better as to be able to crawl out, Father Fabiano was fain to stretch himself on the pallet in his cell. And Fra Simone took it quite as a matter of course in the ordinary order of things, that the father was laid up in his turn with an attack of fever and ague.

It was much about the same time that Father Fabiano had set out on that walk to the forest, from which he had returned in such a state of agitation, that old Quinto Lalli, the prima donna's travelling companion, was made acquainted with the escapade of his adopted daughter. Though she bore his name, the fact was that the old man was in no way related to the famous singer. But they had lived together in the relationship first of teacher and pupil, and then of father and daughter, by mutual adoption ever since the first beginning of the singer's public career; and they mutually represented to each other the only family ties which either of them knew or recognized in the world. The old man had been several hours in bed, when Bianca had returned from the ball, at about five in the morning of that Ash Wednesday. And it was not till he came from his room, between eight and nine, that he heard from Gigia, Bianca's maid, that her mistress had not gone to bed, but had only changed her dress, and taken a cup of coffee before going out with the Marchese Ludovico more than an hour ago in a bagarino.

There was nothing sufficiently strange to the former habits of his adopted daughter in such an escapade, or so unlike to many another frolic of the brilliant Diva in former days, as to cause any very great surprise to the old singing-master—for such had been the original vocation of Signor Lalli. Yet he seemed on this occasion to be not a little annoyed at what she had done.

"And a very great fool she is for her pains," cried the old man, with an oath; "it is just the last thing she ought to have done—the very last. I really thought she had more sense!"

"I am sure, Signor Quinto, she has not had one bit of pleasure all this Carnival. A nun couldn't have lived a quieter life, nor more shut up than she has. With the exception of the old gentleman and the Marchese Ludovico, she has never seen a soul!"

The old gentleman thus alluded to, it may be necessary to explain, was the Marchese Lamberto. "And where's the use of never seeing a single soul, if she throws all that she has gained by it away in this manner?"

"Why, Santa Virgine, Signor Quinto! Where's the harm? Isn't the Signor Ludovico the old one's own nephew?" expostulated Gigia shrilly.

"The old one, as you call him, is not a bit the more likely to like it for that. It is just the very last thing she should have done. I do wonder she should not have more sense," grumbled Quinto.

"Misericordia! why what a piece of work about nothing! The old gentleman will never know anything about it, you may be very sure. He is safe enough in bed and asleep after his late hours, you may swear. Besides, it's both best and honestest to begin as you mean to go on, and accustom him to what he's got to expect," said Gigia, fighting loyally for her side.

"All very well in good time. But it would be as well for Bianca to make sure first what she has got to expect."

"Why, you don't suppose, Signor Quinto, nor yet that old Marchese don't suppose, I should think, that he's going to marry a woman like my mistress, to keep her caged up like a bird that's never to sing, except for him?"

"I tell you, Gigia, and you would do well to tell her, and make her understand, that she is not Marchesa di Castelmare yet, and is not likely to be, if this morning's work were to come to the ears of the Marchese. It is just the very worst thing she could have done; and I should have thought she must know that. I had rather that she should have gone with any other man in the town."

"I am sure," said Gigia, with a virtuous toss of the head, "she would not wish to go with any one of them."

"And she would wish to go with the Marchese Ludovico! There's all the mischief. Just what I am afraid of. I tell you, Gigia, that if the Marchese Lamberto hears of her going off in this manner with his nephew, the game is all up. He would never forgive it."

"You will excuse me, Signor Quinto," said Gigia, with a demure air of speaking modestly on a subject which she perfectly well understood—"You will excuse me, if I tell you that I know a great deal better than that. There's men, Signor Quinto, who are in love because they like it; and there's others who are in love whether they like it or no, because they can't help themselves!"

"And you fancy the Marchese Lamberto is one of those who can't help himself, eh?" grumbled Quinto discontentedly.

"If I ever saw a man who was so limed that he couldn't help himself, it's that poor creature of a Marchese! He's caught safe enough, you may take my word for that, Signor Quinto. He's caught, and can't budge, I tell you—hand nor foot, body nor soul! Lord bless you, I know 'em. Why, do you think he'd ever have come near my mistress a second time if he could have helped himself? He's not like your young 'uns, who come to amuse themselves. Likely enough, he'd give half of all he's worth this day never to have set eyes on her; but, as for giving her up, he could as soon give himself up!"

"Humph!" grunted the old singer, with a shrug, and a sound that was half a sneer and half a chuckle. "I suppose he don't above half like the price he has to pay for his plaything! But that don't make it wise in Bianca to drive him to the wall more than need be. Limed and caught as he is, he's one that may give her some trouble yet. For my part, I wish she had not gone on this fool's errand this morning. Now, I will go and get my breakfast. I shall be back in half-an-hour. I expect Signor Ercole Stadione here this morning."

Signor Ercole Stadione was the impresario of the Ravenna theatre.

"And if he comes before you are back, Signor Quinto?" asked Gigia.

"If he should come before I am back, let the boy call me from the cafe. And, Gigia, whenever he comes, you can let him understand, you know, that your mistress is in her own room, resting after the ball, you know. He's hand and glove with the Marchese."

"I wasn't born yesterday, Signor Quinto, though you seem to think so," returned Gigia, as the old man began to descend the stairs.

Signor Quinto went to the cafe, and consumed his little cup of black coffee, with its abominable potion of so-called "rhum" in it, and the morsel of dry bread, which constituted his accustomed breakfast; and then, as he was returning to his lodging, encountered the "impresario" in the street.

"Well met, Signor Lalli!" cried little Signor Ercole, cheerily. "I was on my way to your house to settle our little matters. I have not seen you, I think, since Sunday night. The bustle of these last days of the Carnival! How divinely she sang that night! If Bellini could have heard her, it would have been the happiest day of his life."

"I am glad that you were contented, Signor Ercole."

"Contented! The whole city was enraptured. There never was such a success. You have got that little memorandum of articles—?"

"No. I've got the paper signed at Milan; but not—"

"Stay, let me see. True, true. I remember now. It remained with the Marchese. We shall want it, you know, just to put all in order. We can call at the Palazzo Castelmare on our way, and ask the Marchese for it?"

"Will he be up at this hour, after last night's ball?" asked Quinto.

"He? The Marchese? One sees you are a stranger in Ravenna, my dear sir. I don't suppose the Marchese has ever been in bed after eight o'clock the last quarter of a century. He is an early man, the Marchese, an example to us all in that, as in all else."

"Very well; then we can call for the paper on our way to my lodging; it is not much out of the way."

So they walked together to the Palazzo Castelmare, talking of the brilliant success of the past theatrical season, and of the eminent qualities and virtues of the Marchese Lamberto; and when they reached the door the impresario desired the servant who answered the bell to tell the Marchese that he, Signor Ercole, wished to speak with him, but would not detain him a moment.

The Marchese, the man said, was not up yet. He, the servant, had been to his door at the usual hour, but had received no answer to his knock; so that it was evident that his master was still sleeping. He had been very late the night before, far later than was usual with him, and no doubt he would ring his bell as soon as he waked.

"The fact is," said Signor Ercole, as he and Quinto Lalli turned away from the door, "that the Marchese has not been well of late. He very often does me the honour of conversing with me, I may say indeed of consulting me on subjects of art;—and I grieve to say that I have of late observed a change in him. He is not like the same man."

"Getting old, I suppose, like the rest of us," said Quinto.

"Like some of us," corrected Signor Ercole; "but, Lord bless you! the Marchese is a young man—a young man, so to speak, he's not above fifty, and a very young man of his years; at least he was so a month or two ago. But changed he is. Everybody has seen it. Let us hope that it is merely some temporary indisposition. Ravenna can't afford to lose the Marchese."

"I suppose we had better put off settling our little bit of business till another time?" said Quinto. "Shall we say to-morrow, at the same hour? And I will get that paper from the Marchese in the meantime," returned Signor Ercole.

"That will suit me perfectly well; to-morrow, then, at my lodgings at ten, shall we say?"

"At ten; I will not fail to wait upon you, Signor Lalli, at that hour. In the meantime I beg you to present my most distinguished homage to the divina Cantatrice," said the little impresario, taking off his hat and holding it at arm's length above his head, as he made a very magnificent bow.

"Servitore suo, stimatissimo Signor Ercole! A dimane!" replied old Quinto, as he returned the impresario's salutation, with a slighter and less provincial bow.

"A dimane alle dieci!" rejoined the impresario; and so the two men parted.

"Not a bad bit of luck," thought the old singing master to himself, as he sauntered towards his lodging, "that the Marchese should be in bed this morning. It gives a chance that he may never hear of this mad scappata with the Signor Ludovico. Lose the Marchese Lamberto! No, per Bacco! there are other people, beside the good folks of the city of Ravenna, who can't afford to lose the Marchese Lamberto just yet!"

CHAPTER VII

An Attorney-at-Law in the Papal States

At a little after twelve o'clock on that same Ash Wednesday morning, a servant in the Castelmare livery brought a verbal message to the "studio" of Signor Giovacchino Fortini, "procurators,"— attorney-at-law, as we should say, requesting that gentleman to step as far as the Palazzo Castelmare, as the Marchese would be glad to speak with him.

The message was not one calculated to excite any surprise either in the servant who carried it, or in Signor Fortini himself. Signor Giovacchino was, and had been for many years, the confidential lawyer of the Castelmare family. And the various business connected with large landed possessions made frequent conferences necessary between the lawyer and such a client as the Marchese, who, among his other activities, had always been active in the management and care of his estates.

Signor Giovacchino Fortini was very decidedly the first man of his profession in Ravenna, as indeed might be expected of the person who had been honoured for more than one generation by the confidence of the Castelmare family. For the lawyer was a much older man than the Marchese, and had been the confidential adviser of his father. And old Giovacchino Fortini's father and grandfather had sat in the same "studio" before him, and had held the same position towards previous generations of the Castelmare family.

For three generations also the Fortini, grandfather, father, and son, had been lawyers to the Chapter of Ravenna; a fact which vouched the very high standing and consideration they held in the city, and at the same time explained the circumstances under which it had come to pass that the "studio" they had occupied for so many years, seemed more like some public building than the private offices of a provincial attorney.

In fact the "Studio Fortini" was a portion of an ancient building attached to the Cathedral, in which some of the less dignified members of the Chapter had their residences. The building in question encircled a small cloistered court, the soil of which was on a lower level than that of the street outside it; and the residences, to which a series of little doors around this cloister gave access, looked as if they must have been miserably damp and unwholesome. But the "Studio Fortini" was not situated in any part of this damp lower floor. In the corner of the cloister nearest to the Cathedral, there was a wide and picturesque old stone staircase, which led to an upper cloister, as sunny and pleasant looking as the lower one was the reverse. There, near the head of the stair, was a round arched deeply sunk stone doorway, closed by a black door, bearing a bright brass plate on it, conveying the information, altogether superfluous to every man, woman, and child in Ravenna, that there was situated the "Studio Fortini."

This black door was never quite closed during the day. It admitted anybody who chose to push it into a small ante-room, on one side of which might be seen through a glass door a long low vaulted room, or gallery rather, running over some half dozen of the inhabited cells below. And along the whole length of it on either side, up to the height of the small round arched windows placed high up in the wall, were ranges of shelves occupied by many hundreds of volumes, all of the same size, and all bound alike in parchment, with two red bands of Russian leather running across the backs of them, and all lettered and dated in black ink, of gradually shaded degrees of fadedness. The place looked like the archive-room of some public establishment, which kept its archives in very unusually good order.

All these were the documents and pleadings in all the lawsuits and other legal transactions of all the clients of the three generations of the Fortini. And it would not have been too much to say, that Signor Giovacchino Fortini would have deemed the destruction of this mass of papers as a misfortune to be paralleled only by that of the Alexandrian library.

On the opposite side to the long gallery the anteroom gave access to a large and lofty vaulted chamber, about one-sixth part of the space of which—that is, a third of the floor and a half of the height—was partitioned off by a slight modern wall and ceiling. Two young clerks occupied the larger unenclosed portion of the large hall, for such its size entitled it to be called, and Signor Fortini's senior and confidential clerk sat on the top of the ceiling, which enclosed the smaller portion. A small wooden stair gave access to this lofty position, which was admirably adapted for keeping an eye on the youngsters on the floor below. Under the same ceiling, in the snug little room thus divided off, sat Signor Fortini himself. And a very snug and bright-looking little room it was, with a pretty stone-mullioned three-lighted casement window opening to the south; and in the wall at right angles to it another window, offering accommodation of a much more unusual and peculiar kind. It opened, in fact, into the transept of the cathedral, and had been intended to enable the occupier or occupiers of the apartment, now inhabited by the lawyer, to enjoy the benefit of attending mass without the trouble of descending into the church for that purpose. If Signor Giovacchino Fortini did not often use it for that purpose, it, at all events, had the effect of imparting an ecclesiastical air to his habitat, which seemed to have a certain propriety in the case of a gentleman whose business connections with the hierarchy were so close, and unquestionably added to the savour of unimpeachable respectability which appertained to Signor Fortini and all belonging to him.

Signor Fortini was a tall, thin, adust old man, with a large, well-developed forehead, a keen, bright hazel eye, and bristling, iron-grey hair, which had once been black, and a beard to match, which seemed as if the barber entrusted with the care of it were always two or three days in arrear with his work. By some incomprehensible combination of circumstances it seemed as if Signor Fortini's face were never seen fresh shaven. His sharp chin and lanthorn jaws appeared to be perennially clothed with a two days' old crop of grisly stubble, two days' growth, neither more nor less!

Long years ago he had buried a childless wife, who was said to have been a wonderful beauty, and to have been in many ways a trouble greater than Signor Fortini knew how to manage, and a trial that made his life a burthen to him. Those old troubles were now, however, long since past and gone; and Signor Fortini lived only for his law and his artistic and antiquarian collections. He was like many of his peers in the provincial cities of the Papal dominions—a great antiquary and virtuoso. Antiquarianism is a "safe" pursuit under a government the nature of which makes and finds very many intellectual occupations unsafe. And this may account for the fact, that very many competent historical antiquaries and collectors are found in the Pope's territories among such men as Signor Fortini.

The son and grandson of thriving lawyers, who had for nearly an hundred years managed the affairs of the Chapter and the estates of the principal landed proprietors of the neighbourhood, was not likely to be otherwise than well off; and it was generally understood that Signor Fortini was a wealthy man. He loudly protested on all occasions that this was a most mistaken notion; but there never occurred an opportunity of adding to his very remarkable collection of drawings of the old masters, or his unrivalled series of mediaeval seals, or his all but perfect library of the Municipal Statutes of the mediaeval Communes of Italy, which found Signor Fortini unprepared to outbid most competitors.

There were very few among his clients whom Signor Fortini would not have expected to call on him at his "studio," instead of summoning him to wait on them. But the Marchese di Castelmare was one of these few, perhaps as much, or more, on the score of old friendship as on that of rank and social importance.

The old lawyer was not more importantly occupied when he received the Marchese's message, than by intently examining a bronze medal through a magnifying-glass; and he sent back word that he would be with the Marchese immediately. The fact was he did not like the look of this summons at all. He, too, had observed the unmistakable change in his old friend; and jumped to the conclusion that what he was wanted for was to make, or to be consulted about making, the Marchese's will.

"To think of his breaking up so suddenly, in such a way as this. No stamina! Why, he must be twenty years my junior; and I don't feel a day older than I did ten years ago, not a day. He has led a steady life too; and seemed as likely a man to last as one would wish to look at. I suppose everything will go to the nephew, legacies to servants, and something, I should not wonder, to the town hospital, not that I think he can have saved much, if any thing. I should like that little cabinet Guido and I don't suppose Signor Ludovico would care a rush about it."

With these thoughts in his mind Signor Fortini presented himself at the door of the Castelmare palace within ten minutes of the time when he had received the summons of the Marchese, and was immediately ushered into the library.

A bright ray of sunshine was streaming in at the large window, and flooding half the room with its comfortable warmth and cheerful light. But the Marchese, though he held a scaldino (a little earthenware pot filled with burning braise) in his hand, and was apparently shivering with cold, sat in his large library-chair, drawn into the darkest corner of the room, cowering over this scaldino, which he held between his knees. He jumped up from his seat, however, to receive his visitor with an air, one would have said, of having been startled by his entrance.

"It is kind of you to come to me so quickly, Signor Giovacchino," he said; and then turning angrily to the servant, who was leaving the room, added in a cross and irritable voice, very unlike his usual manner, "Why are not those persiane shut? Close them directly, and then begone—quick!"

The man, with a startled look, did as he was bid; and the heavy wooden jalousies thus shut reduced the room to comparative darkness.

"I am afraid I find you very far from well, Signor Marchese. Would not a little sun be pleasant this bright morning? the air is quite fresh despite the sunshine."

"I don't like the sun indoors! I don't know how my rascals came to leave the persiane open."

"I thought you seemed cold, Signor Marchese," said the lawyer, kindly.

"So I am cold—very cold," he said, and his teeth chattered as he said it; "but the light hurts my eyes."

"It very often does so when one is not well."

"Not well! I'm well enough, man alive. But I think I must have caught a little cold at the ball last night," rejoined the Marchese, striving hard to speak in his usual manner.

The lawyer, whose eyes had by this time become accustomed to the diminished light, looked hard at his old friend from beneath his great shaggy black eye-brows, with a shrewdly examining glance, and then slightly shook his head.

"Well, I daresay you'll be all right again in a day or two. But any way, I am glad you sent for me all the same. These things have to be done, you know. And a man does not die a bit the sooner for doing them. For my part, I always advise my friends to have all such matters settled while they are in health."

"What, in Heaven's name, are you talking about? I don't know what you mean," said the Marchese, with an angry irritability that was totally unlike his usual manner. "I sent for the lawyer; and you come and talk to me as if you wanted to play the doctor."

"I assure you, Signor Marchese, I have not the slightest desire to play any part but my own. And that I am perfectly ready to enter on. I am ready to take your instructions, and will draw up the instrument to-morrow or the next day. Thank God there is no cause for hurry. And that is one of the advantages of arranging all testamentary dispositions while we are in health. My own will, Signor Marchese, has been made these ten years."

"What is that to me? I may make my will ten years hence, and yet get it done in quite as good time as you have, Signor Fortini. Pray allow me to judge for myself, when I think it right to make my will. I have usually been able to manage my own affairs." He spoke with a degree of anger and petulance, jumping up from his chair, and taking a turn to the window and back again, which seemed to conquer the shivering fit from which he had been suffering.

"Manage your own affairs, Signor Marchese! Who would dream of interfering with your management of them? But did you not send for me to make your will?" said the lawyer, standing also.

"Send for you to make my will! No devil told you I wanted to make my will? I said nothing about making my will."

"I beg your pardon, Signor Marchese. Perhaps I jumped at a conclusion over hastily. I thought it a wise thing to do, and so imagined that you were going to do it;—that's all. Let us say no more about it. What commands have you then to give me?"

The Marchese took another turn across the room before replying; and the observant lawyer saw him, when his back was turned, pass his hand across his brow, with the action of one ill at ease. Then resuming his seat, and motioning the lawyer to take a chair, he said—"If you will take a chair, Signor Giovacchino, I will tell you the business for which I have sent for you. I have thought it my duty—family considerations—in fact, I've been thinking on the subject for a long time—in short, Signor Fortini, I am about to be married."

"Whew—w—w!" whistled the lawyer, without the least attempt at concealing the extremity of his astonishment; and pushing back his chair a couple of feet, as he raised his head to stare into his companion's face.

"And pray, Signor, what is there to be astonished at in such an intention?" said the Marchese, evidently wincing under the lawyer's look.

"I beg your pardon, Signor Marchese, but—the fact is—one is always astonished at what one does not expect, you know. You may depend on it, I am not one bit more astonished than every human being in Ravenna will be," said the lawyer, looking hard at him.

"I am not aware, Signor Fortini, that I have to answer to any one save myself for the wisdom of my resolution," said the Marchese, with a dignity more like his usual manner than he had yet spoken.

"Certainly not, Signor Marchese. Certainly not. But the exception is an important one. You will have to answer for the wisdom of your resolution to yourself," rejoined Fortini, drily.

"That, Signor Fortini, is my affair. As I told you, I have considered the matter well; and I have made up my mind."

"May I ask, Signor Marchese, whether your intention has been communicated to your nephew?" asked the lawyer.

"As yet I have announced it to no one save yourself. As soon as the necessary arrangements with regard to matters of property have been determined on, it will be the fitting time to do so."

"Before any word can be said on that head, of course, it is necessary that your lordship should mention, what you have not yet confided to me, the name of the lady with whom you are about to ally yourself."

"Of course; and it is for the purpose of doing so that I have requested your presence here this morning, Signor Fortini. Before naming the lady, I will merely remark to you, that a man at my time of life may be expected to know his own mind, and has a right to please himself. And bearing these remarks in mind, you will understand that I do not wish to hear any observations on the subject of the choice I have made. My choice is made; and that is sufficient."

The Marchese looked up into the lawyer's face, and paused for some reply to these preliminary observations before proceeding to tell his secret; but the lawyer maintained a look and attitude of silent expectation.

"It is my intention," proceeded the Marchese, "to marry the Signora Bianca Lalli;—the lady whose conduct, as well as her talent, has won the good opinion of the entire city."

The old lawyer flung down on the table, with a clatter, a paper-knife which he had taken into his hand while speaking, and rising abruptly from his chair, took one or two turns across the room before he answered a word. Then coming in front of the Marchese, and still continuing to stand, he said,

"You have warned me, Signor Marchese, not to make any remarks on the communication you have just made to me. There is one, however, which perforce I must make. It is that I must decline to take any instructions, or to act in any way, for the forwarding of such a purpose."

"There are other attorneys in Ravenna, Signor Fortini."

"Plenty, Signor Marchese; plenty who will be abundantly ready to do your bidding. But Giovacchino Fortini will not. Good heaven! I should expect to have my dear and honoured old friend and patron, your father, coming out of his grave to upbraid me. Signor Marchese, you know right well—as well as I do myself—that at this time of day, I don't care two straws, as a mere matter of gain, whether I continue to be honoured with the transaction of your legal affairs or not. But I do care on other grounds. And I do implore you to believe that I am speaking to you more as a friend than as a lawyer;—that I am speaking to you as the whole city would speak, and will speak when it hears of this—this incredible—this monstrous notion, when I entreat you to think yet further on this most disastrous purpose."

Of course when a man speaks as Signor Fortini spoke to the Marchese, he does it not without some hope that his words may produce an effect on the person he addresses. But the lawyer had not much expectation that in the present case what he said would be listened to. He spoke more for the discharge of his own conscience, and because the feelings he expressed were strong within him, than for any other reason. And he fully expected that he should be answered with words of anger and uncompromising rejection of his interference.

It was not without considerable surprise, therefore, that he heard the Marchese's moderate answer to the strong opposition he had offered to his intention. "Well, Signor Fortini, I cannot doubt that what you have said has been, at all events, dictated by a strong regard for my welfare, as you understand it. I have, as I told you, made up my mind upon the subject. Nevertheless, counsel cannot but be useful, and it is well not to be precipitate. I will, therefore, so far accept your advice as to promise you that I will give myself time to deliberate yet further on the step. In the meantime you will note that my first communication to you on the subject was made on this first day of Lent; so that when I again seek your assistance in the matter, you will know that I have at least not acted in a hurry, but have given myself due time for mature reflection."

"I am delighted, Signor Marchese, to have obtained from you at least thus much. It is at all events something gained. And I shall still hope, that further reflection may lead you to change your purpose. Hoping that, I shall, you may depend upon it, breathe no word of what you have said to me to any living soul. But you must understand that, without such hope, I should have deemed it my duty to speak on the subject with the Marchese Ludovico."

"How so, Signor Fortini? A lawyer—"

"Very true, Signor Marchese. A lawyer, as you would observe, is addressed by his client in confidence, and the confidence should be sacred. But you must remember that I have the honour to act in this, as I and my father have done on all other occasions for now three generations, not only for your lordship, but for the whole of the family. I am the legal adviser of the Marchese Ludovico, as I was his father's, and as I am yours. It is my duty, therefore, as I understand it, to look upon myself as bound to consider the welfare and interests of the entire family; and I need not remark to you how cruelly those of the Marchese Ludovico would be compromised by such an event as we were contemplating just now."

"With regard to speaking to my nephew on the subject, Signor Fortini, I can have no objection to your doing so, if you think it your duty. He will, of course, be informed of my intention by myself. Do not forget, however, that my first communication to you on this subject was on the first day of Lent, Ash Wednesday."

"Forget it, Signor Marchese! I am not likely to forget it for a long time to come, I assure you," said the lawyer, not a little surprised.

"I mention it because I am anxious that you should not accuse me of acting with precipitancy in this matter; that when I shall renew my application to you, you may remember that I have had due and sufficient time for reflection. Addio, Signor Giovacchino," said the Marchese, reverting to the more friendly form of address; "addio, ed a rivederci fra poco!"

"Servo suo, Lustrissimo Signor Marchese, a rivederci!"

CHAPTER VIII

Lost in the Forest

Signor Fortini went straight home to his pleasant little snuggery under the wing, it might almost be said, under the roof, of the Cathedral, and sat down in his easy chair to resume the occupation that had been interrupted by the summons from the Marchese. He took up the medal he had been examining, and the magnifying glass, in a manner that implied a sort of ostentatious protest to himself that the calm and even tenour of his own life and occupations was not to be disturbed from its course by all the follies and extravagances of the world around him.

But "mentem mortalia tangunt!" The glass was soon laid aside: the medal remained idly in his hand, and his mind would recur to the things he had just seen and heard.

That an old bachelor should be caught at last by a pretty face, and make a fool of himself in his mature age, was no unprecedented phenomenon. That a man, who had never in any way made a fool of himself at the proper age for such an operation, should, after all, do so when those who did so in their salad days have become wise, was not unheard of. Nevertheless, Signor Fortini, who, in the course of his seventy years, had had a tolerably wide experience of mankind, was astonished that the Marchese Lamberto di Castelmare should have been tempted to act as he proposed to act.

"The very last man," said Signor Fortini musingly to himself, "that I could have suspected of such a thing! The man who has the highest reputation in the city for sound judgment and unexceptionable conduct, to turn out the greatest fool! An old ass! How little he dreams of what he is bringing upon himself. Let alone the terrible fall, the disgrace, in every way, disgrace and contempt and ridicule! It seems impossible, even now, that he should be in earnest. He must be mad! And, davvero, his manner was at times so strange, that I could almost believe he really is not quite in his right mind. Very strange his manner was, very! And very ill he looked, too. Everybody has been saying that he looked ill, that he looked old, that there must be something wrong with him. Wrong with a vengeance! So this was the cause of it all: the Marchese Lamberto is in love!
Bah!—Bah!!—Bah!!!—(with crescendo expression of disgust). Poor devil! Well, I was in love once, or fancied myself so. But then. I was twenty-five years old. Un altro paio di maniche! And I very soon found out my mistake. But he, at his time of life! And such a woman! Well, the Emperor Justinian married Theodora. So, I suppose we Ravennati have authority for madness in that kind. And that poor good fellow, the Marchese Ludovico, too! It is too bad. And all because such a creature as that is cunning enough to know how to drive a hard bargain for the painted face she has to sell. But that is the sort of woman who can make that sort of conquest. A good woman now, who would have made him an honoured and good wife, would never have made such a blind, abject slave of him. He is bewitched! He is mad! and ought not to be allowed to carry out so insane a project! Perhaps it may still be possible to induce him to hear reason. It was very odd, that way, that just at last he promised me he would think of it again before he finally decided. Very odd. Just as if a man has not finally decided in such a matter before he sends to his lawyer! It is all very—very strange. And I have a good mind to speak to Signor Ludovico at once. I think it would be the right thing to do, I do think that would be the most proper thing to do. The old fool ought to be treated as one non compos!"

And then the old lawyer, after spending nearly an hour in such musings, got up and went to his house, not two minutes' walk from his "studio"—to his solitary but comfortable two-o'clock dinner.

By the time he had finished his repast, he had made up his mind that he would at once confer with the Marchese Ludovico on the subject of his uncle's disastrous project. It was by that time nearly half-past three; and Signor Fortini walked out towards the Circolo, having little doubt that he should find Ludovico there at that hour.

But on his way thither he met the man he was in search of in the street. The young Marchese was walking at a hurried pace, and appeared to be scared, troubled, and heated. Nothing could be more unlike his usual easy, lounging, poco-curante bearing. The lawyer saw at once that something was the matter; and thought that, in all probability, the Marchese Lamberto had been already forestalling him, by speaking to his nephew himself on the subject of his projected marriage.

"Oh, Signor Ludovico," said Fortini, as he met him, "I was on my way, to the Circolo, on purpose to see if I could meet with you there."

"Why, what is it? Have you any news to tell me?" said the young man in a hurried manner, that the lawyer thought odd.

"Yes. I wished to speak to you on rather an important matter. Have you seen the Marchese Lamberto this morning?"

"No. I have been out of the town. I am but this moment come back," replied Ludovico, evidently anxiously.

"I should be glad to speak to you for a few minutes before you go to the Palazzo Castelmare. If you are going to the Circolo, I would walk with you, and we could speak there," said Fortini.

"I'll be there in less than ten minutes. But I want first to run just as far as La Lalli's lodging in the Strada di Porta Sisi, only to ask a question," said Ludovico.

"La Lalli again! The devil fly away with her! It was about her that I wanted to speak to you," said the lawyer.

"What about her? Have you seen her? Do you know where she is?" asked Ludovico, hurriedly and anxiously.

"I seen her! No. Where she is? In her bed most likely, after dancing all last night, I should think!"

"Well, I must run and just ascertain whether she is at home!" said Ludovico, again trying to escape. But the old lawyer, partly put a little bit out of temper by the young man's evident wish to get rid of him, partly angered by finding the nephew thus running after the same mischief that was threatening to ruin his uncle, and partly thinking that it was desirable that the news he had to tell should be told before Ludovico should come to speech with his uncle, was determined not to let him escape till he had said what he had to say.

"Very well, Signor. I can say what I have to say in the street as well as anywhere else. Though I confess I expected a somewhat more ready reception of information which concerns you nearly, Signor Marchese, and which I am prompted to tell you by my interest in your welfare. Listen! Your uncle sent for me this morning for the purpose of announcing to me his intention of marrying this Bianca Lalli!"

"So I have been told this very morning," said Ludovico.

"I thought you said that you had not seen your uncle this morning!" returned the lawyer.

"No more I have; but are there not two persons from whom such an intention may be learned?" said Ludovico, with a slight approach to a sneer.

"The lady, you mean?" said Fortini.

"Exactly so—the lady!" rejoined Ludovico.

"The lady herself told you that the Marchese Lamberto had proposed marriage to her?" persisted the lawyer.

"The lady herself told me so," replied the Marchese.

"But I thought you said that you had only just now returned to the city?" objected the lawyer again.

"Really, Signor Fortini, one would think that I was being examined before a police-magistrate! However, since my tongue has let the cat out of the bag, you may take the creature, and make the most of her! I did receive the intelligence in question from the lady concerned, and I have just returned to the city. She communicated the fact to me during a little excursion we made together to the Pineta this morning, after the ball. Now you know all about it," said Ludovico, still in a hurry to get away.

"Not quite!" rejoined Fortini, quite imperturbably. "If you went to the Pineta with her—(did anybody ever hear of such a mad thing?)—and returned this morning, how can you want to go now to her house to ask whether she is there?"

"Because, you very clever inquisitor, though I went to the Pineta with her, I did not say that I had come back with her."

"The deuce you did not! Did another gentleman undertake the duty of escorting the lady back to town? It is all exceedingly pleasant for the Marchese Lamberto, upon my word!—oh, exceedingly! —and really a foretaste to him of the joys to come, quite frankly offered to him on the part of the lady!" sneered the old lawyer.

"Pshaw! how she may have come back, or with whom, I don't know, and can't guess; and that is just what I am anxious to find out," said Ludovico, in provoked impatience.

"I don't understand. Where did you part with the lady?" persisted the lawyer, interested rather by the evident uneasiness of the Marchese Ludovico, than by any care how and in what company Bianca might have found her way back to the city.

"Well, that's just the curious part of the matter. If you want to know how the thing happened, since you know so much already, walk with me to the Strada di Porta Sisi, and I will tell you how it happened. At the ball we spoke of the Pineta, she had never seen it, asked me to show it to her. In short, we agreed to start on leaving the ball, instead of going to bed. I got a bagarino, and drove her to the farmhouse by the edge of the wood, just behind St. Apollinare; left the bagarino there, and strolled into the wood. It was there that she told me of my uncle's purpose. And I was not a little taken aback, as you may suppose. However, that is matter for talk by-and-by. We strolled about a good while, then sat down. She told me a good deal of the history of her life. We must have been talking—I don't know how long; but a long time. Then she said she was so sleepy, she must have a little sleep; she could keep her eyes open no longer. Natural enough! She had been dancing all night—had never closed her eyes for a minute since. The bank we were sitting on was the most delicious place for a siesta that can be conceived. In two minutes she was fast asleep. She slept on and on till I was tired of waiting. No doubt I should have slept too, had not the intelligence she had given me been of a sort to keep me waking, for one while at least. Having my mind full of this, and not being able to sleep, I strayed away from her, and returned in a few minutes, as I think, to the place where I had left her, but could not find her. I could not be sure about the place. One bit of the forest is so much like another, just the same thing over and over again, that I could not feel quite sure of the spot. I still think I went back to the right place; but there she was not. Then I searched the wood all round, far and near, for, I should think, a couple of hours or more. I called aloud, again and again, all to no purpose. And what on earth has become of her I cannot imagine."

"And why you need trouble your head about it, I don't see. I wished the devil might fly away with her just now! And if the devil has taken the hint and done so, I confess it seems to me about the best thing that could happen! Why on earth you, of all people in the world, Signor Ludovico, should be so anxious to recover the lady, I confess I cannot understand. Would it not be the best thing in the world for you if she were never heard of again?"

"Oh, per amore di Dio, Signor Giovacchino, don't talk in that way. Never heard of again! I shall be really uneasy if I don't hear of her again in a very few minutes. It is so extraordinary. What can have become of her?"

"Become of her! Why, she waited, of course: got tired of waiting for you, and so strolled back to the town. That sort of lady does not much like waiting, I fancy."

"That sort of lady does not much like walking so far as from the Pineta here, I fancy. Besides, I should have overtaken her on the road."

"In any case what is there to be uneasy about. No harm can have happened to her. No such luck, per Bacco!"

"Harm! No; no harm can have happened to her, beyond losing herself in the forest. What I am afraid of is that she has strayed and not been able to find her way. And God knows how far she may wander. When I tell you that in wandering away from the place where I left her, for not above a quarter of an hour, I lost my way, and that when I found, as I supposed, the place where we had been, I could not be sure whether it was the same spot or not; you may suppose how easy it is to lose oneself. And I don't suppose the poor girl would be able to walk very far. If she has not returned, I must get help and go back to the forest and search till I find her."

"It's far more likely that you will find that she has returned home. I wish, for my part, that she had never set foot within a dozen miles of Ravenna. Just think what it would be! But I trust—I trust we may yet be able to induce your uncle to listen to reason."

"I'll tell you what, Signor Fortini. I should not be surprised if it should be found more possible to make the other party hear reason."

"What, the lady!"

"Yes, the lady—if we set about the matter in the right way."

"Well, Signor Ludovico, it may be that you may understand such matters and such people better than I can pretend to do. It is not improbable. But my conceptions of the power of persuasion have never risen yet to a belief in the possibility of persuading a dog who has got a lump of butter in his mouth to relinquish it."

"Umph! you are not particularly gallant, Signor Giovacchino. We shall see. But all that must be matter for future conversation. Here we are at her door. Let us see if anything has been heard of her." Ludovico, leaving his companion for an instant in the street, sprang up the stairs to make inquiry; and in the next minute returned looking very much vexed and annoyed, with the information that nothing had been seen or heard of the Diva since she left the house in his company at an early hour that morning.

CHAPTER IX

"Passa la Bella Donna e Par Che Dorma"—Tasso

"What's to be done now? I absolutely must find her," said Ludovico, looking, as he felt, exceedingly puzzled and annoyed.

"Well, yes. Considering the nature of the information she gave you this morning, and bearing in mind that her existence in the flesh promises to be the means of leaving you without the price of a crust of bread in the world, and the further fact she was last seen starting on a tete-a-tete expedition with you at six o'clock in the morning, I admit that it is desirable that you should find her," said the lawyer, with somewhat grim pleasantry.

"For heaven's sake, Signor Giovacchino, don't talk in that sort of way, even in jest," replied the young man, looking round at the lawyer with an uneasy eye. "After all, nothing can have happened to her, you know, worse than losing herself in the Pineta."

"Pooh! happen to her. What should happen to her? Either you did not go back to the place where you left her; or, likely enough, after strolling a little away from it, and not finding you, she sat down, and two to one, fell asleep again. I would wager that she is, at this moment, fast asleep under the shadow of a pine-tree, making up for last night."

"But what had I better do? If she is still either sleeping or waking in the forest, I must find her."

"Let us just step as far as the gate, and make some inquiry there. If she returned to the city she must have come to the Porta Nuova. And she could hardly have entered the town without drawing the attention of the men at the gate. Just let us make inquiry there in the first place."

So they went together to the Porta Nuova, and nothing more was said between them during the short walk. But it seemed as if the manifest uneasiness of Ludovico had infected his companion. Yet it was evident that thoughts of a different nature were busy in their minds. The Marchese Ludovico pressed on faster than the old lawyer could keep up with him, and was very unmistakably anxious about the object of his quest, and the tidings which he should be able to hear at the gate.

Signor Fortini had apparently got some other and newly-conceived thought in his mind. He looked two or three times shrewdly and furtively into the face of the young Marchese; and closely compressed his thin lips together, and drew into a knot the shaggy eye-brows over his clear and thoughtful eyes. Some notion had been suggested to his mind which very plainly he did not like.

At the gate nothing had been seen of the object of their search. The octroi officers perfectly well remembered seeing the Marchese Ludovico, who was well known to them by sight, drive through the gate very early that morning in a bagarino with a lady. One man had recognised the lady as the prima donna at the opera. And they were very sure that she had not returned to the city since, at least by that gate.

But one of the officers volunteered the information that another young lady had that morning passed out of the city on foot a little before the time at which the bagarino had passed with the Marchese and the prima donna. And the men, after some consultation together, were sure that neither had that young lady returned by the gate they guarded.

Ludovico looked at the lawyer, and the lawyer looked at Ludovico; but neither of them could suggest anything in explanation of so strange a circumstance.

"I saw nothing of any such person either in the Pineta or on the road," said Ludovico. "Who could it have been?"

The old lawyer only shrugged his shoulders in reply

"There is a young lady," resumed Ludovico, after some minutes of thought, "a friend of mine—a young artist engaged in making copies from the mosaics in our churches. I know that it was her purpose shortly to begin some work of this kind at St. Apollinare in Classe. It may be that she had selected this morning for the purpose of going out to look at her task, though I almost think that I should have been informed of her intention."

"The plot seems to thicken with a vengeance," said the lawyer, with an impatient shrug, and a slight sneer of ill-humour, provoked by the multiplicity of his young client's lady friends. "I daresay," he added, "the young ladies are not playing hide-and-seek in the Pineta all by themselves."

"But what had I better do?" said the young Marchese, looking with increased anxiety into the lawyer's face; "the fact is—you see, Signor Giovacchino, this new idea, this possibility that Paolina—that is the young artist's name—may be—may have been in the forest—in short, I feel more uneasy than before till I can learn what has become of both of them."

"Do you mean," said the lawyer, with a sneer in his voice, but at the same time looking into his companion's face with a shrewd expression of investigation in his eye, "do you mean that the two ladies may possibly have fallen in with each other, and may in such case not improbably have fallen out with each other? You know best, Signor Marchese, the likelihood of any trouble arising out of such a meeting."

"For God's sake don't speak in such a tone, Signor Giovacchino. I tell you I am seriously uneasy. Should they have met under such circumstances—God only knows—What would you advise me to do, Signor Giovacchino?" said the Marchese, looking into the lawyer's face with increasing and now evidently painful anxiety.

"It is ill giving advice without knowing all the circumstances of a case, Signor Marchese," returned Fortini, somewhat drily, looking hard at the young man as he spoke, and putting a meaning emphasis on the word "all."

"You do know all the circumstances as far as I know them myself. The thing happened exactly as I told you," replied Ludovico.

"You left her sleeping on a bank in the forest, and have never seen her since?" said the lawyer, thoughtfully.

"Exactly so! I returned to the spot where I had left her—at least as far as I could tell it was the same spot—and she was no longer there," replied Ludovico.

"But you were not sure that you did return to the same spot? You could not recognise it again with certainty?"

"So it seemed to me when I was there. I think it must have been the same place. But when I did not find her, I could not feel sure of it. Every spot in the Pineta is so like all other spots. One pine-tree is just like another; and the grassy openings, and the little thickets of underwood, are all the same over and over again. I felt that I could not be sure that the place was the same."

"Was there no fallen tree, no track of road, no specialty of weed or flower, that the spot might be identified by?"

"None I think—none that I am aware of or can remember. There was a little rising of the ground, a sort of bank, and the grass was sprinkled all over with wild flowers. There were violets close at hand,

I know, because I remember the scent of them! But when I came to try, it seem'd to me that I found all these things in a dozen other places."

"Nevertheless, you know at what point you entered the Pineta; it cannot be very difficult to have the whole wood, within such a distance as it is at all likely that she should have strayed to, thoroughly searched. But the best men for the purpose would be some of the foresters in the employ of the farmers of the forest. I dare say that we might find—what is that coming along the road yonder?" said the lawyer interrupting himself.

The two gentlemen had been standing during the above short conversation just on the outside of the gate, and looking down the stretch of long straight road towards St. Apollinare and the pine forest.

"It is a knot of men coming along the road. They are likely enough some of the very fellows we want. In that case we might get them to go back with us without loss of time."

"With us?" said the lawyer, who had not bargained when he left his home, for any such expedition. "Well, I don't mind helping you, Signor Marchese, in your search," he added, after a moment's consideration; "but I am not going to walk to the Pineta this afternoon; and I should think you must have had enough of it for to-day. But I will tell you what I can do. We will send one of these fellows to my house to order my servant to come here with my calessino as quick as he can; and if these men are the people we want—What are they doing? They are carrying something! Why surely—Signor Marchese!" said the old lawyer, looking into his companion's face, while a strange expression of understanding, mixed with a blank look of dismay and alarm, stole over his own features.

"What is it?—What have they got?—Why, heavens and earth! it is—Signor Fortini, is it not a dead body they are carrying? My God!"

The young man griped his companion's arm hard, as he spoke, and the action enabled the lawyer to remark that he was shaking all over.

In another minute the men whom they had seen coming along the road were close to the gate. They were six in number; and they were bearing—somewhat, between them. They advanced beneath the covered gateway, and there, as it is necessary to do in the case of everything brought into the town, they set their burthen down on the flag-stones, at the feet of the officers of the gate, and of the Marchese and the lawyer.

Their burthen was a door lifted from its hinges, and supported by three slender stakes drawn green from a hedgerow. And on the door there lay, covered with a sheet, what was evidently a dead body.

Ludovico, with his eyes starting from his head, and horror in every feature of his face, still clutching one hand of the old lawyer in his, stretched forward with one advanced stride towards the extemporized bier, and with his other hand lifted the sheet.

A shriek of horror burst from him. "Ah! Paolina mia!" he cried aloud; and then with a deep groan, as of one in physical pain, he fell into Signor Fortini's arms, and sunk in an insensible state of sick faintness on the flag-stone pavement beneath the old gateway.

CHAPTER I

How the Good News Came to Ravenna

Such were the events of that last night of carnival, and of the Ash Wednesday that followed it;—an Ash Wednesday remembered many a year afterwards in Ravenna.

The old lawyer, Fortini, standing a pace behind the Marchese Ludovico, when the latter lifted up the sheet from the face of the dead, saw only that it was the face of a woman. Paolina Foscarelli he had never seen; and Bianca Lalli he had seen only once or twice on the stage; the lawyer not being much of a frequenter of the theatre. There could be little doubt that the body lying there beneath the gateway, with the officials standing with awe-stricken faces around it, together with the six peasants who had brought it thither, was that of one or other of those two young women.

Of course there were plenty of persons at hand who were able to set at rest all doubt as to the identity of the murdered woman, for such it was pretty clear she must be considered to be. And of course all interests in the little provincial city were for many days to come absorbed in the terrible interest belonging to the investigation of the foul deed which had been done.

But in order to set before the reader the whole of this strange story intelligibly, and to give him the same means of estimating the probabilities of the questions involved in it, and of reaching a solution of the mysterious circumstances which the authorities, who were called upon to investigate them, were in possession of, it will be expedient to go back to a period some four months previous to that memorable Ash Wednesday.

It was a bitterly cold night in Ravenna, towards the latter end of November, some four months before that Ash Wednesday on which the events that have been narrated occurred. Untravelled English people, who have heard much of "the sweet south," of the sunny skies of Italy, and of its balmy atmosphere, do not readily imagine that such cold is ever to be found in that favoured clime. But the fact is that cold several degrees below the freezing point is by no means rare in the sub-Alpine and sub-Apennine districts of northern Italy.

And Ravenna is a specially cold place. At Florence, the winter, though short, is often sharp enough; and the climate of the old Tuscan city is considered a somewhat severe one for Italy. But the district which lies to the north-eastward, on the low coast of the upper part of the stormy Adriatic, is much colder. There is nothing, neither hill nor forest, between the Friulian Alps and Ravenna, to prevent the north-eastern winds, bringing with them a Siberian temperature, from sweeping the low shelterless plain on which the ancient capital of the Exarchs is situated.

They were so sweeping that plain, and howling fiercely through the deserted streets of the old city, on the November evening in question.

Nevertheless there were several persons loitering around the door of that ancient hostelry, the "Albergo della Spada," in the Via del Monte, then as now, and for many a generation past, the principal inn of Ravenna. They were wrapped in huge cloaks, most of them with hoods to them, which gave the wearers a strange sort of monkish appearance. And they from time to time blew upon their fingers, in the intervals of using their mouths for the purpose of grumbling at the cold.

But they none of them resorted to tramping up and down, or stamping with their feet, or threshing themselves with their arms, or had recourse to movement of any kind to get a little warmth into their bodies, as Englishmen may be seen to do under similar circumstances. However cold it may be an Italian never does anything of this sort. It must be supposed, that to him cold is a less detestable evil than muscular exertion of any kind.

There were some half-dozen men standing about the door; and though they were doing nothing, it was not to be supposed that they stood there in the bitter cold for their own amusement. The fact was, they were waiting for one of the great events of the day at Ravenna, the arrival of the diligenza from Bologna. It was past six o'clock in the evening; and it could not now be long before the expected vehicle would arrive.

It is a distance of some sixty miles from Bologna to Ravenna; the diligence started at five in the morning, and was due at the latter city at five in the evening. But nobody expected that it would reach its destination at that hour. It had never done so within the memory of man, even in the fine days of summer, and now, when the roads were rough with ridges of frozen mud! It was now, however, nearly half-past six—yes, there went the half-hour clanging from the cracked-voiced old bell in the top of the round brick tower, which stands on one side of the cathedral, and by its likeness to a minaret reminds one of the Byzantine parentage of its builders.

Half-past six! The loiterers about the inn door remark to each other, that unless "something" has happened old Cecco Zoppo can't be far off now.

The arrival of the Bologna diligence, the main means of communication between remote out-of-the-way Ravenna and the rest of the world, was always a matter of interest in the old-world little city, where matters of interest were so few. And on a pleasant evening in spring or summer the attendance of expectant loungers was wont to be far larger than it was on that bitter November night, and to include a large number of amateurs; whereas the half-dozen now waiting were all either officially or otherwise directly interested in the arrival. Indeed, there was a very special interest attached to the coming of the expected vehicle on that November night; and nothing but the extreme severity of the weather would have prevented a very distinguished assemblage from being on the spot to hear the first news that was expected to be brought by one of the travellers.

"Eccolo! I heard the bells, underneath the gate-way. Per Bacco, it is time! I'm well-nigh frozen alive," said Pippo, the ostler.

"If they don't keep him an hour at the gate," rejoined a decidedly more ragged and poverty-stricken individual, who held recognized office as the ostler's assistant.

"Not such a night as this! Those gentlemen there at the gate can feel the cold for themselves, if they can't feel nothing else," rejoined the ostler, who was a frondeur and disaffected to the government, in consequence of a drunken grandson having been turned out of the place of third assistant scullion in the kitchen of the Cardinal Legate. "There's the bells again! They've let him off pretty quick. I thought as much," added the old man, with a chuckle.

"Wasn't Signor Ercole's woman here with a lanthorn just now?" said another of the bystanders, a young man, who, though wrapped to the eyes in the universal all-levelling cloak, belonged evidently to a superior class of society to the previous speakers.

"Si, Signor Conte, she is there in the kitchen. Per Dio! she would have had no fingers to hold the light for her master, if she had stayed out here," replied the ostler. And then the rattle of wheels became distinct, and in the next instant the feeble light of a couple of lamps became visible at the far end of the street, as the coach turned out of the Piazza Maggiore into the Via del Monte, and struggled forwards towards the knot at the inn door; it came at a miserable little trot, but with an accompaniment of tremendous whip-cracking, that awoke echoes in the silent streets far and near, and imparted an impression of breathless speed to the imagination of the bystanders, who, being Italians, accepted the symbol in despite of their certain knowledge that the reality of the thing symbolised was not there. Like the immortal Marchioness, Dick Swiveller's friend, in the Old Curiosity Shop, the Italians, when the realities of circumstances are unfavourable, can always manage to gild them a little by "making believe very strong."

"Now then, Signora Marta, bring out your light," called the deputy ostler in at the inn door.

The individual addressed as Signor Conte became evidently excited, and prepared himself to be the first to present himself at the door of the coach as it drew up opposite the inn. The ostler stepped out into the street with his stable lanthorn. Signora Marta, shivering, with a huge shawl over her head, took up her position, lanthorn in hand, behind the Signor Conte, and the ramshackle old coach, rattling over the uneven round cobble-stones of the execrable pavement with a crash of noise that seemed to threaten that every jolt would be its last, came to a standstill at the inn door.

The Signor Conte Leandro Lombardoni—that was the name of the young man hitherto called Il Signor Conte—opened the door with his own hand, and, putting his head eagerly into the interior, cried,

"Are you there, Signor Ercole? Well! What news? Have you succeeded? Let me give you a hand."

"Grazie, Signor Leandro, grazie," replied a high-pitched voice of singularly shrill quality from within the vehicle, "I don't know whether I can move. Misericordia! che viaggio! What a journey I have had. I am nearly dead. My blood is frozen in my veins. I have no use of my limbs. I shall never recover it; never!"

And then very slowly a huge bundle of cloaks and rags and furs, nearly circular in form and about five feet in diameter, began to move towards the door of the carriage, and gradually, by the help of Signor Leandro and Signora Marta, to struggle through it and get itself down on the pavement.

"And this I do and suffer for thee, Ravenna!" said the bundle in the same shrill tenor, making an attempt, as it spoke, to raise two little projecting fins towards the cold, unsympathising stars.

"But have you succeeded, Signor Ercole?" asked the other again, anxiously.

"I have succeeded in sacrificing myself for my country," replied the shrill voice with chattering teeth; "for I know I shall never get over it. I am frozen. It is a very painful form of martyrdom."

"But you can at least say one word, Signor Ercole? You can say yes or no to the question, whether you have succeeded in our object?" urged the Conte Leandro.

Signor Ercole Stadione, however, who was, as the reader is aware, no less important a personage than the impresario of the principal theatre of Ravenna, knew too well all the importance that belonged to the news he had to tell to part with his secret so easily. "Signor Conte," he quavered out, "I tell you I am frozen! A man cannot speak on any subject in such a condition. I know nothing. My intellectual faculties have not their ordinary lucidity. I must endeavour to reach my home. Marta, hold the lamp here."

"And I who have waited here for your arrival ever since the venti-quattro! Per Dio! Do you think I ain't cold too? And the Marchese is expecting you. Of course, you will go to him at once?"

"I don't know that I shall ever recover myself sufficiently to do so. It is useless for the city to expect more from a man than he can accomplish. When I have got thawed, I will endeavour to do my duty. Good night, Signor Conte!" said the little impresario, preparing to follow his servant with the lanthorn, as well as the enormous quantity of wraps around him would allow him to do so.

"Come now, Signor Ercole, you won't be so ill-natured. You know how much interest I take in the matter. Think how long I have waited here for you, and nobody else has cared enough to do that. Come now, be good-natured, and tell a fellow. Just one word. Look here now," added the Conte Leandro, seeing that he was on the point of losing the gratification for the sake of which he had undergone the penance of standing sentinel in the cold for the last hour, and that his only hope was to bring forward les grands moyens, "see now, the only thing to bring you round is a glass of hot punch. Now, while you go home and get your things off, I will go to the cafe and get you a good glass of punch, hot and strong—smoking hot! and have it brought to your house, all hot, you know, in a covered jug. But before I go; you will just say the one word: Have you been successful? Come now. Just one word."

Signor Ercole Stadione, the impresario, would much have preferred not saying that one word just then. He knew perfectly well that the grand object of his questioner was to be the first to carry the great news to the Circolo—the club where all the young nobles of the town were in the habit of congregating; and to make the most of the sort of reputation to be gained by being the first in Ravenna to have accurate information on the matter in question. He knew also that within a quarter-of-an-hour after the news should be told to Signor Leandro Lombardoni it would be known to all Ravenna. Further, he was perfectly aware that, frozen or not frozen, he must wait that evening on the Marchese, of whom Signor Leandro had spoken—the Marchese Lamberto di Castelmare, in order to communicate to him the news which Signor Leandro was so anxious to hear; that not to do so would be as much as his standing and position in Ravenna were worth. And he would have preferred that the Marchese should not have heard what he had to tell before telling it to him himself; which he thought likely enough to happen, if he let the cat out of the bag to Signor Leandro. But the offer of the punch was irresistible. The poor little impresario knew how little possibility there was of finding any such pleasant stimulant in the cold, cheerless, wifeless little quartiere which he and Marta called their home. His teeth were chattering with cold; and the hot punch carried the day.

"Troppo buono, Signor Conte! Truly a good glass of hot ponche would be the saving of me! It is very kindly thought of. Well, then; listen in your ear. But you won't say a word about it till to-morrow morning. It is all right. The thing is done. The writings signed. Have I done well, eh? Have I deserved well of the city, eh? But you won't say a word!"

"Bravo, Signor Ercole! Bravo, bravissimo! Not a word. Not a word. I run to order the punch. Good night. Not a word to a living soul!"

And the Conte Leandro ran off to give a hasty order at the cafe in the Piazza, on his way to the Circolo to spread his important news all over the town.

CHAPTER II

Signor Leandro Lombardoni felt himself to be abundantly repaid for his hour of waiting in the cold street, and for the bajocchi expended on the glass of punch, by the position he occupied at the Circolo all that evening. He was the centre of every group anxious to gain the earliest information respecting a matter of the highest interest to all the society of Ravenna. And the matter belonged to a class of subjects respecting which the Conte Leandro was especially desirous of being thought to be thoroughly well-informed, and to have interest in the highest quarters.

The fact was, that Signor Ercole Stadione, the Ravenna impresario, had undertaken a journey to Milan, in the hope of accomplishing a negotiation in which the whole of the smaller provincial city had felt itself deeply interested. He had gone thither for the purpose of engaging the celebrated prima donna, Bianca Lalli, to sing at Ravenna during the coming Carnival. The pretension was a very ambitious one on the part of the impresario—or, as it may be more properly said, on the part of the city—for the step was by no means the result of his own independent and unaided enterprise. Such matters were not done in that way in the good old times in the smaller cities of Italy. The matter had been much debated among the leading patrons of the musical drama in the little town. The chances of success had been canvassed. The financial question had been considered. Certain sacrifices had been determined on. And it had been settled what terms the impresario should be empowered to offer.

It had been fully felt and recognised that the hope of engaging the famous Bianca Lalli to sing at remote little Ravenna, during a carnival, was a singularly ambitious one. But there had been circumstances which had led those who had conceived the bold idea to hope that it would not prove to be so impossible as it might at first sight appear. There had been whispers of certain difficulties—untoward circumstances at Milan. Ill-natured things had been said of the "divina Lalli." Doubtless she had been more sinned against than sinning. But to put the matter crudely—which, of course, no Italian who had to speak of it, was ever so ill-bred as to do—it would seem that the great singer had placed herself, or had been placed, in such relations with somebody or other bearing a great name in the Lombard capital, that the paternal Austrian government, at the instance of that somebody's family, had seen good to hint, in some gentle, but unmistakable manner, that it might, on the whole, be better that the divine Lalli should bless some other city with her presence during the ensuing season. And then came the consideration, that in all probability most of the great cities of the peninsula had, by that time, made their arrangements for the coming Carnival. Not impossible, too, that the "diva" herself might be not disinclined to allow a certain period of such comparative obscurity as an engagement at Ravenna would bring with it, to pass after her exit from Milan under such circumstances, before re-appearing on other boards where she would be equally in the eyes of all Europe. But this ground of hope, though it may have been felt, was never so much as alluded to in words, in Ravenna. In short, Ravenna had determined to make the bold attempt. And Don Signor Ercole Stadione had returned from the arduous enterprise to announce that it had been crowned with complete success.

None but those who have had some opportunity of becoming acquainted with the social habits and manners of the smaller cities of Italy—and that as they were some twenty years ago, and not as they are now—can imagine the degree in which a matter of the kind in question could be felt there to be a subject of general public interest. From the Cardinal Legate, who governed the province, down to the little boys who hung about the cafe doors, in the hope of picking up a half-eaten roll, there was not a human being in the city who did not feel that he had some part of the glory resulting from the fact that "La Lalli" was to sing at Ravenna during the Carnival. The contadini—the peasants outside the gates—even though they were only just outside it, cared nothing at all about the matter: another specialty of the social peculiarities of the peninsula.

The Cardinal Legate, restrained by the professional decorum of his cloth, said nothing save among his quite safe intimates; but, perhaps, like the sailor's parrot, he only thought the more.

As for the jeunesse doree of the Circolo, to whom Signor Leandro recounted his great tidings with all the self-importance to which the exclusive possession of news of such interest so well entitled him, it is impossible to do justice to the enthusiasm which the news excited among them.

All sorts of pleasing anticipations were indulged in. They were all jealous of each other by anticipation. Already, in the gravest spirit of business, a scheme for taking off her horses at the city gates and harnessing their noble selves to the carriage of the expected guest was discussed.

The reputation enjoyed by the great singer Bianca Lalli at that time was very high throughout Italy. But, perhaps, any one of her rival goddesses would have said undoubtedly, it was a reputation not wholly and exclusively due to her strictly vocal charms. She was, in truth, a woman of more than ordinary beauty; and was universally declared to exercise a charm on all who came within reach of her influence beyond that which even extraordinary beauty has always the privilege of exercising. All kinds of stories were told of her boundless power of fascination. In crude language, again, such as her own countrymen never used concerning her, the reputation of "la diva Lalli" was tout soit peu, a reputation de scandale. And it will be readily imagined that the enthusiasm in her favour of the young frequenters of the Circolo at Ravenna was none the less vehement on this account.

It must, however, be added that she undoubtedly was a very admirable singer. Had this not been the case, the Marchese Lamberto di Castelmare would not have interested himself so much as he had done in the plans and negotiations for bringing her to Ravenna. The Marchese was not a man to be much influenced by the prima donna's reputation for beauty and fascination. But he was "fanatico per la musica." He was the acknowledged leader in all matters musical in Ravenna; the most influential patron of the opera in the city; and all-powerful in the regulation of all theatrical affairs.

The Marchese Lamberto held a rather special position in the social world in Ravenna. His fortune was large; and the nobility of his family ancient. But it was not these circumstances only, or even mainly, that caused him to hold the place he did in the estimation of his fellow-citizens. He was a bachelor, now about fifty years old; and during some thirty of those years he had always been before the public in one manner or another, and always had in every capacity won golden opinions from all men. Though abundantly rich enough to have gone occasionally to Rome, or even to have resided there entirely, if he had chosen to do so, he had, on the contrary, preferred to pass his whole life in his native city. And Ravenna was flattered by this, to begin with. Then his residence in the provincial city had been in many respects a really useful one, not only to that section of the body politic which is called, par excellence, society, but to the public in general. He had held various municipal offices, and had discharged the functions belonging to them with credit and applause. He was treasurer to a hospital, and a generous contributor to its funds. He was the founder of an artistic society for the education of young artists and the encouragement of their seniors. He was the principal director of a board of "publica beneficenza." He was the manager, and what we should call the trustee for the property of more than one nunnery. He was intimate with the Cardinal Legate, and a frequent and honoured guest at the palace. Of course in matters of orthodoxy and well-affected sentiments towards the Church and its government he was all that the agents of that government could desire. It has already been said that he was at the head of all matters musical and theatrical in Ravenna. And besides all this, he gave every year three grand balls in Carnival; and his house was at all times open every Sunday and Wednesday evening to the elite of the society of the city.

Gradually it had come to be understood, rather by tacit agreement among the society which frequented these reunions than in obedience to any desire expressed by the Marchese on the subject, that on the Sunday evening ladies were expected; and on those days a sister-in-law of the Marchese, the widow of a younger brother, was always there to do the honours of the Palazzo Castelmare. The Wednesday evening parties had come to be meetings of gentlemen only. And on these occasions one marked element of the society consisted of all that the city possessed in the way of professors of natural science. For the Marchese was, in a mild way, fond of such pursuits, and had a special liking for anatomical inquiries and experiments.

In one respect only could the world fail to be wholly and perfectly contented with the Marchese Lamberto di Castelmare. At the age of fifty he was still a bachelor! Not that the continuance of the noble line of Castelmare was thereby compromised. The sister-in-law already mentioned had a son, a young man of two-and-twenty, at the time in question, who was the heir to the wealth and honours of the house, and who, it was to be hoped, would also inherit all that accumulated treasure of public esteem and respect which his uncle had been so uninterruptedly laying up. Neither could a social objection to the Marchese's bachelorhood be raised on the score of any such laxity of moral conduct as the world is wont to expect, and to tolerate with more or less of indulgence, in persons so free from special ties. Had the Marchese been an archbishop himself, instead of being merely the intimate friend of one, it could not have seemed in Ravenna more out of the question to mention his respected name in connection with any scandal or inuendo of the kind. There was not a mother in Ravenna who would not have been proud to see her daughter honoured by any such intercourse with the Marchese as might be natural between a father and his child. Proud indeed the most noble of those matrons would have been could she have supposed that any such intercourse tended towards sentiments of a more tender nature. But all hopes of this kind had been long given up in Ravenna. It was quite understood that the Marchese was not a marrying man.

Not that even now, in his fiftieth year, he might not well have entered the lists with many a younger man as a candidate for the favour of the sex. He was a man of a remarkably fine presence, tall, well made, and with a natural dignity and graceful bearing in all his movements, which were very impressive. He had never given in to the modern fashion of wearing either beard or moustache. And the contours of his face were too good and even noble to have gained anything by being so hidden. The large, strong, rather square jaw and chin, and smooth placid cheeks were strongly expressive of quiet decision and dignified force of will. The mouth, almost always the tell-tale feature of the face, seemed in his case rather calculated to puzzle any one who would have speculated on the meanings shadowed forth by the lines of it. It was certainly, with its large rows of unexceptionably brilliant teeth, a very handsome mouth. And it was often not devoid of much sweetness. Nobody had ever imagined that they detected any evil expression among its meanings. But whereas a physiognomist looking at that generally faithful expositor of the moral man, when it was at rest, would have been inclined to say, that it was a mouth indicative of much capacity for deep and strong passion, a further study of it in its varied movements would have led him to the conclusion that no strong or violent passions had ever been there to leave their traces among its lines. The whole face was so essentially calm, unruffled, and placidly dignified.

The loftly noble forehead, the strongly marked brow, the well-opened calm grey eye, all told the same tale of a mind within well-balanced, thoroughly at peace with itself, and thoroughly contented with its outward manifestations, and with every particular of its position.

Clearly the Marchese di Castelmare was a remarkably handsome man. And yet there was something about him, and always had been even as a young man, which seemed to be in natural accordance with the fact that he had never seemed to seek female society, save as an amphytrion receiving all Ravenna within his hospitable doors. There was a kind of austerity about his bearing;—a something difficult to define, which would have prevented any girl from fancying that he was at all likely to want to make love to her; a something which made it as impossible that the refined courtesy of his address should have called a pleased blush to any girl's cheek, or made her pulse move one beat the faster, as that she should have been so affected by the imposition of the hands of the bishop who confirmed her!

Such as the Marchese was, any committee in the world would have chosen him its president, any jury in the world would have named him its foreman, any board in the world have selected him as its chairman, any deputation in the world would have put him forward as its spokesman; any sovereign in the world might have appointed him grand master of the ceremonies; but never at any period of his life would the suffrages of the ball-room have pitched upon him to be the leader of the cotillon.

Perhaps it was that his life had been always too full to spare any space for such lighter matters. He had been left the head of his family when quite a young man, and had at once, in a great degree, stepped into the place he had ever since occupied in the social world of his native city. And what with his music, which was with him really a passion, and what with his dabblings in science, and what with the multifarious business he had always made for himself by real and useful attention to the affairs pertaining to all the functions he had filled, his life had really been a fully occupied one.

Any man, woman, or child in Ravenna would have said, if such an unpleasant idea had crossed their minds, that what Ravenna would do without him it was frightful to think. He was very popular, as well as profoundly respected by all classes of his fellow-citizens. Though certainly a very proud man, his pride was of a nature that gave offence to nobody. He was not only proud of being Marchese di Castelmare; he was very proud of the esteem, the affection and respect of his fellow-citizens. And perhaps this was, next to his love of music, what most resembled a passion in his nature, and what most ministered to his enjoyment of life.

It was to this phoenix of a Marchese that Signor Ercole Stadione, the impresario, having comforted himself with the Conte Leandro's punch, and got somewhat thawed, and having changed his mountain of travelling wraps for a costume proper for presenting himself in such a presence, repaired to report the result of his journey to Milan.

CHAPTER III

The Impresario's Report

It has been said that Signor Ercole Stadione, when he was first introduced to the reader under circumstances somewhat unfavourable to that dignity of appearance and deportment on which he specially prided himself, presented the appearance of a round mass some five feet in diameter. And it may be thence concluded, that when reduced to the proportions familiar to the citizens of Ravenna, his utmost longitudinal dimensions did not exceed that measure. The impresario was in truth a very small man, weighing perhaps seven stone with his boots. But Signor Ercole held, and very frequently expressed, an opinion that dignity and nobility of appearance depended wholly on bearing, and in no wise on mere corporeal altitude. Men were measured in his country (Rome), he said, from the eyebrow upwards. And though Rome is not exactly the place, of all others, where one might expect to find such an estimate of human value prevailing, unless, indeed, smallness of that which a man has above his brow be deemed the desirable thing, it was undeniable that little Signor Ercole carried a mass of forehead which might have been the share of a much taller man.

Nor were the pretensions put forward by the impresario on this score altogether vain. He was no fool;—a shrewd as well as a dapper little man, active and clever at his business, and well liked both by the artists and by the public, for which he catered, despite of being one of the vainest of mortals. Vanity makes some men very odious to their fellows;—in others it is perfectly inoffensive; and though damaging to a claim to respect, is perfectly compatible with a considerable amount of liking for the victim of it.

A very dapper little man was Signor Ercole, as he stepped forth, about eight o'clock, entirely refitted, to wait upon the Marchese at the Palazzo Castelmare. He was dressed in complete black, somewhat threadbare, but scrupulously brushed. He had a large frill at the bosom of his shirt, and more frills around the wristbands of it; one or two rings of immense size and weight on his small fingers; boots with heels two inches high, and a rather long frock-coat buttoned closely round his little body. Signor Ercole had never been known to wear a swallow-tailed coat on any occasion. And spiteful people told each other, that his motive for never quitting the greater shelter of the frock was to be found in his fear of exhibiting to the unkindly glances of the world a pair of knock-knees of rare perfection.

When his toilet was completed, he threw over all a handsome black cloth cloak turned up with a broad border of velvet, which he draped around his person with the air of an Apollo, throwing the corner of the garment round the lower part of his face and over his shoulder, in a manner wholly unattainable by any man born on the northern side of the Alps; and kindly telling Marta that he would take the key, and that she had better not sit up for him in the cold, stepped forth on his errand.

"Ben tornato, Signor Ercole! I thank you for coming to me," said the Marchese, rising from his seat at his library-table, which was covered with papers and books, to receive the impresario.

Despite the extreme cold, this owner of a large fortune, and of one of the finest palaces in Ravenna, was not sitting in an easy-chair by the fire, as an Englishman might be expected to be found at such an hour. The Italian's day is not divided into two portions as clearly as an Englishman's day is divided by his dinner hour into the time for business or out-door exercise, and the time for relaxation, for a book or other amusement. He is quite as likely to apply himself to any business or work of any kind after dinner as before. Still less has he the Englishman's notion of making himself comfortable in his home.

There was a miserable morsel of wood fire in the room in which the Marchese sat; but it was at the far end of it. And in many a well-to-do Italian home there would have been none at all. In order not to be absolutely frozen, he sat in a large cloak, and had beside him, or in his hands, a little earthen-ware pot filled with burning braize—a scaldino, as it is called, the use of which is common to the noble in his palace, and the beggar in the street.

He pointed to a chair near the table, and as he spoke, paid his visitor the ordinary courtesy of offering him his scaldino.

"My duty, my mere duty, Eccellenza," said Signor Ercole, letting his cloak fall gracefully from his shoulders, and declining the proffered pot of braize with an action that might have suited an Emperor. "Of course my first care and object on arriving was to wait on your Excellency. I arrived with barely a breath of life remaining in my body. What a journey! What a journey! But if I had been frozen quite I could not have forgotten that my first duty was to report what I have accomplished to your Excellency."

"Thanks, good Signor Ercole, thanks; you know the interest I take in all that concerns the honour of our theatre, and the pleasures of our citizens; and I may truly add, in all that touches your interest, my good Signor Ercole."

"Troppo buono! Eccellenza! Troppo buono davvero!" said the little man, half rising from his chair, to execute a bow in return for the Marchese's speech, while his cloak fell around his legs.

"I suppose that in such weather as this the diligence was behind its time—E naturale—but I have already heard, in a general way, that you have been successful. I congratulate you on it, Signor Ercole, with all my heart!"

"I trusted that I should have been the first to tell your Excellency the news. I am conscious that it was due to you, Signor Marchese, to be the first to hear the result of my negotiation. But che vuole? There was the Conte Leandro waiting for the coach, and standing at the door as I got out of it, more dead than alive! And there was no way of getting rid of him. I was forced to tell him, in a word, that our hopes were crowned with success. He faithfully promised to keep the fact secret. But, doubtless, all the town knows it by this time! Che vuole?"

"E naturale! e naturale!" returned the Marchese, with a graceful wave of his hand; "naturally they are all anxious to know the result of our impresario's labours. And I was not left in ignorance. My nephew ran in from the Circolo to tell me; he had just heard it from Signor Leandro. But I thought that I should have a visit from yourself, Signor Ercole, before long."

"E come, e come, Signor Marchese; could your Excellency imagine that I could so fail in my duty as to have omitted waiting on your lordship! Had it not been that I was half killed by this awful weather, I should have placed myself at your Excellency's orders an hour ago. Oh, Signor Marchese, such a journey from Bologna hither! I know what is my duty to the city; I know what is expected of me. But—Eccellenza, there are benefactors to their country, who have statues raised to them, that have suffered less in the gaining of them, than I have this day."

"Povero, Signor Ercole! But who knows? Perhaps we may see the day when Ravenna will reward your exertions with a monument. Why not? It must be a statue, life size, nothing less, with 'Ercole Stadione, La Patria riconoscente,' on the base," said the Marchese, with an irony, the fine flavour of which did not in the least pierce, as it was not intended to pierce, the plate armour of the little impresario's vanity.

"Oh, Eccellenza!" said the poor little man, with the most perfect good faith in the propriety, as well as the seriousness, of his patron's proposition.

"And now, then," said the Marchese, "let us hear all about it. She accepts our terms?"

"The scrittura has been signed before a notary, Eccellenza."

"Bravo! she sings—?"

"The whole repertorio, Signor Marchese! What is there she could not sing?"

"And three representations a week?"

"Three representations a week. My instructions were formal on that point, as your Excellency knows."

"Good! quite right! And now what is she, this diva? What is she like? We know that Signor Ercole Stadione is as good a judge of the merits of the lady as of the singer?" said the Marchese, with a smile. "I don't ask you about her singing," he added. "We have all heard all that can be said about that."

"Well, Signor Marchese, if I am to speak my own poor opinion, I take the Signora Lalli to be decidedly the most beautiful woman it was ever my good fortune to see," said Signor Ercole, with a voice and manner of profound conviction.

"Paris himself, if called on to be umpire once again, could require no more conclusive testimony, my good Signor Ercole. But that is not exactly what I mean. Her mere beauty is a matter that does not interest me very keenly. What I want to know, is what sort of a scenic presence has she? Can she take the stage? I do not ask if she is captivating in a drawing-room; but has she the face and figure needed to be effective in the theatre? I need not tell you, my friend, that these are two different things, and do not always go together," said the Marchese, whose interest in the matter was, as he said, wholly theatrical; first, that he and the society of Ravenna should enjoy some fine singing during the coming Carnival; and, secondly that the Lalli should produce such an enthusiasm as should lead all the theatrical world to think and say that a great stroke had been achieved, and a very public-spirited thing done in bringing about the engagement. He was anxious that the step, which he had had a large share in taking, should result in a great and universally admitted success.

"Eccellenza! I have no doubt that your lordship will be satisfied in these respects. Most true it is, as your Excellency so judiciously remarks, that we require something more than merely a beautiful face, or even than a fine figure. And I have never had the good fortune to see 'La Lalli' on the boards. But as far as my poor judgment goes, she is admirably gifted with all the requisites for achieving the result we desire. Then there is the testimony of all Milan! And I succeeded in speaking with an old friend who had seen her the year before last at Naples, and whose report I can trust. The opinion seems to be universal that few artists have ever possessed the gift of fascinating an audience to the degree that she does. Your Excellency may take my word for it, she is a very clever woman. My own interviews with her sufficed to convince me of that fact. And I need not tell your Excellency, that little as some of the empty-headed young gentlemen in the stalls may suspect it, talent, not only the special talent of song but general talent, has much to do with the power of fascination that a gifted actress exercises."

"Most true, mio bravo Signor Ercole; you speak like an oracle; and if she left on you the impression that she is a clever woman, I have no doubt in the world that she is so."

There was no irony in the Marchese's mind when he said this; and the little impresario, highly gratified again, half rose from his chair to bow in return for the compliment.

"As for the specialties of her face and person," continued the impresario, "they appeared to me highly favourable. Very tall, perhaps your lordship or I might say too tall. But—on the stage the prejudice is in favour of a degree of tallness that we might not admire off it. Gestures, bearing, and the movement of the person equally capable of expressing majestic dignity, or heart-subduing pathos. A most graceful walk. In short, a persona tutta simpatica. As for the head—magnificent hair, blonde, which for choice I would always prefer—the true Titian sun-tinged auburn, a telling eye, finely formed nose, and mouth of inexpressible sweetness!"

"Per Bacco, Signor Ercole, a Phoenix indeed! A Diva davvero!" said the Marchese.

"Eccellenza, she'll do," said the little man nodding his head with its top-heavy forehead three or four times emphatically. "If she do not make such a sensation in Ravenna as we have not known here for a long time, say that Ercole Stadione knows nothing of his profession."

"Bravo! bravo!" cried the Marchese, gleefully rubbing his hands. "And now, my good friend, I won't keep you from the bed and the rest you so well deserve any longer. You may depend on it that your zeal in this matter won't be overlooked or forgotten."

"Troppo buono, Eccellenza! But there was one word I wished to say to your lordship," continued little Signor Ercole, dropping his voice to a lower key, and speaking with some hesitation, one little word that I thought it might be useful, or—or—desirable to mention—"

"Yes, speak on, my dear Signor Ercole, I am all attention. What is it? No drawback I hope!"

"Only this, Signor Marchese," said the little man casting a glance round the room, dropping his voice still more, and bringing his head nearer to the ear of the Marchese; "only this:—you see if there had been nothing-disagreeable, nothing untoward, as I may say—your lordship understands, we should never have had La Lalli at Ravenna. There has been a—sort of difficulty—your lordship understands—spiteful things have been said—calumny—all calumny no doubt-the constant attendant of merit, alas! we all know. But—in short—here in Ravenna—it would not be—desirable, your Excellency understands and appreciates what I would say a thousand times better than I can say it. It would be in every point of view better, as your Excellency sees, that no idle chatter of this kind should be set about here. It would be inexpedient for more reasons than one."

"Quite so; quite so. Your ideas on the subject are happily judicious, Signor Ercole. What have we to do with misunderstandings that may have arisen at Milan? Of course, it is not our business to have ever heard anything of the kind. And I'll tell you what I'll do, and that at once, before there is time for any mischief to be done. I will just give my nephew a hint. He can be trusted. He is discreet. And it will be easy for him to put down at once and discountenance any talk of the kind, or any rumour that might find its way among our youngsters."

"The very thing, Eccellenza! The Marchese Ludovico will understand the thing at once. And half a word from him would give the key-note, as I may say, to the tone of talk about the lady. Ravenna must not be thought to be contenting herself with that which Milan rejects," said Signor Ercole, with the air of a patriot.

"I should think not, indeed! And, doubtless, Milan would have been but too glad to retain La Lalli, had it not been for some unimportant contretemps. Ludovico shall put the matter in its right light."

As he spoke, the Marchese rang a little hand-bell which stood on his library table; and on a servant entering from the anteroom, he told him just to step across to the Circolo, and request the Marchese Ludovico to be so good as to come to him for five minutes.

In very little more than that time the man returned, saying that the Marchese Ludovico was not at the Circolo. He had been there for a few minutes at the beginning of the evening, but had gone away without saying whither he was going.

The Marchese knitted his brows when this message was given to him; and after a minute's thoughtful silence, shook his head in a manner that showed him to be not a little displeased. From a look of intelligence that might have been observed in Signor Ercole's eyes, it might have been judged that he understood that the Marchese was more annoyed than on account of the momentary frustration of his immediate purpose, and that he was aware of the nature of his annoyance. But he did not venture to say any word on the subject; and the Marchese took leave of him, merely saying that he would not forget to act on Signor Ercole's caution when he should see his nephew the next morning.

CHAPTER IV

Paolina Foscarelli

The young Marchese Ludovico di Castelmare had in the early part of the evening lounged into the Circolo, as was the habit of most of those of his class, seniors as well as juniors; but he had, as had been correctly reported to his uncle, very shortly left it without saying a word to any one as to how he intended to dispose of his evening. The Marchese Ludovico flattered himself, as people are apt to flatter themselves in similar cases, that his absence would be little noted, and that his reticence would suffice to leave all Ravenna in ignorance as to the errand on which he was bound when he left the Circolo. So far was this from being the case, however, that there was not one, at all events among the younger men, whom he left behind him, who did not know perfectly well where he was gone; and that his uncle, when by the unforeseen accident that has been related he was made aware of his absence from the club, was at no loss to guess what he had done with himself.

But in order that the reader may have a like advantage, it will be necessary to mention very briefly, some circumstances which occurred previously to the period referred to in the former chapters.

Some months before the time of Signor Ercole Stadione's journey to Milan, a wandering Englishman had arrived at Ravenna, and having spent three or four days in examining with much interest the wonderful wealth of Mosaics of the fourth, fifth, and sixth centuries, still preserved in the churches of the ancient capital of the Exarchs, had continued his route to Venice.

There, in the gallery of the Academia, his attention had been attracted by a female student, who was engaged in copying a canvas of Tintoretto. As it so happened that the traveller was a competent judge of such matters, he was struck by the goodness of the work, especially when considered in connection with the appearance of the artist. She was evidently very young, a slim, slender girl, whose girlish figure looked all the more willow-like from the simple plainness, and what seemed to the Englishman the insufficiency, of her clothing For the weather, though not so severe as when it had half frozen Signor Ercole Stadione, was already very cold, cold enough to have depopulated the gallery of its usual crowd of copying artists. At some distance from the young girl's easel, sitting in a corner lighted up by a stray ray of sunshine, there was an old woman busily knitting, probably the girl's mother, or protectress. And besides those two, and the Englishman, and a lounging attendant wrapped in his cloak, there was no other soul in the gallery.

Yet the young student busily plied her task; nor was she surprised into looking up by the stopping of the stranger behind her chair. He did not see her face, therefore; and it would be consequently unfair to imagine that any portion of the interest he could not help feeling in her was to be attributed to the ordinary charm of a pretty face, whereas it was really due partly to the artistic merit of her copy, partly to her bravery in sticking to her work despite the severity of the season, and partly to her youth and very apparent poverty.

Suddenly, as he watched the progress of her work slowly growing beneath the rapid movements of her slender, blue-cold fingers, the idea came into his mind that here might be a favourable opportunity of obtaining what he had much wished to procure when he had been at Ravenna, some drawings of several of the most remarkable of the Mosaics in the churches of San Vitale and St. Apollinare in Classe. He was quite satisfied from what he saw that the young artist was competent to execute the drawings he required. The conscientious determination, which alone could have made her continue her work under such circumstances, was a guarantee to him that she would do her best. It was not probable that the expectations of the girl before him as to remuneration would go beyond such sum as he was willing to pay. And lastly—though truly not least in that Englishman's mind—it might be that such a proposal would be a very acceptable boon to a poor and meritorious artist. So managing to speak to the attendant, when he was at a far part of the gallery, he learned from him that the girl's name was Paolina Foscarelli; that the old woman was, the officer believed, her aunt; that her name was Orsola Steno; and that they lived together at No. 8 in the Campo San Donato.

That same evening the stranger desired his servitore di piazza to make inquiries about Signora Orsola Steno, and her niece, who copied in the gallery; and the next morning he was told that, if he would call upon the Director of the Gallery, that gentleman would be happy to reply to any inquiries about the Signorina Paolina Foscarelli.

The Englishman waited on the Director forthwith, and from him learned that such a commission as he had thought of giving to the young copyist could not be better bestowed in any point of view. The Director spoke highly of her artistic capabilities, and more highly still of her character and worth. She had been left an orphan, wholly unprovided for, several years ago. Her father had gained his living by copying in the gallery. The old woman, Orsola Steno, with whom she lived, was no relation to her, but had been the dear friend of her mother, and had taken the orphan to live with her out of pure charity. They were very poor, very poor, indeed. But Paolina was beginning to do something. She had already sold one or two copies of small pictures. The larger work, on which she was engaged, she had undertaken by the advice of the Director, in the hope of disposing of it when the following summer should bring with it the usual incoming tide of travellers.

The result was that the stranger, taking with him a little note from the Director, went again to the gallery the next day, and finding Signorina Paolina at her post as usual, then and there made his proposition to her.

He was glad, when in doing so he spoke face to face with the girl, that the matter had been settled in his mind before he had seen her. For he was pleased to be sure that his judgment had not been warped in the matter by the irresistible prejudice in favour of a beautiful girl. And had he seen Paolina first, he could have had no such assurance. In truth, the poor Venetian painter's orphan child was very beautiful. It is little to the purpose to attempt a detailed description of her beauty; for such descriptions rarely, if ever, succeed in conveying to the imagination of a reader any accurate presentation of the picture, which the writer has in his mind's eye. She was dark. Hair, brows, eyes, and complexion, were all dark; and the contour of the face was of the long or oval type of conformation—very delicate—transparently delicate—more so, the Englishman thought, not without a pull at his heart-strings, than was quite compatible with a due daily supply of nourishment. Still she did not look unhealthy. At seventeen a good deal of pinching may be undergone without destroying the elastic vigour of youth.

But the chief and most striking charm of the beautiful face was unquestionably imparted to it from the moral and intellectual nature within. There was a calm and quiet dignity in the expression of the pure and noble brow, which may often have been seen in women of similar character, and of some twenty-five years of age. But it is rare to find such at seventeen. Doubtless the having been left alone in the world at so tender an age, had done much towards producing the expression in question. It was added to, moreover, by the singular grace of the girl's figure and mode of standing there before the stranger, as she had risen from her easel on his presenting her with the Director's note.

She was rather above the middle height, and very slender;—more so, the Englishman thought again, than she ought to have been. She was very poorly and even insufficiently clad. But the little bit of quite plain linen around her slim throat was spotlessly clean; and her poor and totally unornamented chocolate-coloured stuff dress was in decently tidy condition, and was worn with that nameless and inexplicable grace which causes it to be said of similarly gifted women that they may wear anything.

And the stranger was delighted, too, with her manner in accepting his proposition. Though she made no attempt to conceal, and, indeed, eagerly expressed her sense of the value to her of the proposal that was made to her, there was a modest, and at the same time self-respecting, dignity about her acceptance of it, which was to his mind an earnest of the highly conscientious manner in which the task would be carried out.

It was therefore settled at once that Paolina, together with her friend and protectress, the Signora Orsola Steno, should proceed to Ravenna as soon as she could conveniently do so. A list of the works of which she was required to make copies was given to her. It included, besides the whole of the very interesting Mosaics in San Vitale, and several of the curious Mosaic portraits of the early bishops of the city in the church of St. Apollinare in Classe, two remarkable full-length figures from the ancient baptistery, the representation of the Saviour as the "Good Shepherd" in the celebrated mausoleum of the Empress Galla Placidia, and the portraits of the Apostles in the private chapel of the Cardinal. Of all these works, exact copies were to be executed on a scale of one sixth the size of the originals; and it was calculated that the work would require at least fifteen months to do it in. A sufficient sum of money was paid in advance to enable Signora Orsola Steno and her ward to move to Ravenna, and to begin their residence there; and satisfactory arrangements were made for subsequent quarterly payments of two-thirds of the price to be paid for the completed copies.

Besides all this, the English patron provided the young artist with a letter of introduction, which he doubted not would make smooth all difficulties which might lie in the way of her obtaining the permissions and facilities necessary for the execution of her task. This letter was addressed to the "Illustrissimo Signor il Signor Marchese Lamberto di Castelmare." The English traveller had brought from Rome a letter of introduction to the Marchese, and had received from him, during his short stay at Ravenna, all that courteous attention and friendly interest in his artistic researches which Englishmen are always sure to meet with in the smaller cities of Italy, even in yet larger measure than in the larger capitals, where strangers of all sorts are more abundant.

Thus equipped and provided, Paolina Foscarelli, accompanied by Signora Orsola Steno, had arrived in Ravenna in the March of the same year, in the November of which Signor Ercole Stadione had made his journey to Milan.

CHAPTER V

Rivalry

The first care of the two Venetian women, on arriving in their new place of abode, which seemed to them almost as much a foreign country as Pekin might seem to an Englishman, was, of course, to present their letter of introduction to the powerful and illustrious protector to whom they were recommended. But there had, thereupon, arisen a difference of opinion between the older and the younger lady. Old Orsola Steno, acting on the wisdom which certain observations of life picked up in her sixty years of passage through it had probably taught her, was strongly of opinion that the important letter should be presented to the Marchese by Paolina in person, or if not that, by both of them together. But Paolina strongly objected to this mode of proceeding; and urged her friend to take upon herself the duty of waiting on the Marchese. Orsola contested the point as strongly as she could. But as it was very rarely that Paolina had ever opposed her in any thing, she was the less prepared to resist opposition on the present occasion. And as Paolina was in this matter obstinate, old Orsola yielded; and set forth by herself to walk to the Palazzo Castelmare. Nobody had ever any difficulty in obtaining access to the popular Marchese; and the Signora Orsola Steno was at once ushered into his library, presented her letter, and was received with all courtesy and kindness.

To receive recommendations of all sorts, to be asked to render all kinds of services, was nothing new or uncommon to the Marchese. He ran over the Englishman's letter rapidly.

"Va bene! va bene! At your service, Signora! I shall be most happy to give you all the assistance in my power. I remember very well that Signor Vilobe (Willoughby was the Englishman's name) was desirous of procuring copies of some of our mosaics. I am very happy he has found so competent a person to execute them."

Signora Orsola made a feeble attempt to point out that she was not herself the artist who was to make the copies in question; but what with her awe of the grand seigneur to whom she was speaking, and what with the strangeness of her Venetian tones to her hearer's ear, and what with the Marchese's hurry, her explanation failed to reach his comprehension.

"Yes! You and your companion will need to find a suitable lodging, the first thing. We must see to it for you. But the fact is, Signora Foscarelli, that I am more than usually busy this morning. I am expecting some gentlemen here on business every minute. If you will excuse me, therefore, I will entrust the commission of finding a proper quartiere for you to my nephew. He will be more likely than I am to know where what you require is likely to be found. He shall call upon you this morning. Where are you? At the locanda de' Tre Re! Very good. Of course you don't want to remain in an inn longer than can be helped. I will tell my nephew to go to you this morning."

So Signora Steno returned to the "Tre Re;" a little alarmed at the thought that she had passed herself off for another person and a somewhat different one, but charmed with the courtesy and kindness of the Marchese. And in less than an hour the strangers from Venice heard two voices below in the entrance of the locanda inquiring for two Venetian ladies who had recently arrived in Ravenna.

Two voices!—for it had so happened that when the servant, whom the Marchese Lamberto had sent to his nephew to request him to undertake this little commission for him, found the Marchese Ludovico at the door of the Circolo, the Signore Conte Leandro Lombardoni was lounging there with him.

"Bah! what a bore? My uncle is always making himself the maestro di casa, the manager, the protector, the servant of all the world. Tell the Marchese I'll go directly," he said to the servant; then added to his companion, "Come, Leandro, don't desert me! Let's go together and see what these Venetian women want."

"I ought to go to the Contessa Giulia at two. She'll be waiting for me, and will be furious if I disappoint her. Never mind, what must be, must be! I Tre Re! Ugh, what a distance; why, it is at the other end of the town?"

"Never mind, come along; it will do you good to walk half a mile for once and away," returned Ludovico, who knew perfectly well how much to believe about the Contessa Giulia's despair at his friend's non-appearance.

Thus the two young men went together to the locanda de' Tre Re to execute the commission entrusted to his nephew by the Marchese Lamberto.

"Yes," said a slatternly girl, who came forth from some back region at the call of the two young men, and who stared at them with an offensive mixture of surprise and understanding interest, when they inquired for the ladies recently arrived from Venice. "Yes, they were upstairs, on the right hand, in No. 13." So they climbed the stairs, knocked at No. 13, were told to passare by the voice of Signora Orsola, and in the next instant were in the room with the two strangers.

The first glance at the occupants of the chamber produced a shock of surprise, which manifested itself in so sudden a change of manner and bearing in the two young men, that it would have been ludicrous to any looker-on. The two hats came down from the two heads with a spring-like suddenness and quickness; and both the young men bowed lowly.

"Ladies," said Ludovico, addressing himself mainly to the elder, but turning also towards the younger as he spoke, while the Conte Leandro stared unmitigatedly at Paolina; "we come to you, sent by my uncle the Marchese di Castelmare, and charged by him to assist you in finding a convenient quartiere for your residence in Ravenna. Permit me to say on my own behalf," he added, turning more entirely towards Paolina, "that I hope it may not be a short one!"

"If the Signorina would make her stay among us as long as we would wish it, she would never leave Ravenna any more," said the Conte Leandro, with a glance from his sharp little eyes, and a bow of his fat person, that were meant to be quite killing.

"It is this young lady, I conclude, who has undertaken to copy some of our mosaics for the Englishman, who writes to my uncle, then?" said Ludovico with a good-humoured and bright smile.

"That is it, Signor—though she is but such a slip of a thing to look at. I was afraid the Signor Marchese had taken it into his head that I was Paolina Foscarelli. Lord love you! I could not make, nor yet copy a picture, if it were to save my life!"

"My uncle will be equally happy to have it in his power to oblige either lady," rejoined Ludovico.

"I am sure the Marchese is too good," said Signora Steno; "we remain here till the Signorina Foscarelli has finished the job she has undertaken, and no longer, nor no shorter. And some place we must find to live in the while. And if your lordship could tell us where we would be likely to find a couple of bedrooms, a bit of a sitting-room, and the use of a kitchen, it would be very kind."

"There will be no difficulty about that, I think, Signora," said the Marchese Ludovico; "I will go at once and inquire! I think I know where what we want may be had. If you will permit me, I will return to you here in less than half an hour."

"Troppo garbato, Signor Marchese!" said Orsola.

"If the Signorina will permit me," said Leandro, "I think I know of just such a little quartierino as would suit her, snug, quiet, and parfettamente libero."

To this offer, Paolina felt herself constrained to reply by a silent little bow. His former speech had received no reply whatsoever.

"I think I had better do what my uncle has told me to do, Leandro," said the Marchese Ludovico, drily.

And Paolina felt sufficiently grateful to him for the amount of snubbing contained in his accent to say the first words she had spoken since they entered the room. "We shall be exceedingly obliged to you, Signore, if you will do so. Any quartiere which the Marchese Lamberto di Castelmare could recommend to us," she added, with a significant emphasis on the words, "would be sure to suit us."

"But perhaps the Marchese Lamberto may not know half as much about such matters as I do, bella Signorina. People forget so many things by the time they come to the age of the Marchese," said the Conte Leandro, with a leering smile, which was meant to establish a confidential understanding between him and Paolina. But the young girl's only answer was to turn in her chair a little more away from him towards the window.

"I think we had better leave the ladies, and see if we can find for them what they require. I should prefer doing myself what my uncle has entrusted to me," said Ludovico, with a frown on his brow.

"Very good—do so. You say you shall be back here in half an hour; if these ladies will permit me I will remain with them till you come back, and then we can all go and look at the quartiere you have found together," said the Conte Leandro.

Poor Paolina, though perfectly determined not to acquiesce in this arrangement, was quite at a loss what to say or do to prevent it from being carried out.

"But you forget your engagement to the Contessa Giulia," said Ludovico; "surely you had better make haste to keep it."

He had no belief whatever in any such engagement, and had a very faint hope that any care for consistency would avail to induce his friend the Conte Leandro to affect the necessity of keeping it. But he also was perfectly determined not to leave him in the room with the strangers, though almost as much at a loss as Paolina how to prevent it.

"Oh, hang the Contessa Giulia! In any case, it is too late to go to her now, and I am sure I shall like much better to stay here," said Leandro.

"Very likely. But you forget that it may not be equally agreeable to these ladies that you should remain here, and they just arrived from a journey too," said the Marchese Ludovico, who was inwardly cursing his folly in having brought his friend with him on this errand, which he unquestionably would not have done had he had the remotest idea what manner of ladies they were that his uncle had deputed him to attend on.

"By-the-by, Leandro," he said, suddenly, as he was moving towards the door, "you must come with me—after all; for now I remember that the rooms I had in my mind were let a short time since, and the best thing we can do will be to go and look at those you spoke of."

"Oh! I will tell you where they are—" said Leandro.

"No, no! that won't do at all; come—come along. I won't go there without you. Come!" said the Marchese.

And this was said in a manner that had the effect of making Leandro take leave of the ladies, with many hopes that they might meet again ere long.

Very soon after the two young men were in the street together, Ludovico protested that he must call at the Circolo before attending to the business they were on; and when he got there he pretended to be obliged to run home for a minute to the Palazzo Castelmare, which was hard by, saying that he would return and rejoin the Conte Leandro in less than five minutes. And very heartily did that deceived gentleman abuse his friend, when he had waited an hour, and found that he did not return at all. Then, poor gentleman! he knew that he had been bamboozled, cruelly treated, as he said himself. And he perfectly well understood his dear friend's object, too!

"Such an intolerable, abominable coxcomb as that Ludovico is! As if he fancied that nobody was to have a chance of speaking to that pretty girl but himself. As if he thought that he had the ghost of a chance with a woman, if I thought it worth while to cut him out!" grumbled the gallant, gay Leandro to himself.

The Marchese Ludovico, meanwhile, the instant he had succeeded in freeing himself from his companion, darted off in search of an apartment, which he thought would just suit his fair clients; hurried back to them, at the inn; and had them installed in their new quarters by that evening.

"I am sure I do not know how to thank you enough for all your kindness, Signor Marchese. I do not know what we should have done without it," said the Signora Orsola.

"For all your kindness!" repeated Paolina, with a look and an emphasis which, while it expressed her gratitude, left him at no loss to understand what part of all he had done for them had chiefly seemed to the pretty Paolina to merit her special thanks.

And these were the facts and the circumstances that had brought about a state of matters which left the Marchese Lamberto and the gossips of the Circolo in no doubt where the young Marchese Ludovico had gone to pass his evening, when his uncle sent for him to the club for the purpose which the reader wots of, and failed to find him there.

CHAPTER VI

The Beginning of Trouble

Nearly eight months had elapsed between that day when the Signora Orsola and the Signorina Paolina were installed in their new lodging and the day when the Marchese Ludovico was sitting in the more than modest little room over a miserable morsel of fire, with the two Venetians, when his uncle sent for him to give him the hint about any inconvenient gossip that might be whispered concerning the Signora Bianca Lalli, in accordance with the suggestion of the impresario.

The Marchese Lamberto had made the personal acquaintance of the young artist, who had been recommended to his protection very shortly after the day on which he had deputed his nephew to find a lodging for her; and he had instantly become aware that he had made a mistake in so doing;—that he would certainly have deemed it better to take that care upon himself rather than have confided it to the young Marchese, if he had had the least idea what sort of person the Venetian artist was. Nevertheless, he had been very strongly impressed with the propriety of Paolina's manner and bearing, and after one or two more interviews, with the thorough modesty of her mind, and purity and dignity of her character. And the Marchese was a man well competent to form a sound judgment of such matters.

He had no reason to think that the young man, his nephew, was as prudent, as steady, as little liable to the influence of female beauty, as cold, if you will, as he himself had been at the same age. On the contrary, the character, which the Marchese Ludovico had made for himself in Ravenna, was a rather diametrically opposite one. But he was strongly of opinion that in any enterprise of an illegitimate nature which his nephew might attempt with the young artist, he would have his trouble only for his pains. And, of course, any enterprise of any other nature was wholly out of the question.

Still, as the months went on he would have been far better contented that his nephew should have been less often at the home of the two Venetians. There were circumstances which made such visits especially inexpedient at the present time. He knew that the young man was there much oftener than he judged to be in any way desirable; and the young man was there much oftener than his uncle knew. The Marchese Lamberto was still very much persuaded that Paolina had not been led by his nephew into any false step of a seriously blamable nature. But this was by no means any reason with the Marchese for approving of his nephew's conduct. The intercourse was altogether objectionable. Talk was engendered, talk of an undesirable description; and this was excessively disagreeable to the Marchese, who had views for his nephew which might be seriously compromised by it. A liaison of the kind, let the real nature of it be what it would, was in any case discreditable to his nephew and heir, and damaging more or less to the position which he wished to see the young man occupy in the town. It was especially so, as has been said, at the present conjuncture.

Then, of course, it could not be otherwise than injurious to the girl. She had, in some sort, been recommended to his care. And it disturbed him much, that the conduct of his nephew should be the means of damaging her reputation.

Yet the Marchese, being a man of sense, knew very well that it would not have done any good to attempt to exercise any such authority over the young man as to forbid him to visit the lodging of the Venetians. In the first place, such a step would, according to the notions and ways of looking at things of the society in which he lived, have placed him himself in a very ridiculous light;—a danger which was not to be contemplated for an instant! And, besides, the Marchese was very well aware that even if such an attempt did not cause his nephew to assume a position of open rebellion, it would only have the effect of making him do secretly and still more objectionably what he did, as it was, comparatively openly.

Comparatively, it must be said; for Ludovico was very much more frequently at the little house in the Strada di S. Eufemia than his uncle wotted of.

Not much more frequently, however, than was very well known by most of his contemporaries and fellow-habitues of the Circolo, by pretty well the whole of the "society" of Ravenna, that is to say. And in the earlier part of the time in question, of the eight months, that is, from the March in which the young artist came to Ravenna, to the November in which Signor Ercole Stadione had made his journey to Milan there had been plenty of joking and raillery about Ludovico's enthralment by the "bella Veneziana," and many attempts to compete with him for so very attractive and desirable a "buona fortuna." But all this had only been at the beginning of the time. Ludovico had taken the matter in a tone and in a humour, that had soon put an end to all such joking and to all such attempts. It was in all ways easy for him to do this. He was popular, and much liked among the young men, in the first place. His social position, as the heir of one of the first families of the province whether for wealth or nobility of race, and of a man of such social standing as his uncle, made it a very undesirable thing to quarrel with him. And even without any of such vantage-ground of position, Ludovico di Castelmare was a man, whose path it would have been dangerous to cross in such a matter as this, and who was very well capable of affording to any woman, in whom he was interested, a very efficient protection against any such offence as the most enterprising of the jeunesse doree of Ravenna might have been disposed to offer her.

The Conte Leandro Lombardoni had made the utmost of the chance that had rendered him the earliest acquaintance of the beautiful Venetian in Ravenna, with the exception of Ludovico himself. He had chattered, and boasted after the manner of his kind. He had succeeded in finding out the lodging, which Ludovico had taken so much pains to conceal from him, and had endeavoured to establish himself on the footing of a visiting acquaintance in the Strada Sta. Eufemia. But it had come to pass, that a degree of intimacy had very quickly grown up between Paolina and Ludovico, which permitted her to let him understand that, he would render her an acceptable service by once again ridding her of the Conte Leandro, as he had done on that first day of their acquaintance. And the result was that, one evening, the gallant Conte, on knocking at the door of the house in the Strada di S. Eufemia, had it opened to him by his friend Ludovico, and further, that he never came back there any more, or was heard again to make any allusion whatever to his Venetian acquaintances.

But what was no longer said jestingly before Ludovico's face was none the less said enviously, sneeringly, or knowingly behind his back. It was perfectly well understood by all the young men in Ravenna that he was desperately in love with the beautiful Venetian artist. As to the terms on which he stood with her there were differences of opinion. But by far the more accredited notion was that the affair was quite a normal and ordinary one; and that the charming Paolina was the young Marchese's mistress.

Would he give her up, when the marriage, which, as was well known to all Ravenna, his uncle had been arranging for him with the young Contessa Violante di Marliani, and which was expected to come off shortly, should be consummated? That was the more interesting point for speculation. Would he, as really seemed not impossible, be mad enough to carry on with the Venetian girl to such an extent as to give umbrage to the family of the Contessa, and perhaps even endanger the match? This also was debated among his young peers of the Circolo, while he was passing the hour in the Strada di Sta. Eufemia.

His uncle was far from being aware how far matters had gone with his nephew in this matter. But he knew enough to make him uneasy about it, and to lead him to endeavour to push on the match with the Contessa Violante by every means in his power: for the marriage with the Lady Violante was, in every point of view, a desirable one. The Cardinal Legate of Ravenna was a Marliani, and the young lady in question was his great-niece—the granddaughter of his only brother. She had lost both her parents at an early age, and now lived at Ravenna with a great-aunt, the younger sister of the Cardinal, under his protection and wing, as it were. The family was not a rich one, but the Cardinal had worn the purple many years. He had held very lucrative offices in the Apostolic Court previously, and had doubtless amassed very considerable wealth, and the Lady Violante was his only heiress. Besides that, of course the position of her great-uncle as Legate rendered her all that was desirable as a match for the noblest of the province—not to mention other grander possibilities in the background. The reigning Pontiff was a very aged man. The Cardinal di Marliani was thought to stand very well at Rome. Who knew what might happen? It would have been too monstrous if the hope of such a marriage as this were to be endangered by a silly fancy for the pretty face and slim figure of a little artist.

The Marchese Lamberto had felt his position to be a difficult one. He really did not know what line it would be wisest to take. Ludovico had spoken among his associates at the Circolo in a manner which had effectually silenced all light allusion to the ladies in the Strada di Santa Eufemia. He could not speak exactly in the same tone to his uncle; but the hints that the Marchese Lamberto had from time to time thrown out to the effect that, under the circumstances of the case, he did not approve of his nephew's intimacy with the Signorina, Paolina Foscarelli, had been received in a manner by the younger man which had warned the elder that some caution was required in the task of guiding his nephew in this matter. He had never had much cause to be dissatisfied with his nephew's conduct, or with his behaviour towards himself: but some years before the present time, he had been made aware that the Marchese Ludovico was one of those whom it is easier to lead than to drive; and that any attempt at a little too much driving would be likely to lead to kicking, and perhaps to an entire breaking of reins and traces.

And, being a man of sense, he had acted on the hints thus given him with considerable success. The Marchese Ludovico had submitted on most occasions to be led with all desirable docility. But now, in this matter, wherein judicious leading was more than ever before in his life necessary to him, he seemed to decline to be led at all.

How could the perplexed Marchese do otherwise than frown when he was told that his nephew was not at the Circolo at that hour of the evening, knowing very well where such absence showed him to be? Yet he probably would have done, or attempted to do, some thing else, or, at all events, the frown would have been a yet heavier and blacker one, could he not only have guessed where his nephew was at that moment, but have also heard what was passing in the little salottino of the Strada di S. Eufemia.

Some account of the conversation there may perhaps serve the purpose of saving all necessity for a detailed account of the intercourse which had taken place between Ludovico and Paolina during the last eight months. The story of it will be sufficiently understood from a peep at its result.

CHAPTER VII

The Teaching of a Great Love

Paolina had been working all day in the church of San Vitale. She had very nearly completed the copies she was to make there; and they were the most important in extent of all she had engaged to execute. It had been necessary to erect a scaffolding for the purpose of bringing the artist sufficiently near to her subject; and the permission to have this done had been obtained by the all-powerful interest of the Marchese Lamberto. Many an hour had Ludovico passed on that scaffolding by the artist's side as she plied her slow and laborious task; and many a "Paul" had the old sacristan pocketed with a grin of understanding, as he had opened the door of the church to the young Marchese, the object of whose visit he had long since learned to understand.

And Paolina herself? Did she approve of these visits made thus in the perfect seclusion of that old church at the hours when its doors were shut to the public? Did she like the hours so spent in tete-a-tete conversation with the handsome young Marchese? She, who had so readily found the means to make the entreprenant Conte Leandro keep his distance, and had succeeded in disembarrassing herself of him altogether, could she find no possible means for avoiding the assiduities of the Marchese Ludovico; could she not at least have induced old Orsola to accompany her in the church of San Vitale, as she had accompanied her in the gallery at Venice?

Perhaps old Orsola did not like climbing up a ladder to a scaffolding. Perhaps she had the superstitious dislike to an empty, and lonely church not uncommon to uneducated Italians. The fact was at all events that, even after Ludovico had, upon more than one occasion, brought the rushing blood into the dark face of Paolina by surprising her at her work on the scaffolding near the vaults of the church, old Orsola never made her appearance there. She was always at her place on one side of the fire during the visits of the Marchese to the quartiere in the Strada di Santa Eufemia in the evening; but it was equally true that she almost always went to sleep.

It is so natural and so desirable that the old should sleep under such circumstances and on such occasions! It is so evidently for the benefit of all the parties concerned, that the tendency may be reckoned among the instances of beneficent adaptation with which the whole order of Nature is filled!

It can hardly be doubted, Ludovico could hardly be blamed for the persuasion—that Paolina did like his visits. It may be pretty safely assumed that those blushes, which greeted the appearance of his head above the planks as he climbed to the scaffolding, were not painful blushes. How early in those eight months it came to pass that her heart leaped at the click of the huge old key in the lock, as the sacristan admitted Ludovico by a turn of it which, as she had well learned, heralded his coming, it might be hard to say. Paolina herself could not probably have told this to her own heart. But that such had come to be the case long before the evening when the Marchese Lamberto sought his nephew at the Circolo, and could not find him, can hardly be doubted.

Thus much having been admitted, it seems as if there might be reason to fear that Paolina may appear worthy of censure to those of her own sex, to whom her story is here commended, to a degree which truth, and an acquaintance with times, places, and national manners, would not quite justify. But in these matters of national appreciation, of fitness and unfitness, and of propriety and impropriety, the nuances are so fine and subtle, that it is somewhat difficult, in trying to explain them, to say just what one means without seeming to say more than one means.

One thing is clear. Paolina was as thoroughly and essentially modest and innocent a girl as ever breathed; but she was so "by the grace of God,"—from natural idiosyncrasy and instinctive purity of heart, that is to say, rather than from teaching of any kind, or from any knowledge of good or evil. She was an orphan, the child of parents who were "nobody," and she was left in the world to find her own way in it as she could. So much the more, replies the prudent English matron, ought she to have been extra careful lest the breath of misconception should even for a passing moment sully her. It is the sentiment of a people, who, "aristocratic" as they may be, do really feel that that which is best and purest in the highest lady of the land may be, and should be, also the heritage of lowliest. But such is not practically the feeling in those social latitudes where Paolina was born and bred.

The breath that tarnishes the clear mirror of a noble damsel's name, says and teaches that social feeling, brings dishonour to a noble race; and she has failed in her duty to her race. But who could be injured by any light word spoken or light thought of such an one as poor Paolina? She was an "artist." What treason to art, what lese-majeste against the beautiful in every one of its manifestations, to conceive that in that fact any reason was to be found why a less nice conduct in such matters should be expected of her! And yet, for reasons which it would take a volume to elucidate, so it is, that in the countries where art is deemed to be most at home, and where it is in the largest degree the occupation of large sections of the people, it is deemed that a less strict rule with reference to the matters under consideration is laid on them than on others. What if a young female artist "perfectly free from ties," as would be urged, and whose conduct in such a matter could hurt nobody, what if such an one chose to form a tie not recognized by the Church? The Church herself would look very leniently on the venial fault. And though Paolina was such as she has been described, it was impossible but that such notions, not specially set forth or taught, but pervading all the unconscious teaching of the world around her, should have rendered her less sensitively anxious as to the possibility of misconception lighting on her, than an equally good English girl would have been. Could she have been indifferent to the danger that slander should tarnish her good name? asks an Englishwoman. But the whole world in which she lived would not have felt it to be slander. It would have been too much in the ordinary course of things.

How Paolina felt in the matter, Ludovico was made to understand on that evening which has been so often referred to; and the reader may gather from the conversation that passed between them.

Paolina had worked hard all day. The mosaics in San Vitale were nearly finished. Ludovico had been with her on her scaffolding during the few hours of light of the short afternoon. He had become sensible that the intercourse between him and Paolina had latterly been growing to be less frank, unreserved, and easy than it had been. He had once been quite sure that Paolina loved him with the whole force of a thoroughly virgin heart. He had latterly begun almost to think that he had been mistaken in her. She would turn from him. She would fall into long silences. She was embarrassed in speaking to him; and it had often happened lately that talk had passed between them, which had seemed as if they were speaking at cross-purposes—as if there were something not understood or misunderstood between them.

And Ludovico had come to the house in the Strada di Sta. Eufemia that evening, safely relying on the expectation that the Signora Orsola would go fast asleep, and determined to bring matters to an understanding between him and Paolina.

"You can hardly, I think, doubt, Paolina mia, that I love you dearly, far more dearly than anything else on the face of the earth. Do you not see and know that all my life is devoted to you? You do not doubt, darling, do you?" said Ludovico, as he sat holding one of her hands in his.

She sat silent for awhile, and with her face turned away from him, though she made no attempt to take her hand from his.

"You do not doubt it, Paolina?" he asked again.

"If I did doubt it, if I had doubted it, Ludovico, you could not have taught me the lesson which you have taught me—the lesson which you well know you have so thoroughly taught me, to love you. We neither of us doubt of the love of the other. But—."

She still continued to sit with her face averted from him; and, after another pause, finished her speech only by a little sad shake of her head.

Now the truth was that Ludovico often did doubt very much whether Paolina really loved him. He did not understand the position in which they stood towards each other at all. Here was a little utterly unpretending artist, dependent on no one but herself, owing no duty to any one, to whom he had been making love for the last eight months, as he had never in his life made love before, who assured him that she loved him; how was it that she had not been his mistress months and months ago? How to account for so strange a phenomenon? He knew very well, that if the exact truth of his position with regard to the little Venetian artist were known or guessed at by any of the men with whom he lived, he would have appeared to them an object of the utmost ridicule, a dupe, a fool of the very first water. What on earth could he have been about all the time?

And there were moments in which he was tempted to think the same of himself; bitter moments of cynical world-wisdom, in which he scoffed at himself for having been led to play the part he had played for these last eight months. He would resolve at such moments to "speak plainly" to Paolina; and, if such plain-speaking failed of the effect it was intended to produce, to put her out of his mind and never waste a minute or a thought upon her again.

But such plain-speaking had never got itself spoken, had seemed, when he was in presence of the intended object of it, utterly impossible to be spoken. And as for the other alternative, he knew at the bottom of his heart, that it was as much out of his power to put it in practice, as it was to forget his own identity.

Something there was in the girl different from anything he had ever known in any other specimen of the sex he had ever become acquainted with. Something too there unmistakably was in his feeling towards her very different from aught that he had ever felt before. What spell had come over him? And what the deuce was the nature of her power over him? And what the deuce was her own meaning, and feeling, and the motives of her conduct?

It really was necessary, however, that they should in some way come to understand each other. If he had been becoming for some time past discontented with the state of matters between them, it was evident that Paolina had been becoming ill at ease and unhappy also. In some fashion or other some more or less plain speaking was evidently needed.

And Paolina herself? What was her feeling on the subject? Whence did her unmistakable malaise, distraught behaviour in Ludovico's presence, paling cheeks, hours of reverie, when she should have been busily at work—whence did all this come? What was really in her mind when she told him that doubtless they both loved each other, and then ended her words with a "but," and a sad shake of her drooping little head?

She had found this man, her first acquaintance, in a strange land, good-natured, pleasant, kind, useful, handsome, protecting and, at the same time, deferential in his manner; and she had liked him. He had delivered her from the Conte Leandro, and there had come into her mind comparisons between the two men. He had been on her side in that matter; they had wished the same thing, and had accomplished it against a third person; there had been, as it were, a secret between them on the subject; and hence had grown a bond of union. She had advanced from liking to admiring. Thence to the consciousness that she was admired. She had gone onwards through the usual phases of surprising herself in the act of thinking of him at all sorts of hours, and gradually discovering that he filled an immense portion of her lonely life there in the strange city, till she came to the stage of mingling the avowal "Gli voglio tanto bene" with her last prayers to Mary Mother by her bedside at night, and meditating on the words he had said and the looks he had looked, after she had laid her head upon the pillow.

She had thus quietly walked onwards into the deep waters of a great love, before any question had ever suggested itself to her as to whither she was going, and whether there might not be danger of perishing in those deep waters.

Now nothing is clearer or more undoubted by every good and well-conditioned girl among ourselves, than the certainty that any man who unmistakably seeks to win her love either means and hopes to make her his wife, or is merely fooling her for his own abominably selfish amusement, or is insulting her and endeavouring to injure her in a manner that makes it at once her duty and her inclination to spurn him from her with horror and loathing.

But here, again, as the lawyers say, "locus regit actum." That which the English girl feels, under such circumstances, so naturally, that she deems it an inseparable part of her nature that she should so feel, she feels because of the teaching of the whole social atmosphere in which she has lived. The Italian girl, in the position of Paolina, does not feel it, because she has lived in a very different social atmosphere.

It is quite certain that Paolina, if the question, whether it was in anywise on the cards that the Marchese Ludovico di Castelmare had conceived, or was likely to conceive, any project of marrying her, Paolina Foscarelli, had suggested itself, or had been suggested, to her at any time during those eight months, would at once have replied to her own heart or to any other person, that such an idea was utterly preposterous and out of the question.

But he had been striving to convince her that he loved her by every means in his power for months past, and had succeeded in so convincing her. Was he merely playing with her? That idea never entered into her head. As she, with sad and transparent frankness, had told him, neither of them could doubt the love of the other. What doubt could remain, then, as to the alternative? What doubt of the atrocious nature of his designs and intentions towards her? No doubt at all. Ought she not, therefore, with the intensest scorn of what-do-you-take-me-for-sir indignation to have repelled the insult offered to her?

Poor Paolina had no conception that any insult at all was offered to her or intended. Ludovico was minded to offer to her that which it was in his power to offer, for her to accept if it suited her, or to decline if it suited her not. The species of tie that he offered her was all he could offer her. It was one very frequently offered and very frequently accepted in similar cases. Had the possibility that she might one day accept such been suggested to her, it would have produced no horror in her mind. She had no conviction during all these eight months that she never could or would accept such a position from any man. Why, then, did not matters proceed harmoniously and smoothly between them? Why had not Paolina become Ludovico's mistress before this time? What was the meaning of the averted face, and of that broken off "but—" which she had found it so difficult to follow with a completed sentence?

The meaning was, that Paolina's own heart, during those hours of reverie filled with the meditation of her love, during those pourings forth of her confessions of love to her heavenly confidant in her bedside prayers;—during her nightly review of the love-passages of the day, her own heart, as it became clearer to her, had revealed to her, that she could not accede to any such proposal as that which, she was well persuaded, the Marchese could alone offer to her;—had revealed it to her, not in obedience to any moral principle; not by any what-do-you-take-me-for process of indignant virtue; but by an instinctive feeling irresistible and not to be gainsayed, that the love she had to bestow must possess its object wholly and entirely, or not at all. It was quite a matter of course that Ludovico would marry some lady in his rank of life. She was not ignorant of the position in which he stood with regard to the Contessa Violante. And his openness to her on this subject is a curious indication of the very wide difference between the mode in which the whole subject would be looked at by both parties in the world in which they lived, and in our own.

Philosophers, as the result of much learned observation and long reasonings, come to the conclusion that monogamy is best suited, on the whole, to the nature, the requirements, and progressive improvement of mankind. A pure-hearted woman, who loves with a true and great love, finds a shorter cut to the same conviction.

And the growing depth and earnestness of Paolina's love had arrived at teaching her this with unmistakable clearness. She might pine, might die—might compel her heart to turn to stone;—might seek the refuge of a cloister, which is the southern equivalent for suicide;—but she could not—she felt she could not live and be content to share her lover's love with another. It was not any sensation of the nature of jealousy so much as an unconquerable feeling that not to have all was to have nothing;—that she must have all and for ever; that she and he must be one;—one flesh and one spirit.

Of course all this ought to be taught, and is taught to all respectably educated young persons in more regular and didactic fashion. But to poor little unschooled Paolina it was taught not less authoritatively by the greatness and the purity of her own love.

CHAPTER VIII

A Change in the Situation

"Neither of us can any more doubt the love of the other, Ludovico mio!" Paolina had said in reply, to his pleading, "but—"

But what, tesoro mio? What 'but' can come between us, if there is no such doubt to come between us?" urged Ludovico, gently drawing her towards him by the hand he still held locked in his own.

Again Paolina paused some minutes before replying, less apparently from hesitation to speak what was in her mind, than because she was applying her whole mind to the better understanding of her own meaning.

"It is not, that I doubt whether you love me, Ludovico mio!" she said at length, but still without turning towards him; "I know you love me truly and well. But I sometimes think, that you do not love me in the same way that I love you. I never knew before that there could be different ways of loving. But now it seems to me, and I have thought so much, oh, so much of it, that somehow you look less to the whole, of everything, how can I say what I mean?—less to all our lives, and all our selves, in your love, than I do."

"What can you mean, Paolina? A different way of loving! I know but of one way!" said Ludovico with a somewhat banal flourish.

"What would become of me, Ludovico mio," she said, now looking round into his face, with a look in her deep true eyes, that made him feel for the moment as though all the world were truly as nothing to him, in comparison with her love;—"what would become of me, if you were to cease to love me? I should wither away, and die. It is probably what will happen to me!"

"Paolina!" he exclaimed, in a voice of strong reproach.

She put her hand upon his shoulder, as if to beg him to let her complete what she wished to say, and continued, "But what would happen to you, if I were—it is impossible, but if I were—to cease to love you? would not that show you, that there is a difference between ways of loving?"

"No, cara mia, it would shew no such thing. Look now, Paolina! They tell of lovers' perjuries. But I never said one word to you that I did not believe to be true. Nor will I ever do so. Were you to be taken from me, by your own heart, and your own act, or in any other way, I do not believe that I should wither and die. But it does not follow, that I should suffer less. I should live on, not because my love is weaker, but because my body is stronger than yours. God grant that such a lot may never befall me."

"It never can befall you, amor mio! but, Ludovico, you could not only live, but you could love—some other woman;" she uttered the words with a little gulp of emotion, and continued: "Do you imagine, that if I lived to a thousand years, I could ever love any other than you?"

"What right have you to say, Paolina, that I should ever, or could ever love another but you?" said Ludovico, indignantly.

"Nay, Ludovico, must you not do so always? Are you not professing to do so even now? Are you not promising your love to the Contessa Violante? will she not have a better right to your love than I?"

Ludovico started, and drawing himself a little back from Paolina, looked at her with reproachful surprise. It was not that he was surprised at learning that she was aware of his engagement to the Contessa. He had, as has been said, concealed nothing from her in that respect. But he was vexed, and surprised at the feeling she manifested on the subject.

"You surprise me, Paolina!" he said. "Would it have been better if I had concealed all this from you? Many men, most men perhaps, in similar circumstances would have done so. But I cannot treat you in that way. I have been, and would always be open and sincere to you in all things. You know all about this match. You know that it is a family arrangement managed by my uncle. You know, that if I wished it ever so much, I can't avoid it. You know, or ought to know, that it is not, and cannot be a matter of affection in any way. You know that in the world such marriages are arranged and are known and understood to be arranged, for reasons, and on ground with which love has nothing to do. Does not all Ravenna know, including the lady herself doubtless, that I am to marry her because she is the great-niece of the Cardinal Legate? Can I be expected to love her, because she is the Cardinal's niece? Surely, my Paolina, you are not speaking or thinking of this matter, with your usual good sense!"

"I can't help it, Ludovico; I am, at all events speaking with my whole heart!" she said in a tone of profound sadness. "If what you say is true, and do not imagine, dearest, that I have the smallest doubt that all you say to me is entirely and perfectly true, just think of the lot of that povera Contessa Violante! Poverina! I dare say she, think of the wrong I should be doing her! Think how she would hate me!" She shuddered as she spoke. "Nobody, I think, ever hated me yet," she continued; "and it seems to me so horrible to be hated. And more horrible still to know that I should be justly hated! And then, tesoro mio!—Mio!—How could I ever say mio? Never, never, never, mio!" she cried, bursting into passionate tears. "No, never mine! The very word itself, which comes so naturally to my lips, tells me, like a knell in my heart, that it can never be!"

"But, Paolina, angiola mia," said Ludovico, who had heard her with a look of consternation, "what has thus changed you? For it is a change. You knew all these things before. What has occurred to put such notions into your mind all of a sudden?"

"Not all of a sudden, Ludovico! The blessed Virgin knows for how many sad and solitary hours I have been thinking, and thinking, and thinking of all this! She knows how many nights I have passed in tears to think of it. What has put it into my head, you say? Ludovico, it is my love for you that has put it into my head! It is my strong love that has opened my eyes, and made me see that I cannot—cannot—I mean—that I cannot share your love with another!"

The words came forced from her with a great effort, and with a sob that seemed as if it would choke her.

"Oh my Paolina, what words are these?" said he, his own voice trembling with trouble and emotion.

"It is true, Ludovico! It is my true love that has opened my eyes. I fear that I have done very wrong; and the blessed Saints know that I shall have my punishment! I have done wrong in loving you, and letting you love me! But I did not know it, I did not think, I did not see where I was going! I ought to have known that love was not for a poor girl like me! I ought to have known that evil and misery would come. But till I loved you with my whole, whole heart, Ludovico; and till I found out that I did, I did not know that—that it would be so, that I should feel as I feel now."

Ludovico got up from his seat, and began walking up and down the floor of the little room, sighing deeply, and passing his hand again and again across his forehead. Presently he sat down again, bringing his chair so as to front her fully as he sat.

"Paolina," he said, looking sadly into her eyes with a deeper meaning in his own than she had ever seen there; "your words have made me very, very miserable! I never in all my life was so unhappy as I am now. You must listen now, my Paolina, to what I am going to say; and you must think well before you answer me. You see, dearest, that it is necessary that we should quite understand this matter, and understand each other. Many men, if they had been told what you have now told me, would begin to reproach a girl with not loving them, to say that it was clear she did not care for them. I will not do so. I will not pretend to think that you do not love me. I know that you do, as well as you know that I love you with my whole heart. And with this knowledge in both our hearts, think what is the meaning and the end of what you have been saying. You know that this marriage is inevitable! And the consequence of it is to be that we two are both to be broken-hearted, to condemn ourselves to pass loveless lives, to give each other up, see each other no more, make all the future a blank to both of us. Good God, Paolina! You cannot mean that!"

"When you have married, Ludovico mio, when I have said those dear words for the last, last time, you will have plenty of things to make you forget your poor Paolina! And for me, I shall be heart-broken doing no wrong to any other, instead of heart-broken and doing terrible wrong all the time! And, dearest, it would be worse than heart-break. I could not—it is stronger than I am! It seems like a new horrible thing shown to me, which I never saw or thought of before! When it comes close to me I shudder at the thought—."

"At what thought, Paolina? At the thought of my being married to the Contessa Violante?" asked Ludovico, looking steadfastly into her eyes.

She bore his gaze without withdrawing her sad, still eyes for awhile, thinking deeply before she answered.

"No, Ludovico; not at the thought of your being married to the Contessa Violante! That is a thought which may break my heart. But it does not make me shudder, as that other thought does;—the thought of—of—of loving one, who—who—who owes his love to another; the thought of taking by stealth whatever share of love may be given to me stolen from the rightful owner. Never! never! never! Would you then be mine, all mine, for ever, and ever, and ever! Oh, my love, my love! If you don't understand this, love has not opened your eyes as it has mine. Do you think that I could endure the thought of being married to another man? The bare notion is horror—horror—HORROR! Would I not rather die this minute; ay, or die a thousand times!"

Again Ludovico got up from his chair and paced the room, sometimes stopping abruptly in apparently deep thought, and sometimes resuming his walk with every appearance of despair in his face and gestures. It is needless to say that Paolina had spoken the very inmost truth that was in her heart in all its entirety; but she had also succeeded in making him feel that it was so.

There is often a feeling in a man's mind on such occasions—a feeling too closely allied to selfishness—which leads him to be dissatisfied with what seems to him the unwillingness of a woman to make sacrifices to her love. And often a woman, knowing this, and calculating mostly falsely, is urged to yield by a desire of proving that she does not deserve such a suspicion. But Ludovico had no such thought in his mind. He knew that Paolina had not only spoken truly, but had represented her mind accurately. It was not that she "respected herself." The poor child had never received any lessons which could teach her such respect. She had been perfectly ready to accept the social position of Ludovico's mistress, until the power of a great, true, and pure love had unsealed the eyes of her understanding, of her imagination, and of her heart to the nature—not of the social position of such a tie as that proposed to her—but of the absolute imperious necessity of sharing such a love with none. Putting all notion of principle, of duty, of the understood expediency of conforming to laws divine, and human, out of the question, such a love as Paolina felt demands this with a cogency of insistence that cannot be set aside. And the man who hopes, or flatters himself, or suffers himself to be persuaded that such a love has been given to him upon any other terms, is—he may rely upon it with the certainty due to an eternal law of nature—deceived. The quality of the love which may have so been given to him is of a different kind.

After awhile Ludovico came again and stopped directly in front of the chair in which Paolina was sitting; but he remained standing, and placing his two hands, one on either of her shoulders, and looking down into her face with moist eyes, he said, "My love, my true and best—my only love! I cannot lose you, Paolina; I cannot give you up. Truly—truly I had rather that any other thing—any other evil that could happen, should happen to me. We are, and we must be, all in all to each other, my Paolina, now and ever. There is no alternative possibility to this. Love has opened my eyes, too, my darling angel! Your love has opened my eyes; I will know no other love, no other woman—call none other wife but you! Paolina, you will be mine?—my all? my only one?"

"Ludovico!" she exclaimed, looking up at him with an ecstasy of joy, and yet with a great terror upon her face; "but what will happen—what will happen to you? What will be done to me?"

"We must see, my heart's treasure! We must have patience; you must trust to me. You do trust me, non e vero? I must put off this marriage; then find means to break it. And, after all, what can my uncle do? I am dependent on him while he lives; but I must succeed to all he has when he dies. My promised wife! Are you mine—mine for ever? Will you now put your dear little hand in mine, and promise me, and have faith in me, and wait for me, and have patience till I can see my way, and love me all the time, my own—my darling?"

"I am your own, Ludovico;—yours, any way: to live for you, if such a lot may be mine; to die still yours, if it may not! Wait! Patience! What shall tire my patience? So I know that you are loving me—me only—all the time, I shall ask nothing more! But, oh, I am so frightened! And then I shall be a cause of such mischief and trouble to you. Would it not have been better for you if you had never seen poor Paolina?"

"No, no, no, no! It would have been a thousand million times worse for me! Be of good heart, my treasure; nothing can hurt you. We must keep our secret for a while; and nothing will hurt me, if we manage well. But I must think; my mind is in a confusion;—a joyful confusion, dearest! But I must think it all over. If you see me less often, be sure that it is because I am planning for our happiness. And now, darling, my own, my own, now really and for ever, my own—one kiss to seal our contract! You won't refuse me that. I take you thus in my arms, my Paolina; for the first time as your promised husband. Good-night—good-night—my own! I trust I may be able to think of what I am doing at the Palazzo tonight. Good-night, my own!"

And thus the Marchese Ludovico returned that evening to the Palazzo Castelmare, about an hour after Signor Ercole Stadione had quitted it; pledged to find some means of breaking off the match with the Contessa Violante Marliani, to which all Ravenna was looking forward, and engaged to be married to the little obscure Venetian orphan artist.

CHAPTER IX

Uncle and Nephew

Ludovico di Castelmare did not see his uncle that evening. He returned to the Palazzo, thoughtful enough, direct from the house in the Strada di Santa Eufemia, and there learned that the Impresario had been with the Marchese; that he had brought the good news of his success in having engaged "La Lalli" to sing at Ravenna during the coming Carnival; and that he, Ludovico, had been sent for by his uncle from the Circolo. What for, the servant could not tell him. He could only say that the Marchese had seemed much put out at the Signor Marchese Ludovico's absence, and that he had shortly afterwards gone out to pass the remainder of the evening at the palace of the Cardinal Legate.

Ludovico was by no means so anxious to see his uncle as to wait to do so till he should return at night. He betook himself to his own quartierino, locked the door, and sat down to think.

He had said no more than the truth to Paolina when he professed that he had never spoken a word with the intention of deceiving her. Nor had he been otherwise than entirely sincere in all that he had just been saying to her. Nevertheless he felt, somewhat more strongly and clearly, perhaps, than while he had been looking into Paolina's eyes, that he had undertaken rather a tremendous task in declaring that he would break off the projected marriage with the Lady Violante, the great-niece of the Cardinal, a match which both families considered to be definitively arranged, and which was expected and looked forward to by all Ravenna, and that for the purpose and with the view of making so terrible a mesalliance as that he contemplated. The Marchese Ludovico felt all the weight of the inheritance of a great name and a still greater social position, which devolved upon him from his uncle. It was bad enough to contemplate the effect which would be produced, as regarded himself, by the step he contemplated. But it was perfectly terrible to think of the effect it would produce on the Marchese Lamberto. Ludovico was proud, in his more easy-going way, of the position he occupied as his uncle's nephew in the society of the city; but it was not to him the breath of his nostrils as it was to his uncle.

He felt, as a weak man is apt to feel in similar positions of difficulty, that the best and quickest, and, above all, the easiest, way out of all embarrassment would be to run away from it—to quit Ravenna, and give it up—it, and all its inhabitants for ever. He could do this. He felt that Paolina would be worth such a sacrifice. But how to accomplish such a step while his uncle lived?

As it was all he could do was to procrastinate, he thought of the old Italian proverb, "Gain time, and you will pull through," and he determined to profit by the wisdom of it. Even procrastination would not be without difficulty. But something might be done in that way, some time might be gained. And then there was always that never-failing resource and consolation of those who, in the words of Horace, limit their ambition to adapting themselves to circumstances instead of adapting circumstances to them, something might turn up; though, for the present, it was difficult to see what that something could possibly be, unless it were the death of his uncle, a perfectly robust and healthy man in the fiftieth year of his life.

Might possibly the something take the shape of a change or mitigation of Paolina's resolve? No sooner did the idea cross his mind than he felt ashamed of it, and his heart smote him for having for a moment harboured a thought that involved falseness to his promise to her. Nevertheless, it was not the last time that the thought recurred.

The next morning he met his uncle.

"I had Stadione with me yesterday evening," said the Marchese, "and I wanted to speak to you about something he said. I was sorry to be told that you were not at the Circolo."

"I was sorry that Beppo did not find me. What was it? Signor Ercole has succeeded in his mission, I hear."

"Yes; and it was on that matter I wanted to speak to you; but this morning will do as well for that. It was not that that vexed me, Ludovico. I won't ask you to tell me where you were, and I don't want to play the inquisitor; but the fact is, I know very well without asking. And, my dear nephew, I cannot but tell you that you are acting unwisely, imprudently even."

"What have I done that is wrong, sir? Is it not fitting that I should show some attention to people, who came here recommended to you, and whom you yourself first commissioned me to assist?" said Ludovico.

"What is the good of answering in that way, Ludovico. Just as if we both did not know better than that, and know too what we both mean? Pay some attention! Pshaw! Do you think that I am quite a fool? As if I did not know what you go there for, and what you have been going there for these eight months past, since first I was blockhead enough to throw that pretty girl in your way. Now, figliuolo mio, it is my duty to tell you that that sort of thing won't do—just at present. I don't want, as I said, to play the inquisitor, nor do I wish to play the preacher. When you are married you must guide your own conduct as you may think fit; but now every consideration of propriety and prudence should teach you that you must not continue to run after that young person in the sight of all the town in the way you do. Here you are on the point of contracting a marriage, which—"

"On the point, uncle? We are surely a long way from that yet?" said Ludovico.

"A long way! I don't know what you mean by a long way; if we are not further advanced, it is your own fault. We might bring the negotiation to a conclusion at once. It might all be settled this Carnival.

"This Carnival, uncle? Impossible! I must have a little time. There are so many things to be thought of."

"What is there to be thought of, that has not been thought of already? They are in no hurry; they look upon the matter as arranged. But in decency, we cannot show any backwardness; it does not look well.

"Well, uncle: at all events, let this Carnival pass over. Let me have this last Carnival; then Lent is of no use: after that we will see about it."

"Well, be it so. But, my dear boy, you know all the importance of this marriage! You know how desirable it is in every point of view; family, rank, station, influence, money, though that happily we have no need to seek; why, it was only last week, this is a secret, and must go no further, but I know I can trust to your discretion;—only last week, that I got a letter from my old friend, Monsignore Paterini at Rome, in which he speaks in almost open terms of the chance, and even probability, that our Cardinal might—ahem!—find the next conclave a particularly interesting one. You know how Paterini stands at Rome, and that a hint from him is as good as a volume from another; and just think of the possibilities that such a contingency might open before you! I won't say any more; but do now during this Carnival, show yourself a little more at the palace, and pay a little attention, and let the world see that you occupy the place with regard to the Contessa Violante, that you really do occupy. Basta!"

"I will do the best I can, sir, to merit your approbation," said Ludovico, feeling that he was expected to say something, and not well knowing how to do it.

"And now about the matter I wanted to speak of last night. La Lalli comes to us, you see, for the Carnival: it is a great triumph for Ravenna. She is certainly the first singer in Italy, since England with its brute power of money, robbed us of poor Sparderini. But between you and me, figliuolo mio, we should never have got her, if there had not been certain difficulties—certain scandals, che so io?—at Milan. All that is no business of ours, you know, tutt' altro! But there has been talk;—stories have got about!—mere calumny probably, as Signor Ercole very justly remarked, but it is very desirable that such things should not be the talk of the town here. It is mauvais genre to chatter about such matters. You can make it mauvais genre among the youngsters at Ravenna, if you choose. Do so; you understand! That's all."

"Perfectly, uncle! Lasci fare a me! I'll see to it; though I confess I do not quite understand why we need trouble ourselves about any such gossip," said Ludovico, delighted to be able to fall in with his uncle's wishes in something.

"Well, I should have thought that you might understand. In the first place I don't want it to be said or imagined, either here or elsewhere, that Ravenna has taken up with a singer, who could not get an engagement elsewhere. Not that that is the case by any means. But don't you see, if it is said that she was obliged to leave Milan, it puts us in the position of a pis aller! And I don't like that. In the next place, I don't want to have light talk about a person whom I have had so large a share in bringing to the city. These are things you ought to learn to think of, caro mio!" replied the Marchese, a little annoyed at having to put his feelings on the subject into such plain words.

"I'll take care that things shall be as you wish. When is she to arrive?" asked Ludovico.

"About the end of the year—in a month's time or thereabouts. Stadione did not mention whether the day of her coming had been fixed. Her first appearance will be on the night of the Beffana, the 6th of January."

"Because they were talking at the Circolo of getting up some little matter of welcome, taking the horses from her carriage, and drawing her in, or some thing of that kind, and a serenata of course. Leandro is busy already with a poem for the occasion, you may swear!"

"Bravo! bene! If only our good friend the Conte keeps his muse within tolerable limits! It would not do to quite smother her in verse on her first arrival; and, you know, our good Leandro has rather a special gift that way. Well, get up any kind of dimostrasione you like for the occasion, it will all help to give eclat to our opening. You can arrange all about the when, and the where, etc., with Stadione. We are going to have a meeting of the Belle Arte Committee here this morning. They'll be here directly!" said the Marchese Lamberto, pulling out his watch.

"One word more, uncle, before I'm off," said Ludovico.

"What is it?—money, I suppose?" said the Marchese, again taking out his watch.

"No, sir; not money this time, unless, indeed, you insist on it," said the nephew, laughing.

"Not at all, not at all! I won't press it on you by any means!" said the uncle in a similar tone; "but what were you going to say?"

"Why, with reference to what you were saying just now, about the Signorina Foscarelli," replied Ludovico, in quite a different tone. "I am always anxious to shape my conduct in accordance with your advice, uncle. You see La Foscarelli has all but finished her work at St. Vitale, you know: she is to do her copying in the Cardinal's Palace next, for you have kindly arranged for her permission to do so. Now, she can't very well go to the palace, for the first time, alone, you know! If you had not expressed the opinions you have on the subject, I should have gone with her, thinking no harm. But perhaps—to the palace, you know;—it would be better, if you would not mind it, to accompany her, for the first time, yourself."

"Very right, very properly thought of, my dear boy! Yes; I can go with her—or I can send Burini, which will come to the same thing."

"No, uncle; not the same thing—to send a mere maestro di casa, a servant! It would not be nice for the poor girl; it would make all the difference with the servants and people at the palace: if I avoid going with her to please you, you will go with her yourself, won't you?"

"Very well, very well; I'll go with her. If any man has more to do of his own than all the rest of the city put together, there are sure to be other folk's affairs thrust on him also; it has been sowith me all my life. Well, I will find half an hour somehow."

"Thanks, uncle! Good-by, I wish you well through your meeting."

"We shall see each other at dinner?"

"Yes. A rivederla!"

CHAPTER X

The Contessa Violante

The Contessa Violante Marliani lived, as has been said, with her great-aunt, a sister of the Cardinal. They occupied a small house nearly contiguous to the palace, which was almost more their home than their own dwelling. The Marchesa Lanfredi, the Cardinal's sister, though a great-aunt, was not yet sixty years old. She had been left a childless widow, very scantily provided for, early in life, and had retired from Bologna, her husband's native place, to live first at Foligno, of which city her brother had been bishop, and afterwards at Ravenna, to which he had been subsequently promoted. The Cardinal was six or seven years her senior. His elder brother, the grandfather of the Lady Violante, had inherited the family estates in the neighbourhood of Pesaro, and had died, leaving them to his only son, Violante's father, when the latter was a very young man.

This Conte Alberto Marliani had married for love, as it is called. That is to say, that he had not married for any of the reasons for which marriages among people of his rank and his country are usually made; but had been attracted by a pretty gentle face seen in a Roman ball-room. The pretty gentle face had remained always gentle; but had soon ceased to be pretty.

The Contessa Marliani was inclined to devotion. The Conte was very much disinclined to anything of the sort. He soon got tired of his wife, repented of his marriage, and commenced an active system of breaking her heart. It was not a very difficult task, for she was as gentle in spirit as in face. He completed it when his only child Violante was about nine years old. But he had also completed, much about the same time, the entire dissipation of the never very large Marliani property. And it so happened that, very shortly afterwards, his own career was brought to a conclusion, which his relatives felt to have overtaken him a few years too late! He was travelling from Rome down to Pesaro to complete the sale of the last portion of the estates, the proceeds of which had been anticipated, when he was very opportunely drowned in attempting to cross the Tiber swollen by flood.

The little Violante, thus left an almost destitute orphan, was nevertheless a personage of some importance. She was the only remaining scion of the family; and the position of her great-uncle seemed to promise a renewed period of prosperity and fortune to the old name. Violante was the Cardinal Legate's natural and sole heir. The Cardinal was a very rich man; and in amassing wealth and attaining honours, he had, like a true Italian, never thought the less of the additions to, and provisions for, the fortunes and splendour of the family name, which he was winning, because he was himself a priest, and would leave no heirs of his name. The peculiarities in the position of a sacerdotal aristocracy have engrafted the passion of nepotism in the hearts, as well as the practice of it in the manners, of the members of Rome's hierarchy.

Generally the family tie is a stronger one among the Italians than among ourselves. In the upper classes, it is certainly so; and, probably, among all classes. It may be thought strange, perhaps, that this should be the case with a people whose lives are supposed to be less pervaded by the sentiment of domesticity than our own. The explanation may, however, perhaps be found in the greater and more frequent disruption of family ties, which is caused by that more active social movement, which pushes our younger sons away from the parental stock in search of the means of founding families of their own.

And one of the results of the Italian mode of living and feeling is seen in the very common family ambition of Churchmen.

The little Violante then, as has been said, was a personage of some importance, at least in the eyes of the Cardinal and his sister; and when she was left an orphan, was at once taken to live with her great-aunt, under the auspices of her Cardinal great-uncle. Both of those remaining members of the family would have preferred that the one remaining scion of the race should have been a boy; but—when the young Contessa should be married, of course her name should be thenceforward borne as part of that of the family; into which she should marry, as is so commonly the case in Italy, (many of the oldest and most illustrious names in the peninsula having survived to the present day solely by virtue of such arrangements); and the Marliani be thus saved from extinction.

The young Contessa Violante, when she reached the age of young-ladyhood, had not the "fatal gift of beauty." Some people think that such a deprivation is the most unfortunate from which a woman can suffer. Others maintain that the absence of beauty is, upon the whole, no real misfortune. But however philosophers may settle this question, it can hardly be doubted that no young girl devoid of beauty, was ever yet persuaded that to be unattractive in appearance, was otherwise than a very, very sore affliction and misfortune. Nature often kindly mitigates the blow by making the unlovely girl unconscious of her want of beauty. But this was not the case with the young Contessa Violante Marliani.

Violante knew that she was not beautiful, or even pretty. Probably in her own estimate of herself she exaggerated her plainness. She was one of those persons who have not the gift of self-deception. Neither was she elegant in person. And yet there was something about her bearing, which would have prevented any one from imagining that she was other than a high-born lady. There was strong evidence of intellect in her face; and it was doubtless from within that came that quiet dignity of bearing that marked her.

And it was a dignity compatible and combined with the most perfect gentleness and almost humility of manner;—a dignity arising not from the consciousness of any high position or high qualities, but from the consciousness of that sort of gentle passive strength, which knows that no external circumstance, or difficulty, or pressure will avail to make its owner step but a hair's breadth aside from the path which conscience has marked as that of right and duty.

Violante was tall and slender, but her figure was not graceful. People did not say of her that she was slender; they said she was thin. And that was incontestably true. She was very thin. But her shoulders were high and square, and there was a sort of angularity and harshness about all the lines of her person. Her head seemed somewhat too large for her body; and the upper part of it seemed too large for the lower portion. She had a large, square forehead, white enough, but strongly marked with inequalities of surface, which, however much they might have delighted a phrenologist, were not conducive to girlish comeliness. Her hair was of the very light reddish quality, which has not a single touch in it of that rich sunny auburn, which makes so many heads charming, red though they be. Her face was perfectly white, yet not clear of complexion. And the pale grey eyes beneath their all but colourless brows completed the impression of a general want of vigour and vitality.

A little before the end of that year in which the Ravenna impresario performed his memorable journey to Milan with the results that have been recorded, Violante di Marliani reached her twenty-third birthday; a few months before that day the Marchese Ludovico had reached his twenty-second. It was a difference on the wrong side, but not so great as to form any serious objection to the proposed match. But twenty-three is a rather mature age for an Italian noble lady to reach unmarried. That such should have been the case with the Signora Violante was by no means because no suitor for her hand had ever presented himself. Several such aspirants had entered the lists. For the Contessa Violante was the great-niece of her great uncle. But some of these had appeared objectionable to the Cardinal and his sister;—who also were not at all likely to forget all that was due to the prospects arising from such a relationship, and all that it implied; and all of them had been objectionable to the young Contessa herself.

Violante's expectations, indeed, in that line, or in any other of all the different ways in which happiness may come to mortals in this world, was very small. For the first nine years of her life she had lived the only companion of a very miserable mother. And all that mother's misery had apparently come from the fact of her having a husband. Those first years of the child's life had been very sad; very monotonous, very depressing. Perhaps the effect of them did but confirm the speciality of an idiosyncrasy, which would have been much the same without them. But, at all events, when the child was brought to the house of her great-aunt, it seemed as if her mind and character had been too long and too uniformly toned to accord with sadness, for happiness to have any power of taking hold of her.

The old Marchesa Lanfredi, who took the young Contessa under her roof, and under her care, was not a bad sort of woman in the main; but she was thoroughly and consistently worldly, and judged everything from a worldly point of view. The Contessa Marliani was an important little lady in her eyes; and was treated, by her with an indulgence and consideration which she would have considered out of place in the case of a child not born to such expectations and such a destiny. She was not contented with her young relative; but was more perplexed and puzzled by her than angered. And as Violante grew towards womanhood, her great-aunt understood her less and less.

In the first place, she had a much stronger tendency towards devotion than the Marchese Lanfredi thought either natural or becoming in a young woman. Of course it was right and proper to pay due attention to one's religious duties; there was no necessity to tell her, a Cardinal Archbishop's sister, that, it was to be supposed. But she had a strong objection to excess in such matters. And to her mind Violante carried her devotional practices, and yet more her devotional ideas, to excess. Of the latter, indeed, the old Marchesa Lanfredi disapproved altogether. Young people had no ideas upon the subject in her time;—and the world was certainly a better world then than it had been since.

And then, worst of all, it gradually became evident to the Marchesa's mind that there was a more or less direct connection in the way of cause and effect between her niece's religious notions and feelings and the strange readiness she had shown to find objections to both of the two persons who had been judged by her family to be admissible suitors for her hand. The Marchesa began to entertain a strong apprehension that her niece had conceived the idea of "entering into religion;" i.e. of becoming a nun.

It had been necessary at the time of Violante's first coming to live with her aunt, to select a governess for her; and a lady had been found fitted to teach her all that it was proper for a noble young Italian lady to know. But when she became seventeen it was judged expedient to change this lady for another. A different sort of person was required. Custom and the habits of life and convenience of the Marchesa made it expedient that a duenna should be provided to attend on the young Contessa; but she was supposed no longer to need an instructress.

The person selected for this trust was not perhaps altogether such as might have been desired. By some fatality, arising probably from some latent incompatibility between the institution itself and the eternal order of things, it would seem as if the persons entrusted with that responsible situation rarely did turn out to be exactly the right people in the right place. Perhaps in the case of the young Contessa Violante her great-aunt had sought to find some attendant and companion for her who should have a tendency to correct that too great proclivity to retirement from the world—to a life in which religion was the chief interest and occupation, and to a sad and unhopeful view of the world around and before her—which she lamented in her niece. If so, the choice she made was not followed by the results she hoped from it; and was attended by other inconveniences.

The Signora Assunta Fagiani, the widow of a distinguished Bolognese professor of jurisprudence, was certainly quite free from all those dispositions which the Marchesa regretted in her niece. But she was not altogether discreet or judicious in the method she adopted for reconciling the young girl to the world, and to worldly views and hopes and objects.

She very soon perceived that to Violante the consciousness of her own want of personal attractions was, despite her yearning for a life to be filled with thoughts and objects to which beauty could contribute nothing, a source of bitter and ever-present mortification. There was inconsistency, doubtless, in regret for the deficiency of personal attraction in persons who, with perfect sincerity, declared to themselves that to enter a convent was their greatest object in life. But Violante was not aware that if the beauty had been there the devotional aspirations would not have been there! That, which causes more deeply implanted in her nature than she knew of were impelling her to desire and to yearn for, the imperfect teaching of the world around her had led her to imagine to be unattainable save by the gifts of personal beauty. And, knowing that if that were so there was no hope for her, her bruised heart had sought the only refuge which seemed to be open to such misfortune.

The Signora Fagiani's first attempt at finding a remedy for this state of things consisted of a vigorous endeavour to persuade her pupil that her own estimate of her personal appearance was altogether a mistaken one. All the former experience of the old lady led her to consider this an easy task. And she was much surprised to find that her insinuations, assertions, and persuasions on this subject were totally thrown away on her pupil. The precious gift of personal vanity had been denied to poor Violante; and she saw herself somewhat more unfavourably than others saw her.

Then the duenna changed her tactics; and strove to point out how very little a pretty face signified to any girl in the position of the Contessa di Marliani. To a poor girl, indeed, whose face was her fortune, it was another matter. But the niece of the Cardinal Legate! Bah! Did she imagine that she would lack suitors? She had nothing to do but to make the most of the advantages in her hand, and she would see herself surrounded by all the beaux, while the prettiest girls in the room might go whistle for the smallest scrap of attention, And then, when married, with rank, station, wealth at her command, what would it signify?

And in urging all these considerations, the Signora Assunta Fagiani spoke at least sincerely, and expended for the benefit of her pupil the best wisdom that was in her.

Partly, however, she was working for her own purposes, as well as for the advantage, as she understood it, of her charge. Of course, as she judiciously considered, her position gave her, in a great degree, the valuable patronage of the disposal of the Lady Violante's hand in marriage. And, of course, this advantage of her position was equally well understood by others; and among these by a certain Duca di San Sisto, a Bolognese noble, whose sadly-dilapidated fortunes much needed the aid that might be derived from the coffers of the wealthy Cardinal Legate. The Duca di San Sisto had interests at Rome also, which might be most importantly served by the influence of the Cardinal Marliani. So that a marriage with the Lady Violante seemed to be exactly the very thing for him. But the cautious, and carefully-masked inquiries which the Duke had set on foot, after the fashion in which such things are done in Italy, had brought him the information that a marriage was almost as good as arranged between the lady in question and the Marchese Ludovico di Castelmare, an old acquaintance of the family. Were it not for that impediment, the Duke thought that he might have good reason to hope that his plan might succeed.

Now it so happened that the Signora Assunta Fagiani was an old friend of the Duca di San Sisto; and when the widow of the professor of jurisprudence was promoted to the important post she held in the household of the Marchesa Lanfredi, that nobleman did not fail to find means for securing the continuance of her friendship. It was the object and purpose, therefore, of Signora Assunta Fagiani that the Lady Violante should become in due time Duchessa di San Sisto, and not Marchesa di Castelmare. But she understood her position quite well enough to be aware that the end she had in view must be approached cautiously and patiently.

Violante had, of course, been informed at the proper time that her family destined her to become the wife of the young Marchese Ludovico di Castelmare. Now, if Violante's temper and disposition had been other than it was; had she been able to think of herself differently from what she did; had it been possible for her, in a word, to have supposed that the Marchese Ludovico loved her, he was the man whom she could most readily have taught herself to love. They had been, to a certain degree, acquaintances from an early period of their childhood. He was the only young man she had ever known with anything like the same degree of intimacy; and Ludovico, as we know, was not devoid of qualities calculated to win a lady's love.

But Violante knew right well that Ludovico did not love her, and that there had never been any probability that he should do so; and, had she any lingering doubt on the subject, the good Assunta took very good care to dispel it. And there was a bitterness in this knowledge which did much towards producing in Violante the state of mind that has been described. She was not in love with Ludovico, but she had liked him—he was the only man she had ever liked at all. She knew that she was to be married to him if he could be persuaded to marry her, and if she were sufficiently obedient to marry him. She thought that no man could ever love her, and she knew very certainly that this man did not. Her own hope and firmest purpose, therefore, was, if such resistance to the higher authorities might in any way be possible to her, to avoid a marriage with Ludovico di Castelmare: if possible to her, she would fain escape from any marriage at all. If this should be altogether impossible, then the Duca di San Sisto, as well as anybody else. It was not that she had any hope that the Duca di San Sisto would love her: but, at least, it had not been proposed to him to love her, and found impossible by him to do so. At least the unloving husband would not be the one man whom she felt she might have loved had he deemed it worth his while to ask her love.

Yet, with all this, Violante had not learned, as perhaps most women in her place would have done, to hate Ludovico for having found it impossible to love her, for having condemned her to feel the spreta injuria forma, which so few of the sex can ever forgive. Had she ever reached the point of loving him it might, perhaps, have been otherwise. As it was, she was too gentle, too humble, in her estimate of her own worth and power of attraction to be angry with him: and yet she was sufficiently interested in the matter to listen not unwillingly to all the gossip that the Signora Assunta poured into her ear about Ludovico, tending to show that he was unworthy of pretending to her hand.

Assunta's object, of course, was to break the match with the Marchese di Castelmare for the sake of bringing on one with the Duca di San Sisto.

Violante's object, it has been said, was to avoid any marriage at all—specially that immediately proposed to her; and the stories, which from time to time Assunta brought her of the goings on of Ludovico, had a double interest for Violante. In some sort, all such intelligence was acceptable to her, as tending to make it unlikely that her only escape from a loveless marriage with him would be by her own resistance to the wishes of her family. Yet, at the same time, it was bitter to her, and ministered an unwholesome aliment to her morbid self-depreciation.

On the first day of the New Year, according to long-established custom, there was a grand reception in the evening at the palace of the Cardinal Legate. It was to be, as always on that occasion, a very grand affair. All the diamonds, and all the old state carriages, and all the liveries in Ravenna were put in requisition. Old coats, gorgeously bedizened with broad worsted lace of brilliant colours, and preserved for many a year carefully, but not wholly successfully, against time and moth, were taken by fours and fives from the cypress-wood chests in old family mansions, where they lay in peace from year's end to year's end if no marriage or other great family solemnity intervened to give them an extra turn of service, and were used to turn dependants of all sorts into liveried servants for the nonce; and nobody imagined or hoped that anybody else would look upon this display as anything else than absolute and frank ostentation. Nobody supposed that any human being would be led into believing that this state indicated the ordinary mode of life of the persons who exhibited it. Everybody in Italy has been for so many generations so very much poorer than his forefathers were, that such a state of things has long since been accepted by universal consent as a normal one; and it is understood on all hands that these fitful displays of the remnants of former grandeur, this vain revisiting of the glimpses of the moon by the ghosts of long-departed glories, shall be taken and allowed as protests on behalf of the bearers of old noble names to the effect that their ancestors did really once live in a style conformable to their ideas—that they perfectly know how these things should be done, and would be found quite prepared to resume their proper state, if only the good old days of prosperity should come again.

And there is the good as well as the seamy side (not, alas, to the old liveries! for they had been mostly turned and turned again too often); but to the feelings and social manners which prompted such a manifestation of them. At least, in such a condition of social manners and feelings mere wealth was not installed on the throne of Mammon in the eyes of all men. If one of the old coaches was more pitiably rickety than the rest; if the ancient-fashioned coat of some long-descended marchese was itself as threadbare as the old family liveries; if some widowed contessa had crept out from the last habitable corner of her dilapidated palazzo, where she was known to live on a modicum of chicory-water, brought in a tumbler from the nearest cafe, and a crust; not on any such account was there the smallest tendency towards a derisive smile on the lip, or in the mind of any man, at these pitiable attempts to keep up appearances, which everybody considered it right to keep up. Not on any such account was the stately courtesy of the Legate's reception in the smallest degree modified. It was subject, indeed, to many modifications; but these were wholly irrespective of any such circumstances.

There is a peculiar sort of naivete about Italian ostentation, which robs it of all its offensiveness. Nobody exhibits their finery or grandeur for the sake of crushing another; nobody feels themselves crushed by the exhibition of it. The old noble who turns out his gala liveries and other bedizenments on a festal day, does it to make up his part of the general show, which is for the gratification of all classes, and is a gratification to them. But it is a curious commentary of the past history of Italy that, as between city and city, there is the feeling, the wish, and the ambition, to crush and humble a rival community by superior magnificence.

Nobody expected much immediate gratification from attending the Cardinal's reception. There was little to be done save to bow to the host and to each other. Ices were handed round—none the less because it was bitterly cold—and cakes and comfits. Old Contessa Carini, who had a grandchild at home, and no money to buy bonbons with, emptied half a plateful of them into her handkerchief, the old servant who handed them helping her; and the Cardinal, who happened to be standing by, smilingly telling her to give the little one his benediction with them. The brave old Contessa still kept her carriage, as it became a Carini to do; though she starved her poor old shrivelled body to enable her to keep her half-starved horses. And "society" gave her its applause for struggling so hard to do that which it became her to do in the state of life to which it had pleased God to call her; and no soul in the room dreamed of thinking the less of her because of the sharp poverty that confessed itself in her eagerness to make the most of the opportunity of the Legate's hospitality.

The Conte Leandro Lombardoni had a bilious headache the following morning in consequence of overcramming himself with cakes and sweetmeats. One active-minded old gentleman originated the remark that the cold was greater than had been known in Ravenna for the last seven years; and this fact, repeated again and again by most of the company to each other, supplied the material of conversation for the first half-hour. Then somebody, alluded to the circumstance that, whereas it had been said that La Lalli was to have arrived before the end of the year, the fact was, that she had not yet come: and thereupon the Marchese Lamberto had authoritatively declared that the lady had been detained by an unforeseen circumstance of no importance, and would infallibly reach Ravenna on the evening of the 3rd.

And thenceforward this interesting news formed the sole topic of conversation till the carriages were ordered; and all the finery was taken home again to be laid up in lavender till that day twelvemonth.

There was to be, also according to annual custom, the first ball of the Carnival at the Palazzo Castelmare on the following evening; but for this the state trappings reserved for the Legate's reception on the Capo d'Anno, were not required.

The balls given by the Marchese Lamberto di Castelmare every Carnival were the grand and principal gaieties of Ravenna. The whole of the "society" were invited, and to be prevented from going by illness or any other contretemps was a misfortune to be lamented during all the rest of the year. At the Palazzo Castelmare people really did expect to enjoy themselves. There was dancing for the young, cards for the old, and eating and drinking for all. For the Palazzo Castelmare was the only house in Ravenna at which suppers were ever given. There three balls and three handsome suppers were provided for all the society of Ravenna every year! And the first of these always took place on the 2nd of January; the Capo d'Anno being left for the state reception at the Legate's palace.

Well might little Signor Ercole Stadione say, what would become of Ravenna if anything were to happen to the Marchese Lamberto!

All the people came much about the same time; and there was then half an hour or so, before the dancing commenced, during which the main object and amusement of the assemblage was to escape from misfortune, which it was well known the Conte Leandro meditated inflicting on the society. He was known to have written a poem for the opening of the new year, which was then in his pocket, and which he purposed reading aloud to the company, if he only could get a chance! He was looking very pale, and more sodden and pasty about the face than usual, from the effects of his excesses at the Legate's the night before. But his friends had no hope that this would save them from the poem, if he could in anywise obtain a hearing.

"Take care, he is putting his hand in his coat-pocket! That's where it is, you know; he'll have it out in half an instant, if we stop talking! Oh, Contessina, you are always so ready! Do invent something to stop him, for the love of heaven!" said a young man to a bright-looking girl next him.

"Oh, Signor Leandro, since you are riconciliato con bel sesso," said the Contessina, alluding to words which, to the great amusement of all Ravenna, Leandro had written in the album of a lady who asked the poet for his autograph, "since you are reconciled to the fair sex, will you be very kind and see if I have left my fan where I put off my shawl in the ante-room?"

"Bravo, Contessina; now let us get to another part of the room, before he gets back. Oh, Ludovico," he continued, addressing the young Marchese Castelmare, whom they encountered as they were crossing the room, "for the love of heaven, let us begin! Make the musicians strike up, or we shall have Leandro in full swing in another minute!"

"I assure you, Signor Ludovico, the danger is imminent!" said the Contessina.

"When I saw him at work last night at the Cardinal's pastry, I thought he must have made himself too ill to come here to-night," said the former speaker; "but I suppose poets can digest what would kill you or me!"

"If Leandro begins to read, I vote we all are seized with an invincible fit of sneezing," said another of the grown-up children.

"Well, we may as well begin at once; I will go and tell the Contessa Violante that we are ready," said Ludovico, moving off.

It was a matter of course, that he should open the ball with the Contessa Violante, not only by reason of her social standing in the city, but because of the position in which he was understood to stand towards her.

Violante was sitting at the upper end of the room between her great-aunt and the sister of the Marchese Lamberto, Ludovico's mother. She was very handsomely dressed in plain white silk, but was looking pale and dispirited. When Ludovico came up and offered his arm, bowing low as he did so, she rose and accepted it without speaking.

"I had almost made up my mind," she said as soon as they had moved a pace or two towards the middle of the large ball-room, "not to dance at all to-night: I am not well."

"Oh, Signorina, how unfortunate! What a disappointment! But it would be cruel to force you to dance, when it is against your inclination," said Ludovico, with a very unsuccessful attempt to put a tone of tenderness into his voice.

"I will not do so, after this dance," said Violante; "but I suppose we must dance the first dance together!"

"I am sorry it should be a matter of such disagreeable duty to you, Signora Violante," said Ludovico in a tone of pretended pique.

"It is equally disagreeable to me to dance with any other partner; I am not well, as I have told you, Signor Ludovico; I have no business to be here; I think my health becomes weaker from day to day. And the blessed Saints only know when it may be possible to think of carrying into effect the arrangements desired by our parents!"

"I am sure that mine would not wish to urge you on the subject to—to decide more quickly than you would wish to. I can assure you, Signora, nothing would be more contrary to my own feelings than to do any such violence to yours. Indeed I may say—"

"Yes, yes! I think I understand all about it, Signor Ludovico. Might it not be possible to find means of pleasing all parties in this matter, if only all parties understood each other, Signor Ludovico?"

She dropped her voice almost to a whisper as she said these last words, with a rapid furtive glance at his face.

"And now," she added, speaking in a louder tone, "we had better give our minds to the present scene of the farce, and perform the opening quadrille, as is expected of us!"

"I am truly sorry, Signora, that you should be called upon to do this sort of thing, when you are so unwell, as to make it even more disagreeable than it might be to you otherwise. But believe me," continued he, speaking in a low voice, and with an emphasis that indicated that his words had reference rather to what she had spoken to him in a similar tone than to the words of his own which had immediately preceded them, "believe me that it is my wish to meet your wishes in all respects."

There was a jesuitism in this speech, which did not recommend it or its speaker to the Contessa Violante. She would have been far better pleased by a more open reply to the confidence which she had half offered. She only said in reply:

"I am disposed to think, that such is the case in the matter which more nearly concerns us both, Signor Ludovico, than anything else. But—although we knew just now that we had to dance together, it was you who had to ask me, you know, and not I you. Very little active power of influencing her own destiny is allowed to a girl; come, we had better attend now to the business in hand!"

There was nothing more, except such ordinary words between each other or the others dancing in the same set, as the dance itself led to, spoken by the Contessa and Ludovico. The former declined all other invitations to dance, and went home at the earliest moment she could induce her aunt to do so.

There was much talk going on in all parts of the room as to the announced coming of the great singer on the morrow. The young men settled together the last details of their plans for the triumphal entry of the "Diva;" and the ladies were by no means uninterested in hearing all that their cavaliers had to tell them on this subject. Much was said, too, about the qualities of La Lalli both as a singer and as a woman. Everybody agreed that she was admirable in the first respect; and there was not a man there, who had not some anecdote to tell, which he had heard from the very best authority, tending to set forth the rare perfection of her beauty, and the wonderful power of fascination she exercised on all who came near her.

She was to arrive quite early on the morrow. It was understood that she purposed passing the previous night, that night in short, which those who were discussing her were spending at the Castelmare ball, at the little town of Bagnacavallo, a few miles only from Ravenna. Such a scheme looked, or would have looked in the eyes of any other people than Italians, rather ridiculously like the ways and fashions of royal progresses, and state entries into cities. But the Ravenna admirers of the coming "Diva" neither saw nor suspected the slightest absurdity; and it is to be supposed that La Lalli knew all the importance of first impressions, and that she did not choose to show herself to her new worshippers for the first time under all the disadvantages of arriving tired and dusty from a long journey.

CHAPTER XII

The Arrival of the "Diva"

On the morrow of the Marchese's ball was the great day of the arrival of the divine songstress. And it was as lovely a day for the gala doings, which had been arranged in honour of the occasion, as could be desired. A brilliant sun in a cloudless sky made the afternoon quite warm and genial, despite the general cold. An Italian sun can do this. Where he shines not it may be freezing. As soon as he has made his somewhat precipitous exit from the hard blue sky, the temperature will suddenly fall some ten degrees or more. But as long as he is in glory overhead, it is summer in the midst of winter.

Three o'clock had been named as the hour at which the coming "Diva" would reach the city gates. But the plans which the young habitues of the Circolo had arranged for receiving her, had been in some degree modified. The scheme of harnessing their noble selves to her chariot-wheels had been abandoned; and instead of that it had been understood that the Marchese Lamberto would himself go in his carriage to meet her a few miles out of the city and bring her in. The Marchese Ludovico and the young Barone Manutoli were to accompany the Marchese Lamberto, and to assist in receiving the lady; but were to return to the city in the carriage which she would leave, on getting into that of the Marchese, or in any other way that might seem good to them. The Marchese Lamberto and the lady alone were to occupy his handsome family equipage. There was to be a band of music in attendance, which would precede the carriage as it entered the city; and some half-dozen young officers of a regiment of Papal cavalry, which chanced to be then stationed at Ravenna, intended to ride at each door of the carriage as it returned to the city. Altogether it was to be a very brilliant affair. And all the gay world of Ravenna was on the tiptoe of expectation and delight.

The Marchese Lamberto, indeed, looked upon his share in the pageant as a great bore. He had had put off one or two more congenial occupations for the purpose of doing on the occasion his part of that which he deemed his duty to the city. Professor Tomosarchi the great anatomist, who was at the head of the hospital, and curator of the museum, was to have come to the Palazzo Castelmare that morning to show the Marchese an interesting experiment connected with the action of a new anodyne; and Signor Folchi, the pianist, was to have been with him at one, to try over a little piece of the Marchese's own composition. And both these appointments, either of which was far more interesting to the Marchese Lamberto than driving out in the cold to meet the stage goddess, had to be set aside.

Nevertheless, he had deemed it due to his own position, and to the occasion, to grace this little triumphal entry with his presence. If he had left it wholly in the hands of his nephew, and the other young men, it might have been the means of starting the Signora Lalli amiss on her Ravenna career in a manner he particularly wished to avoid. After that little hint on the subject, which the impresario had given him, he was specially desirous that anything like an occasion for scandal should be avoided in all that concerned the sojourn of the Signora Lalli in Ravenna. He, the Marchese Lamberto, the intimate friend of the Cardinal, and the most pre-eminently respectable man in Ravenna, had had a very large—certainly the largest—share in bringing this woman to the city; and he was anxious that the engagement should lead to no unpleasant results of any kind.

It might be very possibly that the little matters at which the impresario had hinted, were not altogether calumnious;—that the lady might be one of those members of her profession who seek other triumphs besides those of her own scenic kingdom, and the story of whose lives in the different cities they visit is not confined to the walls and to the records of the theatre. It might very well be that a little caution and looking after was needed in the matter, It would be as well, therefore, to take the thing in hand at once in a manner that should put the lady on a right course from the beginning;—all which could be excellently well accomplished by at once taking her, as it were, into his own hands; and would, on the other hand, be endangered by throwing her from the first into those of the youngsters who purposed going out to meet her.

So the Marchese sacrificed himself; put off the anatomist and the musician; spent the morning in arranging all the details of the proposed cavalcade with the young men who were to compose it; and at two o'clock got into his open carriage to drive out towards Bagnacavallo. The young Barone Manutoli and Ludovico were in the carriage with him. But it was understood, as has been said, that they were to leave it when they met the heroine of the day, who was to enter Ravenna with the perfectly safe and unattackable Marchese alone in the carriage with her.

"I wonder whether she is as lovely as she is said to be?" said Manutoli, as they drove out beyond the crumbling and ivy-grown brick wall, which had helped to repel the attack of Odoacer the Goth; but which had, some thirteen hundred years ago, failed to keep out the mischief brought into the city by the comedian Empress Theodora, whose beauty had promoted her from the stage to the throne.

Absit omen! And what, indeed, can there be common between Goths and Greeks of the Lower Empire, who lived thirteen hundred years ago, with the good Catholic subjects, and the quiet Catholic city of our Holy Father the Pope, in the nineteenth century!

At all events, it may be taken as very certain that no omen of the sort and no such thoughts were present to the minds or fancies of any of those who were about to form the escort of the modern actress.

"All who have ever seen her, speak in the most rapturous terms of her great beauty," said Ludovico, in reply to his friend's remark.

"Don't be too sure about it, figliuoli mio, or it is likely enough you may be disappointed," said the Marchese Lamberto. "People repeat such things one after the other; there is a fashion in it. I have always found that your stage beauty is as often as not no beauty, at all off it; and then you know stage work and the foot-lights are terribly quick users-up of beauty. And La Lalli is not at the beginning of her career. But what have we to do with all that! che diavolo! She is a great singer; she comes here to delight our ears, not our eyes!"

"But time and work make havoc with the voice as well as with the face and figure, Signor Marchese!" said Manutoli.

"Not to the same degree, Signor Barone, and not quite so rapidly," replied the Marchese, with the manner of one laying down the law on a subject of which he is an acknowledged master. "Of course a voice which has done much work, is not the same thing as a perfectly fresh one? A chi lo dite? though, observe, you very often gain more in knowledge, and in perfection of art, than you lose in freshness of organ. But with proper care, voice, though a perishable thing, is not so rapidly and fatally so, as mere beauty of face; that is sure to go very soon. I have not troubled myself to inquire, as you may imagine, much about the state of La Lalli's good looks. But I have informed myself of the condition of her voice, as it was my duty to do. And I think that in that respect, which is the only one we need care about, the city will find that we have not done badly."

"For my part, I confess a romanzo comes very specially recommended to my ears from a lovely mouth!" said Ludovico; "and I fully expect to find La Lalli quite up to the mark in this respect. I shall be disappointed if she is not."

"From all I have heard, we shall none of us be disappointed!" said Manutoli.

"We shall see in a few minutes!" returned Ludovico, looking at his watch.

"There's something in the road now, I think, as far as I can see!" said Manutoli, who had stood up in the carriage, holding the rail of the driver's seat with one hand. The road stretched long and flat, in a perfectly straight line before them for a great distance. "Yes," continued he, "there is certainly something coming along the road;—a carriage by the quickness with which it nears us: now for it!"

"Tell him to draw up, Ludovico; and he might as well turn round so as to be ready to drive back. We will wait here till she comes; and our friends on horseback may as well remain here too," said the Marchese.

So the little party drew up, and all eyes were turned to the small cloud of dust rapidly approaching them.

"Yes: it is a carriage, and no mistake; and coming along at a good pace too!" said Manutoli.

"It is she, no doubt; she was to sleep at Bagnacavallo," returned Ludovico.

"Signori!" said the Marchese, addressing the four, or five mounted officers, "will you kindly put your horses across the road, so that the lady's driver may see that he is to stop, and that there may be no mistake."

And then an open carriage became clearly visible, and in the next minute, it could be seen that it was occupied by two persons;—a lady and another figure—an old man apparently—muffled in a huge blue travelling-cloak.

Then in another instant the travelling-carriage, finding the road blocked before it, had stopped, and in the next, the Marchese Lamberto, hat in hand, was standing at the door of it, on the lady's side;—the two young men standing immediately behind him, and the horsemen crowded round, craning over the necks of their horses.

Oh! per Bacco! There is no mistake about it; she is startlingly beautiful. Report had not said half enough. And, somehow or other, it appeared as if a travelling-costume was specially becoming to her. At least, it seemed so to the innocent youths who so first saw her. Had there been any women present their minds would have at once gone back from the splendid effect produced to all the details of the artfully combined causes which had gone to the producing of it. But there were no ladies present, save the "Diva" alone.

Such a Diva! She wore a little blue velvet hat, with a white feather in it very coquettishly placed on a superb wealth of hair of the richest auburn tint. She was very delicately fair, with just such an amount of the loveliest carnation on her cheeks as might be produced by the perfection of health and joyousness and youth; or might be, a lady critic would have whispered, by some other equally effectual means. She had large—very large—wide-opened, clear, and limpid light-blue eyes, with that trick of an appealing look in them which always seems to say to every manly heart, "You, alone of all the harsh, cold, indifferent crowd around us, are he to whom I can look for sympathy, comprehension, and fellow-feeling." And now these eyes looked round from one to another of those around her with a look of smiling, innocent surprise and inquiry that demanded an explanation of the unprecedented circumstances with a childish freshness the most engaging.

She wore a bright blue velvet pelisse, trimmed with ermine, which admirably showed to the greatest advantage her magnificently shaped bust, and round slender waist; and bent forward towards the Marchese, as he stood at the carriage-door, with inimitable grace of gesture, and a smile on her sweet lips that would have utterly defeated and put to shame any St. Antony exposed to such temptation.

"Signora," said the Marchese, who looked very handsome, as he stood with his hat in his hand, and bowed with stately courtesy, "Ravenna welcomes you, and places itself at your feet in our persons. Permit me to present to you these gentlemen, who have had the good fortune to be selected among many aspirants to that honour, to assist me in welcoming you to our city: the Barone Adolfo Manutoli; my nephew, the Marchese Ludovico di Castelmare."

"E Lei dunque e il Marchese Lamberto di Castelmare?" said the lady, in the sweetest possible of silvery tones, and with an air of humble wonder at the greatness of the honour done her, mingled with grateful appreciation of it, that was inimitably well done; and held up two exquisitely-gloved slender little hands, as she spoke, half joining them together in thankful astonishment, and half extending them towards him with an almost caressing movement of appeal.

"Si, Signora; I am the man you have named; I am fortunate that my name should have reached your ears; more fortunate still in having had a part in making the arrangements that have brought you here;—and most fortunate of all if I shall be so happy as to make your sojourn among us agreeable."

"Signor Marehese! Lei e troppo garbato, troppo buono; ma troppo buono, davvero!" said the pretty creature; and the appealing eyes looked into his with the semblance of a tear of emotion in them.

"Will you allow me the pleasure, Signora, of conducting you to the city in my carriage?" said the Marchese, with a graceful wave of his hand towards his handsome equipage. "I have thought it might possibly be agreeable to you to place it and myself at your disposition on this occasion."

"Ma come? It is too great an honour, davvero. But to make my first appearance in your city under such auspices will go far towards assuring me such a success at Ravenna, as it is my most earnest wish to attain."

The Marchese put out his hand to assist her to alight, as he added, "Perhaps you will allow these gentlemen to return in your carriage, Signora? They have no other here. I did not think it necessary to bring a second carriage."

"Come loro commandano!—as their lordships please," said La Lalli with a graceful bow; though the young men were of opinion, that her eyes very plainly said, as she glanced towards them, that she would have preferred that they should have returned in the same carriage together.

She rose, as she spoke, and giving her hand to the Marchese, put one foot on the carriage-step in the act of descending, and then paused to say, as if she had forgotten it till that moment:

"Will you permit me, Signor Marchese, to present my father to you, Signor Quinto Lalli? I never travel without his protection!"

The old man in the corner moved slightly, and made a sort of bow with his head. He had remained quite still and passive in his cloak and his corner all through the rest of the scene, taking it all apparently as something very much in the common order of things. Perhaps the piece that was being played had been played too often in his presence to have any further interest for him.

While thus presenting her father, as she called him, to the Marchese, the beautiful actress had remained for the moments necessary for that purpose, with her matchless figure poised on the one dainty foot, which she had stretched down to the step of the carriage. The attitude certainly showed the svelte perfection of her form to advantage; and from the unavoidable circumstances of the position, it also showed one of the most beautifully formed feet that ever was seen, together with the whole of the exquisite little bottine that clothed it, a beautifully turned ankle, and perhaps as much as two inches of the silk stocking above the boot.

The mere chance that caused the lady to bethink herself of presenting her father just at that moment, was thus quite a piece of good fortune for the young men on foot and on horseback, who were standing around, which no other combination of circumstances could have procured for them.

Then the Marchese handed her with graceful gallantry to his carriage, took the place in the back of it by the side of her; and the little cavalcade began its return to the city. At a small distance from the walls, they found the band stationed, and thus preceded by music, and passing through all the elite of the population in the streets, the Marchese conducted her to the Palazzo Castelmare, and handed her up the grand staircase to the great saloon, where all the theatrical world of Ravenna, and many of the more notable patrons of the theatre, were assembled to receive her.

Signor Ercole Stadione, the little impresario, was there of course, and in high enjoyment of the triumph of the occasion, and of the importance which his share in it reflected on him. He buzzed about the large saloon from one group to another, raising himself on tiptoe as he looked up into the faces of his noble friends and patrons, and rubbing his hands together cheerily in the exuberance of his satisfaction.

"You had the happiness of accompanying the illustrissimo Signor Marchese to receive our honoured guest to-day, Signor Barone!" said he to Manutoli, who was giving an account of his expedition, and of the first appearance of the new "Diva," to a knot of young men grouped around him; "mi rallegro! Mi rallegro! Ravenna could not have had a more worthy representative than yourself, Signor Barone! But is she not divine! What beauty! What a grace!"

"Why, Signor Ercole, one would think you had begotten her yourself. She is a pretty creature certainly. What a smile she has!"

"Eh bene, Signori miei! Are you satisfied? Are you content? Have we done well?" said the little man, buzzing off to another group. "Che vi pare? Is she up to the mark, or is she not?"

"Bravo, Signor Ercole! We are all delighted with her!" said one.

"If she sings as she looks," cried another, "Ravenna has a prima donna such as no other city in Italy has."

"Or in Europe, per Bacco!" added a third.

"What do you think of her, Signor Leandro? Did I say too much?" asked the happy impresario, moving off to a console, against which the poet was leaning in an abstracted attitude, while his eye, in a fine frenzy rolling, managed nevertheless to look out for the manifestation on the Diva's face of that impression which he doubted not his figure and pose must make on her.

"What a bore she must find it having to talk to all those empty-brained fellows that have got round her there, just like buzzing blue-bottle flies round sugar-barrel! I wonder it does not occur to the Marchese that it would be more to the purpose to present to her some of the brighter intelligences of the city. She must think Ravenna is a city of blockheads! And one can see, with half an eye, that is the sort of woman who can appreciate intellect!"

"It will be for you, Signor Conte, to prove to her that our city is not deficient in that respect. Sapristi? Would you desire a better subject? What do you say to an ode, now, on the rising of a new constellation on the shores of the Adriatic? Hein! Or an inpromptu on seeing the divine Lalli enter Ravenna through the same arch under which the Empress Theodora must have passed?"

"I had already thought of that," snapped the poet, sharply.

"Of course you had," said the obsequious little man. "An impromptu, by all means! You could have it ready to present to her at the theatre to-morrow."

"Unless the Marchese thinks fit to present me to the lady presently, I shall decline to write anything at all," rejoined Signor Leandro, thus unjustly determining, in his ill-humour, to punish all Ravenna for the fault of one single individual.

The Diva was, in the meantime, winning golden opinions on all sides. She had bright smiles, and pretty captivating looks, and courteous, prettily-turned phrases for all. But amid all this she contrived unfailingly all the time, by means of some exquisitely subtle nuance of manner, to impress every person present with the unconsciously-conceived feeling that there was something more between her and the Marchese and his nephew than between her and anybody else in the room; that she in some sort belonged to them, and was being presented to the society under their auspices. She remained close by the side of the Marchese. She would look with an appealing and inquiring glance into his face at each fresh introduction that was made to her, as if to ask his sanction and approval. She had some little word from time to time either for his ear, or that of his nephew, spoken in such a manner as to reach those of nobody else; while, gracious to all, she delicately but markedly graduated the scale of her graciousness towards those who were introduced to her, according to the degree of intimacy which seemed to exist between them and the Marchese. The result was that the Marchese, without having been in the least conscious by what means and steps it had been brought about, felt, by the time the gathering was at an end, a sort of sense of proprietorship in the brilliant and lovely artiste;—it was so evidently he who was presenting her to the city! She herself so evidently felt that it would become her to rule her conduct in all respects at Ravenna according to the Marchese's wishes and ideas, and there was so sweet and so subtle a flattery in the way in which she made this felt, that when, after all the crowd had retired, and she was about to take leave of the Marchese to go to the lodging that had been prepared for her, she ventured to take his hand between both hers, while looking up into his face to thank him, in a voice quivering with emotion, for his kindness to her, there passed a something into the system of the Marchese from that contact of the palms that he found it very difficult to rid himself of.

BOOK III

"Sirenum Pocula"

CHAPTER I

"Diva Potens"

Quinto Lalli was the name by which the prima donna had presented the old gentleman who had shared her travelling-carriage to the Marchese Lamberto as her father. And Quinto Lalli was his real name; but he was not really her father. Nor had she any legitimate claim to the name of Lalli. She had never been known by any other, however, during the whole of her theatrical career; and there were very few persons in any of the many cities where the Lalli was famous, who had any idea that the old man who always accompanied her was not her father. Indeed, Bianca had so long been accustomed to call and to consider him as such, that she often well nigh forgot herself that he held no such relationship to her.

The real facts of the case were very simple, and had nothing romantic about them. Old Lalli was a man of great musical gifts and knowledge. He had been a singing-master in his day; an impresario too for a short time; and sometimes a kind of broker, or middle-man between singers in want of an engagement and managers seeking for "available talent;" and a hunter-up of talent not yet available, but which, it might be hoped, would one day become such.

It was in the pursuit of his avocations of this latter sort, that he had one day, about fifteen years before the date of the circumstances narrated in the last chapter, chanced to meet with a little girl, then some twelve years old, on the hopes of whose future success he had resolved to build his own fortunes. It was time that he should find some foundation for them, if they were ever to be built at all, which most of those who knew Signor Quinto Lalli deemed not a little improbable; for he was of the sort of men who never do make fortunes.

He was fifty years old when he had met with the little girl in question, and had done nothing yet towards laying the foundations of any sort of fortune. Unstable, improvident, unthrifty, fond of pleasure, and not fond of work, nothing had succeeded with him. Nevertheless, a cleverer man in his own line, or a shrewder judge of the article he dealt in, than Quinto Lalli did not exist in all Italy. And his judgment did not fail him when he fell in with little Bianca degli Innocenti.

Persons unacquainted with Italian things and ways might suppose that the above modification of the "particle noble" in Bianca's family name was indicative of a very aristocratic origin. Italians, however—and specially Tuscans—would draw a different conclusion from the premises. The family "Degli Innocenti" is very frequently met with in Tuscany; but the bearers of the name do not, for the most part, take great heed of their family ties. The "Innocenti," in a word, is the name of the foundling-hospital in Florence; and those of whose origin nothing is known save that they have been brought up by that charity, are often called after it, and known by no other name. Little Bianca's father, or possibly her grandfather, must have been some such Jem, Jack, or Bob "of the Foundlings," and left no other patronymic to his race.

Quinto Lalli fell in with the child one day in the dirty and miserable little town of Acquapendente, just on the Roman side of the frontier line dividing the Papal territory from Tuscany, as he was travelling from Florence to Rome. He was travelling by the diligence, which always used to remain a good hour or more at Acquapendente, for the transaction of passport and dogana work. There, strolling, for want of something better to do, through the dilapidated streets of the poverty-stricken little town, which in those days told the traveller most unmistakably how great was the difference between prosperous Tuscany, which he had just left, and the wretched Pope's-land which he was entering—Quinto Lalli heard a child's voice, and instantly stopped and pricked up his ears.

Looking round, he saw a little creature, barely clad, happy amid the surrounding squalor, sitting with its little bare feet and legs dabbling in the sparkling water in the broken marble tank of a once magnificent fountain. There she sate alone in the sunshine, and carolled, with wide-opened throat, like any other nature-made songster.

Quinto Lalli, with startled ear, listened attentively; got round to where he could see the child's face; marked well, with knowing eye, the little brown feet and legs bare to the knee; and then determined to abandon the fare paid for the remainder of his diligence journey to Rome.

The business for the sake of which he made that sacrifice was easily and quickly done. A bargain is not difficult when that which is coveted by one party is deemed a burden and encumbrance by the other. And Quinto Lalli became the fortunate purchaser of the article of which he had so judiciously appreciated the value.

Quinto had his little purchase well and carefully educated—educated her himself in a great measure, as far as her voice was concerned—and took care that every attention was paid, not only to her musical culture, and to the preservation and enhancement of her beauty—which, with great comfort as regarded the ultimate issue of his speculation, he saw every year that passed over her develop more and more—but also to her intellectual cultivation. For Lalli was a clever man enough to know, that if a stupid singer with a fine voice can charm so as to be worth a hundred, an intelligent singer with an equally fine voice, can charm so as to be worth two hundred.

And the old singing-master was good and kind to his pupil: firstly, because he had no unkindness in his nature, and secondly, because it was in every way his interest to conciliate the girl. She had been brought out at eighteen, and had now been nine years on the stage—nine years of success, which ought to have enriched both teacher and pupil.

They had very soon come to understand each other in matters of interest. Lalli had begun by taking all her large earnings. But Bianca very quickly let her protector understand that such an arrangement did not meet her views at all. The ingratitude, when she owed everything to him alone! No, Bianca had no intention to be ungrateful—anzi! she looked upon Lalli as her father, and hoped she always should do so; but she had no intention of being treated like a child. So long as she could earn anything, her adopted father should want for nothing. She asked nothing better than to continue to live with him, and work for both of them.

And, in truth, her grateful kindness and fondness for the old man whom she had so long looked on as a father was Bianca's strongest point in the way of moral excellence. In all their nine years of partnership she had worked for him as much as for herself. But her nine years of success ought to have made both the old man and his adopted daughter comfortably well off. And it had done nothing of the kind.

They had laid by nothing. Old Quinto had all his life been recklessly extravagant and thriftless; and his mode of education had not made Bianca less so. If he was fond of dissipation and pleasure, she was not less fond of them on her side. Careful as her education had been, it was hardly to be expected that it should have been eminently successful in forming a high standard of moral character. The demands made by society upon its members in general in the clime and time in question were not of a very exacting nature; and the expectations of society in this respect from a person in Bianca's position were more moderate still. Nor were the precepts, counsels, example, or wisdom of her protector at all calculated to guide the beautiful singer scatheless through the dangers and difficulties incidental to her position.

In short, for nine years Bianca had worked hard—had earned a great deal of money, and had spent it all (except what Lalli had spent for her) in dissipation, the sharers in which had been chosen by the beautiful actress—as kissing goes—by favour, and not with any view to their ability to pay the cost.

And now La Lalli had reached her twenty-seventh year; and was very nearly as poor as when she began her career. And certain small warnings, unimportant as yet, and wholly unsuspected, save by herself and old Quinto, had begun to suggest to her the expediency of thinking a little for the future. She and Quinto Lalli had had a very serious conversation on the subject just before the commencement of that season at Milan, which, as has been hinted, had ended somewhat disagreeably for the charming singer.

The real truth of the matter was that the difficulty in question had arisen not from any tendency in the lady to behave in the Lombard capital with more reprehensible levity than, it must unfortunately be admitted, she had been very well known to have behaved in other places and on other occasions; but from a change in her manners in a diametrically opposite direction. It was a change of tactics, which the strictest moralist must have admitted to involve an improvement in moral conduct, that got the hardly treated Diva into trouble.

The Austrian Government, as we all know, is, or was, a paternal government-a very paternal government. And the governor who ruled in the Lombard capital was quite as much intent on playing the "governor," in the modern young gentleman's sense of the word, as good old paternal Franz himself in his own Vienna. But this paternal government was not of the sort which ignores the well-authenticated fact that "young men will be young men." On the contrary, it proceeded always, especially as regarded its more distinguished sons, on the largest recognition of this truth. Wild-oats must be sown; the "governor" knew it, and the law allowed it. But they should be so sown as to involve as little prejudicial an after-crop, as may be—as little prejudicial especially to those distinguished sons who cannot be expected to refrain from such natural sowing.

And enchanting Divas may assist in such sowing, and be tolerated in so doing by a not too rigidly exacting paternal government—may be held in so assisting not to step beyond the sphere of social functions assigned to them by the natural order of things in a manner too offensive to the mild morality of a paternal government, as long as such joint wild-oat cultivation shall in nowise threaten to interfere with the future tillage of less wild and more profitable crops by those distinguished young scions of noble races, to whose youthful aberrations a paternal government is thus wisely indulgent.

So long, and no longer. Mark it well, enchanting Divas. Enchant if you will; 'tis your function. But do not think to enchain? Enmesh a young Marchese in the tangles of Neaera's hair. A paternal governor puts his fingers before his eyes; and lets a smile be seen on his lips beneath them. But do not seek to bind him by less easily broken ties. A vigilant and moral governor frowns on the instant; and a paternal government well knows how to protect its distinguished sons by very summary and effectual process.

But when for a poor Diva there comes also the time when that pleasant wild-oat sowing seems no longer a promising pursuit, what does the paternal wisdom decree as to her future? Why, she must reap as she has sown—or helped to sow. See ye to it, Divas. Such providence is beyond our function.

And thus it had come to pass that the trouble had arisen which had resulted in inducing the Diva Bianca to turn her back on ungrateful Milan, and her face towards welcoming Ravenna. In that conference between Bianca and her old friend and counsellor, which has been mentioned, it had been fully brought home to the Diva's conviction that for her the pleasant time of wild-oat sowing had come to an end. "Would that the year were always May." But old Quinto Lalli knew that it wasn't. And it had been concluded between him and his adopted daughter that it was high time for Bianca to take life au serieux;—to understand thoroughly that noctes coenaeque deum, with champagne suppers and love among the roses, must be, if not necessarily abandoned, yet steadily contemplated as a means and not an end.

What if—
Love, free as air, at sight of human ties,
Shakes his light wings, and in a moment flies?

The warning of the verse teaches that the skittish god must not be scared by a premature exhibition of the noose hid beneath the sieve of corn. Champagne suppers and love among the roses—yes. But there should be, also, cunningly hidden, the noose among the roses.

And to this wisdom the Diva her well-trained mind did seriously incline, during that last Milan campaign. Nor did her moral aim seem to be without good promise of success. The sleek young colts with their shiny coats, glossy, with the rich pastures of the Lombard plains, pranced up and nibbled, all unconscious of the hidden noose. One fine young unsuspecting animal, the noblest of the herd, came so close to the noose that Bianca thought her work was done, and was on the point of casting it over his lordly head—and he all but enchanted into such docility as to submit to it, even seeing it.

When lo! with sudden swoop of hand, sharp vibrating police decrees, an unsleeping paternal government darts down the fabric of our hopes, sends off the nearly captured prey, loud neighing and with heels kicked high in air, but safe, to his ancestral Lombard pastures, and whirls away the too dangerous enchantress into outer space.

Sorrowfully the baffled fair goes forth (a graceful picture somewhere seen of paradise-banished Peri with pretty stooping head, recalls itself to my mind as I write the words); sorrowfully but not despairing, and wiser than before.

And yet before she goes seeking fresh fields and pastures new, and meditating new emprise, wealthy Milan shall itself equip her for the next campaign. For much of such expedient outfit Milan can supply, which, in remote Ravenna, might in vain be sought. There, beneath the shadow of those marble walls, where once the sainted Borromeo preached, the cunningest Parisian artists may be found—so rich in corn and wine and silk are Lombard plains-modists and mercers, corset-makers, lacemen, skilled so to clothe the limbs of beauty, that every fold shall but display the perfect handiwork of nature, yet add to it the further grace of art. Makers of tiny slippers and such dainty bootlets as show forth and enhance the separate beauty of each inch of outline of rounded ankle, arched instep, and slender length of foot, shall lend their help. And if envious Time have something done to blur the bloom upon the cheek, or blot the clear transparent purity of skin, sunt certa piacula, there are not wanting means for helping a mortal Diva to some of the prerogatives of immortality in these respects.

And thus equipped, everything is ready, Quinto mio; we turn our backs on haughty Milan, and nova regna petentes cras ingens iterabimus aequor, that is to say, the wide plains of Lombardy.

So Bianca and her faithful Quinto journeyed forth on that interminably long flat monotonous Emilian road, with no accompanying sound of music on their departure, but with the much-improved prospects, which have been described, on their arrival.

CHAPTER II

An Adopted Father and An Adopted Daughter

When Bianca, on the evening of her arrival at Ravenna, rejoined Quinto Lalli at the handsome and convenient lodging which had been provided her, after having passed an hour or two, as has been related, in being presented to the notabilities of the city, and receiving a great deal of homage at the Palazzo Castelmare, she had already learned many useful things.

Imprimis, she had learned that the Marchese Lamberto was a bachelor; that he was—though what young girls call an old man—still almost in the prime of life, for a man so healthy and well preserved; that he was a remarkably handsome and dignified gentleman; that he evidently occupied the very foremost place in the esteem and respect of his fellow-citizens; that he was rich; and that he appeared from all those little signs and tokens of manner, which such a woman as La Diva Bianca can interpret so readily, the last man in the world likely to fall in love with such a travelling Diva as herself. She had learned, further, that the Marchese Ludovico was his heir; that the said Ludovico might be judged, by all those same signs and tokens, to be very much such a man as might be likely to fall over head and ears in love with a beautiful woman, who should make it her business to cause him to do so; and yet further, that this Marchese Ludovico was just the sort of man, whom, if she might permit herself to join pleasure with business, she would very well like so to operate on. She had heard a poem read to her by the Conte Leandro, and had decided that, if he were the wealthiest man in all Ravenna, no sense of her duty to herself could prevail to make her do anything but run away from him at the first warning of his approach. Nevertheless, from him, even, she had learned something. She had become acquainted with the fact, whispered in his own exquisitely felicitous manner, and with the tact and judicious appreciation of opportunity peculiar to him, that Ludovico di Castelmare was, to the great sorrow of his friends and family, enslaved by a certain Venetian artist, then resident in Ravenna, a girl really of no attractions whatever.

Thus much of the carte du pays of that new country, in which her own campaign was to be made, and of which it so much imported her to have the social map, she had learned, when she found Quinto Lalli waiting for her to take possession of their new home.

"Well, bambina mia, my baby," for so the old man often called her, "what sort of folk have we come among? How do you like the appearance of the country?"

"Eh, papa mio, che volete? I have seen only a bit of it. It is rather early to judge yet," said Bianca.

"Not too early for your quickness, bambina mia. Besides, you may be sure you have seen most of what you are likely to see, and what it most concerns you to see. The Cardinal Legate was not likely to come out to meet you, I suppose; nor does it much matter to you to see his Eminence."

"Well, what I have seen, I like. As for the theatre, that Marchese Lamberto, whom you saw, knows what singing is as well as you do. I shall please him on the stage; and, if so, as I see very well, I shall please all the rest of Ravenna. But—"

"But what? There is always a 'but.' What is it this time?" said the old man.

"As if you did not know as well as I!" said Bianca, with a little toss. "Is what I can do on the theatre of Ravenna the thing that is most in my thoughts?"

"'Twas you who mentioned it first," said Quinto. "I spoke of it merely with reference to that man, the Marchese Lamberto di Castelmare. He is one of the first, if not the very first, man in the city; and everybody is cap in hand before him. Evidently a rich man."

"And he is a musician, you say?" rejoined Quinto.

"Fanatico! But what matters that; except, indeed, as a stepping-stone? What has music done for me? The Marchese Lamberto is a bachelor, Quinto."

"Ha! what, the old man?" said Quinto, looking sharply at her.

"Yes, the old man, as you call him. Not so old but he might be your son, friend Quinto. But there is the young man, the Marchese Ludovico, whom you also saw, when they met us on the road. He is the nephew and heir to the other—a bachelor too—and as pretty a fellow as one would wish to see into the bargain; a charming fellow."

"So was the Duca di Lodi at Milan," said the old man, quietly; "a very charming fellow—charming and charmed into the bargain. But—"

"Yes! I don't need to ask the meaning of your 'but.' We know all about that; but what is the good of going back upon it?" said Bianca, throwing herself at full length upon a sofa, and tossing her hat on to the ground, with some little display of ill-temper, as she spoke.

"Only for the sake of the light past mistakes may throw on future hopes," replied Quinto, with philosophic calmness.

"Bah-mistakes—what mistake? There was no mistake, but for that infamous old wretch of a governor," said Bianca, with an expression which the individual referred to would hardly have recognized as beautiful, if he could have seen it.

"Yes! I know. May the devil give him his due! But, bambina mia, there are wretches of governors here too, it is to be feared, no less infamous."

"What do you mean? What did we come here then for?" cried Bianca, rearing herself on her elbow on the sofa, and looking at her old friend with wide-opened eyes of angry surprise.

"In the first place, cara mia, because it was necessary to go somewhere; and, in the second place, because I should be very much at a loss to name any place where the governors are not infamous wretches, every whit as bad as at Milan. 'Tis the way of them, my poor child. But you see, Bianca dear, to return to what we were saying, there was a little mistake at Milan. The Duca di Lodi did not go off into the country, and leave you plantee la, to please himself."

"Who ever thought he did? No, poor fellow, he was right enough. But what was the mistake, I want to know?"

"You could bring no influence to bear, except upon himself, you know."

"Of course not. How should I? E poi?"

"And he could not do as he pleased," said Quinto, with a slight shrug of his shoulders. "That was the mistake, cara mia, to endeavour to bring about an object, by influencing some one who had no power to act for themselves in the matter."

"A very pleasant Job's comforter you are to-night, Quinto. I don't know what you are driving at?" said Bianca, staring at him.

"Only this, my precious child. I was set thinking of the mistake at Milan by what you said of these two men, the uncle and nephew. Has it not come into your clever head, mia bella, that we might find here the means of avoiding a repetition of that error?"

"Ah—h! Now I see what you are at. The uncle—hum—m—m," said Bianca, meditatively; and then shaking her head with closely shut lips.

"And why not the uncle, bambina mia? I am sure the few words you have said about him are sufficient to point out that an alliance with the Marchese di Castelmare would be an advantageous one for any lady in the land," said old Quinto, with a demure air, that concealed under it just the least flavour in the world of quiet irony.

"I won't deny, papa mio, that, being humble as becomes my station," replied Bianca, in the same tone, "I should be perfectly contented with the style and title of Marchesa di Castelmare. But what reason have we for thinking that there would be any less difficulty in becoming such than in becoming Duchessa di Lodi? That, between ourselves, is the question."

"And what difficulty lay in the way of becoming Duchessa di Lodi? Certainly none that arose from the Signor Duca. Governors and fathers, and uncles and aunts, and police commissaries, and the devil knows what, all interfered to keep two young hearts asunder, and spoil the game. And why did they interfere?—the devil have them all in his keeping! Because all the world agrees to believe that such springalds as the Duca di Lodi can't take care of themselves. Because it is considered that the titles and acres of such, if not their persons, should be protected against—against the impulses of their warm hearts, shall we say? Now, do you think that the world would consider any such protection necessary in the case of the Marchese Lamberto? Would any governors, or fathers, or uncles, or aunts, or commissaries, interfere to prevent him from doing as he pleased in such a matter?"

"No, I suppose not!" replied Bianca, thoughtfully; "but if no father or uncle did, a nephew might. It is always the way; people get out of the leading-strings put on them by their elders, only to be entangled in others wound round them by their sons and daughters and nephews and nieces! The poor old man is beguiled. We must prevent him from making such a fool of himself! And the interference is all the worse, and the more fatal, because the poor old man would not only make a fool of himself, but beggars of his protectors."

"Ha, ha, ha!" laughed old Quinto Lalli with a quiet, almost noiseless laugh; "it is very well and shrewdly said, bambina mia. But between the two times of interference, my Bianca, there is a happy medium; an intervening space, a high table-land, we may say, after the dominion of fathers and uncles has been escaped from, and before that of sons and nephews begins—a short time, during which a man may and can please himself. Now, it seems to me, that your Marchese—pardon me for the anticipation, it is a mere figure of speech, your Marchese di Castelmare, I say, seems to me to be just in that happy position!"

"I don't know that, I have not seen enough to be sure about that yet. That young fellow, the Marchese Ludovico, does not look to me a likely sort of man to stand by quietly and see himself cut out of houses and lands! And besides, it strikes me—"

"Speak out your thought, bambina mia; I am sure it is one worth hearing. And between us, you know—"

"Well, between ourselves then," continued Bianca; while a smile, half of mockery and half of pleasure, writhed her lips into changing outlines, each more bewitchingly pretty than the other, and her eyes were turned away from Quinto to a contemplation of the slender dainty foot peeping out from beneath her dress, as she lay on the sofa; "between ourselves, papa mio, from one or two small observations, which I chanced to make to-day, it strikes me that the Marchese Ludovico might possibly feel other additional objections to the establishment of any such relations, as you are contemplating between me and his uncle, besides the likelihood that they might be the means of cutting him out of his heirship."

"Ha, I see, I see; nothing more likely! Per Dio, bambina mia, you lose no time! Brava la Bianca! And perhaps I may conclude, from one or two small observations that I have been able to make myself, you would prefer to win on the nephew! Eh, cara mia" said the old man, looking at her with a sly smile.

"Pshaw!" cried Bianca, with a toss of her auburn ringlets, and a shrug of her beautiful shoulders; "I must do my duty in that state of life to which it has pleased God to call me, as the nuns at St. Agata taught me. But between uncles and nephews, I suppose any girl would say, nephews for choice!"

"But you see, my child, the devil of it is that it would be the Milan story over again. You would have all the family to fight against. A Cardinal Legate can be quite as despotic, and disagreeable, and tyrannical as an Austrian governor. You may be very sure that these people have some marriage in view for this young Marchese, the hope of the family! We know that the Marchese Lamberto is hand and glove with the Cardinal. And there would be an exit from Ravenna after the same fashion as our last!"

"I know for certain already, that there is a marriage arranged between the young Marchese and no less a personage than the niece of the Cardinal Legate himself," said Bianca.

"Well then; that is not very promising ground to build on, is it, bambina mia!" replied Quinto.

"It may be, that as far as the man himself is concerned, the match that has been made for him would be rather the reverse of a difficulty in the way," rejoined Bianca.

"But the difficulty will not come from the man himself, cara mia! It would be doing you wrong to suppose that to be at all likely. I don't suppose it; but—do you imagine that the Cardinal Legate will permit you to snatch his niece's proposed husband from out of her mouth! It would be a worse job than the other," said Quinto, shaking his head emphatically.

"So that you are all for the uncle, papa mio?" rejoined Bianca; yawning, as if she were tired of discussing the subject.

"Well, I confess it seems to my poor judgment the better scheme, and indeed a very promising scheme. Depend upon it, my child, an old man, who is his own master, is the better and safer game," replied Quinto.

"Very well! Have at the old man then, as you call him; though, as I have told you, Quinto, he is not an old man—not over forty-five I should say; at all events the right side of fifty, I'd wager anything! But I tell you fairly, that a less promising subject I never saw. A man, who has lived till that age a bachelor, though the head of his family, and a bachelor of the out-and-out moral and respectable sort, mind you, the great friend of the Cardinal; trustee to nunneries, and all that sort of thing!—a man who looks at you and speaks to you as if he was a master of ceremonies presenting a Duchess to a Queen, a man, I should say, who had never cared for a woman in his life, and was very unlikely to begin to do so now," said Bianca, yawning again as she finished speaking.

"Bambina mia," replied Quinto, "you are a very clever child, and you know a great many things. But you have not yet sufficiently studied the elderly gentleman department of human nature. If the Marchese Lamberto is as you describe him, it may be, it is true, that he is one of those men for whom female beauty has no charm, and on whom any kind of attack would be thrown away and mere lost labour. But it is far more likely that the exact reverse may be found to be the case! A thousand circumstances of his social position, or even of his temper and turn of mind, may have kept him a bachelor, may have kept him out of the way of women altogether. He may be found cautious, haughty, backward to woo, requiring to be wooed, in love with the respectabilities of his social standing; but depend upon it, bambina mia, if you can once awaken the dormant passion of such a man, you may produce effects wholly irresistible, you may do anything with him! His love would be like a frozen torrent when the thaw comes! It would dash aside every opposition that could be offered it. The calculated and calculating tentatives, and coquettings and nibblings of your practised lovers, who have been in love a dozen times, would be as a trickling rill to an ocean wave, compared to what might be expected from the passion of a heart first strongly moved at the time of life the Marchese has reached. Fascinate such a man as that, and in such a position, bambina mia, and all the governors, and all the Cardinals that ever mumbled a mass, won't avail to prevent him from being your own!"

"Well, I suppose you are right, Quinto. And I suppose that that is what it must be!—But—well! it is time to be going to bed, I suppose; I am tired and sleepy!" said Bianca, rousing herself after a pause from a reverie into which she seemed to have fallen, and yawning as she got up from the sofa.

CHAPTER III

"Armed at All Points"

The quartiere which La Lalli found prepared at Ravenna for her and her travelling companion was a very eligible one. It consisted of a very nicely-furnished sitting-room, with a bed-room opening off on one side for herself, and another similarly situated on the other side for her father. There was also, behind, one little closet for a servant to sleep in, and another, still smaller, intended to serve as a kitchen.

On the morning following the conversation related in the last chapter Bianca, hearing Quinto coming out of his bed-room into the sitting-room about nine o'clock, called out to him from her bed:

"Oh, papa! I forgot to tell you last night that the Marchese and Signor Stadione are to be here at one o'clock to-day to hear me, and settle about the night of the 6th, you know."

"All right, bambina mia! I will be back in time. I'm going to the cafe to get some breakfast," called out Quinto through the door.

"Yes. But, papa, be here at one o'clock, and do not come back before that. E inteso? And send me a cup of chocolate from the cafe."

"Inteso! I'll be here at one, and not before," said the old man through the door, with special emphasis on the last words.

Then Bianca called her maid, told her to bring the chocolate to her as soon as it came from the cafe, and then to come and dress her at ten. Whether the intervening time was spent in sleep or meditation may be doubted; but, at all events, when the hour for action came Bianca was ready for it.

By means of the skilled and practised assistance of Gigia Daddi, the maid who had been with her ever since the first beginning of her stage career, the Diva had completed her toilette by half-past eleven. But she had had, to a certain degree, a double toilette to perform. All the component parts of a rich and very becoming morning-costume had been selected and assorted with due care, and minute attention to the effect each portion of it was calculated to produce in combination with the rest; and then they had been not put on, but laid out in order on the bed. The more immediate purpose of the Diva was to array herself differently—differently, but by no means with a less careful and well-considered attention to the result which was intended to be produced.

The magnificent hair was brushed till it gleamed like burnished gold as the sun-rays played upon it. But when ready to be coiled in the artistic masses, which Gigia knew well how to arrange, variously, according to the style and nature of the effect designed to be produced, it was left uncoiled, streaming in great ripples over back and shoulders in its profuse abundance. An exquisite little pair of boots, of black satin, clasping ankle and instep like a glove, were chosen to match the black satin dress laid out on the bed: but, like the dress, were not put on. The place of the black satin dress was supplied by a wrapper of very fine white muslin, edged with delicate lace, so shaped with consummate skill that, though the snowy folds seemed to lie loosely within the girdle that confined them at the waist, no part of the effect of the round elastic slimness of the waist was lost; open at the neck, from a point about a span beneath the collar-bone, it allowed the whole of the noble white column of the grandly-formed throat to be visible from its base above the bosom to the opening out of the exquisite lines about the nape of the neck into the tapering swelling of the classically-shaped head. The exact arrangement of the shape of this opening of the dress, from the throat down to about a hand's-breadth above the girdle, was very carefully attended to; the lace-edged folds of the muslin being three or four times drawn a little more forward so as to conceal, or a little back so as to show, a more liberal glimpse of the swelling bosom on either side, by the doubting Diva, as she stood before the glass.

"E troppo, cosi." she said to her attendant at last. "Is that too much so?"

Gigia looked critically before she answered, "To receive, yes, a little, perhaps. But to be caught unawares, no; and then with a handkerchief, you know—"

"Oh, yes! One knows the exercise," said Bianca, with a laugh; "blush and call attention to it by covering it with one's handkerchief, which falls down as often as one chooses to repeat the manoeuvre. A chi lo dite?"

"Style?" said Gigia.

"Sentimental, eyes soft and dreamy; therefore the very faintest blush of rouge. Yes; not a shade more."

"You won't put your bottines on?"

"No; there'll be time afterwards. Give me a pair of bronze kid slippers. After all, there is nothing that shows a foot so well: and look here, Gigia, draw this stocking a little better; I'd almost as soon have a wrinkle in my face as in the silk on my instep. That's better! The narrow black velvet with the jet cross for my neck, nothing else. Now, you understand? Anybody who comes after one o'clock may be admitted; before that you will let in no soul save the Marchese Lamberto, in case he should come. I don't at all know that he will. And, Gigia," continued her mistress, as she passed into the sitting-room, "draw this sofa over to the other side of the fireplace, so as to face the window; ten years hence, when you have to place a sofa for me, you may put it just contrariwise—so, with the head at the side of the fireplace, and push the table a little further back so as to leave room for the easy-chair there to stand near the foot of the sofa facing the fire. That will do. Now, be sure of your man before you let him in. The Marchese Lamberto, mind, an elderly gentleman—not the Marchese Ludovico, who is a young man. If he or anybody else should come before one o'clock tell them that I can see nobody till that time. Now, don't bring me the wrong man; and, Gigia, if he comes, don't announce him, you know. Just open the door quietly, and let him walk into the room without disturbing me—you understand?"

"A chi lo dite, Signora mia! Lasciate fare a me! Is it the first time?" said Gigia.

"If only one could hope that it would be the last," returned her mistress with a half laugh, half sigh.

By the time all these arrangements were made it was nearly twelve o'clock; and Bianca, dismissing her maid, placed herself, not without some care in the arrangement of her delicate draperies, on the sofa.

The judicious Gigia had said that the extent of snowy bosom exposed was not too liberal, due consideration being had to the circumstance that the Diva was to be caught by an unexpected surprise in an undress. So, as Bianca meant to be very much surprised, she carefully, and with dainty fingers, drew back the muslin on either side just a thought, so as to permit to an exploring eye merely such a suggestive peep of the swelling curves on either side as might furnish an estimate of the outline of the veiled heights beyond. She smiled, half with pleased consciousness and half with self-mockery, as she did so: then carefully arranged her drapery so as to allow two slim ankles to be visible just at the point where they crossed each other in a position which exhibited the curved instep of one slender foot in a full front view, and the side of the other negligently thrown across it. The pose was artistically perfect. Lastly, with one or two dexterous touches and shakes, she so arranged her wealth of hair as to combine an appearance of the most perfect negligee with a thoroughly artistic disposition of it, which, while it displayed to the best advantage the tresses themselves, served also to heighten the effect of the contours of neck and bust, which they partly showed and partly concealed.

And then the Diva waited patiently.

She had, as she had said to Gigia, no certain knowledge that he would come, nor even any very clear reason to believe that he would do so—that he would come, that is to say, earlier than one o'clock, at which hour it had been arranged that he should meet Stadione there. Nevertheless, Bianca had a strong persuasion that he would come earlier. Despite what she had said to Quinto Lalli of the circumstances and signs which seemed to indicate that the Marchese was not a man likely to be exposed to danger from such attacks as the Diva meditated making on him, despite the fact that she had said to herself also all that she had said to her old friend, there had been something about the Marchese's manner—something in that last pressure of palm to palm that had set Bianca speculating as to the meaning of it. It was not a mere manifestation of admiration; the Diva was used enough to that in all its forms, and could read every tone of its language. It was more like wonder and curiosity, at all events, it was not indifference. She had seen with half an eye, and without the slightest appearance of seeing it, that the Marchese could not keep his eyes away from her. During the drive to the city, and afterwards at the Palazzo Castelmare, while she was making the acquaintance of the principal people of the city, it had been the same thing. And nothing could be further than was the Marchese's manner, from the bold, unabashed staring, which such beautiful Divas as Bianca have often to endure. He evidently was devouring her with his eyes on the sly. Evidently he did not wish to be observed looking at her as he did look. Whenever her own eyes caught him in the fact, his were on the instant withdrawn: to return, as Bianca well marked, on the next instant.

Then, after those first words, which he had addressed to her at their meeting in the road, she had noted that he did not speak to her, as she sat by his side in the carriage, with the simple ease and freedom of indifference. There was almost something approaching to a manifestation of emotion in his manner of addressing her. It could not be that this elderly gentleman, this very mature Marchese, had fallen in love with her already. Such an idea would have been too absurd! Yet his whole bearing was odd and ill at ease.

It had seemed to himself as if some subtle material influence affected him, as he sat by her side, as if a magnetic emanation came forth from her that mounted to his brain, and disordered his pulses, and the flow of his blood. He had sat by the side of women as beautiful before now, and never been conscious of being affected in any similar manner. What it was that produced such an effect upon his nervous system, what was the matter with him, he could not for the life of him imagine. It was unpleasant; he did not like it at all. And yet some irresistible stimulus and curiosity drove him to prolong rather than to avoid the sorcery.

Bianca was by no means fully aware of the power and of the strength of the sorcery which she was exercising on the Marchese. But she understood a great deal more about it than he did. And when, in making the appointment for him and the impresario to call on her at one o'clock, he had asked her if that was too early for her habits, and she had replied, that she was always afoot much earlier than that, Bianca had felt persuaded that he would be at the door at an earlier hour.

And her experience, or her instinct, with reference to such matters had not deceived her.

The quarter-past twelve had not struck, when the Diva heard a knock at the door of her apartment.

CHAPTER IV

Throwing the Line

In the next instant Bianca heard the door of the room in which she was sitting opened very gently; it was Gigia who opened it, so gently as to enable her mistress to keep her eyes on a book she held in her hand, apparently unconscious that she was not alone. The Marchese Lamberto advanced two paces within the room, and then stopped gazing at the exquisite picture before his eyes. Bianca knew that all her preparatory cares were doing the work they were intended to do. But no sound had yet been made to compel her to recognize her visitor's presence; and she remained as motionless as a recumbent statue.

"I fear, Signora—," said the Marchese, after a few instants given to profiting by the rare opportunity a singular chance had given him, "I fear, Signora—"

"Santa Maria, who is there!" cried Bianca in a voice of alarm, starting to her feet as she spoke with a bound, that none but so skilled an artist and so perfect a figure could have executed with the faultless elegance with which she accomplished it.

"A thousand pardons, Signora; your servant—"

"The Marchese Lamberto! It is unpardonable in the woman—to have so failed in her duty-towards your Excellency! It is I who have to beg your indulgence, Signor Marchese. Can it be one o'clock already? In truth I had no idea it was so late; and I have still to dress! How can I apologize to your Excellency sufficiently for appearing before you in this dishabille?"

"Nay, Signora, it is in truth I who have to apologize; it is not yet one o'clock, it is not much past twelve! And I feel that I am guilty of an unwarrantable intrusion. But I hoped for the opportunity of having a few words of conversation before the hour named for our little business with our good Signor Ercole. Permit me to assure you, Signora, that if your servant had given me the least hint that you were not yet—ready to see any visitor—"

"If only your Excellency will excuse—the fact is, I have so rarely any visitors that the poor woman does not understand her duty in such matters. Really I am so covered with confusion,"—she continued, putting up her delicate little hand with a feeble sort of little attempt to draw her dress a little more together across her throat. "I cannot forgive her! She has exposed me to seem wanting in respect towards your Excellency; I will dismiss her from my service!"

"Let me intercede for her, poor woman!" said the Marchese, advancing into the room; "indeed it was mainly my fault, I ought to have asked if you were visible."

"One word from la sua Signoria is enough. If you can forgive me, I must forgive her! But you will own, Signor Marchese, that it is—what shall I say—?" She hesitated and cast her eyes down with a bewitching smile and a little movement of her head to one side, "that it really is—embarrassing! Such a thing never happened to me before!"

"But now it has happened, Signora," said the Marchese, emboldened by the smile, and by a shy sidelong glance, which she shot from under her eye-lashes with a laugh in her eyes, as she spoke; "now it has happened that I have been permitted to see you in a toilet all the more exquisitely charming in that it wants the formality of the costume in which the world is wont to see you, may I not say what I came for the purpose of saying?"

"Will you be very discreet, Signor?" she said, putting a slender rosy finger up to her smiling lips; "and never, never let it be known to any human being, that I ever received you save in the fullest of full dress, as would become me in receiving the honour of a visit from your Excellency!"

"Not a syllable, not a whisper!" replied the Marchese, taking her tone, and putting his own finger on his lips. "And then, I may say, Signora, that in Ravenna a visit at any hour from old Lamberto di Castelmare would do your fair name no harm!" he added, taking the arm-chair by the side of the sofa to which she pointed, as she resumed her former place and attitude on the couch.

"I dare say it might not, if I am to judge of his position in the society from your own, Signor Marchese. But I did not know, that there was any old Signor Lamberto di Castelmare. I supposed you were the head of the family, your uncle, perhaps?" said Bianca, very innocently.

"I have no uncle, Signora! I am the oldest Castelmare extant," said the Marchese.

"And you call yourself old Lamberto, Marchese! Why I would wager my pearl necklace, and that is the most valuable possession I have—against a daisy chain, that you are not ten years older than I am. I shall be called old Bianca Lalli next, at that rate!"

"And how many years, since you are ready to wager on it, have gone to the bringing the face and form I see before me to their matchless perfection?" said the Marchese.

"Who was ever before so prettily asked how old she was?" said Bianca, suffering her large blue eyes to rest fully on the Marchese's face for an instant, and then dropping them with an air of conscious embarrassment. "Well, a frank question deserves—or at least shall have—a frank answer! I shall never see my twenty-fourth birthday again?"

"And you judge me then to be thirty-four!" said the Marchese, looking at her laughingly.

"Certainly I don't think any room full of strangers would judge you to be more than that," replied Bianca, looking at him seriously.

"Ta!—ta!—ta! Add fifteen years to that; and you will be nearer the mark. So you see, bella Signora, that you may safely trust yourself to a tete-a-tete with me under any circumstances."

"Ta!—ta!—ta!" said Bianca, repeating his own phrase, with a merry laugh in her eyes, and shaking her rich auburn curls at him. "It seems impossible, utterly incredible! But I am very glad if it is so, very glad. There is nothing so intolerable to me as the young lads who come buzzing about one circumstanced as I am, and whom it is as difficult to drive away as it is to drive away flies in summer. There is no trusting to them; they would compromise a poor girl as soon as look at her, if she was fool enough to let them. And I have had lessons in the necessity of caution, Signor Marchese. I have been cruelly treated, very cruelly calumniated!" And Bianca, knowing, it is to be supposed, that, if it is not always the case that "Beauty's tear is lovelier than her smile," as the poet says, yet that it is a phase of beauty often more potent over a male heart than the sunniest smile, raised a corner of her daintily-embroidered handkerchief to her eyes.

The Marchese was an old man of the world, as the cynical phrase goes, and of what a world?—an old Italian Marchese of the beginning of the nineteenth century, a period when, if crime was less rife than in former and stronger ages, morality was never at a lower ebb. He was a man whose musical tastes had made him conversant with the Divas of the stage, and familiar with the interior aspects of Italian theatrical life;—one, too, whom circumstances had caused to become specially well acquainted with the antecedent history of this particular Diva now stretched on the sofa before him. Yet none the less for all this did "beauty's tear," enhanced by beauty's laced pocket-handkerchief, exercise on him its usual glamour.

Calumniated!—that lovely creature of matchless purity before him, matchless purity! so white was her throat; so round and slender her waist; so daintily snowy her muslin drapery. Calumny! Of course it was calumny. And how he could have poignarded the calumniators, and taken the poor, fluttering, persecuted Diva to his bosom. The desire to execute that latter portion of retributive and poetical justice was making itself felt stronger and stronger within him every minute, as he sat beside the sofa exposed to the full force of the magnetic poison-current which was intoxicating him.

"Signora—" he said, putting his hand out to take hers, which she readily gave him. His own hand shook, and he paused in his speech, overcome for a moment by a sort of dizziness and a sudden rush of the blood to his brow and eyes, a veritable electric shock caused by the contact of her hand with his.

"Signora," he continued, recovering himself, "no such slander—no such insults will follow you here; none such shall follow you here. Lamberto di Castelmare can, at least in Ravenna, promise you that much. Nor if they did follow you, would such stories here be believed."

"Generous! Just!" murmured Bianca behind the laced pocket-handkerchief in a broken voice, just loud enough to reach the neighbouring ear of the Marchese, while she suffered her slender fingers to press the hand which held hers just perceptibly before withdrawing it from him;—"just," she continued in a louder tone, taking her handkerchief from her face, and raising her shoulders a little from the sofa, so as to turn more fully towards him, while her eyes fired point blank into his a broadside of uncontrollable gratitude and admiration;—"just, because generous and noble. Oh, Signor Marchese, those who have never known what it is to suffer from a slanderous tongue can never know the delight—the sweet consolation of meeting with such generous appreciation."

The poor Diva was quite overcome by her own emotion; and, sinking back on the cushions of the sofa, again lifted her handkerchief to her face, while one or two half-stifled sobs showed how deeply she had been moved;—and how perfect was the form and hue of the beautiful half-covered bosom which this emotion caused to heave beneath its gauzy veil.

Just at that minute there came, to the infinite disgust of the Marchese, a discreet tap at the door.

Bianca rapidly passed her fingers over the tresses above her forehead, resettled her pose on the sofa, and gave the Marchese a meaning look of common intelligence and mutual confidence, which set forth, as well as a volume could have done, and established the fact that there existed thenceforward a bond of union and a fellowship between her and him, such as shut them in together, and shut out in the cold all the rest of Ravenna, and then said "Passi," and admitted, as she knew very well, no more startling an interrupter than Gigia.

The well-trained servant said nothing and looked at nothing; but silently handed to her mistress two cards.

"Of course you told these gentlemen that I was not visible, Gigia?"

"Diamine! Signora; of course I should not have let any gentleman pass this morning more than any other morning of the year if you had not specially told me to admit the Marchese Lamberto at any hour he might come," said Gigia with a niaise simplicity, as she left the room.

Bianca covered her face with her pretty hands and shook a gale of perfume from her sunny locks, as she exclaimed, sotto voce, "Oh, the stupidity of these servants! Signor Marchese," she continued, looking up shyly, but with a gay laugh in her eyes, "what must you not imagine?—not, at all events, I hope, that I contemplated the possibility of receiving you in this dishabille? But I will do as other criminals do;—confess when they are found out. I did think," she continued, casting down her eyes, and hesitating with the most charmingly becoming and naive confusion; "I had some little hope—no; I don't mean that;—I did not mean to put that into my confession;—it did occur to me as possible," she went on, hanging her pretty head, and playing nervously with the folds of her dress in a manner which had the accidental effect of causing it to leave uncovered an additional inch of silk stocking—"it did occur to me as possible that the Marchese Lamberto might come to me sooner than the time named for the meeting with the impresario;—for the sake of giving me any hints that his perfect knowledge of the subject might suggest; and I fully intended to be dressed and ready to receive him if he should show me any such condescending kindness—and so told my maid to make an exception in his case to my invariable rule! And then the minutes slipped away; and I fell into a reverie, thinking—thinking—thinking; and then, all of a sudden, before I knew that there was any one in the room—if you think of the devil—and I suppose it is equally true if you think of an angel;—but there, again, that was not intended to be any part of my confession. I think I shall give up confession, at all events to you, Signor Marchese, for the future. But now I have confessed myself this time, and told the whole, whole truth—may I hope for absolution?"

There was an adorable mixture of candour, and gaiety of heart, and child-like simplicity in the beautiful features as she looked up into his face when she finished speaking, together with an expression of appealing confidence and almost tenderness in the eyes that achieved the final and complete subjugation of the Marchese.

Again he took her hand, and again his head swam round with the violence of the emotion caused by the contact of palm with palm, as he said,

"Ah, Signora, if I were equally candid perhaps it would turn out that it was for me to confess, and for you to grant absolution—if you could. Do you think you could?" he said, raising her hand to his lips as he said the words.

"Ha! Signor Marchese, that would quite depend upon the nature of the confession. When I have heard it I will do my best to be an indulgent confessor. But, however curious I may be to hear you in the confessional, it must not be now; or I shall really not be ready to receive Signor Stadione. Heavens! It wants only ten minutes to one now. I must run and dress as quickly as I possibly can. To think that almost an hour should have run away since you came here; and it seems like ten minutes. May I beg your indulgence, Signor Marchese, if I ask you to wait for me while I dress? I will be as quick as I possibly can."

"On no account hurry yourself, Signora. It is my fault for having detained you. And if I had to wait ten hours instead of one, would not the one I have passed be cheaply purchased? Never mind Stadione; I will explain to him that you are dressing—"

"And that you have been made to wait some time already by my abominable unpunctuality," said Bianca, holding up one fore-finger and giving him a look of mutual intelligence.

"Of course—of course. A chi lo dite!" returned the Marchese, giving her once more his hand to help her to rise from the sofa.

As she did so she put into his hand, without any word of comment, but with a slight smile and a little momentary raising of her eyebrows, the two cards that Gigia had, a little while before, handed to her. They bore the names of the Barone Manutoli and the Marchese Ludovico Castelmare; and Bianca handed them to the Marchese with a matter-of-course air that seemed to say that, in the position which the Marchese Lamberto and she had assumed towards each other, it was natural and proper that he should see who had called on her.

He merely nodded as he looked at them; and then, for the second time, kissing the tips of the fingers he still held, as she got up from her couch, he bowed low as she passed him to go towards the bedroom; and she, before quitting the room, made a sweeping curtsey, half playfully, and then kissed the tops of her fingers to him as she vanished into the inner room.

CHAPTER V

After-Thoughts

The Marchese Lamberto and Signor Ercole Stadione quitted the house in which the prima donna had her lodging, together, when the business matters, which they had come thither to arrange, had been settled.

"A wonderful woman, Signor Marchese," said the little impresario, trotting along with short steps by the side of the Marchese, and rising on his toes in a springy manner, that made his walk resemble that of a cock-sparrow. "Truly a wonderful woman. I have seen and known a many in my day, Signor Marchese, as you are well aware, sir; but such a one as that, such an out-and-outer, I never saw before."

"She is evidently a lady, whose education and manners entitle her to be treated with all respect," replied the Marchese, more drily, the little man thought, than his great patron was usually in the habit of addressing him, and somewhat quickening his stride at the same time, as if he wanted to walk away from the impresario.

"Most undoubtedly, Signor Marchese, and every sort of respectful treatment she shall have. There shall be a stove and a new looking-glass put into her dressing-room this very day. If she don't draw, say Ercole Stadione knows nothing about it. A very singular thing it is, Signor Marchese, and you must have observed it, Signor, as well as I, there's some women whose singing, let 'em sing as well as they will, is the smallest part of their value in filling a theatre. There's no saying what it is, but they draw—Lord bless you, as a bit of salt will draw the cattle after it! And this Lalli is one of that sort. I know 'em, when I see 'em. Won't she draw, that's all!" said the little man again, rubbing his hands together, and chuckling with infinite glee.

The Marchese Lamberto would have been at a loss probably if he had been required to state clearly why he felt angry and annoyed with the impresario that morning, and thought him a bore, and wished to be quit of him. But such was the case. And presently, when the well-skilled and business-like little man began to canvass the capabilities of certain parts in his repertorio, for the most advantageous showing off of the personal advantages of the new acquisition, the Marchese could stand it no longer, but replied hastily:

"Well, well. All these matters had better be submitted to the lady herself. I think, Signor Ercole, that I will say good-morning now. You are going to the theatre, and I am waited for at the palazzo."

And the Marchese did return to the palazzo, though nobody was specially waiting for him there. On the contrary, he told the servant in the hall to admit nobody, and when he reached his library, he shut the door and bolted it. And then he threw himself into an easy chair to think.

The first thing that his thinking made clear and certain to him was that something had happened, or was happening to him, which had never happened to him before, something respecting the exact nature of which all his previous experience afforded him no light.

In love! He had never been in love; but he knew, with some tolerable accuracy, what was generally understood by the phrase. He had read the poets, who describe the passion under sufficiently various phases; and he had heard plenty of lovers' talk among a people who are not wont to suffer, or to exult, or to be happy in silence. Was he in love with this woman? Did he, in his heart, love her—in his heart, as he was there in the solitude of his own room, at liberty and at leisure to examine his heart upon the subject. A heavy frown settled on the Marchese Lamberto's brow, and an unpleasant change came over his face, as he proceeded with the task of asking his heart this question. There rose up feelings and promptings within him, which almost drove him to the fierce assertion to himself that he hated this woman, who was thus occupying his thoughts against his will.

What had become of all that warm chivalry of feeling that had urged him, with all perfect earnestness of sincerity, to declare that no breath of calumny or insult should come near her, beneath the aegis that he could and would throw over her? Where was it gone? All clean gone. He knew, with tolerable accuracy, the story of the former life of this woman. They were facts which he knew, certainly knew. But they had all vanished from his mind, had been as though they were not, while he had sat there by her sofa, looking at her and listening to her, had all vanished, even as the ardent chivalry, which had then been caused by some sorcery to spring up in his mind, had vanished now.

It was passing strange.

That he was very sorely tempted—as he had never before in his life been, tempted—to make love to this actress, as it is called, to make love to her after the fashion, not so much of those poetical descriptions which have been referred to, as after the fashion of those prosaic settings-forth of the passion, which were familiar enough to his ears, was clearly recognizable by him. He knew very certainly that he desired that.

And was what he desired so much out of his reach? Surely all that had happened, all that he had seen, all that he had heard at the interview with Bianca that morning, was not calculated to lead him to think so. And why should it be? It would be all very much according to the ordinary current of events in such matters. He was a bachelor. He was wealthy. He was the most prominent noble of the city. He was brought specially into contact with the lady by his theatrical connection and habitudes. His patronage and protection were by far the most valuable that could be offered to her in Ravenna. The Diva herself was—such as Divas of her sort and time were wont to be. It would seem to be all very easy and straight-forward. What was the worst penalty wont to follow from such peccadilloes to persons in his position? The loss of a little money, of a good deal of money perhaps. But he had plenty and to spare.

But none of these considerations availed to smooth the frown from the Marchese's brow, or to make the future at all seem clear before him.

In the first place to make this singer his mistress, simple and little objectionable as such a step might seem to most men of his country, and rank, and period, and freedom from ties, was not an easy matter, or an agreeable prospect to the Marchese, on purely social considerations. He had placed himself on a special pedestal, from which such a liaison would involve a fall. And such a fall, or the danger of such a fall, was very dreadful to the Marchese. There was the Cardinal; there were the good nuns, whose affairs he managed, and who looked on him as a saint on earth. Worst of all there was his nephew. How preach to him (terribly necessary as such preaching might be) under such circumstances?

To be sure, there was no need of doing whatever he might do in such sort that the whole town should be his confidant. He had as good opportunities for secrecy as could be desired. Theatrical business and his recognized connection with it was an abundant and unsuspected excuse for as much conversation with the lady, as many interviews as he might wish. It seemed safe enough upon the whole.

And yet these considerations did not avail to take the frown from the Marchese's brow, or bring his perplexed self-examination to an end. The very evident disposition of the lady to be kind did not avail to please him. Instead of being pleased and triumphant at the probable prospect of so enviable a bonne fortune, he was displeased, unhappy, irritated, angry—angry with himself and with the sorceress who had thrown this spell on him. How was it? By what charm had she bewitched him so? Already he was impatient, longing to be back again in her presence. And yet he was angry with her, doubted whether he did not rather hate her than love her.

At last he started from his chair and swore that he would retain the mastery over his own self; that he would think no more of the abominable woman, see her no more!

Taking his hat he rushed out of the house, with an instinctive desire for bodily movement as a means of stilling the tossing fever that was raging within him; walked through the streets at such an unusual pace, that the people turned round to look after him as he passed; walked by the door of the house in the Via di Santa Eufemia in which Paolina lived, saw Ludovico coming from it, who was surprised indeed at thus seeing his uncle; and more surprised still to find, that the Marchese passed him without seeming to notice him, walked out into the country, and returned only at supper-time, tired and worn out; and then, when the supper was over, and Ludovico had gone out to the Circolo as usual, after pacing his room, and swearing to himself at every turn, that he would see the creature no more, slunk out of his own palazzo, feeling afraid of being seen by his own servants, and wandered to her lodging!

And what were Bianca's meditations, when the business visit of the impresario was over, and he and the Marchese left her room together?

First and foremost, the Marchese Lamberto was in love with her; and that not as dozens of youngsters in many a city had been; but madly, desperately, in love with her. That fact admitted of no doubt whatever! It was strange, curious enough, that she should have succeeded so brilliantly, so entirely, and so immediately in spite of all the signs and tokens which had led her not small experience to expect so entirely different a result. Clearly the still larger experience of old Quinto Lalli had been more far-sighted. His view of the matter had been the true one!

But still, how far was his view of the question a correct one? What was the success, which had been very unmistakably so far achieved, in reality worth? It was very plain that this Marchese Lamberto had been caught, captivated, fascinated! But what then? There was no doubt at all that he would very willingly suffer her to add him to the list of her previous admirers and lovers. It never entered into the Diva's head to conceive, after the very unmistakable testimony she had received of the evident admiration of the Marchese, that very grave difficulties, objections, and hesitations would, on his side, stand in the way of his accepting any such position. She doubted not that this conquest was perfectly within her reach; and that there would be no difficulty at all in drawing large supplies from the Castelmare wealth towards recruiting the needs of the Lalli exchequer.

But this, as has been explained, was not what Bianca wanted. "Major rerum sibi nascitur ordo!" She was intent on playing a higher and greater game. Was it likely she would be able so to fix the harpoon she had successfully thrown in the very vitals of the prey, so to make this man feel that she was absolutely essential to his happiness, as to induce him to marry her? That was the question! And Bianca did not delude herself into imagining that anything that had passed between herself and the Marchese that morning entitled her to consider the battle which should lead to that victory as even begun.

The Diva did not conceal from herself the greatness and arduous nature of the task before her. She knew what a Marchese of mature age, of noble lineage, and of unblemished reputation, was; and she knew what she was. But she did not appreciate those extra difficulties in the case, which arose from the special social position, and still more from the special character and temperament of the man, and these were the greatest difficulties of all!

On the whole, she was sanguine; and what was perhaps more to the purpose, old Quinto, when they talked the matter over together, and the general result of the morning interview had been reported to him, was sanguine too.

"Depend upon it, bambina mia," he said, "it is the best game—the real game. Young fry will rise to the bait more readily; but they also wriggle off the hook much more easily. It is the old fish who, when he has it once fixed in his gills, cannot get rid of it, struggle as he may. You play your game well, neither relaxing, nor yet too much in a hurry, and I prophesy that I shall live to see you Marchesa di Castelmare."

"And many a year afterwards, I hope, papa mio. And you may depend on my teaching my husband to behave like a good son-in-law," said Bianca, with a bright laugh.

"As for the nephew," continued Quinto, "I can understand that it would be more agreeable to make your attack on him—"

"I don't know that at all, papa mio," interrupted Bianca. "You may laugh, if you will, and think that I am making a virtue of necessity—and small blame to me if I were—but the truth is, I do like the Marchese. I like him better, as far as I can yet tell, than any man I ever knew. Yes! you may make grimaces, and look as wicked as you please! But it is true. And, if you ever do see me Marchesa di Castelmare, you will see that I shall make him a very good, ay, and a very fond, wife."

"Who could doubt it, Signora, that has the advantage of knowing you as well as I do?" said the old man, with a mocking bow.

"You may sneer as much as you like, Quinto; but you understand nothing about it. The Marchese is a man any woman might love. You call him an old man? I tell you he is younger for a man than I am for a woman, God help me! It isn't only years that make people old."

"That's true, bambina mia, poveretta. And I am sure I have nothing to say against it if you can fancy this Marchese a gay and handsome young cavalier."

"Handsome he is, as far as that goes. I swear he is the handsomest man I have seen here! His nephew is good-looking enough, but he is not to be compared to his uncle either in face or person."

"Well, whether you have succeeded or not in making the Marchese in love with you, cara mia, I begin to think that you have succeeded already in falling in love with him," said Quinto, looking at her with raised eyebrows.

Bianca remained silent awhile, nodding her head up and down in a sort of reverie, and then said, rousing herself with a shake of her flowing curls as she looked up, "No; not quite that. But I won't say that it is impossible that if I am to make him love me, I may come to love him in the doing of it. You see, amico mio, it is something new. It is not the old weary mill-round. He did not come to me with the set purpose of making love to me, as all those young fellows have done, and do, just because they have nothing else to amuse them; because it's the fashion; because it's a feather in their caps; because it's the thing to have a prima donna for their mistress! If the Marchese has fallen, or falls, in love with me, he does so because he cannot help himself, he does it in despite of himself; and that flatters a woman, Quinto. Well, we shall see," she added, after another pause: "one thing, at all events. I swear that there shall be nothing between me and the Marchese—of—the old sort."

"It is wisely said, bambina mia. That is the road which must lead, if any can, to the winning of your game."

CHAPTER VI

At the Circolo

There was, at all events, one man at Ravenna who was entirely pleased and satisfied with the famous prima donna in all respects: and this was Signor Ercole Stadione.

The Carnival campaign of La Lalli had been thus far brilliantly successful, and the Carnival was now about half over. She "drew," as the little impresario had prophesied she would, to his heart's content. It was many a year since there had been so successful a season at the theatre. Each part she sang in was a more brilliant success than the last; and the public enthusiasm was such as enthusiasm on such subjects never is save in Italy.

In every respect, too, her ways and behaviour had been unexceptional. Her attention was never distracted from her business by the visits of young men behind the scenes—a torment which, during the reigns of other Divas, had often driven the poor little impresario, who dared not get rid of such intruders as he would have liked to do, almost wild. Bianca would permit no visits of the kind. She had never behaved herself to any of the young men in such sort as to cause any of those rivalries and jealousies which are sometimes apt to manifest themselves in hostile partisanship, when the Diva is on the boards—another fruitful source of trouble to much-tried impresarios.

She had walked circumspectly and prudently in all respects—a most moral and highly satisfactory Diva.

She was understood to receive no visitors at home—at least, none of a compromising kind. The Marchese Lamberto was often with her: of course, naturally! He was well known to be always a sort of second amateur manager: neither the theatre nor little Ercole Stadione could go on without him.

And then the Marchese Lamberto was—the Marchese Lamberto! If he had chosen to sit by the bedside of any prima donna in Italy night after night, it would only have been supposed that he was giving her possets for the improvement of her voice.

Occasionally, also, she would receive the visits of the Marchese Ludovico; evidently by reason of the unavoidable intimacy of his uncle in the house. And Ludovico reported to them all at the Circolo that she was a most charming woman indeed—full of talent, merry as a young girl, companionable, and fond of society, but wholly devoted to her art, and quite inaccessible in the way of love-making. He assured the jeunesse doree of Ravenna that they lost nothing in any such point of view by their exclusion from her intimacy, for that all their enterprises in that line would be quite thrown away.

The Conte Leandro Lombardoni, indeed, always carried about with him in his breast-pocket, a carefully preserved little letter on pink notepaper, which he gave the world to understand was part of a correspondence carried on between him (reconciled as he was to the bel sesso) and the Diva; and had more than once contrived to be seen hanging about the door of her house at hours when honest Divas, as well as mortals, ought to be in bed and asleep. But nobody believed him, or imagined that anything save a bad cold was at all likely to result from his vigils beneath the cold stars. He showed, indeed, with many mysterious precautions against the remainder of the letter being seen, that the little pink sheet of notepaper did indeed bear the signature of "Bianca Lalli." But when one of the ingenuous youth picked his pocket of it, it was found to be a very coldly courteous acknowledgment of a copy of verses, which the Diva promised to read as soon as her avocations would permit her to do so!

"Any way," said the discomfited poet, "that is more than any of you others have got. And it's not so small a matter, when you come to think of it!"

"Per Bacco, no! Leandro is in the right of it!" said the young Conte Beppo Farini; "a small matter to find somebody who promises even to read his verses! I should think not, indeed! Where will you find another to do as much?"

"Riconciliato col bel sesso! I should think you were, indeed!" cried another; "she absolutely thanks you for sending her your rhymes! Nobody ever did as much as that before, Leandro mio! No wonder you haunt the street before her door!"

"I don't haunt the street before her door. Envy, Jealousy, ye green-eyed and loathsome monsters, how miserably small and mean can ye make the hearts of men!" said Leandro, lifting up hands and eyes.

"Bravo, Leandro, bravo! get upon the table, man!" cried Farini.

"Get home to bed, rather. It is too bad, because no human being will read his poetry, he takes to spouting it!" said the other.

"Let us look what she says," cried Ludovico di Castelmare; putting out his hand to take the little note. "Upon my word she writes a pretty hand. It is a very neatly expressed note."

"Oh, you can see that much, can you?" returned Leandro. "I should think it was too! Is there any one of you here can show such a note from any woman, let her be who she may? She says she will read the poem I have been good enough to send her—good enough to send her, mark that!—as soon as she can find time to do so! What could she say more, I should like to know? Of course she is occupied. It stands to reason. But she will read my poem; and then you will see!"

"Ay, then we shall see our little Leandro duly appreciated at last!" said the Barone Manutoli. "As soon as the Diva has found time to read the poem there will come another little pink note, adorably perfumed: he will be summoned to her august presence, and installed as her poet in ordinary, and who knows what else besides, her Magnus Apollo? It is a pity there are not eight other prime donne to make up the sacred number. Then we should see our Leandro in his true position and vocation. Give me a sheet of paper, and I will show you a new presentation of Apollo and the Muses. They are all presenting him with pasticcerie and bonbons. He has one hand on the lyre, and the other on his stomach, for the homage of the goddesses has made him somewhat sick; his eyes, you observe, are cast heavenwards, partly by reason of poetic inspiration, and partly by reason of nausea!"

"Bravo! bravo, Manutoli!" cried a chorus of voices.

"Envy and jealousy, envy and jealousy, all envy and jealousy. It is pitiable to see what they can reduce men to," cried the poet, foaming at the mouth.

"Never mind them, Leandro mio—never mind them. It is the universal penalty of true merit, you know; the same thing all the world over," said Ludovico.

"But, I say, Ludovico," rejoined Manutoli, "in the meantime, till our Leandro's poem shall have been read and duly appreciated, you are the only one who has been admitted to the privacy of La Lalli. What is your report to us Gentiles of the outer court? Is she really so unapproachable? And is she as adorable behind the scenes as before them?"

"Well, you ought to be able to answer that question yourself, Manutoli," replied Ludovico; "you were with lo zio and me that day when we went out to meet her; I am sure you had a fair look at her then."

"A look? Yes; and I looked all I could look. I saw a charming face, younger and fresher looking than might have been expected from the length of time she has been on the boards, a very pretty figure, as far as her travelling-dress would show it one; and the loveliest foot and ankle I ever saw in my life. I could swear to that again at any time. Don't you remember how she stood with her foot down on the step, when she was getting out of the carriage. I thought at the time that she knew what she was about very well."

"Of course she did. Do you think they don't always know very well, every one of them, off the stage or on the stage?" said Farini.

"But I want to know what sort of body, she is?" returned Manutoli; "I don't need to be told that she is a very lovely woman; but of what sort is she? Why does she keep us all at a distance? What is her game?"

"Upon my life I don't know," answered Ludovico, "unless it's a devouring passion for Leandro. I protest I have no reason to think she cares a button for anything but her own art. I never tried; but it's my impression that if I had ever whispered a word in her ear I should have got a flea in my own for my pains."

"You don't want to make us believe that you have been seeing her frequently all this time, passing hours with her a quattro occhi, and have never made love to her, Ludovico?" said Farini.

"No; I don't want to make you believe don't care a straw whether you have it or not; but it is the the fact, for all that," returned Ludovico.

"Ludovico has enough on his hands in quarter. What would they say about it in the Via Santa Eufemia if he were to bow down to new and strange goddesses?" said Manutoli.

"That, if you please, Manutoli, we will not discuss either now or at any other time," said Ludovico, with a look that showed he was in earnest. "But, as for La Diva Bianca, I have no objection to tell all I know to anybody. My belief is that she is as correct and proper, and all that sort of thing, as a Vestal."

"Che!"

"Che!"

"Che!"

A chorus of protestations of incredulity in every tone of the gamut met the monstrous assertion.

"What, after all we heard of her doings at Milan—after all the histories of her goddess-ship in every city of Italy?" said Manutoli.

"Well, what did we hear of her doings at Milan? The fact is, we know nothing about the matter; and as to her previous history—of course I don't suppose that she is, and always has been, a Diana; but it may be that she has come to the time when she has thought it well to turn over a new leaf. Such times do come to such women; but all I know is, that I firmly believe that since she has been here she has lived the life of a nun," said Ludovico, in the simple tone of a man who is stating a truth which he has no interest in causing his hearers to credit or discredit.

"Per Bacco, it's queer!" said Farini, slapping his hand against his thigh. "I have heard," he continued in the tone of one speaking of some strange and almost incredible monstrosity, "I have heard of such women taking a turn to devozione. It's not that with La Lalli, is it?"

"Che! Nothing of the sort; she is as full of frolic as a kitten—up to any fun. And she is a very clever woman, too, let me tell you—a good deal of education. If you will put making love to her out of your head, I never knew a woman who was pleasanter company," said Ludovico.

"And you really mean that you have never tried to make love to her in any way?" reiterated Manutoli.

"I do mean it, upon my soul; but I don't care a rap whether you believe it or not," rejoined Ludovico.

"And you are with her very frequently?" persisted Manutoli.

"Yes, I have seen a good deal of her altogether. I like her; and I fancy she likes me to go there; she seems to wish me to come. Perhaps it is a novelty to her to have a man about her who doesn't try to make love to her."

"The Marchese Lamberto sees her a good deal?"

"Yes; naturally. If it had not been for that I should probably never have made acquaintance with her at all. Lo zio is continually there. He ought to have been an impresario. In fact, he is the real impresario. Little Ercole only does what my uncle tells him. I don't believe she ever sings a note on the stage that he has not heard and approved beforehand."

"Suppose he is the dark horse; suppose she is his mistress all this time; and he takes care to keep her all to himself," said Manutoli.

"What, lo zio. Bah! I should have thought that you knew him better than that, Manutoli. To him a woman is a voice, and nothing else. If the same sounds could be got out of a flute or a fiddle he would like it much better, and think it far more convenient. I don't think my uncle Lamberto ever knew whether a woman was pretty or plain. I wish to heaven he would get caught for once in his life; it would suit my book very well. He would have less leisure to think of other things."

The fact was that the Marchese had, in truth, had less leisure to think of those other things from which Ludovico desired that his attention should be drawn away. His visits to the Via Santa Eufemia had been more frequent than ever; his visits to the Marchesa Anna Lanfredi and her niece rarer than ever. And he had received neither lectures nor remonstrances for a long time past. In truth, the Marchese had his mind too full of other matters to think much of his nephew's affairs or doings. And, besides that, there was a quite new and hitherto unknown feeling in the heart of the Marchese Lamberto which made him shrink from any such encounter with his nephew, as remonstrances respecting his conduct with regard to Paolina would have occasioned;—a feeling which made it seem to him that he was the watched instead of the watcher; that suggested to him the fear that the first word he might utter upon the subject would be met by references to doings of his own.

An utterly unfounded fear. But so it is that conscience doth make cowards of us all.

CHAPTER VII

Extremes Meet

The Marchese was uneasy in the presence of his nephew. But the fact was that he was uneasy and unhappy altogether, and at all times. From being one of the most placidly cheerful and contented of men, he was becoming nervous, anxious, and restless. People began to remark that the Marchese was beginning to look older. They had said for years past that he had not grown a day older in the last ten years. But this winter there was a change in him!

It did not occur to anybody to connect any change that was observable either in the Marchese's manner or in his appearance, with the frequency of his visits to the quartiere inhabited by the prima donna and Signor Quinto Lalli, in the Strada di Porta Sisi. The ordinary habits of the Marchese, and his functions as a patron of the theatre and amateur impresario were so well known and understood, that it seemed perfectly natural to all Ravenna that he should be very frequently with the prima donna. And on the other hand, the almost monastic regularity of his life, and his character of long standing in such respects, would have made the notion that he had any idea of flirting with the singer appear utterly absurd and inadmissible to every man, woman, or child in the city, if it had ever come into anybody's head.

The fact was, however, that the Marchese was much oftener in the Strada di Porta Sisi than anybody guessed. Besides the morning visits, which were patent to all the world, who chose to take heed of them, the Marchese very frequently spent those evenings there, when the "Diva" did not sing; slinking out of the Palazzo Castelmare, and taking all sorts of precautions to prevent any human being—nephew, servants, friends, or strangers—from guessing the secret of these nocturnal walks.

Such precautions were very needless; if anybody had noticed the Marchese Lamberto passing under the shadow of the eaves in any part of the city after nightfall, it would only have been supposed that he was bound on some mission of beneficence, or good work of some sort! And if even it had become known to a few persons given to prying into what did not concern them, that the Marchese Lamberto di Castelmare was not more immaculate in his conduct than his neighbours, the only result would have been a few jests which he would have never heard, and a few sly smiles which he would have never seen.

But the Marchese could not look at the matter in this light. He felt as if his fall from the social eminence on which he stood would have been as a moral earthquake in Ravenna. The idea that such jests and such smiles could exist, however unseen and unheard, would have been intolerable to him. And the Marchese was, accordingly, a miserable man.

A miserable man, and he could not help himself! Each time that he quitted the siren, the chain that bound him was drawn more tightly around him. At each visit he drank deep draughts of the philtre, that was poisoning the fountains of his life. Again and again he had made a violent struggle to throw off the enchantment and be free. And again and again the effort had been too great for his strength, and he had returned like the scorched moth, which comes back again and again to the fatal brightness, till it perishes in it.

In his hours of solitary self-examination he loathed and mocked himself to scorn! He, Lamberto di Castelmare, to risk and to feel humiliation, and to suffer for the love of a woman, whose light affections had been given to so many! He, who had been smiled on by many a high-born beauty in vain! Love! did he love her? Again and again he told himself that what he felt for her was far more akin to hate. He marvelled; he could not comprehend himself! He was often inclined to believe that the old tales of philtres and of witchery were not all false, and that he was in truth bewitched; and he struggled angrily against the spell, and at such times hated the beauty that had tangled him in it!

And in all this time Bianca had not yet ventured to show clearly her real game. Nor had it yet occurred to the Marchese that such a preposterous thought as that he could marry her could have entered into her mind. Yet it was clear to him that he made no progress towards making her his own upon any other terms. The alternations between beckoning him on and warding him off had been managed with such skill, that they appeared to be the result of the Diva's internal struggle with her own inclinations. What was he to understand by it? If she had been, had always been—of unblemished character! But it was not so; he knew better!

That her conduct at Ravenna had been correct was undeniable. Still, even with regard to that, the Marchese was not spared the pangs of jealousy, in addition to all the rest. Ludovico continued to frequent the house in the Strada di Porta Sisi. It seemed, as he had said at the Circolo, as if Bianca wished him to come there. In fact, he had spoken to the young men at the Circolo with perfect truth in all respects as to his relations with the Diva. There had never been any word of love-making or even flirting between them. Yet, in a sort of way, she seemed to wish to be agreeable to him and to attract him. But she never made any secret of his visits from the Marchese, although it was unmistakable enough that it was disagreeable to him to hear of them.

Had he been free from the spell himself he would have rather rejoiced that his nephew had met with an attraction, which would be likely to have the effect of making him faithless to Paolina. As it was, it was an additional source of irritation to the Marchese, another drop of gall in his cup, to hear it constantly mentioned by Bianca in the most innocent way in the world, that Ludovico had been here with her, or there with her, or passing the morning with her!

It was drawing towards the end of the Carnival, which the late fall of Easter had made rather a long one that year, when, on one Saturday night, Bianca sat by her own fireside, expecting a visit from the Marchese. She doubted not that he would come, though no special appointment on the subject had been made between them. There were few "off evenings" now, that he did not spend with her. Saturday in most of the cities of Italy is, or was, an off night at the theatre, being the vigil of the Sunday feast-day. The ecclesiastical proprieties are less attended to now in matters theatrical, as in other matters in Italy. But Saturday used, in ante-revolutionary times, to be an evening on which actors and actresses and their friends could always reckon for a holiday.

Bianca was sitting, exquisitely dressed, it need hardly be said, in a style which combined with inimitable skill all the requirements of the most strict propriety with perfect adaptation to the objects of showing off every beauty of face, hair, hand, figure, foot to the utmost, and attracting her expected visitor as irresistibly as possible.

Quinto Lalli had been sent to enjoy himself at the Cafe, with stringent directions not to return before he should have ascertained that the Marchese had left the house, let the hour be as late as it might.

Bianca meditated deeply, while she waited her lover's coming.

Her lover! yes, there was no doubt about that. Bianca had felt perfectly assured that she was justified in considering the Marchese as such on that first morning, when he had come to her an hour in advance of the time appointed for his visit in company with the impresario. But it was high time that some better understanding of the footing on which they stood as regarded each other should be arrived at.

Hitherto no direct proposals of any kind had been made to her by the Marchese. He was not good at any such work. Any one of those distinguished sons of paternal governments, who had constituted the material of Bianca's experiences of that division of mankind, would have long since said what he wanted, and have very clearly indicated the terms on which he was willing to become the fortunate possessor of the coveted article. And Bianca would have perfectly well known how, under the present circumstances, to answer any such proposals, as she had known under the other circumstances of past days. But the Marchese made no proposals. What he wished, indeed, was abundantly clear to her. But his mode of making it clear rendered the task of dealing with him a somewhat difficult one.

Partially, Bianca understood the nature of the case. She was partly aware why the Marchese was slow to say that which so many, whom she had known, had made so little difficulty of saying. She understood that, whatever his years might be, he was a novice at that business. She comprehended that he was, in many respects, a younger man than many a coulisse-frequenting youth whom she had known. But she was far from conceiving any true notion of the Marchese's state of mind on the subject. She was very far from imagining that he looked with disgust and with terror at the position which she conceived him to be but too ready to accept to-morrow, if only he knew how to ask for it, or if it could be offered to him without his asking. She little guessed that his feeling towards her oscillated between the maddest desire and the fiercest hatred; that reveries, filled with pictured imaginings and fevered recollections of her beauty, alternated with the most violent efforts to cleanse his mind and imagination of the thought of her.

She understood nothing of all this, and it was impossible that she should understand it. In truth, she was innocent of any conduct which could have justified such sentiments. Why should he hate her? It was true that she sought to attract him, true that she was scheming to lead him to a point at which he might find it so impossible to give her up, that, being well convinced that he could have her on no other terms, he might offer her marriage. But was there anything worse in that than men had been treated "since summer first was leafy?" How many men had married women in her position—women less capable of doing credit to the position to which they were raised than she was? How many men had been treated in such matters very much worse than she had any thought of treating him? She fully proposed to make him a good and true wife, and fully thought that she should do so. She was not deceiving him in any way. She made the best of her past life—naturally; but was it to be for a moment supposed that such a man as the Marchese could, or did, imagine that she, Bianca Lalli, whose career, for the last eight years, was known to all Italy, was in the position of a young contessa just taken from her convent?

It is abundantly clear that there were difficulties in the way of the desirable understanding being arrived at, greater than either the lady was aware of, or than might usually be expected to attend similar negotiations.

Bianca waited without impatience the coming of the Marchese. She was a study for an artist as she lay perfectly still on her sofa, turning the minutes of expectation to profit by arranging in her mind her plan of attack in the coming battle; for she was thoroughly determined that that evening should not pass without some progress towards the understanding having been accomplished.

One lamp on the table alone lighted the small but comfortable-looking room; but the flame was leaping cheerfully among the logs on the hearth, and the sofa was so placed that the fitful light from the fire glanced in a thousand capricious reflections on the Diva's auburn hair and rich satin dress. It was black of the most lustrous quality, and fitted her person with a perfection that showed the shape of the bust, and the lithe suppleness of the slender waist to the utmost advantage. The dress was made low on the superb shoulders—the dazzling whiteness of which, as seen contrasted with the black satin, was now covered with a slight silk scarlet shawl, a most artistic completion of the harmonious colouring of the picture, which yet was not so fixed in its position as to be prevented from falling from the snowy slopes, it veiled at the smallest movement of them.

Presently the now well-known step and well-known tap at the door were heard, and the Diva, without stirring a hair's-breadth from her charmingly-chosen attitude, spoke, in a silver voice, the "Passi" which admitted her visitor.

CHAPTER VIII

The Diva Shows Her Cards

"Ah, Signor Marchese," she said, with a sweet, but somewhat sad, smile, extending to him a long, white, slender, nervous-looking, ungloved hand, but not otherwise moving from her position. "Ah, Signor Marchese, then I am not to be disappointed this evening? I was beginning almost to fear that the fates were against me."

He advanced to the head of the sofa and took her hand, and held it awhile, while he continued to stand there looking down from behind her shoulder on the beautiful form as it lay there beneath his gaze—on the parting of the rich golden hair; on the snowy forehead; on the still whiter neck; on the gentle heaving of the bosom beneath its light veil of scarlet silk; on the tapering waist; on the exquisitely-formed feet peeping in their black satin bottines from beneath the extremity of her dress! It was all perfect: and the Marchese held the soft warm hand that served as a conductor to the stream of magnetic poison that seemed to flood his whole being as he gazed.

For an instant all the room seemed to swim round with him. The blood rushed to his brow. He shut his eyes, and a nervous crispation caused the fingers of his hands to close themselves with such force, that the grasp of that which held her little palm hurt her.

"Ah, my hand! you hurt my hand!" she said. "You don't know how you squeezed it, you are so strong. You don't know the quantity of force you put out!"

"Pardon—a thousand pardons, Signora! I am such a clumsy clown! Have I really hurt you, Bianca?"

"Not to the death, Signor," she said, with a charming smile, and holding up to him the injured member, shaking it as she let it dangle from the slender wrist. "But see! it is really all blushing red from the ardour of your hand's embrace!"

"Poor little hand!—indeed, it is!" said the Marchese, taking it gently and tenderly between both of his; then, suddenly throwing himself on his knees by the side of the sofa, while he still held it, he said, "And how can the great cruel hand that did the harm make fit amends?"

"Ah, Signor Marchese, it might find the way to do that, if it were so disposed. It would not be so far to seek. But you are seeking in the wrong direction," she continued, drawing herself back from him on the sofa, as he, leaning forward against it, had brought himself so near to her, that the back of the hand in which he held hers touched her waist. "You are seeking amiss. It is not so that any remedy can be found; and—pray rise, Signor, and take your usual chair. This must not be, I am sure you would not willingly give me pain, Marchese, and you are paining me. Pray leave the sofa."

She had drawn herself back away from him as far as the breadth of the sofa would allow, yet without withdrawing her hand from him; and she looked at him certainly more in sorrow than in anger, looked into his face earnestly with grave, sad eyes, and heaved a long sigh as he, after pressing the hurt hand to his lips, rose from his knees and took the chair she had pointed to.

"Pain you, Bianca?" he said, as he sat down; "why should I pain you? You do me no more than justice when you say that I would not do so willingly; but have you thought how much pain you inflict on me by thus keeping me at a distance from you? I think you must know that. Is there aught to offend you in anything that I have done, or said, or hoped, or wished?"

"I think, Signor Marchese," she said, dropping her large eyes beneath their long fringes, and looking adorably lovely as she did so, "I am afraid that what you have wished is—what some might deem offensive to a lady."

And as she spoke she looked out furtively from behind her eyelashes.

"Bianca, is that reasonable?" he said, in a tone of remonstrance. "Diamine, let us talk common sense; we are not children. Have you always found such wishes as mine offensive in others?"

"Yes, always—always offensive, always cruel," she said, with extreme energy; "but—can you not understand, Signor Marchese, can you not conceive that what from one man passes and makes no mark, and leaves no sting, may from another—What cared I what all the empty-headed young fops who came in my way could say or do; they were nothing to me. But—I did not expect pain from the Marchese Lamberto di Castelmare. I—I thought—I hoped—I—I flattered myself—fool, idiot fool that I have been!" she exclaimed, bursting into violent sobs, and hiding her face with her hands.

The Marchese was startled and utterly taken aback for a minute or two. He was genuinely at a loss to interpret the cause or the meaning of the lady's emotion. His puzzled embarrassment did not, however, prevent him from seeing that she looked, if possible, more fascinatingly beautiful in her grief and her tears than he had ever before seen her. And, again, despite what she had said, he knelt down by the side of the sofa, and gently removing her hands from before her face, murmured in her ear, "Bianca, what is it—what is moving you so? Don't you know that you are dear to me;—that I would—Don't you know that I would do anything to be agreeable to you rather than give you any sorrow or pain? What is there within my power that I would not do? Bianca, let me tell you—let me speak the truth—I cannot keep it in my own heart any longer—I love you! You have come to be all that I care for in the world. Bianca, do you hear me? For your love I would sacrifice all, everything in the world; I die without it; I must have it—I must! You have been loved before; but never as I love you—never, never! And, Bianca, I—I—Bianca, you are my first love—my only love. Never, till I saw you, did I care to look on a woman for a second time; I never felt love. But, when I saw you—the first time—the first hour—Bianca, I must have your love or die; I thirst—I hunger for it. Since I have known you all my nature is changed; all my old life is flat and unmeaning, and without interest to me. I care for none of the things I used to care for; all—all has melted and slipped away from me, and nothing remains but one great devouring rage and passion—my love for you!"

He had spoken like a torrent, which, for a long time dammed up, at last becomes too powerful for restraint, and bursts forth, overthrowing all obstacles with its headlong flood.

Bianca turned her face away from him towards the back of the sofa; but she slowly, and with an uncertain intermittent movement, drew his hand over to her lips, and pressed it against them.

A light came into the Marchese Lamberto's eyes;—a gleam almost, one would have said, rather fierce than fond, as he felt the pressure of her lips; and a shock as from an electric spark ran through all his body, making him quiver from head to heel.

"Bianca, Bianca! You are mine—you are mine!" he cried, pantingly, with his mouth close to her ear, and encircling her waist, as he spoke, with the hand which she had relinquished after she had kissed it in the manner that had been described.

But she sprang away from him, pushing him from her, by putting her flat hand against his forehead, with her face still turned towards the back of the sofa, away from him.

"No, no, no!" she cried, violently; "it cannot be, not so—not so! I cannot—I cannot!"

"Bianca," he cried, starting to his feet as if he had been stung; "what does this mean? What am I to understand? What is it you wish? You know my position. I tell you that there is no sacrifice that I am not willing to make. I am rich; name what you would wish."

"Spare me—spare me, I deserve all; but spare me! I deserve to suffer, but not at your band," she cried, in words interrupted by her sobs.

"Spare you what, Bianca? In truth, I do not understand you," said the Marchese, genuinely mystified.

"Do you not understand?" she said, turning round on the sofa, so as to face him, and looking into his face with those great appealing eyes suffused with tears; "do you not understand? Can you not comprehend? A woman would understand, I think; but I suppose men feel these things differently."

"Upon my honour, Bianca, I do not know what you mean. Every word I have spoken to you has been spoken from the very depth of my heart. I am ready to—"

"Hush, hush, Marchese! No more of that; I could not bear it," she said, with a great sigh that seemed as if it would burst her bosom; "it is very—very painful to me; but I must endeavour to bring your heart to understand me, it must be your heart, Lamber—your heart, Signor Marchese; for one does not arrive at the understanding of such things with the head. See, now, I will put myself in the place I deserve to occupy—in the dust at your feet! You may trample on me, if you will. I say I have deserved the shame and the misery I am now suffering. I deserve them because I have no right to resent the—the—the proposals which you—wish to make to me. I have suffered much from calumny and evil tongues—much from unhappy circumstances and evil surroundings. Yet it may be that I-have—more right to—resent—what—I have heard from you than you imagine. But let that pass. You know—or think you know—that I have accepted from others that which I have said I cannot accept from you; and you cannot imagine why this should be so. Oh, Marchese, does your heart lend you no aid to the understanding of it? What were those men, those empty creatures whose gold could not repay the disgust occasioned by their presence, what were they to me? Did they love—pretend even to love—me? Did I love them? Love! Alas, alas, alas! Ah, Marchese, a poor girl exposed to the world, as I have been from my cradle upwards, has to suffer much that might well move the pity of a generous heart; but it is nothing—nothing—nothing to the tragedy of the misery, the shame, the remorse that comes upon her when at last the day shall come that her heart speaks and shows to her the awful chasm—the immeasurable gulf that separates such—I cannot, Lamber—pardon, I don't know what I am saying; I cannot go on—I cannot put it into words! Do not you—cannot you understand the difference?"

"I do understand, Bianca mia; povera anima sofferente—I do understand. Do you imagine that I would judge you harshly—severely? I know too well all that you would say; I know the difficulties, the impossibilities of your position. Do you think that I cannot make allowances for all the fatalities attending on such a combination of circumstances? And, trust me, the difference between what has been, and what I so earnestly hope may be now, is greater, I feel it to be greater, not less than you can feel it to be. Truly there is nothing in common between the all-devouring passion which consumes me, and—such love-vows as you have spoken of. Do I not understand the difference. And remember, Bianca, dearest, that the protection I offer you would be the means of placing you out of the reach, far out of the reach of any such disgusts, such suffering for the future."

Bianca let her head fall on her bosom, and covered her face with her hands, and remained silent for some moments. Then, lifting her face slowly, and shaking her head, she sighed deeply as she looked with a wistful earnest glance into his eyes; she said, "You are good, you are, very good and kind to me; perhaps it might have been better for my happiness if you had been less so. But bear with me yet a little, Signor Marchese. Sit down there, there where I can see your face,"—pointing, as she spoke, to a spot exactly in face of the sofa, "and let me see if I can explain myself to you. It is difficult; it is very difficult. A woman, as I said, would understand it at once; but men—are so different. You have told me, Signor Marchese, that you love me; that you never loved before; that I am the first woman who has ever moved your heart. Eh, bene, Signor Marchese! If I, having heard those protestations, were to confess that—that it was with me even as with you,"—she dropped her eyes and sighed as she made the confession;—"that I, too—that you have taught me now for the first time what it is to love, though I might speak it less eloquently than you have done, the words would be equally true, equally true, Signor," she repeated, slowly nodding her head. "And when I have confessed that it is so," she continued, speaking more rapidly, "can you wonder—can you not understand that it is impossible to me—that it would be a horror unspeakable to—to renew with the object of a true love—the first—the first, as God sees my heart—the degradation that has left nothing but bitterness and humiliation behind it? Shall the name of Lamberto di Castelmare be written in my memory in the hateful list of those who have been to me the occasion of remorse, of self-condemnation, of bitterness immeasurable? Never, never, never! Come what may there shall be one pure place in my heart; one unsoiled spot in my life; one ever-dear remembrance unlinked with sorrow and with shame; one memory which, however sad, shall not be humiliating."

She put her handkerchief to her eyes as she ceased speaking, and appeared to be entirely overcome by her emotion.

The Marchese rose from his chair in a state of hardly less agitation. He walked across the room;—returned to the sofa, and seemed for a moment as if he were going to take her hand; then turned away, and stood on the hearth-rug with his back to the fire. He was much moved, puzzled, pained, disappointed, goaded and lashed more violently than ever by the furies of passion; more than ever wishing that he had never seen the beautiful creature lying there before him, and more than ever writhing in mind under the consciousness that to give her up was beyond his power.

At length he again stepped up to the side of the sofa and took her hand.

She started; and plucked it from him.

"Go, Signor Marchese—go, and leave me. It would perhaps be better so for both of us. I am not used to show to anybody the very inmost secrets of my heart, as I have been doing to you, I know not why. Forget what I have said. Go, and forget me;—forget the poor comedian to whom your goodness, your nobleness, and—your love—seemed for a passing minute to open a blessed glimpse of a heaven upon earth; but never—never again propose to me to associate the name of Lamberto di Castelmare with names that I would—oh, so fain—forget!"

Still the Marchese had not realized the nature of the position or seen the only outlet from the cul-de-sac into which he had been driven. It involved too monstrous an impossibility to seem to him to be an outlet at all. What was the real meaning of all this? Then suddenly an in-rushing suspicion flashed across his mind like a blasting lightning brand, bringing with it a sharp pang, as of a dagger stab in the heart. What was the meaning of all these protestations of admiration and affection, coupled with a denial of all that his passion drove him there in search of? Did it perchance mean that this woman, so terrible in the power of her beauty, so dangerously irresistible, would fain have the protection which his position could give her, the supplies which might be drawn from his purse, while her love—such love as he wanted from her—would be given to a younger rival?

Suddenly he asked her, "When was the Marchese Ludovico here last?"

"The Marchese Ludovico?" said Bianca, carelessly; "oh, he is often here. When last? Let me see: he was here this morning. As good and noble a gentleman as any in Italy he is, too. He is worthy to bear your name, Marchese, though it is only a poor girl like me that says it."

"He seems to have won your good will, anyhow," said the Marchese, frowning heavily. "What answer, I wonder, would he get if he were to speak to you as I spoke just now?"

"He would never speak so, Signor Marchese; he would know that, whatever might have been the case in past years, alas! it would be useless or worse to speak so now. I do not say, indeed, that—I have a sincere regard for the Marchese Ludovico. This much you may be very sure of, Marchese, that the feelings which you have surprised me into confessing would make it quite impossible for me to listen to any such words from the Marchese Ludovico. But, if ever the Marchese Ludovico were to say any word in my ear, it would not be," continued Bianca, dropping her voice and speaking as if more to herself than to him—"it would not be to offer me what his uncle was offering me just now."

And now it flashed upon the Marchese for the first time what the real drift of Bianca's words and conduct had been. She wanted to be Marchesa di Castelmare. And the meaning of her last words, with their reticences and their half-uttered expressions spoken out at length might, he thought, be read thus: If you, Marchese Lamberto, do not make me Marchesa di Castelmare, your nephew will be ready enough to do so. The scandal, the wrong done to the family name, the chatter of all the tongues in Ravenna will be none the less. The matter would be, indeed, worse instead of better. For it would involve the grave injury that would be done to the Lady Violante, and the destruction of all the hopes built upon that alliance. All this seemed to be revealed to him as by a lightning flash. But the pang of jealousy, which had stung his heart, still remained the foremost and most prominent occupation of his mind.

"If you imagine, Bianca," he said after a while, "that my nephew would, or could, however much he might wish to do so, make any other kind of proposal to you, you are labouring under a delusion. I speak in all sincerity of heart."

"And I have spoken to you, God knows, with all sincerity, Signor Marchese. I have spoken as I have never before spoken to any human being. I have opened my heart to you to the very bottom of it. But the effort of doing so has been a painful one. It has terribly overset me; I feel like a wrung-out rag; and would fain rest. You will not be offended if I ask you to leave me now. It is getting late, too; and I expect my father home every instant. Good-night, Signor Marchese. Forgive me if I have said aught that I should not have said; if I have in any way offended you. I think you know how far the wish to do so is from my heart. Good-night."

"Good-night, Bianca," said the Marchese, taking the hand she held out to him, and retaining it in his own for some instants, despite his intention of specially abstaining from any demonstration of the kind—"Good-night, Bianca. We shall meet to-morrow morning."

"Yes, on business," said Bianca, looking up into his face with a sad smile. "Signor Ercole said he should be here at midday."

And then the Marchese left her, and, carefully shunning the more frequented parts of the city, returned to his own home.

CHAPTER IX

One Struggle more

The Marchese reached the Palazzo Castelmare unobserved by any one, save old Quinto Lalli, who had been for some time past watching the door of his adopted daughter from a neighbouring corner, in order to ascertain when he might go home to his bed without infringing the order that had been given him.

"And what do you think of it now, papa mio?" said the Diva, when she had very faithfully, though summarily, recounted the scene which had just passed, to her old friend and counsellor.

"Well, I see no reason to despair of the result," said Quinto. "You did not expect him to jump at the idea of making you Marchesa di Castelmare, I suppose? Of course he was a little staggered; and, probably, his own notion at this moment is, that he would rather never see your face again, than dream of such a thing. Ma, ci vuol pazienza! My notion is, that you will have him nibbling at the hook again before long. That little hint about the nephew was masterly. Depend upon it that will do its work."

"But, Quinto, I did not say a word to him that was not true—hardly a word. I do like him better, by a hundred times, than any other man I ever knew; and if I succeed, you see if I do not make him a good wife; I swear I will! As for Signor Ludovico, that is all trash and nonsense. He belongs to his Venetian, body and soul: and he has enough to think of, poor boy, in scheming to get out of the marriage they have planned for him."

"What! he wants to marry the Venetian, does he?" asked Quinto.

"Yes; they have engaged themselves to each other; she would not hear of anything else."

"Lord bless me! how moral and respectable the world is growing. I suppose Cupid himself will be attended by a gentleman in cassock and bands before long, and Mars will make Venus an honest woman, as the phrase goes. Well, I am not sorry I had my day in the old time. It would be rare fun, though, if these grand Signori, the uncle and the nephew, were both to be hooked in the same fashion at the same time."

"There is nothing against the character of the Venetian of any sort," said Bianca, with a sigh.

"Ta, ta, ta! I'd back your chance of the uncle against her chance of the nephew, any day of the week."

"Ludovico is solemnly engaged to her."

"I'd hold to my bet, all the same for that; and now let's get to bed, you have to sing to-morrow night."

"Yes, and I'm regularly tired out; good-night."

The Marchese Lamberto was probably hardly less in need of rest, when he reached the Palazzo Castelmare. But he did not equally feel that it was within his reach. He shut himself into his room; and throwing himself into an easy chair, with one hand pressed to his fevered brow, strove to think; set himself to think out the possibilities of the present, and the prospects of the future, as far as the blinding volcano bursts of passion, which ever and anon threatened to sweep all power of thought away, would permit him to do so.

So this was the meaning of all the difficulties, which Bianca had made. She had absolutely conceived the idea of his marrying her. Heavens and earth! Was she mad? But, at all events, if this notion had been the cause of all her fighting off of his advances for the last month past, it was not necessary to attribute her conduct to any preference for some more favoured lover; she had assured him that she loved him—loved him as she had never loved another. And, gracious heaven, how lovely she looked as she said it!

He pressed his hands before his eyes, and saw again in fancy the beautiful vision; gloated on the eloquent movement of her person in the earnestness of her confession; looked again into those large appealing honest eyes, which seemed to be so incapable of lending their voucher to a lie. Surely it could not be that all those protestations and assurances were false, mere comedy got up for the purpose of deluding him. That she was worldlily anxious to secure so great a prize as that which she was trying for was natural enough—was matter of course. But surely, surely there was genuine affection in that glance. Was it not likely to be genuine, that feeling that she could not be to him what she had been to others? It must have been abundantly clear to her that had she chosen to accept from him what he had offered her, she might have amply satisfied any mercenary views, the most exorbitant. Therefore her views and her feelings were of a different order.

And then the thought of being so loved by such a creature—of being really loved for himself—loved as she had never loved before, made for the moment all other thought impossible to him: he started from his chair, and paced the room with rapid disordered strides. What was all the world to the ecstasy of such a love? All—all that he had hitherto lived for, was it not flat, stale, poor, puerile, in comparison to it? Why not leave all, and seize a happiness so infinitely greater than any he had ever known or imagined? Why not marry her, and be hers for ever, as she was anxious to be his? Nobles of higher rank than his had done as much before. Why not?

What would they all say and think? All his world, that he had lived among, and lived for, from his cradle upwards: the Cardinal, his sister, his nephew, Violante? The whole society which had looked up to him as some one altogether above the sphere of human frailties and follies: how could he face them? What say to them? Why face them at all? Why not leave all, and make a new world for himself and the one dear companion of it? Marry her, and take her safe away from all her past, and from all his. Why not?

But would she consent to that? Would that be her idea of a marriage with the Marchese di Castelmare? Was it not likely that she would prefer to be Marchesa di Castelmare in the Palazzo Castelmare, in Ravenna, where—ha!—where Ludovico was, for whom she had so much regard? who was so frequently with her. That poor Violante! Of course he knew that there could be no love between her and his nephew. Ludovico had promised that that marriage should be made. Ay, marry the uncle, to be the nephew's mistress with all convenience! Such things had often been; there was nothing new in the arrangement—nothing original in the idea—why, the very stage was full of such examples: he to be the old duped husband of the farce; he saw it all.

And as these thoughts also suggested themselves to his mind, his heart seemed as though it were clutched by a hand of ice, while his brow throbbed and his head burned with the pulsing blood.

He threw himself on to his chair again, and tore his hair with rage and anguish; and all those vivid and palpitating love-representations which passion had but now painted on the retina of his eye, were reproduced by jealousy with the difference that Ludovico instead of himself was the actor in them.

It was maddening; his brain seemed to reel; a cold sweat broke out all over him. The fear dashed across his mind that he should really lose his reason.

Was there, he thought to himself, as the terror of this made him shudder—was there that night in all Ravenna so miserable a being as himself? And that miserable man, cowering there in the restlessness of his agony, was the Marchese Lamberto di Castelmare; he whose whole life had been one placid scene of happiness, prosperity, and content. Never had he known a passion strong enough and forbidden enough to cause him a pang or a sleepless hour till now. Had not his life been happy? What did he want with more? Ah, if he could but blot out for ever all that the last month had brought with it. If he could but be again as he had been before this woman had cast her sorcery on him. Ah, would to God that his eyes had never seen her!

Was it yet too late? Could he not even now tear her from his mind, shut his eyes to the recollection of her, so command his imagination that it should never again present the image of her to his fancy?

And thereupon forthwith uncommanded fancy was busy with every detail of the beauties that had so made him their slave. The line of the neck and shoulder which he had looked down on as he stood at the sofa head; all the white ivory from the fresh innocent rosy little ear to the swell of the curves about the bosom; the intoxicating perfume from the heavy tresses of the hair; the lithe slender waist, round and yielding; the slight nervous hands, the touch of whose fingers fired the blood, as a match fires gunpowder; the exquisite feet; and, oh God! that face, whose every feature, as he last looked on it, was harmonized in an expression of love.

Quite still he sate for some minutes, conscious of nothing save the pictures which memory was passing before his eye. Then suddenly, with a bound, he sprang from his chair, and away from it, and beat his head against the opposite wall of the large room.

"Fool, fool; enslaved, besotted idiot! I am lost, spelled; the victim of sorcery I cannot fight against. What am I to do, what am I to do? Surely I can keep my steps from going near her. If I were to swear now that I will never set eyes on her more?"

And then he recollected that it was impossible for him even to seek that means of safety without giving rise to all kinds of observations, and wonder, and speculation in the city. He was to see the prima donna on the following day. His habits in such matters, well known to all the town, brought him into frequent contact with Bianca, as with other ladies who had been similarly engaged in Ravenna. What would be thought, or guessed, or said, if he were suddenly to refuse to hold any further communication with her?

And would he not thus be simply leaving the coast all free to his nephew? To be sure. There, there, he could see it all. And that was the worst hell of all. Anything, anything was preferable to that. Come what would that should never, never, never be. Rather—rather anything. He gnashed his teeth, and clenched his hand; and a sudden agony of hatred for both Bianca and his nephew seemed to steal like a snake into his heart, and maddened him.

And thus the miserable man passed the greater part of the night in useless strugglings with the bonds that bound him.

It was near morning before he crept, still sleepless, but utterly worn out, to his bed.

He did sleep, exhausted as he was, after awhile; but it was only to see again in dreams all that he had so bitterly wished that he had never seen at all. Sometimes he was himself by Bianca's side, licensed to revel to the full in her every charm. And then the dream would change. It was Ludovico he saw in her white arms; and he started from his fevered sleep bathed in perspiration and quivering in every limb.

The next morning he was, in truth, quite ill enough to have furnished a very sufficient and unsuspected excuse for not going to meet the impresario at Bianca's house according to appointment. He thought at first that he would do so. But as the time drew near, he dragged himself from his bed, haggard, fevered, and looking very ill, and crawled to the appointed meeting.

BOOK IV

The Last Days of the Carnival

CHAPTER I

In the Cardinal's Chapel

Paolina was industriously pursuing her task in the chapel of the Cardinal's palace. Ludovico was not so frequently with her there as he had been while she was at work in San Vitale. But there were evident reasons why this was necessarily the case. The chapel in question is a private one, and is accessible only by passing through a portion of the Cardinal's residence. At San Vitale Ludovico needed to take nobody into his confidence, when he climbed to Paolina's scaffolding to be by her side while she worked, save the old sacristan. But to have joined her at her work in the Cardinal's palace, he must have knocked at the door of the residence, and told the servants what he wanted.

And that would have been obviously inconvenient, even without mentioning the fact that the Lady Violante, to whom the gentleman ought to have been addressing himself, passed much of her time at the palace, and might very possibly have been met by him there.

It was true that, ever since the ball at the Castelmare palazzo, on the second day of the year, Ludovico had felt pretty nearly sure that Violante was as desirous of escaping from the marriage which had been arranged as he was himself. But it did not at all follow that it would be an easy matter to break it off. Of course it was not to be expected that Violante herself could take any active step towards refusing to fulfil the promise that her family had made for her. That would be for him to do. And except as regarded his intercourse with the lady, and her personal feelings, the task of doing so was hardly rendered any the easier by the knowledge that he would be consulting her wishes as well as his own.

It would hardly, therefore, have done in any way for him to have been visiting the young artist in the Cardinal Legate's chapel.

The intercourse, however, between Ludovico and Paolina was much pleasanter and more unrestrained than it had been before that explanation, which had ensued between them. He was a frequent visitor at the house in the Via di Sta. Eufemia in the evening; and the happy hours were passed by them on the perfectly understood footing of mutual betrothal.

And Ludovico was perfectly honest and sincere in all that he said to Paolina. He said nothing to her that he did not equally say to himself. And if his conduct under the circumstances was not exactly what a father or brother of Paolina might have desired it to be, the fault arose from the indecision of character, which belonged to a weak man accustomed to self-indulgence. There was difficulty and annoyance before him; and instead of meeting it, as a strong man would have done, he turned from it, and was content to put off the evil day, contenting himself with the enjoyment of that which was passing. He marvelled somewhat at the ease, with which he was permitted to pass evening after evening with his mistress, at the absence of surveillance, of which he was conscious, and at the silence of his uncle as to both his visits to Via di Sta. Eufemia, and his no visits to the Lady Violante.

But he troubled himself little to account for this, or to question the reason of the goods the gods provided him. It was not in his character to do so. Paolina, on her side, was, upon the whole, trustful and contented. Yet there had been moments at which she had suffered a passing pang from little gossipings which had been, perhaps injudiciously, repeated to her by Orsola Steno. Of course the great prima donna, the celebrated Lalli, who was blessing Ravenna by her presence, was often talked of in the Via di Sta. Eufemia, as she was in every other house in the city. That was quite a matter of course. And then Orsola would speak of the strict conduct of the lady; of the fact that no one of the young nobles of the place was permitted to visit her—except, indeed, the young Marchese Ludovico; and how people did say that half-a-dozen would be safer company than one; and that the young Marchese was finishing the sowing of his wild oats before becoming a married man by a flirtation with one of the most celebrated beauties of Italy.

There was very little cause for this gossip beyond what the reader is aware of. Still, upon the whole, it might have been better if Ludovico had seen less of the fascinating singer. He had given cause enough for spiteful tongues to make mischief if they could do so; and it may probably be supposed that he was not insensible to the fascinations of Bianca—perhaps not to the glory of the fact that he was the only young man admitted to her society, and that he had occasionally done that which, being repeated, might not unnaturally give umbrage to Paolina.

It was now within ten days or so of the end of Carnival; and, while almost everybody else was amusing themselves in some way or other, Paolina stuck close to her work in the chapel, intent on her silent and solitary task, while, from time to time, the voices of revellers in the streets would reach her in her seclusion.

But all her hours of work there had not passed in utter solitude.

The Contessa Violante was in the habit of spending much of her time in the palace of her great-uncle the Cardinal Legate. It presented, among other advantages, that of being pretty well the only place in which she could escape for awhile from the companionship of the Signora Assunta Fagiani, her duenna. Certainly, it would not have been consistent with that lady's conception of her duty to allow her charge to visit any other house whatever in the city, without the protection of her companionship, but the palace of a Cardinal Legate—and that Legate her great-uncle. Besides that, her great-aunt, the Cardinal's sister, was also often at her brother's residence; and, having this facility close at hand, Violante was wont very frequently to avail herself of the privacy, comfort, and warmth of her uncle's chapel for the morning's devotions, which she never missed.

One morning she found a small portable scaffold or estrade of deals standing in one corner of the chapel; and, on inquiring for what purpose it had been placed there, she was told that it was to enable an artist to make a copy of some of the mosaics on the vault of the little apartment. She learned further that the artist in question was a young Venetian lady: that she was a protegee of the Marchese Lamberto; and that the permission to execute the copies in question, and to have that scaffolding placed there, had been obtained by him.

Then Violante knew right well who the Venetian artist was. The worthy Assunta Fagiani had taken care that all the gossip of Ravenna which connected this girl's name with that of Ludovico di Castelmare should reach her ears. And she was glad of the easy opportunity which thus offered itself to her of gratifying her natural curiosity respecting the stranger—the girl who could win that love which had been promised to her; but which she had been unable to inspire.

This Paolina Foscarelli—she well knew her name—was, in some sense, her rival. Ludovico di Castelmare was bidden to love her, the Contessa Violante, and instead of doing so, had given his love, as she had been assured, to this Venetian. She knew, indeed, quite well that had the stranger never come near Ravenna, Ludovico would not have loved her the more. She did not love Ludovico. She was anxious to be quit of the engagement it had been proposed to make between them; and it might be very likely that this girl might be serviceable to her, rather than otherwise, in helping to bring about such a consummation.

Nevertheless, there was a certain amount of bitterness—such bitterness, more akin to self-depreciation, as could find place in the gentle heart of Violante—in the thought of what might have been; in the thought that she was irrevocably excluded from that which it had been so easy for this poor stranger artist to attain; and, above all, there was a strong curiosity to see the beauty which had accomplished this; to hear the voice which had been able to charm; and, further, in her own interest, to ascertain, if that should be possible, whether the tie which she had been told existed between this girl and the man who had been assigned to her for a husband, was, or was not, of a nature likely to lead to a marriage between them.

At first sight this would have seemed impossible to the aristocratic notions of the Cardinal Legate's niece. But Assunta Fagiani, whose object had been simply to convince Violante that no union between herself and Ludovico would ever take place, despite all appearances to the contrary, had given her to understand that it was whispered as a thing not impossible—such was Ludovico's infatuation—that he might even go the length of making such an alliance.

One morning, soon after the commencement of her work in the chapel, whither she had been escorted on her first going thither by the Marchese Lamberto himself in person, in accordance with his promise, Violante, on entering the chapel, saw that the little scaffold had been pulled out from its corner and placed immediately under one of the medallion portraits of the Apostles, on the vault of the building. She looked up, and perceiving the artist above her at her work, paused, hesitating before kneeling at the footstool in front of the altar.

In an instant a light step tripped down the steps of the wooden erection, and a little figure, clad in a brown holland frock, which wrapped it from head to foot, stood by her side.

Paolina knew very well who the lady that had entered the chapel was: and, as may be easily imagined, she too was not without her share of curiosity.

"Do I disturb you, Signorina?" said Paolina, in a sweet, gentle voice. "If you would prefer it, I will wait till you have finished your prayer. I can kneel here too the while."

Violante looked at the girlish face, bright not only with the elements of material beauty, but with the animation of intelligence and the informing expression of talent. One would have said that nothing could well be less becoming than such a long shapeless wrapper as that which the artist wore. There was the band at the waist, which showed that the figure was slight and slender; but, for the rest, a less ornamental costume could not well be imagined. Nevertheless, Violante perfectly well perceived and understood at a glance that this girl had what she had not—a something by virtue of which it was possible for her to win a man's love, while for herself it was, or seemed to her appreciation of herself, impossible.

"Oh, no, Signorina," answered Violante, gently, "the knowledge that you were painting up there would not suffice to distract my thoughts. But will you not let me look at your work? It must be very difficult to copy these strange old wall-paintings. May I climb up? I know your friend the Marchese Lamberto well. Do you know who I am?"

"Pray, come up, Signorina, if you have any curiosity. Oh, yes, I know your ladyship. I saw you once in the Cardinal's carriage. You are his niece, the Contessa Violante," replied Paolina, blushing a little at the name of the Marchese Lamberto, only because, though assuredly not the rose, he lived close to it.

So the two girls climbed the steps of the estrade together.

"How came you to know the Marchese Lamberto?" asked Violante, after they had matured their acquaintanceship by a little talk about the subject of Paolina's work.

"Only because the Englishman, who employed me to copy these mosaics, gave me a letter to him. He seems to be very highly esteemed."

"More so than any other man in all Ravenna, except my uncle the Cardinal, I suppose I ought to say; he is a most excellent man in all ways. But you know his nephew also, the Marchese Ludovico? non e vero?" said Violante, looking down on the ground, while a pale blush came over her white cheeks.

"Yes," replied Paolina, flushing crimson, and similarly looking down, but stealing a side-glance under her eyelashes at her companion, "yes; I became acquainted with him also in the same manner—at least, on the same occasion; and, in truth, I have seen more of him than of his uncle, for the Marchese Lamberto is always so busy, and he commissioned his nephew to do all that he could to assist us, when we were first settling ourselves here."

"And you found him kind, too; as kind as his uncle?" said Violante, stealing a sidelong glance at Paolina.

"Yes, indeed, Signorina," said she, feeling not a little embarrassment.

"Paolina—you see I know your name, and I think it such a pretty one—Paolina," said the Contessa Violante, yielding to a sudden impulse, and taking the hand of the blushing girl, who kept her eyes fixed on the ground, "shall we be friends, and speak openly to each other? I should like to."

"Oh, Signorina! so should I, so much. There is nothing I should like so much—almost nothing," replied Paolina, looking up into her face, with her own still crimson.

"Tell me, then, if you ever heard my name mentioned in connection with that of the Marchese Ludovico?" said Violante, looking with a rather sad and subdued, but yet arch, smile into Paolina's eyes.

"Yes, Signorina, I have so heard," said Paolina, raising her head with a proud movement, and looking, with well-opened eyes and clear brow, into Violante's face as she spoke. "I have heard that it was intended by both your families that you and the Marchese Ludovico should be married."

"Yes; everybody in Ravenna, I believe, expects to see such a marriage before long; do you? We are to be friends, you know, and speak frankly to each other; do you expect it, Paolina?" asked Violante, still holding her hand, and looking with a smile, half shrewd, half sad, into her face.

Paolina remained silent a minute or two, again dropping her clear honest eyes to the ground. Then raising them again, she said in an almost whispered voice, but looking straight at her companion,

"No, Signorina, I do not expect that; for he has promised to marry me."

"Ah—h! it is a relief to hear you say so. My dear Paolina, I am so glad," said the elder girl, putting a hand on each of Paolina's shoulders, and kissing her on the forehead—"I am so glad; much for your own sake, somewhat, too, for his, and much for my own sake. For, Paolina, I could not marry Ludovico. If he asked me to do so, it would be only done in obedience to the will of his uncle. He does not—no, 'tis no fault of yours, my child—never has loved me."

"Signora, when first I—allowed him to teach me to love him, I knew nothing of any duty that he owed elsewhere. And when I did know it I determined, even if it should break my heart, to refuse any such love as should have been stolen from a wife," said Paolina.

"That was the part of a good and honest girl. And for me, I have to thank you for it. Paolina, I hope you may be happy. We shall often meet here, shall we not?"

"Not often here, Signora. My task here is not a long one; and I hope by the end of Carnival to have finished it, so that I may go to St. Apollinare, outside the town, where I have to make several copies. It is very desirable not to go there later; because when the warm weather comes it becomes so unhealthy there."

"Yes; but we have some days yet before the end of the Carnival; and till then you will be at work every day here?"

"Si, Signora; I hope so."

"Then I hope we shall have several more opportunities of seeing each other. And now I must not keep you from your work any longer. Shall we be friends?"

"Oh, Signorina; it is too good of you to ask me, a poor artist. And when—it would be my greatest pride to have such a friend."

And then the girls kissed and parted: Violante to kneel for her daily devotions, at the footstool before the altar; and Paolina to continue her copying. And after that they had frequent meetings in the little chapel, and learned to become fast friends.

The Carnival was now drawing near its end; and the city had been promised that before the time of cakes and ale should be over, and that of sackcloth and ashes should begin, the divine prima donna should appear in one more new part. And, after much deliberation and debate, it had been decided that this should be Bellini's masterpiece, La Sonnambula. She was to sing it on one night only—the last Sunday of the Carnival; and the attraction on that night was proportionably great. The Sonnambula, then in the first blush of its immense popularity, had never yet been heard in Ravenna. It was one of the favourite parts of the Diva; and all the city was on the tiptoe of expectation.

It was a matter of course that all the "society" would be there. The entire first row of the boxes, the "piano nobile," as it is called in Italian theatres, was the private property of the various noble families of the city, which each had its box, with its coat of arms duly emblazoned on the door thereof, in that tier. Nobody who did not belong to "the society" of the town could in any way show his intruding face in the "piano nobile." But above this sacred hemicycle there was another range of boxes; equally private boxes; as all the boxes of an Italian theatre are;—and the key of one of these upper "loggie" had been secured by Ludovico, and presented to Signora Orsola and Paolina for the great evening.

Of course he himself would be obliged to be in his proper place in the Castelmare box, which was the stage box on the left hand of the stage.

"Whether I may be able to run up and pay you a little visit in the course of the evening, I don't know. You may be very sure I shall if I can; but there will be all the world there, of course, and lo zio in the box—unless, indeed, he should choose to go behind the scenes. Talking of that," he added, as he was on the point of leaving the room, "I don't know what to make of lo zio of late."

"Has he said anything?"

"Not a word; but I don't like the look of him. He never was more amiable as far as I am concerned; but he is not well; I never saw him as he is now. He is haggard, feverish, restless; an older man in appearance by a dozen years than he was at the beginning of Carnival."

"I suppose he has been raking too much, and wants a little rest. Lent will be good for him."

"What, he! The Marchese Lamberto raking! You don't know him. But he seems quite broken down; I should say, that he had got something on his mind, if it was not impossible. He never had any trouble in his life; and never did anything he ought not to do, I believe. But I confess he puzzles me now. Good-night. God bless you, Paolina mia!"

That was on the Friday; and the Diva's last appearance was to take place on the following Sunday.

CHAPTER II

The Corso

The institution of Carnival and Lent in Italy seems very much as if it arose from a practical conviction in the minds of the Italians that they cannot serve two masters, at least at the same time, Mammon in all his forms is to be the acknowledged and exclusive lord of the hour during the first period, on condition that higher and holier claims to service shall be as unreservedly recognized when the second shall have set in.

"Let us have wine and women, mirth and laughter,
Sermons and soda water the day after."

Byron has given us the rule with the most orthodox accuracy. Whether the second portion of the prescription is observed as heartily, punctually, and universally as the first, may be doubted. But in all outward form and ceremony the violence of the contrast between the two seasons is acted out to the letter; is, or was, as may be perhaps more correctly said now-a-days; for both Carnival jollity and licence, and Lent strictness, are from year to year less observed than used to be the case. At Rome, Mother Church exhorts her subjects to feast and laugh in Carnival, in nowise less earnestly or imperatively than she enjoins on them fasting and penances for having laughed in Lent. But her subjects will do neither the one nor the other. And when one hears reiterated complaints in Roman pulpits of pipings to which no dancers have responded, and the vain exhortations of the ecclesiastical authorities to the people to Carnival frolic and festivity, one is reminded of our own Archbishop's "Book of Sports," and led to make comparisons, by which hangs a very long tale.

Great Pan died once upon a time. And Carnival, as it used to be, is with much else dying now in Italy. But in the days to which the incidents here narrated belong, the difference between Carnival and Lent was as marked as that between day and night.

More marked indeed. For between day and night there is twilight, but the transition from Carnival to Lent is as sudden as a plunge from sunshine into cold water. Carnival ends at twelve o'clock on the night of Shrove Tuesday. And the theory of its observance is, or was, that the fun and revelry should grow ever more fast and furious up to the last permitted moment. Then, the clock strikes; the lights are put out, Carnival dies amid one last hurrah. And maskers and revellers go home to rise the next morning with grave and perhaps yellow faces.

In Ravenna, as has been said, a great reception of all the society at the Palazzo Castelmare on the Sunday evening was as much an institution as the High Mass on a Sunday morning. And this was the course of things during all the year, except in Carnival time. Then, in order to leave Sunday evening—the great time for balls and theatres, and pleasure of all sorts free, the reception at the Palazzo Castelmare was changed to the Monday. The programme, therefore, for the three last grand days of the Carnival in Ravenna, on that occasion, stood thus:—On the Sunday, a grand gala Corso from four to six in the afternoon. (That is to say, that every available carriage of every sort in Ravenna would be put in requisition, and would be driven in procession, at a slow foot pace, up and down the long street called the Corso; and those who had servants and liveries and fine horses would display them and rejoice; and those who had none of these things would mingle with the grand carriages in broken-down shandridans, and rejoice also at the sight of the finery, without the smallest feeling of shame at their own poverty. This is a Corso.) On the Sunday evening, the grand representation of the Sonnambula, with the theatre lighted (according to advertisement) "with wax-candles, till it was as light as day!"

Secondly, on the Monday, another Corso, with throwing of flowers and "coriandoli" (i. e. what was supposed to be comfits, but in reality little pills of flour made and sold by the hundredweight for the purpose) from the carriages to each other, and from the windows and the balconies of the houses. Then in the evening, a grand gala reception at the Palazzo Castelmare, at which it was understood masks would be gladly welcomed by the host.

On the night of the Tuesday, thirdly, the last great day of all, there was to be a grand masked ball at the Circolo dei Nobili; that ball of which and of its consequences on the Ash Wednesday morning, the reader already wots. And this was to be the wind-up of the Carnival.

The Corso on the Sunday was a most successful one. The weather was all that was most desirable; bright, not too cold, and free from wind and dust. The Marchese Lamberto turned out with two handsomely appointed equipages. He and his sister-in-law occupied one carriage, and the Marchese Ludovico and the Conte Leandro Lombardone, who was not a rich man, and had no carriage of his own, sat in the second.

It could not be said that the Marchese Lamberto "looked like the time!" And, in truth, he would have given much to escape the ordeal he was called upon to go through. But that was out of the question; unless he had been confined to his bed—in which case the whole town would have been at the palazzo door with inquiries, and all the doctors at his bedside in consultation—it could not be that he should not show himself at the Corso.

Both the Castelmare carriages had the front seats laden with huge baskets of bouquets prepared for throwing at friends and acquaintances in other carriages, and at windows and balconies. The occupants of the carriages seemed to be embedded in a bank of flowers. And there sat the

Marchese amid this wealth of rainbow-colours, looking positively ghastly, so changed, so drawn, so aged was he. And his painful attempts to enter into the spirit of the scene, and act the part which he was expected to act, would have been pitiable to any eye which had observed them closely.

He had left Bianca only just before it had been necessary to return to the palazzo to get into his carriage for the Corso: and the interview between them had been an important one. He had gone thither fully purposed to explain to her, finally, the utter impossibility of his doing as she would have him do. He meant to point out to her how exceptionally difficult it would be for him, in the peculiar position he occupied, to make her his wife. He intended to show her that such a step would have the effect of pulling him down rather than that of pulling her up. He had purposed endeavouring to induce her to accede to such proposals as he could make to her by the exhibition of the most unstinting generosity. And he had determined, fully, finally, and irrevocably determined, that if all that he could say to her on these points should fail to persuade her to accede to such an arrangement, as he had it in his power to propose to her, he would that day, and from that hour, give her up, and swear to himself never to let the image of her cross his memory again.

The visit had been long, and occasionally even somewhat tempestuous. The Marchese had been eloquent; and now driven to bay, had been unequivocal enough in his declarations, his determinations, and his promises. The Diva had shown herself a Diva at every point. She had wept, she had smiled, she had been scornful, she had been suppliant, she had been repellent, she had been loving! And in every mood she had seemed to the fascinated eyes of the Marchese more lovely than in that which preceded it. Finally, she had conquered. Instead of coming away from her, never to see her again, he came away leaving her with the offer of his hand.

And there had been a moment of supreme triumph and ecstasy when permitted, for the first time, to take her in his arms, and press that lovely bosom to his own, and glue his own to those heavenly lips; it had seemed to him as if the prize that was his was worth a thousand times all that he was paying for it. It was all for love, and the world well lost. For not for an instant did the Marchese blind himself to the fact that his world must be lost by such a marriage as he was contemplating. But what did he care for all that had been hitherto to him as the breath of his nostrils? He now felt, for the first time, what of joy and real happiness life had in truth to offer. He would go away, far away with his Bianca and live only for her, and for the delights of her love! Fool that he had been to hesitate. And blessed a thousand times was her sweet, her dear insistence, that had led him to better things!

Such was the state of the mind of the Marchese, while he held his Diva in his arms; and it lasted in full force, almost till he had left the door of her house behind him as he hastened to the palazzo to discharge the Corso duty, which was one of the most prominent functions of his present social position.

And then it seemed as if suddenly, with a suddenness equal to that of a tropical sunset, the scales had fallen from his eyes, and he was another man.

Great God! What had he done? Had he been smitten with sudden madness? What—what was the fatal power this fearful woman had over him? Were then the old witchcraft and philtre tales really true? Surely he must be the victim of some spell, some horrible enchantment. Marry her! Heavens and earth! He hated her. He felt as if he could with pleasure take her by that beautiful throat and squeeze the noxious life out of her.

He pressed his burning hand to his yet hotter forehead, as soon as he found himself in the quiet and solitude of his own room, swallowed a large glass of water, and strove to obtain such little command over himself, for the moment at least, as might suffice to enable him to go through the task before him.

A servant knocked at the door and put his head in to announce that the carriages were at the door. The miserable man started from his chair as if he had been caught in some crime, and answered that he would be down directly. A second time he swallowed, hastily, a large glass of water, for his throat felt parched with thirst; and then, with a vigorous effort to appear gay and at his ease, which produced only the semblance of a fixed unnatural grin on his face, he went down to the carriage.

It was painful to him to pass between the servants who stood in the hall, painful to have to take his seat by the side of his sister-in-law, and most painful of all to meet the gaze of all the town assembled for the Corso. He could not help thinking that all eyes were turned on him, with glances of surprise and suspicion. He felt ashamed to meet and be seen by his acquaintances. He, the Marchese Lamberto di Castelmare, who had never, till that hour, known what it was to shun the eye of any man, who had been accustomed to be the cynosure of all eyes, and to feel that they were all turned on him with respect and regard.

The occasion, and the part he was expected to fulfil in it, made it necessary for him to recognize and return every minute the salutations and greetings of his friends and those who knew him. And who in Ravenna did not know the Marchese Lamberto? There was a good-natured word wanted here, a gallant little phrase there, a salutation with the speaking fingers to this carriage, a more formal bow to the occupants of another, a gracious nod to one person, and a smile to a second.

And all this the unhappy man essayed to perform, as he had so often performed it happily, easily, and successfully in other days.

It was impossible for anybody, whose eye rested on the Marchese for an instant, as he sat amid the flowers in his carriage, to avoid seeing that there was something wrong with him—that he was very unlike his usual self. And every eye, as the carriages passed each other in the long procession, forming two lines as one passed down the street while the other moved in the contrary direction, did rest on him. But it never for an instant entered into the head of a single human being there, to guess at anything like the real cause of the change in the Marchese.

"Time begins to tell on the Marchese; he takes too much out of himself; always busy—no rest—a bad thing!" said one.

"The Marchese Lamberto looks knocked up with this carnival. Quite time for him that Lent was come," said another.

"The fact is that the Marchese is growing old, and he wants more rest. He has not a minute to himself, too many irons in the fire at once, said a third.

"I dare say he has been worried out of his life in getting this new Opera put upon the stage. You'll see he'll be all right enough at the ball to-morrow night."

"Is she in the Corso—La Lalli?"

"Altro. I should think so—and looking so lovely. What a woman she is!"

"Whereabouts is she?"

"About twenty carriages further ahead. You'll see her presently, when we are near the turn, sitting buried up to her waist nearly in flowers—a regular Flora, and such a representative as the Goddess never had before."

"Who has she got with her in her carriage?" asked the first speaker. "I expected to have seen the Marchesino Ludovico there, but he is with the Conte Leandro, in one of the Castelmare carriages."

"Che! catch her compromising herself in any such manner. I wonder how much some of our friends would have given to have the place beside her to-day? But not a bit of it: she has got the old man she calls her father with her."

"Funny, isn't it? I wonder what her game is?"

"Simply to work hard at her vocation, and make as much money as she can, I take it. Probably you would find, if you got at the truth, some animal of a baritono robuato, who owns the Diva's heart, and for whom she works and slaves."

"Poverina! there are the Castelmare carriages coming round again."

The manner of an Italian "Corso" is this: A certain street, or streets—the most adapted to the exigencies of the case that the city can supply—is selected for the purpose; and when the line of carriages reaches the end of this, it turns and proceeds back again to the other end; turns again, and so on. Thus, at each turn, every carriage in the line meets every other once in each circuit.

The second Castelmare carriage, in which the Marchese Ludovico and Leandro Lombardoni were sitting, was following next after that occupied by the Marchese Lamberto and his sister-in-law; and thus each carriage in the line proceeding in a contrary direction to them, passed first the Marchese Lamberto and then his nephew. The carriage occupied by the latter was a wholly open one with a low back. But that in which the Marchese Lamberto sat, though also an open carriage, and entirely so in front, had a half roof at the back, so that it was not so conveniently adapted as the other for seeing those following it as well as those preceding it.

The Marchese and his sister-in-law threw bouquets into almost every carriage that passed them; and the stock with which they had started was soon very much diminished. But one specially magnificent and large bouquet, which conspicuously occupied the centre of the front seat of the carriage, was evidently reserved. Everybody who saw it knew very well for whom that was intended. Of course it was for none other than the Diva of the theatre. And the known interest which the Marchese took in such matters, his musical fanaticism, and the large share he had had in bringing La Lalli to Ravenna, made it quite natural, and a matter of course, that he should pay her such a compliment.

Presently he descried her in the opposite string of carriages, coming towards him. Her carriage was an entirely open one, and she sate in it, with old Quinto Lalli by her side, literally, as one observer had said, half buried in flowers. And most assuredly neither the labours nor the dissipations of the carnival, nor time, nor care, nor any other circumstance, had dimmed the lustre of her beauty, or lessened the verve and spirit of enjoyment with which she took her part in the pageant. She was brilliant with vivacity, beauty, and happiness.

The Marchese might have been seen, had anybody been observing him closely at the moment, to turn visibly paler as her carriage approached his. As far as any clear thought had been in his mind, or any power of thinking possible to him, his latest idea in reference to her had been a desperate resolve that he would never speak to her again. And now, again, as he saw her, in a new avatar of loveliness, he once again knew that to keep such a resolution was above his power.

What he had to do at the moment was to be done, in any case, with the best grace he might. Taking the huge mass of skilfully-arranged flowers in both hands, as her carriage came opposite to his, he leaned out as far as he could, and Quinto Lalli, who sat on the side nearest to him, stretched out to meet him, and then handed the offering to the Goddess. She smiled brilliantly and bowed low, sending a coquettish, sidelong glance of private thanks under eyelashes as she bent her graceful neck.

The carriages rolled on, and passed each other; and there rushed into the Marchese's head a sudden pulse of blood, which turned his previous pallor into a dusky crimson, and seemed to make all the scene swim before his eyes. Partly to hide the evidences of the emotion of which he was conscious, and partly because he felt as if he needed the support, he threw himself back into the corner of the carriage, turning himself away from the scene in front of it as though to shelter his face from the sun that was then so low in the sky as to begin to throw its slanting rays under the hoods of the carriages. This position, as it chanced, brought the Marchese's eye to bear on the little glass window made in the back of the hood of the carriage, after the old-fashioned manner of coach-building.

And what he saw through the little window was this.

A something—a white paper packet, it looked like—was in the act of being thrown to the Diva's carriage from that immediately behind his own, in which, it will be remembered, were his nephew and the Conte Leandro; and the Goddess herself was leaning far out of her carriage in the act of throwing a bouquet to the Marchese Ludovico: The Marchese Lamberto also saw the magnificent flowers he had himself just given to Bianca roll from her carriage on to the pavement, an accident caused by the movement of her person as she leaned forward to throw her flowers to the other carriage.

With what an added torment to the hell that raged within him the unfortunate Marchese returned from that miserable Corso to his palazzo, may be well imagined.

Nevertheless, there had been as little meaning in what he had seen as there often is in many things that make the madness of a jealous man's jealousy.

With the white paper packet—for such it in truth was—the Marchese Ludovico had nothing whatever to do. It had been thrown by the poet Leandro, and contained an attempt to improve the occasion after a fashion, such as he hoped must draw some reply from the Diva. Bianca had taken the opportunity—somewhat coquettishly, but according to the laws and customs of such occasions, quite permissibly—to pay Ludovico the compliment in the eye of all Ravenna of throwing some flowers because she liked him, and because she chose to mark the fact that she threw none during all the Corso to anybody else. She would have done the same if it had so happened that it had been in front of the Marchese Lamberto's carriage instead of behind it; but, of course, to the passion-blinded brain of the latter, this circumstance made all the difference.

As to the rolling of his own superb bouquet on the pavement, it had been quite accidental, and much regretted by Bianca. To recover anything of the kind on such an occasion is, it must be understood, quite out of the question. Any such fallen treasure—and half the things thrown do fall short of the hands for which they are meant—becomes the instant prey of the small boys who throng the streets, and are constantly on the look-out for such windfalls around the carriages.

It may be easily imagined that the Marchese returned from the Corso very little disposed to take any pleasure in the treat to which all Ravenna was looking forward, and which he would have enjoyed more than any one else under other circumstances—the performance at the theatre on that Sunday evening. Nevertheless, the duty of attending it had to be done. All Ravenna would have been astonished, and have wanted to "know the reason why," if the Marchese had been absent from his box on such an evening. "Society" expected it of him that he should be there, and he had been all his life doing everything that "society" expected of him; besides, his presence there really was needed, and poor little Ercole Stadione would have despaired inconsolably if he had been deprived, on such an occasion, of the support of his great friend and patron.

But if none of these reasons had existed—if the Marchese, when he reached the shelter of his own roof after that horrible Corso, had been entirely free to go to bed and escape the necessity of facing the eyes of all the world of Ravenna, which seemed to him to be from hour to hour growing into a more terrible ordeal, would he have gone to bed and abstained from attending the theatre?

It might have been very confidently predicted that he would not have done so. He began, in an unreasoning animal-like sort of way, to recognize the fact that every hour that he spent away from this woman was bare, barren, and of no value to him at all. He was conscious that he could be said to live only in her presence. He was beginning to give himself up as a lost man, and to acquiesce, half-stunned and stupid, in a fatality which he could not struggle against.

And now he was longing—burning not only to have his eyes on her again, but to speak to her. He would have plenty of opportunities of doing so at the theatre in the green-room, or in her dressing-room, and every minute seemed to him an age till he could find such an opportunity.

If he had been asked at that minute—if he had himself asked of his own mind—what he meant to do—to what future he was looking, whether he meant to marry La Lalli or to give her up, he would probably have repudiated either alternative with equal violence. His mind was in a state of chaos; and what was to come in any future, except the most immediate one, he had become incapable of considering. Now he was going to see, to hear, to breathe the same atmosphere with her again, and to go through the wretched task of striving to behave as usual, and look as usual in the eyes of all Ravenna.

The performance was to commence at half-past eight o'clock, and the Marchese, reaching the theatre nearly half-an-boar before that time, found Bianca sufficiently nearly dressed for him to be admitted to her dressing-room. She was putting the finishing touches to the platting of her magnificent hair, after the fashion of a Swiss village-girl, for the completion of her toilette as Amina. He thought that, in this new costume, she looked more irresistibly attractive than he had yet seen her.

"Bianca," he said, as soon as her dresser had left her, and shut the door, "you have made me so miserable to-day. I must tell you openly at once what is in my heart. I saw, to-day, at the Corso—by no means intending to look at all at your carriage after it had passed mine—I saw my poor flowers thrown away by you, while you were throwing a bouquet to my nephew and receiving from him something thrown in return. Bianca, is that the conduct of a woman who has the very same morning accepted the hand of another man? Bianca, I warn you to beware; you do not know what such a love as mine, if it should discover itself to be betrayed, might be capable of."

"Marchese, do not look at me in that way; you frighten me, and what have I done? It is all a mistake, entirely a mistake!" said the poor Diva, really frightened at the manner of the Marchese.

"Did I not see you throw the flowers I had given you from your carriage; evidently for the purpose of gratifying another person?"

"Oh, Marchese! how is it possible that such a thought should enter into your head? Ah, how little you know. If you knew how I had grieved over the loss of the beautiful bouquet that had come from your hand! It fell from the carriage by accident; and it was snatched up, and a boy ran off with it, all in a moment; I would have given anything to get it back again."

"But how came the accident? It was caused by your leaning out of your carriage to throw a bouquet yourself."

"Yes, exactly so; to the Marchese Ludovico. He was the only person to whom I threw a bouquet in all the Corso."

"And why should you throw one to him?"

"To him, to your nephew? Why not, I should not have thought of doing so to another. But to him—"

"And what was it, pray, that he threw to you? I wonder whether he thought, too, that he should not dream of throwing anything to anybody except you."

"The Marchese Ludovico threw nothing to me. Just at the same moment that troublesome idiot, the Conte Leandro, threw a packet into the carriage. I have not even opened it; you may have it unopened the next time you are in the Strada di Porta Sisi, if you like. No doubt it contains some of his charming verses. It is not kind of you, Signor Marchese, to say such things, or to have such thoughts in your head!" said Bianca, turning away her face and putting her handkerchief to her eyes. "And now," she added, "you have made my eyes all red just before I have to go on the stage!"

Of course once again the unhappy Marchese was entirely routed, and the Diva was victorious. "Forgive me, Bianca,", he whispered; "I think only of you from the morning to the evening, and from the evening to the morning again. And it would be impossible for any man to love, as I love you, without a liability to jealousy. I am jealous of your love, Bianca!"

"But it is wonderful that you should not perceive how little cause you have for any such feeling. Oh, Marchese, how can you doubt me? Surely you must have seen and known how entirely my love is yours. You must not wring your poor Bianca's heart by such cruel suspicions."

And then the three knocks, which announced the raising of the curtain, were heard; and the Marchese again murmuring a request to be forgiven, as he kissed her hand, hurried away to take his place in his box.

The house was already nearly full, for the occasion was a notable one; and the opera was new to Ravenna; and everybody wished to hear every note of it. The Marchese Ludovico was not, however, in the Castelmare box, when his uncle reached it, but he came in a minute afterwards. He had been up to the upper tier of boxes to say a word to Paolina and her old friend, who were in the box he had provided for them, which was on the opposite side of the house to the Castelmare box; and exactly over that in the "piano nobile" in which were the Marchesa Anna Lanfredi, and her niece the Contessa Violante.

There was a little noise in the house of people not yet seated during the opening chorus of villagers; but when the prima donna came on the stage as Amina, after the prolonged and repeated rounds of applause, which greeted her appearance, had subsided, a pin's fall might have been heard in the theatre.

The Marchese Ludovico had joined cordially and boisterously, and the Marchese Lamberto more moderately, in the applause which had saluted the entrance of the Diva; and after that the latter had placed himself in the corner of the box, with his back to the audience, and his face towards the stage, and with an opera-glass at his eyes, he sat perfectly still, feeding his passion with every glance, every change of feature, and every movement of the woman who had enthralled him.

Then came the famous song of Amina, the happy village-bride about to be married on the morrow to her lover—the tenor of course. The Diva sang it admirably, and acted it equally well. The purest girlish innocence was expressed in every trait of her features and manifested itself in every gesture and every movement. The perfect, trusting, happy love of a fresh and innocent heart could have had no better representative.

The recitative, "Care compagne," etc, addressed to the assembled villagers, fell from her lips with a purity of enunciation that made each syllable seem like a note from a silver bell. And then the air, "Come per me sereno," held the house entranced till the final note of it. And then burst forth such a frantic shout of applause and delight as can be heard only in an Italian theatre.

Ludovico leant far out of the stage-box in which he sat, and joined vociferously in the plaudits with both hand and voice. But the Marchese remained quiet in his corner, with his face half-shaded by his hand, conscious as he was that the expression of it might need hiding from the others in the box. He need not have heeded them; for their attention was too exclusively occupied with the stage for them to expend any of it on him. Had it been otherwise his hand, covering the lower half of his face, would not have sufficed to conceal his emotion.

Now again the hot fit of his love was in the ascendant. Never had Bianca more thoroughly captivated him. Never had it seemed to him less possible to live without her. What to him were all these dull and empty blockheads for whom he had hitherto lived, and who were now—the foul fiend seize them!—sharing with him the delight of seeing and hearing her for the last time. Yes, it should be for the last time. He would make her his, all his own; and carry her far away from all that could remind either her or himself of their past lives. And then a scowl of displeasure came over his face as his glance lighted on his nephew's noisy and unrestrained manifestations of enthusiastic admiration.

Presently, towards the end of the first act, came the duet between Amina and her lover, who has been made causelessly jealous, and Bianca sang the pretty lines—

"Son, mio bene, del zeffiro amante,
Perche ad esso il tuo nome confido.
Amo il sol, perche teco il divido,
Amo il rio, perche l'onda ti da,"

with a sweetness of expression perfectly irresistible. The Marchese in his corner, half-shrouded from the observation of the house by the curtain, which, though undrawn, hung down by the side of the box, but fully facing the stage, was perfectly aware that the singer had specially addressed herself to him; and he felt the full force of the loving rebuke for the unreasonable displeasure he had so recently manifested in her dressing-room. His heart went out towards her; and he felt that if it were to be done that moment, he could have led her to the altar in the face of all Christendom.

At the end of the act the plaudits were again vociferous, and four times was the smiling and triumphant Diva compelled by the calls and clamour of her worshippers to return before the curtain to receive their applause and salute them in return for it. The Marchese Ludovico again loudly and enthusiastically joined in these manifestations; and then, when they were over, and the noise in the house had subsided, he quietly slipped out of the box, and springing up the stairs which communicated with the upper tier of boxes, entered that occupied by Paolina and the Signora Orsola Steno.

"What did you think of that, Paolina mia?" he said, sitting down by her side, and making the action of applauding with his hands, as he spoke. "Did you ever hear a thing more charmingly sung? Is she not divine?"

"There is no mistaking your opinion on the point, at all events, amico mio. I never saw anybody manifest such unbounded admiration as you did just now. But the Diva was not thinking of you, I can tell you," said Paolina, with just the slightest possible flavour of pique in her tone.

"Thinking of me; I should imagine not indeed. But what upon earth have you got into that dear little head of yours, my Paolina? Did not you think both singing and acting very fine?"

"Certainly I think her voice is perhaps the finest I ever heard in my life; and she is no doubt a great actress—a very great actress; but—she is not simpatica to me. I don't know why, but—somehow or other—I don't like her."

"What can you have got into your head, tesoro mio? You know nothing of her; you have nothing to do with her except to see and hear her on the stage."

"No; thank heaven! I should not like that she should come any nearer to my life than that," replied Paolina, with a little shudder.

"Come, Paolina, you must admit that that is being prejudiced and unreasonable," said Ludovico smiling at her.

"Yes; I suppose it is. But—Ludovico mio, just ask any other woman—any other good woman—in the house; and see if they have not the same feeling. The Contessa Violante, for example—ask her," said Paolina.

"Just because she is splendidly handsome: women cannot be just to each other when that comes in the way. But you might afford to be charitable even to so beautiful a creature as the Lalli, my Paolina."

"No, Signor, I won't be bribed by compliments, even from you," she whispered, with a look that showed that the value of the bribe was not unappreciated; "and I think that what you say is unjust to women in general."

"But I wonder what it is then that has prejudiced you against the Lalli?"

"I don't know. Really nothing that I can tell. One feels sometimes what one cannot explain. She is not simpatica to me, that is all."

"But what on earth put it into your head, Paolina mia, to say that she was not thinking of me when she was singing her part? Why should she think of me—or of anybody else, except the primo tenore, who was singing with her? What is it you mean?" said Ludovico, much puzzled.

"You said she was a very good actress as well as a fine singer," returned Paolina; "and I think she is. This is a capital box for seeing all that goes on the opposite side of the theatre. And I can tell you who the Lalli was thinking of, and who she was singing at during her duet at the end of the act—your uncle, the Marchese Lamberto; and he knew it very well, too."

"What parcel of nonsense have you got into your little brains, Paolina? Sing at the Marchese? Of course they all do; of course they all know that his suffrage is of more importance to them than all the rest of the theatre put together. But as for my idea of—lo zio—of all men in the world. Ha, ha, ha! If you had lived in Ravenna instead of Venice all your life, carina mia, you would know how infinitely absurd the idea seems of there being anything between the Marchese Lamberto and a stage singer, or of its being possible for him to regard her in any other light than that of a singing machine."

"I dare say you are right, caro mio. Still I can't quite think that the Marchese would look at any one of the fiddles quite as I saw him look at her," said Paolina.

And then the immense interval, which occurs between one act and another in Italian theatres, and which is tolerated with perfect contentment by Italian audiences, came to an end; and Ludovico hurried down to take his place again in the Castelmare box.

The next point in the opera which excited the special enthusiasm of the house was the impassioned finale to the second act, in which Amina on her knees strives to convince her lover of her innocence of having ever harboured a thought inconsistent with entire devotion to him. She sang as if her whole soul were in her words; and the entire theatre was electrified by the power of her acting; the entire theatre, with the exception of one intelligent and observant little face in a box on the upper tier, exactly opposite to that of the Marchese Lamberto.

From that vantage-ground of observation Paolina saw perfectly well both the singer on the stage and the Marchese in the box; and again felt sure that the actress was specially addressing herself with an implied meaning to the latter; and that he was aware that she was doing so. She felt no doubt that the motive for this was exactly that to which Ludovico had attributed it. It was important to the Diva to flatter and make a friend of so powerful a theatrical patron as the Marchese; and she took this very objectionable method, Paolina thought, of attaining that end. Paolina thought nothing more than this; but, nevertheless, it made her conceive a dislike for the Diva greater, perhaps, than the cause would seem to justify.

The interval between the second and the third act Ludovico thought himself obliged to pass in the box of the Marchese Anna Lanfredi, in which Violante was sitting with her aunt. There, too, he found the ladies not quite disposed to be as frantically enthusiastic in their praises of the singer as the whole male part of the audience. The Marchesa Lanfredi thought that La Lalli was nothing at all in comparison with some singer who had charmed all Bologna some forty years before. And Violante, admitting that she had an exquisite voice and perfect method, confessed much as Paolina had done, that she did not quite like her, she hardly knew why.

In the third act, the song sung by the sleep-walker in her state of unconsciousness—"Ah non credea mirarti,"—was a great success. And most fascinatingly lovely the Diva looked in her white night-dress, with her wreath of rich auburn tresses hanging in luxuriant curls around her shoulders.

Shortly after this had been sung a liveried servant entered the Castelmare box, bearing a most superb bouquet of choice flowers, tied with a long streamer of broad rose-coloured ribbon, and deposited it on the front of the box.

And then came the joyful finale "Ah non giunge." And in that the Diva seemed to surpass herself. It was a passionate carol of love, and joy, and triumph in which she seemed to pour the whole force and energy of her soul into the words and sounds that told the truth, the entirety, the perfection of her love, and the overwhelming happiness the recognition of it by its object gave her.

For many minutes the vociferous applause continued. The stage was covered with flowers flung from all sides of the house. The Marchese Lamberto whispered a word or two to Ludovico; and then the latter, leaning far out of the box, presented the magnificent bouquet to Bianca, who was smiling and thanking the public for their plaudits by repeated curtsies, and who came for it to the side of the stage. She made a very low and graceful curtsey to Ludovico, as she took it from his hand; but her eyes thanked the Marchese Lamberto, who still remained close in his corner, for the gift.

The fact was that he was too much moved by violent and contending emotions to dare to trust himself to hand the flowers himself. He knew that he was shaking in every limb; and, therefore, had told his nephew to give the bouquet; which, indeed, it was quite a matter of course that a successful prima donna should receive from that box on such an occasion.

Again and again the curtain had to be raised after it had descended in obedience to the cries of the spectators, who were determined to make the Diva's triumph complete. Again and again she had to step back on the stage and make yet one more bow and smile—yet one more gracious smile.

During this delay the Marchese Lamberto slipped from his box and made his way behind the scenes. "Can you feel as Bianca what you can so divinely express as Amina?" he whispered in her ear as he gave her his arm to lead her to her carriage at the stage-door.

"Try me as Amina was tried; and reward me as Amina was rewarded, and then see," she replied in the same tone.

And so ended Bianca Lalli's Carnival engagement at Ravenna.

CHAPTER IV

The Marchese Lamberto's Correspondence

The next morning—the morning of the Monday after the gala performance at the theatre—the post brought to the Palazzo Castelmare a letter from Rome, before the Marchese had left his chamber. The servant took it to his master's room, found him still in bed, though awake, and left it on the table by his bedside.

The Marchese Lamberto was, and had been all his life, far too busy a man to be a late riser. Italians, indeed, who do nothing all day long, are often very early risers. Their, climate leads them to be so.

They sleep during hours which are less available for being out of doors—for your Italian idler passes very little of his day in his own home—and they are up and out during the delicious hours of the early morning. But the Marchese Lamberto, whose days were filled with the multiplicity of occupations and affairs that have been described in a previous chapter, was wont, at all times of the year, to rise early.

On the present occasion, a sleepless night—and such nights, also, were a new phenomenon in the Marchese's life—might have been a reason for his being late. But he was not sleeping when his servant took the letter in to him. The frame of mind in which he returned from the theatre has been described. It lasted till he fell into a feverish sleep, soon after going to his bed.

The dreams that made such sleep anything but rest may be easily guessed. He was startled from them by the fancy that the kisses of Bianca burned his lips; that it was a scorching flame, that he was pressing in his arms, the contact of which turned all his blood to liquid fire.

He slept no more during the night. And the good that had seemed to him, as he sat in his box at the opera, more desirable than all the other goods the world could give, seemed good no longer; seemed, in the dark stillness of his night-thoughts, like a painted bait, with which the arch-tempter was luring him to his ruin and destruction.

Restlessly turning on his bed with a deep sigh, and pressing his hot hand to his yet hotter brow, he took the letter that had been brought him, and saw that it was from his Roman friend and correspondent, Monsignore Paterini:

"Illusmo Signor Marchese E Mio Buono E Colendmo Amico," the letter ran—"Seeing that the subject of my letter is matter adapted rather to Carnival than to Lenten tide, I hasten to write so that it may reach your lordship before the festive season is over. That your friends in Rome are never forgetful of one, who so eminently deserves all their best thoughts and good wishes, I trust I need not tell you. But in this our Rome, where so many interests are the unceasing care of so many powerful friends and backers, it needs such merit as that of your lordship to make the efforts of friends successful."

"Understand, then, that his Holiness has been kept constantly aware of all that Ravenna—the welfare of which ancient and noble city is especially dear to him—owes to your constant and intelligent efforts for the advancement of true civilization and improvement, as distinguished from all that innovators, uninfluenced by the spirit of religion, vainly, boast as such. Specially, our Holy Father has been pleased by the energy, tact, and truly well directed zeal, with which you have succeeded in bringing to a satisfactory conclusion the thorny and difficult business of the Spighi property, on which all the welfare of our well-beloved Sisters in Christ the Augustines of St. Barnaba so greatly depends. The lady superior of that well-deserving house is, as you are aware, the sister of his Eminence the Cardinal Lattoli; and so signal a service rendered in that direction is, as I need hardly tell your lordship, not likely to be forgotten."

"It is under these circumstances that I have the great satisfaction of having it in my power to inform your lordship, that it is the gracious purpose of our Holy Father to mark his approbation and satisfaction at the conduct of your illustrious lordship in this matter, in a manner that, while it manifests to the whole world the care of his Holiness for every portion of the dominions of the Holy Church, will, I doubt not, be highly gratifying to yourself at the present time, and will redound to the future glory and distinction of your noble family. It is, in a word, the intention of the Holy Father to confer on your lordship the Grand Cross of the Most Noble Order of the Santo Spirito. And it is further the benignant purpose and wish of his Holiness to present you with this most honourable mark of his approbation with his own sovereign hand."

"We may therefore hope—myself and your numerous other friends in this city—to see you here before long. Doubtless the tidings, which I have been anxious to be the first to give you, will be very shortly communicated to you in a more official manner. I fancy, indeed, that I shall not have been able to be much beforehand with the official announcement. Make your arrangements, then, I beseech you, to give us as long a visit as you can steal from the grave cares of watching over the interests of your beloved Ravenna. There are many here who are anxious to renew their acquaintance, and, if he will permit them to say so, their friendship with the Marchese di Castelmare. And, if I may venture to do so, my dear friend, I would, before closing my letter, whisper that, with due care and a little activity, the present favour of our Holy Father may be but the earnest of other things."

"The future, however, is in God's hands, and man is but as grass. Nevertheless, as far as it is permissible to judge of the human agencies by which the Heavenly Providence brings about its ends, I should say that your Legate, his Eminence the Cardinal Marliani, was, of all the present Fathers of the Church, one of the most deserving of our regards and respect. Should you have a fitting opportunity of allowing his Eminence to become aware how strongly such have always been my sentiments, and how unceasingly I endeavour to impress them on others, I should esteem it as a favour. It is well that merit even so exalted as his should know that it is appreciated."

"Omit not, my friend, to offer to the Marchese Ludovico, your nephew, the expression of my most distinguished regard and respect; and believe me, Illusmo Signor Marchese, of your Excellency the devoted friend and most obedient servant,"

"Giuseppe Paterini"

Before the Marchese had read the wordy epistle of his correspondent half through, he raised himself briskly to an upright sitting posture in his bed, his head was lifted with a proud movement from its drooping attitude, and an expression of gratified pride and pleasure came into his eyes. The much-coveted distinction which was now, he was told, to be his, had long been the object of his eager ambition. And the manner in which it was to be conferred on him—the attitude he should stand in with reference to his friend the Cardinal Legate—all contributed to make the occasion gratifying to him.

He rang his bell sharply for his servant, and said he would get up at once.

The valet said that there was a servant from the Legate's palace below, with a letter for the Marchese from the Cardinal—that, fearing his master was not well, and might be getting a little sleep, he, the valet, had been unwilling to bring the letter up; but that the man was waiting his Excellency's pleasure, as he had been ordered to ask for an answer.

Doubtless this was the official communication of which Paterini spoke, or the forerunner of it. The Marchese desired his man to bring him the Cardinal's letter directly.

Yes; the pleasant duty having fallen to the lot of the Cardinal of making a communication to the Marchese, which would doubtless be highly gratifying to him, his Eminence was anxious to seize the earliest opportunity of performing so agreeable a task; and would be happy to see the Marchese at one o'clock that day, if that hour suited his lordship's convenience.

"Delighted to have the honour of waiting on his Eminence at the hour named."

The Marchese put the two letters on his toilet-table, and proceeded to dress. They were large letters. That from Monsieur Paterini was written on a sheet of foolscap paper, and addressed in a large strong hand, with the word RAVENNA in letters half an inch high. That from the Cardinal was contained in a large square envelope, sealed with a huge seal bearing his Eminence's arms under a Cardinal's hat, with its long many-tailed tassels hanging down on either side.

What a triumph would be this journey to Rome. What a yet greater triumph the return from it. The Legate would certainly hold a special state reception to welcome him back, and give him an opportunity of showing the new order to all his fellow-citizens. What a proud hour it would be.

The Marchese was indulging in these thoughts; dressing himself the while, and looking every now and then at the two letters lying on his table, when a footman tapped at the door and handed to the valet, who was attending on his master, yet a third epistle. Unlike the Cardinal's servant, the man who had brought it had simply left it, and gone away without saying anything about an answer.

This third letter did not resemble its two predecessors—at least on the outside—at all. It was a very little letter; not a quarter of the size of either of the others; and the seal wherewith it was sealed was not a tenth of the size of that of his Eminence; also, instead of being white like the Cardinal's, or whity-yellow like the Prelate's, it was rose-coloured, and delicately perfumed. And the superscription, "All' Illmmo Sigr il Sigr Marchese Lamberto di Castelmare," was written in very daintily pretty and delicate small characters; as unmistakably feminine a letter as ever a gentleman received.

The Marchese's face changed visibly as the little missive was put into his hands. Yet he opened it eagerly, and opened his nostrils to the perfume, which exhaled from it, with a greedily sensuous seeming of pleasure.

This letter ran as follows:—"Dearest And Best, If you were not indeed and indeed so to me, could I have ever suffered the vow that binds us mutually to each other to have been uttered?—Dearest and best, I write mainly, I think, for the mere pleasure of addressing you. For I am sure that it is not necessary to ask you to come to me. You can guess how eagerly I wish to speak to you; to hear from you that you have dismissed for ever those horrid thoughts that you vexed me with at the theatre last night. I longed so to have sung the words I had to utter for your ears—to your ears only: 'Amo il zeffiro, perche ad esso il tuo nome confido.' Ah, Lamberto, if you knew how true that is. It is often—how often—the singer's duty to utter on the stage the words of passion. But what a thing it is—a thing I never dreamed before—to feel them as I utter them. The opera did not go badly, did it? I think the success was a legitimate one. But what is any success or any applause now to me, save yours? I felt that I was singing to one only, as one only was in my heart and in my thoughts. Do not let many hours pass before you come to me, my love, my lord! For they go very slowly and heavily, these hours; and as I trace the movement of the tardy hour-hand on the clock, I grow sick with longing, and with hope deferred. Come to me, my dearest and my best. Your own,"

"Bianca"

"P. S.—I have mentioned our engagement to no soul save my father; of course you did not wish me to exclude him from our confidence. He is fully worthy of it."

The Marchese sunk down into the chair that stood before his toilet-table, with the little letter in his hand; and his hand shook, and his eyes were dizzy, and there was a buzzy ringing in his ears. And still the perfume from the pink paper rose to his nostrils, and seemed to his fancy as though it were a poison that he had neither the power nor the will to defend himself from.

He had put the little pink note down on the table where the two other letters were, and sat looking at the three. They were manifestly, fatally incompatible. Either the two big letters must be thrown to the winds—they and their contents for ever—together with all thought of honours, high social standing, and admiring respect of the world; or the little pink note must be crushed at once and for ever, and its writer—ah!—made to understand, to begin with, that the Marchese di Castelmare did not know his own mind; that his offer and his plighted word were not to be trusted.

The letters lying there on the table before him, as he sat gazing at them almost without the power of anything that merited to be called thought, represented themselves to his fancy as living agencies of contrasted qualities and powers. The two large missives from his ecclesiastical friends were creditable and useful steeds; harmless, wholesome in blood and nature, big and pacific, apt for service, and good for drawing him on to honour, success, and prosperity. The little pink note was a scorpion with a power a thousand-fold greater, for its size—a sharp, venomous, noxious power, stinging to the death, yet imparting with its sting a terrible, a fatal delight, an acrid fierce pleasure, which once tasted could not by any mortal strength of resolution be dashed away from the lips.

He took the sweet-scented little paper in his hand and read it through again. And his veins seemed to run with fire as he read. Then for the first time he saw the postscript. It had escaped his notice before. That old man had been informed that he had offered marriage to the girl he called his daughter and had been accepted.

It might not be so easy to crush the little pink scorpion note, and liberate himself from the writer of it. Proof? There might be no legal evidence to show that he had ever made such a promise. Yet, to have such an assertion made by Bianca and her father, to have to deny the fact, knowing it to be true!—he, Lamberto di Castelmare! Great God! what was before him?

Then there was that woman, the servant, too. Might it not well be that she, too, knew the promise he had made; overheard him possibly; set to do so—likely enough! What was he to do?—what was he to do?

Something he must do quickly. The Cardinal Legate was expecting him at one o'clock, and—would it be best to drive Bianca from his mind till afterwards? Go to her he must in the course of the day!

Then, suddenly as a lightning-flash, he saw her before him as he had gazed on her at the theatre overnight in her white night-dress, uttering those words of passionate love—love which she told him was all addressed to him, which she was pining to speak to him again.

That, then, it was in his power to have, and to have now, now at once. "Ahi, ahi!" he gnashed, through his ground teeth, closing his eyes as the besieging vision postured itself in every seductive guise before the suggestions of his fancy. Ah, God! what were Cardinals, and Crosses, and place and station, or all the world beside, to one half-hour in those arms?

Come what come might, he would see her first before going to the Cardinal.

Snatching his hat, cane, and gloves, breakfastless as he was, he hurried out of the house half mad with the passion that was consuming him, yet with enough of the old thoughts about him to turn away, on quitting his own door, from the direction of the Porta Sisi, and to seek the goal of his thoughts by the most unfrequented route he could find.

Quinto Lalli and Bianca were sitting together in the parlour of their apartments in the Strada di Porta Sisi, that same Monday morning just after the little pink note had been despatched to the Marchese. Bianca was having her breakfast—a small quantity of black coffee in a drinking-glass, brought, together with a roll of dry bread, from the cafe. Old Lalli was not partaking of her repast, having previously enjoyed a similar meal, with the addition of a modicum of some horrible alcoholic mixture, called "rhume," poured into the coffee at the cafe in the next street.

"That will bring him fast enough," said the old man, alluding to the note which had been just despatched. "The game is quite in your own hands, as I told you from the beginning it would be. That postscript was a capital thought."

The postscript in question, which, it may be remembered, had not added to the pleasure the billet had given the Marchese, had been added at the suggestion of old Lalli himself.

"I would rather not have written it," replied Bianca, peevishly. "It looked too much like putting the screw on—I don't like it."

"Be reasonable, bambina mia, whatever you are. How, in the name of all the Saints, do you imagine that you are to become Marchesa di Castelmare without putting the screw on—and that pretty sharply too? The man is as thoroughly caught as ever man was caught by a woman; and I tell you, therefore, that the game is in your own hands. But you don't suppose that he is burningly eager to solicit the honour of your alliance, che diamine?"

"Don't, Quinto; don't go on in that way. I tell you I hate it all," returned Bianca.

"Cars mia, you are in an irrational humour this morning. Do you like the old game better? It don't pay, bambina mia, as you have found out; and, above all, it won't last. But I am sure you have reason to be satisfied with your success this season in any way. I never heard you sing better in my life than you did last night; and, to say the truth, these people seemed to appreciate it."

"I tell you, I hate it all—all—all!" said Bianca, as she swallowed the last drop of her coffee, and threw herself on the sofa in an attitude of languor and ennui.

"You are unreasonable, Bianca, you are not like yourself this morning; I don't know what is come to you. What in the world do you like, or what do you want?" said the old man, looking at her with a puzzled air.

"Did you see the Marchese Ludovico in a box on the right-hand side on the second tier with that Venetian girl, the artist?"

"The Marchese Ludovico was in the left-hand stage-box with his uncle."

"Of course he was; but I mean between the acts. I saw him from the wing by the side of that girl with her face the colour of mahogany, and her half-alive look. I hate the look of her, and I know she hates me!"

Old Quinto looked at his pupil curiously for a minute before he replied to her.

"What do you mean, Bianca mia?" he said, at last; "and what, in the name of all the Saints, is the Venetian girl to you, or you to her? Did you ever speak to her? Why should she hate you?"

"I tell you, she does. We women can always see those things without needing to be told them; and she knows, you may be very sure, that I hate her."

"But why? What is she to you?" reiterated the old man.

"You asked me, just now, what I wanted. I want, if you must know, what I can never have—what the Venetian girl last night was getting."

"And what was she getting? I don't understand you, upon my soul!" said Quinto, staring at her, and utterly puzzled.

"What was she getting? Love!—that was what she was getting! Ludovico loves her," said Bianca, raising herself on her elbow, and speaking with fierce bitterness.

"Tu, tu, tu, tu, tu, tu!" whistled Quinto, between his pursed-up lips. "But I thought, bambina mia, that you were going to love the Marchese Lamberto, and be a good wife to him, and all the rest of it, according to the rules and practices of the best-regulated domestic family circles; and I—I was so rejoiced to hear it," said the old reprobate, casting up his eyes and hands.

"Don't, Quinto; don't talk in that manner, or you'll drive me beyond myself. I can't bear it."

"But did you not say that you loved the Marchese Lamberto?" persisted Quinto, dropping his mocking tone, however.

"I said that I liked him better than any of the men I have known; that I admired him as a fine and noble gentleman; that I would be a good and true wife to him, and should love him," she added, with a burst of bitterness, "better than he ever will, or can, love me."

"Well, come now, bambina mia. If you think that the Marchese is not enough in love with you, you must have a strong appetite, indeed, and be very hard to content. Why, if there ever was a man thoroughly caught, fascinated—"

"Bah! Love! Ludovico loves the Venetian," said Bianca, with an expressive emphasis on the verb.

"Ludovico, again! I protest I don't understand you, Bianca. But there, when a man has come to my age he don't expect ever to understand a woman. You did not want Ludovico, as you call him, to love you, did you?"

"No: but—"

And Bianca stopped short, and seemed to fall into a sort of reverie.

"But what? If you mean that you wanted to have the uncle for a husband, and the nephew for a lover, that is intelligible enough. The game would have been a dangerous one. But there is no reason why you should not say it plainly between friends."

"I tell you, Quinto, I won't hear you speak to me in that tone," said Bianca, turning on him fiercely, and with flashing eyes. "Did I ever do anything to attract him?" she added, "did I try to make him love me? Do you think that the Venetian would have stood in the way if I had chosen to do so? I never did! I meant, if the Marchese would make me his wife, to be true and loyal to him; though he himself seems to think it impossible that I should be so. You know that I have never attempted to attract Ludovico in any way."

"Very well then; let his Venetian have him in peace," said Quinto, shrugging his shoulders.

"Why, then, does that girl hate me as she does? What harm have I ever done her?" returned Bianca.

"Why should you think she does hate you?" expostulated Quinto.

"I have told you that I saw it. I saw it in her eyes when Ludovico was handing me the bouquet;—which he only did because his uncle told him to do it. She would have blasted me to death with her look at that moment if she could have done it;—I have a good mind—a very good mind—"

"Be guided by me this once for the last time, as you have so often been before; bambina mia," said Quinto, who thought that he now understood the real state of the case; "make sure of your own game first. Make all safe with the Marchese Lamberto. When you are the Marchesa di Castelmare it will be time to take any revenge on the Venetian you please."

"Ah—h—h—h!" sighed Bianca, shaking her head with an expression of disgust; "you understand nothing about it, Quinto; you can't—of course you can't. Gia," she continued, after a pause of thought; "yes, I could take from her, poor fool, what she has; but could I, Bianca Lalli, take it and keep it for myself? Ah me, it is weary work! You might as well go and flaner, Quinto; for I must dress ready for the Marchese, in case he comes this morning."

"He'll come sure enough," said Quinto; as he prepared to leave the room.

"It's quite time, then, that I made myself ready to receive him," returned Bianca, getting up from the sofa.

"Amo il zeffiro, perche a lui suo nome confido," she sang, as she turned listlessly to go to her chamber; and despite what she had said—and said with perfect sincerity to her adopted father—it may be feared that the suo did not refer in the singer's mind to the Marchese Lamberto.

Quinto Lalli was in the act of shutting the sitting-room door behind him, when the outer door of the apartment opened and Ludovico appeared in the doorway. He was the very last man whom Quinto, with the ideas in his head which the above conversation with Bianca had put into it, would have wished to see there. And perhaps there was something in his manner of meeting the visitor that enabled the Marchesino to perceive that he was not just then welcome.

"A thousand pardons," he said, in an easy, careless manner, "for coming at so indiscreetly early an hour; but I could not refrain from just saying one word to the Signorina Bianca on her last night's triumph, and I shall have no opportunity of seeing her later in the day."

"Bianca," called out Quinto, re-opening the door he was closing, and putting his head back into the room, "here's the Marchese Ludovico wishes to speak to you." If the old man had not been a little bit out of humour with his adopted daughter he would probably have found some excuse for getting rid of the inopportune visitor.

"Pray let the Signor Marchese come in," returned Bianca, turning back from the door of her bed-room, rather to the surprise of Signor Quinto;—and Ludovico passed on into the sitting-room as the old man went out and shut the outer door behind him.

Bianca, as she had said, had been about to dress to receive the Marchese Lamberto; and Ludovico thus caught her (really surprised this time) in her morning toilette. But there was nothing in her dress to prevent her from being with propriety presentable, or, indeed, to prevent her from looking very charming in her dishabille. Nevertheless, she did not intend, as we have seen, to present herself without further adornment to the Marchese Lamberto; and it was not without a certain feeling of bitterness at her heart that she said to herself, "What does it signify?" as she cast a glance at her looking-glass before stepping back into the sitting-room to receive her visitor.

"Really, Signora, I don't know how to apologize sufficiently for thus breaking in upon you," said Ludovico, coming forward to meet her; "but I could not refrain from calling to say one word of congratulation. Can you forgive me?"

"I hardly know whether I can," said Bianca, half pouting and half laughing, and looking wholly beautiful; "to be seen when they are not fit to be seen is an offence which we others, women, find it difficult to forgive, you know."

"But that is an offence which, in the nature of things, cannot be committed against the Signora Bianca Lalli," retorted Ludovico, with a low bow, half earnest and half in fun, and a look of admiration that was entirely sincere. "But the fact is," he continued, "that I really was impatient to be the first to make you my compliments on last night's immense success. To tell you that I never heard a part sung as you sang that of Amina last night would, perhaps, appear to you to be saying little. But I do assure you the whole city is saying that there never was anything like it. It was superb! Perfect! Perhaps the praise of all Ravenna is not worth very much to one who has had that of all Italy. But, at all events, my uncle is a competent judge—and he is not an easy one. And I do assure you he was moved as I never saw him moved by music before."

"He is very good—too kind to me. He was good enough to see me to my carriage at the theatre last night; and he said some word that makes me think he purposes doing me the honour of coming here to give me the advantage of his criticism on last night's performance," said Bianca, who was anxious to let her visitor understand the desirability of avoiding being caught there by his uncle.

"Yes, I am sure he would not fail to bring his tribute of admiration this morning," returned Ludovico, carelessly; "but he will not be here yet awhile. He is an early man in general, lo zio; but he has not been well lately. You must have seen yourself, Signorina, how changed he is since you have known him. I really begin to be uneasy about him. You must surely have observed how ill he is looking."

"I am so grieved to hear you say so. Of course any change must be far more evident to those who have known him all his life. But I should have said that I had rarely or never seen so remarkably young-looking a man for his years. The Marchese happened to tell me once that he is fifty or not far from it. It seemed to me impossible to believe it," said Bianca, who understood perfectly well how and why it came to pass that the Marchese should lately be a changed man.

"Three months ago he might have well passed for five-and-thirty; but, per Bacco, he looks his years now every day of them—and more, too, il povero zio."

"Nay, Signor Ludovico, I think your regard for your uncle makes you think him worse than he is. I thought he was looking very well at the theatre last night," replied Bianca, knowing nothing more to the purpose to say.

"At the theatre. Ah! perhaps. He was pleased and excited. I did not specially remark him last night. But, the truth is, I am not easy about him."

"I feel very much persuaded, Signor Ludovico, that you are alarming yourself unnecessarily. Your fears are excited by your affection for your uncle. I doubt whether many nephews in your position, Signor Marchese, would feel as much anxiety about the health of an uncle whose heirs they were; not that I mean, of course, Signor, to insinuate that you are dependent on your uncle," added Bianca, who felt considerable curiosity to know how matters stood in the Castelmare family in this respect.

"Faith, though, I am dependent on him," returned Ludovico, with the most careless frankness. "I have not a bajocco in the world but what comes to me from him. But lo zio is more generous than uncles often are to their nephews who are to be their heirs. And I am in no hurry to succeed to him, I assure you."

"I am sure that would not be in your nature in any case, Signor Ludovico," returned Bianca; "but there is some excuse for those being in a hurry whose future depends on the caprice of old people," she added, fishing for further information.

"But my future does depend upon his caprice—in one way, at all events. Suppose my uncle should take it into his head to marry, and have a family. There is nothing to prevent him. Many an older man than he by a great deal has done so. And if that were to happen, there is not a beggar in all Ravenna who is a poorer man than I should be. Only that lo zio is about the most unlikely man to marry in all Italy, it is a thing that might happen any day."

"Why should the Signor Marchese be so unlikely to marry? One would say, to look at him, that it was not such an unlikely thing. Suppose some designing woman were to make the attempt?"

"There does not exist the woman who could have the faintest shadow of success in such an enterprise, Signora. If you could tell how often the thing has been tried! He is seasoned, lo zio is. Besides, he never was a man given much to falling in love at any time of his life. I don't think he is much an admirer of the sex, to tell you the truth. No; there is no fear of that."

There was a silence of some minutes, and Bianca seemed to have fallen into a reverie; till, suddenly, raising her eyes, which had fallen beneath their lashes, while she had been busy with her thoughts, she said, looking up archly into Ludovico's face:

"Your attention, at all events, was not so fully occupied by the performance last night, Signor, but that you had plenty of thoughts and eyes at command for other matters."

"What do you mean, Signora? I am sure I was not only an attentive but a delighted listener," said he, while the tell-tale blood flushed his cheeks.

"Ah! I saw which way your glances and thoughts were wandering. We artists see more things in the salle than you of the world before the foot-lights think for. A very pretty little brunette, in No. 10 on the upper tier, was quite equally aware of the direction of the Marchese Ludovico's thoughts and looks."

"You might have seen not only my thoughts but me myself in the same box, Signora, if you could have continued your observations after the curtain was down. The lady you saw there is one for whom I have the highest possible regard," said Ludovico, with a very slight shade of hauteur quite foreign to his usual manner, in his tone.

It was very slightly marked, but not so slightly as to escape the notice of Bianca, who perfectly well understood it and the meaning of it.

"I dare say she well deserves it; she looks as if she did," said the Diva, with a pensive air, and a dash of melancholy in her voice. "I have often wondered," she continued, after a moment's pause, "whether you others, grand signori, ever ask yourselves, when you bestow such regards as you speak of on a poor artist—I know who she is, merely an artist like myself—what the result to the woman so loved is likely to be?"

"Signora!" cried Ludovico, provoked, exactly as Bianca had intended he should be, into saying what he would not otherwise have allowed to escape him, "permit me to assure you that, however pertinent such speculations may be in other cases, which have doubtless fallen under your observation, they are altogether the reverse of pertinent in the present instance. The lady in question is, as you say, a poor artist; not, perhaps, as you were also kind enough to say, one quite of the same kind as yourself, neither so successful nor so celebrated"—he hastened to add as he saw a sudden paleness come over the face of the singer, and an expression sudden and rapidly repressed and effaced, of such a concentration of wrath and hatred in her eyes, that momentary as it was, pulled him up short with something very much akin to a feeling resembling fear—"an artist neither so successful nor so celebrated as the Signora Lalli, but, nevertheless, a lady whom it is the dearest wish of my heart to call my wife."

"She is indeed, then, a most fortunate and happy woman," said Bianca, who had perfectly recovered herself, with grave gentleness; "and I am sure that neither I nor any sister artist have any right to envy her her happiness. Would it seem presumption in a poor comedian to express her earnest wish that you, too, Signor Ludovico, may find your happiness in such a marriage?"

"Nay, don't speak in that tone!" said Ludovico, putting out his hand and taking hers, which she readily gave him. "I accept your good wishes, Signora, most thankfully. I do hope and think that I—that we shall find happiness in our mutual choice. But, pray observe, Signora, that our talk has led me into confiding a secret to you, that I have, as yet, told to no living soul, and that it is important to me it should be kept secret yet awhile longer. I know I may trust you; may I not?"

"Depend on it, Signor Marchese, your secret shall be quite safe with me. But are you sure it is a secret? And then, do you know," continued the Diva, resuming her air of pensive thought, "when I hear a man in your position speaking with such noble truthfulness, the converse of the thought that I angered you—very innocently, believe me—by expressing just now, comes into my head. And I ask myself, if women in such a position as the lady we speak of, are apt to take themselves to task with sufficient strictness, as to what they are giving in return for all that is offered to them."

"I don't quite understand your meaning, Signora," said Ludovico, who really did not perceive the drift of his companion's words.

"I mean that a woman, so circumstanced, ought to be very sure that she is giving her heart to the man who asks for it, and not to his position, not to the advantages, to the wealth he offers her. She ought to feel certain that, if all this—the advantages—the wealth were to vanish and fly away, her love would remain the same. Suppose now—it is out of the question, you tell me, but the case may be imagined all the same—suppose your uncle, the Marchese, were to marry, would the Venetian lady's love suffer no tittle of falling off?"

The red blood rushed to Ludovico's cheeks and brow, and then came an angry gleam into his eyes. It was not that he resented the liberty which his companion took in thus speaking to him. It was not, either, that he felt indignant at the doubt cast, even hypothetically, on the purity of his Paolina's love. It was rather the unreasoning animal anger against the person who had given him pain. It was a stab to his heart, this germ of a doubt thus placed there for the first time. He was conscious of the pang, and resented it. In the next minute the hot flush passed from his face, and he became very pale.

Bianca saw, and understood it all, as perfectly as if she could have seen into his heart and brain.

"The doubt, you put before me, is so horrible an one that I could almost wish it might be put to the test you speak of. But I have no such doubt. However much your questioning may be justified by other examples, it is not justified in the case of Paolina. I know her; I know her heart, and the perfect truthfulness that wells up from the depths of her honest eyes."

No amount of ready histrionism was sufficient to prevent a very meaning, though momentary, sneer from passing over the beautiful face of the singer as Ludovico spoke thus. But he was too much excited by his own thoughts and words to perceive it.

"I trust that you may be right, Signor Marchese. I have no doubt that you are right. Believe me that I have ventured to speak as I have spoken, solely from interest in the welfare of one who has been so uniformly good and kind to me as you have. Will you believe me, Signor Ludovico, that I would do a good deal and bear a good deal to be able to conduce to your happiness in any way?"

She put out her hand to him, as she spoke the last words, with her eyes dropped to the ground, and with a feeling of genuine shyness, that was quite surprising and puzzling to herself.

"Dear Signora, I will and do believe it with all my heart; and, in truth, I am deeply grateful to you for your good will," said Ludovico, really touched by the evident and genuine sincerity of her words.

"And now, I must ask you to leave me. I must dress myself and lose no time about it. The Marchese will be here in a minute or two. And I could not, you know, venture to receive him in the unceremonious manner which you have been good enough to excuse."

She gave him a little sidelong look with half a laugh in her eyes, as she said the latter words; and Ludovico, putting the tips of her fingers to his lips before relinquishing her hand, bowed, and left her without saying anything further.

CHAPTER VI

Paolina at Home

Ludovico had run up in a hurry to Bianca's lodging, as has been seen, merely because it happened to be in his way, and because he had been desirous, as he told her, of paying her his compliments on the success of the preceding evening. He was hastening to pay another visit, in which his heart was far more interested, and had not intended to remain with La Lalli above five minutes. The conversation between them had extended to a greater length; and the Marchesino, eager as he was to get to the dear little room in the Via di Sta. Eufemia, would have made it still longer, had not the Diva dismissed him.

The talk between them had become far more interesting than any which he had thought likely to pass between him and the famous singer. This horrible doubt—no, not a doubt—he had not, would not, could not doubt; but this germ of a doubt deposited in his mind by the words she had spoken? Could she have had any second motive for speaking as she had done? Surely not; surely all her manner and her words showed sufficiently clearly that she was actuated by kindly feelings towards him and by no unkindly feeling towards Paolina. Yet unquestionably Paolina's instinctive prejudice against her would not have been diminished by a knowledge of what the Diva had said. Ludovico thought of the bitter and burning indignation with which his darling would have heard the expression of the possibility of a doubt of the uncalculating purity and earnestness of her love.

Nevertheless he felt that he should have liked to talk further with Bianca on the subject; of course only to convince her of the absolute injustice of her suspicions. Still she was a woman, a fellow artist; placed in some respects in the same position in relation to the world to which he belonged, as his Paolina—in some respects similar; but oh, thank God, how different! Yet women understood each other in a way a man could never hope to understand them. What immediately struck Bianca, struck her naturally and instinctively in this matter of a marriage between him and the Venetian artist, was the idea that Paolina, almost as a matter of course, was at least biassed in her acceptance of his love by a consideration of the material advantages she would gain by it. It was the natural thing then, the thing a priori to be expected, that a girl in Paolina's position should be so influenced. Ludovico would fain have questioned and cross-questioned La Bianca, his experienced monitress, a little more on this point.

Yes, to be expected a priori. But when one knew Paolina; when one knew her as he knew her, was it not impossible? Could it be that Paolina, being such as he knew her in his inmost heart to be, should even adulterate her love with interested calculations? He knew it was not so; and yet—and yet other men had been as certain as he, and had been deceived. In short the germ of doubt had been planted in his mind. And Bianca well knew what she had been about when she planted it there.

Why had she done so? She spoke with perfect sincerity when she had told him that she would do much and suffer much for his happiness. And yet she had knowingly placed this thorn in his heart. Why could she not let him, as Quinto Lalli had expressed it, have his Venetian in peace? She spoke truly, moreover, when she said that, married to the Marchese Lamberto, she fully purposed to make him a good and true wife; truly, when she declared to old Lalli, and also to her own heart, that she really did like and admire him much. And yet there was something in the sight of the love of Ludovico and Paolina that was bitter, odious, intolerable to her.

Ludovico hastened to the house in the Via di Santa Eufemia on quitting that in the Via di Porta Sisi, not unhappy, not even uneasy; with no recognized doubt, but with a germ of doubt in his mind.

Signora Orsola had gone out per fare le spese, to make the marketings for the day; and he found Paolina alone. Such a tete-a-tete would have been altogether contrary to all rules in the more strictly regulated circles of Italian society. And it would have been all the more, and by no means the less contrary to rule in consequence of the position in which Ludovico and Paolina stood towards each other. But the world to which Paolina belonged lives under a different code in these matters. And ever since the day in which the memorable conversation between her and her lover, which has been recorded in a former chapter, had taken place, Paolina had never felt the smallest embarrassment or even shyness in her intercourse with him. And she received him now with openly expressed rejoicing, that the chance of Orsola's absence gave them the opportunity of being for a little while alone together.

"I called at this early hour, tesoro mio," said Ludovico, "mainly to tell you that I have made all the necessary arrangements at St. Apollinare in Classe, and you can begin your work there as soon as you like. What a dreary place it is. To think of my little Paolina working, working away all by herself in that dismal old barn of a church out there amid the swamps!"

"Oh, I shan't be a bit afraid. I am so accustomed to work all by myself."

"No, there is nothing to be afraid of! Do you think I should let you go there alone, if there were? You will find the scaffolding all ready for you."

"Thanks, dearest, I am so much obliged to you; I should never have been able to get my task done without your help. Ah, how strange things are! To think, that that Englishman, in sending me here, should have been—"

"Should have been sending me my destined wife. Who ever in the world did me so great a service as this Signor Vilobe, who never had a thought of me in his mind."

"And if I had chanced not to be in the gallery at the Belle Arti that day," rejoined Paolina, with a shudder at the thought of what the consequences of such an absence would have been.

"You will have the great church entirely to yourself, anima mia," said Ludovico; "there is not a soul near the place, save the old monk, who keeps the keys, and a lay-brother, who was ill, the poor old frate said, when I was there. It is a dreary place, my Paolina, and I am afraid you will find your task a weary one. I fear it will be cold too."

"Oh, I don't mind that much! What is more important, is to get the job done before the hot weather comes on. They say it is so unhealthy out there, when the heat comes. What is the old frate like?"

"He is a very old, old man, and he looks as if fever and ague every summer and autumn had pretty nearly made an end of him. He seemed quite inclined to be civil and obliging. If he were not, you could knock him down with a tap of your maulstick, I should think, though it be wielded by such a tiny, dainty little bit of a hand," said Ludovico, lifting it to his lips between both his as he spoke. "And now tell me," he continued; "what did you think of the third act last night? Did she not sing that finale superbly?"

"Superbly, certainly the finest singing I heard. But—"

"What is the 'but,' anima mia? I confess I thought it perfect."

"So I suppose it was. But I think that perhaps I should have had more pleasure in hearing a less magnificent singer, who was more simpatica to me. I can't help it, but I do not like her; and I am sure I can't tell why. I have no reason; but do you know, Ludovico mio, there was one moment when, strange as it may seem, our eyes met—hers and mine—in the theatre last night. It was just as she turned away from your box, when you had put the bouquet into her hand. She looked up, and our eyes met; and I can't tell you the strange feeling and impression that her look made upon me. And I am quite sure that, for some unaccountable reason or other, she does not like me. She looked at me—it was only half a moment with a sort of mocking triumph and hatred in her eyes, that quite made me shudder and turn cold.

"If it were not so entirely impossible, I should think you were jealous, my little Paolina. If I were to—what shall we say?—if I were to set out on a journey with la Diva, tete-a-tete, to travel from here to Rome, should you be jealous?"

"With La Bianca?"

"Yes! with La Bianca."

"I don't know. I don't think that I should in earnest. I know in my inmost heart, my own love, that you love me truly and entirely; I feel it, I am sure of it. But all the same, I should rather that you did not travel from here to Rome alone with La Lalli."

"That means that, to a certain degree, you are jealous, little one. Do you think I should be uneasy if you were called on to travel under the escort, for example, of our friend the Conte Leandro?"

"The Conte Leandro!" cried Paolina, laughing, "I am sure you ought to be uneasy at the bare thought of such a thing, for you know how terrible it would be to me. But is it quite the same thing, amico mio? La Lalli is indisputably a very beautiful woman; and the Conte Leandro is—the Conte Leandro. But it is not that she is beautiful. I don't know what it is. There is something about her—ecco, I should not the least mind now your travelling to the world's end, or being occupied in any other way, with the Contessa Violante."

"She is not a beautiful woman, certainly."

"She is, at all events, fifty times more pleasing-looking, as well as more attractive in every way, than the Conte Leandro. But that is not what makes the difference. I take it, the difference is, that one feels that the Contessa Violante is good, and that nobody would get anything but good from her. I have got quite to love her myself."

"And yet you see, Paolina mia, somehow or other it came to pass that I could not love her, when I was bid to do so; and, in the place of doing that, I went and loved somebody else instead. How is that to be accounted for, eh?"

"I am sure that is more than I can guess, Ludovico."

"One thing is clear—and a very good thing it is—that Violante has no more desire to marry me than I have to marry her. As soon as ever Carnival is over, my own darling, I mean to speak definitively to my uncle, and tell him, in the first place, that he must give up all notion of a marriage between Violante and me."

"As soon as Carnival is over. Why, that will be the day after to-morrow,"—said Paolina, flushing all over.

"Exactly so; the day after to-morrow. But I mean only to tell him, in the first instance, that I cannot make the marriage he would have me. Then, when that is settled—and some little time allowed for him to get over his mortification, il povero zio—will come the announcement of the marriage I can make. I have quite fixed with myself to do it the day after to-morrow. But—I don't know what to make of my uncle. He is not in the least like himself. I am afraid he must be ill. I fully expected that I should have to fight all through Carnival against constant exhortations to pay my court to the Contessa. But he has never spoken to me a word on the subject."

"Perhaps he has discovered that the lady likes the proposal no better than you do," suggested Paolina, with a wise look of child-like gravity up at her lover's face.

"No; it's not that. He never dreams of her having any will in the matter apart from that of her family. I can't make him out. There's something wrong with him. He looks a dozen years older than he did; and his habits are changed too."

"Do you think—that is—it has just come into my head—do you remember, Ludovico, what I said to you last night at the theatre about the way La Lalli sung her love verses at him?"

"La Lalli again. Why, she has fascinated you at all events. You can think of nothing else. La Lalli and lo zio. Dio mio! If you only knew him. All the prime donne in Europe might sing at him, or make eyes at him, or make love to him, in any manner they liked from morning till night without making any more impression on him than a hundred years, more or less, on the tomb of the Emperor Theodoric out there. No, anima mia, that's not it. No, il povero zio, I am more inclined to think that he is breaking up. It does happen, sometimes, that your men, who have never known a day's illness in their lives, break down all of a sudden in that way. Everybody in the city has been saying that he is changed and ill. But I must be off, my darling. I only came to tell you that all was in readiness for you at St. Apollinare. At least that was my excuse for coming. But now I must go and see about all sorts of things for the reception to-night. We shall have all the world at the Palazzo to-night. And lo zio asked me to see to everything. Addio, Paolina mia. You know where my heart will be all the time. Addio, anima mia."

CHAPTER VII

Two Interviews

After Ludovico had passed into the sitting-room in the Via di Porta Sisi to pay his visit to Bianca, Quinto Lalli prepared to leave the house in accordance with her suggestion that he should dispose of himself out-of-doors for the present. But before going he called Gigia the maid, and said, as he stood with the door in his hand:

"Gigia, cara mia, the Marchese Lamberto is coming here presently; just make use of your sharp ears to hear what passes between him and Bianca; and take heed to it, you understand, so as to be able to give an account of it afterwards if it should be needed. You need not say anything about it to la bambina till afterwards; I have no secrets from her, you know, and, as soon as the Marchese is gone, you may tell her that you have heard everything, and that I directed you to do so; but better to say nothing about it beforehand. Inteso?"

"Si, si, Signor Quinto! Lasci fare a me!"

And, with that, the careful old man went out for his walk, and it was not half-an-hour after Ludovico left the house before the Marchese made his appearance.

Bianca, now having completed her toilette, started from her sofa, and went forward to meet him with both hands extended, and with one of her sunniest smiles.

"This is kind of you, Signor Marchese. I hoped, ah! how I hoped, that you would come. If you had not, I don't know what would have become of me. My heart was already sinking with the dreadful fear that my little note might have displeased you. But, thank God, you are here: and that is enough."

"Of course, Bianca, I came when you begged me to do so," said the Marchese, looking at her with a sort of sad wistfulness, and retaining both her hands in his. He advanced his face to kiss her, and she stooped her head so as to permit him to press his lips to her forehead.

"Was it of course, amore mio?" she said, with a gushing look of exquisite happiness, and a little movement towards clasping his hand, which still held hers, to her heart. "Was it of course that you should come to your own, own Bianca when she begged it? But you are looking fagged, harassed, troubled, mio bene: have you had anything to vex you? Henceforward, you know, all that is trouble to you is trouble to me. I shall insist on sharing your sorrows as well as your joys, Lamberto. What is it that has annoyed you, amore mio?"

"I have much on my mind—necessarily, Bianca mia; many things that are not pleasant to think of. Can you not guess as much?"

"I have had but one thought, amico mio, since I heard from your lips the dear words that told me that henceforward we should be but one; that our lives, our hopes, our fears, would be the same; that, in the sight of God and man, you would be my husband, and I your wife. Since then, I have had but one thought, and it is one which would avail to gild all others, let them be what they might, with its brightness. Is the same thought as sweet a source of happiness to you, my promised husband?"

"That's clear enough, I hope," thought Gigia, outside the door, to herself. "Che! If nothing had been said the other day, that would be enough; and I think Quinto might trust nostra bambina to manage her own affairs. She knows what she is about, the dear child: not but that it is a good plan to be able to remind a gentleman in case he should forget. Gentlemen will forget such things sometimes."

"You cannot doubt my love," said the Marchese, in reply to her appeal.

Those five words may possibly, in the course of the world's history, have occurred before in the same combination. But the phrase served the occasion as well as if it had been entirely new and original.

"Indeed, I do not, Lamberto; nor will you again, I trust, ever doubt mine as you seemed to do last night. Ah, Lamberto! you do not know how bitterly I wept over the remembrance of those cruel words when I had parted from you. You will never, never say such again. Tell me you never will."

"Doubts and fears, my Bianca, are the inevitable companions of such a love as mine," said the Marchese, with a somewhat sickly smile; "but the few words you said last night sufficed to dissipate them, as I assured you."

"But there is still something troubling your mind, Lamberto. See, I already take the wifely privilege you have given me to wish to share all that annoys you. What is it? Come and sit by me here on the sofa, and tell me all about it."

And then the Marchese sat himself in the seat of danger that had been proposed to him, and, in a certain degree, explained to Bianca the difficulties attending a marriage with her. He tried hard to recommend to her favourable consideration the plan of a secret marriage—of a marriage to be kept secret, at all events, for awhile for the present; but such an arrangement, as may easily be understood, did not, in Bianca's view, meet the requirements of the case. That was not what she wanted. It may also be easily understood that the Marchese, occupying the position which the enemy had assigned to him, carried on the contest at an overpowering disadvantage, and was finally routed, utterly conquered, and yielded at discretion.

On her side the advantages of the situation were made the most of with the most consummate generalship. The limit between that which was permitted to him, and that which was denied to him, was drawn with a firmness and judgment admirably conducive to the attainment of the end in view. He was permitted to encircle the slender, yielding waist with one arm as he sat by her side on the sofa, and to retain possession of her hand with the other; but any advanced movement from this base of operations was firmly and unhesitatingly repressed. At one moment, when the attacking party seemed to be on the point of pressing his advances with more vigour than before, it chanced that the Diva coughed; and it so happened that, in the next instant, Gigia entered the room, bringing wood for the fire in her arms—a diversion which, of course, involved the execution of a hurried movement of retreat on the part of the enemy.

The whole of Bianca's tactics, indeed, were admirable. And the result was, as usual, victory. Once again, as long as he was in her presence and by her side, the unfortunate Marchese felt that the spell was irresistible—absolutely irresistible by any force of volition that he was able to oppose to it. Once again it seemed to him that the only thing in the world that it was utterly impossible to him to relinquish was the possession of Bianca. The hot fit of his fever was on him in all its intensity; and there was nothing that he could do, or suffer, or undergo that he would not rather do, or suffer, or undergo than admit the thought of giving her up. It really seemed as if there were some physical emanation from her person—some magnetic stream—some distillation from the nervous system of one organization mysteriously potent over the nervous system of another, which mounted to his brain, mastered the sources of his volition, and drew him helpless after her, as helplessly as the magnetized patient obeys the will of his magnetizer.

Suddenly both of them heard one o'clock strike from the neighbouring church. To the Marchese it was a knell which, with horrid warning-note, dragged him forcibly back from his Circean dalliance to the thoughts, the things, and the people whose incompatibility with the possibility of such dalliance was driving him mad. It was the hour at which he had promised to wait upon the Cardinal. It was absolutely necessary that he should go at once; and he tore himself away from that fatal sofa-seat with a wrench, and a reflection on the purpose of his visit to the Legate, which seemed to him really to threaten to disturb his reason.

Slinkingly he stole from the house in the Strada di Porta Sisi, and hurried to the Cardinal's palace. His mind seemed to reel, and a cold sweat broke out all over him as he rang the bell at the top of the great stone stair of the Legate's dwelling.

This business that he was now here for—those high honours which were about to be lavished upon him—would they not all make his position so much the worse? The higher he stood, would not his fall be the more terrible? What would be said or thought of him? At Rome, immediately after the high distinction shown him, what would they not say? Here, in Ravenna, how should he look his fellow-citizens in the face? Impossible, impossible. Could he venture even to accept the high distinction offered to him? Would there not be something dishonourable—a sort of treachery in suffering this mark of the Holy Father's special favour to be bestowed upon him, while he was meditating to do that which, if his intention were known, would make it quite impossible that any such honour should be conferred on him?

And how fair was life before him, as it would be if only this fatal woman had never crossed his path? And was it not even yet in his own power to make it equally fair again? Was it not sufficient for him to will that it should be so?

What if he never saw Bianca again? What could avail any nonsense she or her pretended father might talk of him? If they were to declare on the house-tops that he had promised marriage to La Lalli, what human being in all the city would believe them? The very notion that such a thing could be possible would be treated as the impudent invention of people who clearly had not the smallest knowledge of the man they were attempting to practise on. No, he had but to will it to be free. If only he could will it.

And with these thoughts passing through his mind he entered the receiving-room of the Legate.

It was impossible to be received more cordially than he was by that high dignitary. His Eminence felt sure that his old acquaintance and highly-valued good friend the Marchese was aware how great his (the Cardinal's) pleasure had been in discharging the duty that had devolved upon him. The letter he had that morning received from the Cardinal Secretary was a most flattering one. Perhaps he (the Cardinal) might take some credit to himself for having performed a friend's part, as was natural, in keeping them at Rome well acquainted with the singular merits of the Marchese. He would, indeed, have been neglecting his duty if he had done otherwise.

Then, after alluding lightly and gracefully to the special interest he could not but feel, in his private capacity, in any honour which tended yet more highly to distinguish a family with which he trusted his own might at no distant day be allied, he told the Marchese that it was probable that nothing would be done in the matter till after Easter.

It was the gracious wish of the Holy Father to enhance the honour bestowed by conferring it with his own apostolic hand; and, doubtless, as soon as Lent should be over, it would be intimated to the Marchese that the Holy Father was desirous of seeing him at Rome. When he came back thence his fellow-citizens would, in all probability, wish to mark, by some little festivity or otherwise, with which he, on the part of the government, should have great pleasure in associating himself, their sense of the honour done to their city in the person of its most distinguished citizen.

The Marchese, while the Cardinal Legate was making all these gracious communications, strove to look as "like the time" and the occasion as he could. At first it was very difficult to him to do so at all satisfactorily. The influence of that other interview, from which he had so recently come, was too strong upon him. All the images and ideas called up by the Cardinal's words were too violently at variance, and too incompatible with those other desires and thoughts to affect him otherwise than as raising additional obstacles and piling up more and more difficulties in the path before him. But, as the interview with the courteous and dignified churchman proceeded, as the genius loci of the Cardinal's library began to exert its influence—as all the hopes and ambitions and prospects which were opened before his eyes, falling into their natural and proper connection of continuity with all his former life, so linked the present moment with that past life as to make all that had filled the last few weeks seem like a fevered dream, gradually the Marchese entered more and more into the spirit of the Cardinal's conversation. Gradually all that he had hitherto lived for came to seem to him again to be all that was worth living for. Old habitual thoughts and ideas, the growth and outcome of a whole life, once again asserted their wonted supremacy; and the Marchese Lamberto marvelled that it should be possible for that to happen to him which had happened to him.

Ah! if only weak men were as prone to run away from temptation as they are to run away from the difficulties that are created by yielding to it. But they are ever as brave to run the risks of confronting the tempter, as cowardly to face the results of having done so.

The Cardinal had not failed to mark the air of constraint and dispirited lassitude which had characterized the Marchese during the commencement of their conversation. And he, as others had done, attributed it to the supposition that the Marchese was very rapidly growing old—likely enough, was breaking up. Nor did he less observe the very notable change in him as their interview proceeded—the result, as the churchman flattered himself, of the charms of his own eloquence and felicitous manner. He was himself a good twenty years older than the Marchese; but he had been put into great good humour that morning by private letters accompanying the official despatch that has been mentioned, which had hinted at favourable possibilities in the future as to certain ambitious hopes that had rarely failed to busy his brain every night as he laid it on the pillow for many a year. So he smiled inwardly a gentle moralizing smile as he thought how gratified ambition had power to stir up the flagging passions and stimulate the sinking energies even as the golden bowl is on the eve of being broken.

The Marchese, however, left the Cardinal's presence a much happier man for the nonce than he had entered it, his mental vision filled with pictures of ribbons, stars and crosses, with, perhaps, a statue—between the two ancient columns in the Piazza Maggiore would be an excellent site—in the background.

Ah! if only he could have had the courage to run away from temptation.

CHAPTER VIII

A Carnival Reception

On that Monday night all the world of Ravenna were assembled in the suite of state-rooms on the piano noble of the Palazzo di Castelmare. The cards of invitation had announced that masks would be welcomed by the noble host; and a large number of the younger portion of the society accordingly presented themselves in dominoes and the silk half-masks which are usually worn in conjunction with them. But very few of either ladies or gentlemen came in character. Such costumes were mostly reserved for the ball, which was to take place at the Circolo dei Nobili on the following evening. That was of course the wind-up of the Carnival; and besides it was felt, that a shade or two more of licence and of the ascendancy of the Lord of Misrule might fitly be permissible at the Circolo, than was quite de mise in the rooms of so grave and reverend a Signor as the Marchese Lamberto di Castelmare.

A few determined revellers would lose no opportunity of enjoying the delight of dressing themselves up in costumes, which they deemed specially adapted to show off to advantage either their physical perfections or their intellectual and social pretensions. Sometimes, as may have been observed by those who have witnessed such revelries, it unfortunately happens that both the above desirable results are not quite compatible. Our friend the Conte Leandro, for instance, having determined to appear at the Circolo ball in the character of Dante—which, for a poet at Ravenna, was a very proper and natural selection—presented himself at the Palazzo Castelmare in that of Apollo—an equally well-imagined presentation; had it not been that the happy intellectual analogy was less striking to the vulgar eye, than the remarkable exhibition of knock-knees and bow-legs resulting from the use of the "fleshings;" which constituted an indispensable portion of the god's attire.

He carried in one hand what had very much the appearance of a gilt gridiron; but was intended to represent a lyre; and in the other a paper, which was soon known to contain a poem of congratulation addressed to the host, on the announcement which, all the city well knew by this time, had been made to him that morning.

The rooms were thronged with black dominoes, and white dominoes, and pink, and scarlet, and blue, and parti-coloured dominoes. Violante was there in a black domino, and Bianca in a white one. There was very little dancing, but plenty of chattering and laughing. One main thing to be done by every person there was to congratulate the host on his new honours. Our Conte Apollo, among the rest, would fain have read his poem on the occasion. But as he approached the Marchese for the purpose, a white silk domino, that was standing by the Marchese's side, burst into such an uncontrollable fit of silvery and most musical, but too evidently uncomplimentary laughter, that the poor god of song was too abashed by it to make head against it.

"Surely never had Apollo such a representative before," said the Marchese to his companion, as the mortified god turned away.

"The voice, the face, the lyre, and the legs; oh, the legs!" said the silvery voice of the white domino in return.

The words of both speakers had been uttered sotto voce; but the Conte Leandro had unfortunately sharp ears; and not only heard what was said, but was at no loss to recognize the voice of the second speaker.

The poor poet was destined not to find the evening an agreeable one. A little later he was passing by an ottoman in one of the less crowded rooms, on which the Marchese Ludovico was sitting with the Contessa Violante. She had, at an early period of the evening, abandoned all pretence of keeping up her incognito, and was dangling her black mask from her finger by its string as she sat talking to Ludovico. Leandro turned towards them to pay his compliments to the Contessa, and possibly in the hope of being allowed to read his copy of verses. But here again mortification awaited him.

"What, Aesop, Leandro! What put it into your head to choose the old story-teller for a model? You look the part to perfection, it is true; but what is that thing you have got in your hand?"

Again his lordship was fain to retreat.

"What a shame to torment the poor man so, in your own house too, Signor Ludovico," said Violante, who, nevertheless, could not help laughing.

"Not a bit, he's used to it. He is too absurd for anything; an egregious vain ass," returned Ludovico; with very little precaution to prevent the object of his animadversions from hearing them. And again Leandro's acute ears did him the ill service of carrying every word that had been said to his understanding.

"Indeed I think her perfectly charming," said Violante, in continuation of the conversation, which had been interrupted by the bow-legged vision of Apollo; "extremely pretty of course, but a great deal more than that. She is fresh, ingenuous, modest, full of sensibility, and as honest-hearted as the day. You are a very fortunate man, Signor Ludovico, to have succeeded in winning such a heart."

"How came it about at first, that you spoke to her?" asked Ludovico.

"Oh, I went into the chapel in the morning, as I very often do, to recite the litany of the Virgin, and if she had remained on her scaffolding I should probably not have noticed her. But she ran down in the most obliging manner, fearing that she might disturb me, and offering to suspend her work, as long as I should remain at my devotions. It was so pretty of her, and so prettily said!"

"And then you answered her as prettily, I suppose, Signora?"

"Nay, it is not in my power to do that," said Violante, with a touch of bitterness; "but I told her, that she did not disturb me in the least; and I spoke to her of the work she was engaged on; and she asked me to come up and look at it; and so we talked on till we became very good friends."

"And then you were kind enough to converse with her on several subsequent occasions?"

"Oh, yes, we had several long talks; and I liked her so much. I am sure she is thoroughly good. I rejoice with all my heart that a destiny, so much more brilliant than anything that could have been expected for her, is likely to be hers."

"I wish, Signora Contessa, that it was more than likely to be hers; I wish that our path lay clearer before us!" said Ludovico, with a sigh.

"Including me in the 'us'? I wish it were with all my heart. But remember, Signor Marchese, how much is possible to a man, and how little to a woman. All, that the strong expression of my own wishes and feelings can do, shall be done when the proper time comes for the doing of it. But you must not trust to that, or to me. You ought to save me from being compelled to act at all in the matter. You are free to speak. And now that another besides me is so vitally concerned, I think you ought to do so without further delay."

"And I have fully made up my mind to do it, Signora Contessa. I have told Paolina, this very day, that I purpose speaking very seriously to my uncle on the subject on the day after to-morrow—the first day in Lent. I thought I would let this Carnival time pass by first without breaking in upon it, with business that cannot, I fear, be otherwise than painful. I have promised Paolina, and am fully determined to speak to my uncle on Wednesday."

"And what do you purpose saying to him?" asked Violante, looking into his face with quiet eyes.

"In the first instance I have no intention of speaking to him on the subject of Paolina—"

"No!" interrupted the Contessa, changing her look to one of surprise.

"Not to begin with, I think. To speak of my intention to make a marriage, which I cannot hope will meet his approbation, would only make my rejection of the alliance, which he hopes to see me form, the more difficult."

"Yes, that seems true; but I doubt whether you are right there. You will begin, then, by telling him—?"

"I shall begin by saying that it seems clear to me, that I have little hope of any success in the quarter in which he has wished me to—"

"Nay, that will not be quite fair, Signor Marchese," interrupted Violante, speaking very quietly. "Can you honestly tell your uncle that you have made any very strenuous efforts in that direction?"

"But I thought, Signorina," said Ludovico, hastily; I surely had reason to suppose that I should be speaking in support of your sentiments—quite as much as—"Stay, Signor Marchese; excuse my interrupting you, but it is exactly on this point that I wished to talk with you. Let us clearly understand each other. It is, no doubt, quite true that if you and I had been left to ourselves, if no family-considerations had intervened to suggest other views, neither of us would have been led by our own inclinations, it is best to speak openly and frankly, neither of us, I say, would have been led by our own inclinations to think more of the other than as an old and valued acquaintance. This is the truth, is it not?"

"Nay, Signorina, can I say—"

"It is not fair, you would say," interrupted Violante again, "that I should force your gallantry to make so painful an avowal. Nonsense! Let us put aside all such trash: the question is, not—how we shall mutually make what the circumstances require us to say to each other agreeable to the self-love of either of us, and to silly rules of conventional gallantry, but there is a real question of fairness between us; and it is this: how much should each of us expect that the other will contribute towards the difficult task of liberating both of us from engagements we neither of us wish to undertake. You see, Signor Marchese, I have made up my mind to speak clearly; more clearly than I could, I think, have ventured to do, had I not the advantage of having had those conversations with my friend Paolina in the Cardinal's chapel."

"In what respect did it seem to you, that what I proposed saying to my uncle in the first instance, was unfair, Signorina?"

"In this it would be unfair. To talk of your want of success in obtaining what you never sought to obtain, is simply to throw on me the burden and the blame of disappointing the wishes and plans of both our families. I am ready to do my part; but it would be unreasonable to expect that it can be so active or so large a part as your own. It will not be for you to let it be supposed that you are ready and willing to offer your hand to the Contessa Violante Marliani, trusting to my refusal to accept it in the teeth of the wishes of my family. It is your duty to say openly and plainly that you cannot make the marriage proposed to you. If I were in your place—if I might venture to suggest, what I would myself counsel—I should add, as a reason—an additional reason—that I had given my heart elsewhere."

"But, Signora, you forget that the marriage between us was proposed before I ever saw or heard of Paolina," said Ludovico, with a naivete that should certainly have satisfied his companion that he was no longer attempting to shape his discourse according to the rules of conventional gallantry.

Violante, despite her gravity, could not forbear smiling, as she said in reply:

"Not at all, Signor. I do not in the least forget that before Paolina ever came to Ravenna, you were no whit better disposed to second the wishes of our families."

"Nay, Signorina. I declare—"

"What, again! Do let us leave all such talk. Don't you see that we may frankly shake hands on it. Don't you see that any pain that your indifference might have occasioned is entirely salved by the consciousness that I have been as bad as you. We are equally rebels against the destiny arranged for us. Let us fight the battle together then. I think that you would act wisely in telling your uncle at once that it is impossible you should make any other woman your wife than her who has your entire heart and affection. I think that this course is due to Paolina also."

"I only wished to spare my uncle, as much as possible, in breaking to him what I know will give him pain."

"People, who will wish what they ought not to wish, must endure the pain that the frustration of such wishes entails. It is certainly your right to marry according to your own inclinations."

"Yes; and in truth, as far as real power goes, there is nothing to prevent my doing so. It is truly a desire to break to my uncle, as gently as I can, that which will certainly be a blow to him. He is not well, my uncle. He is deplorably changed since the beginning of this year. Look at him, as he passes us," he added, as he observed the Marchese Lamberto approaching the place where they were sitting, with the white satin domino on his arm.

"He is looking changed and ill, certainly," said Violante, when the Marchese had passed, apparently without noticing them; "he looks thin and worn, and yet feverish and excited. Who is the lady on his arm? She must be very tall."

Many of the assembled company had by this time, like the Contessa Violante, discarded their masks, finding the heat, which always results from the use of them, oppressive, and not perceiving that any further amusement was to be got by retaining them. But the white domino, leaning on the Marchese's arm, still retained hers. It is not likely that Bianca herself could have had any objection to its being seen by all Ravenna that she monopolized the attention of the Marchese during the entire evening. And it is therefore probable that she had retained her disguise in compliance with some hint given to that effect by the Marchese Lamberto.

"I take it it must be La Lalli, the prima donna. I know she is here to-night and in a white domino, though I have not yet spoken to her. I am afraid my uncle must be tired and bored with her. He always makes a point of showing those people attention; and besides he had so much to do with bringing her here. I dare say we shall hear her once or twice again in this house before she leaves Ravenna. My uncle is fond of getting up some good music in Lent, when he can."

"The Marchese Lamberto did not look to me as if he was tired or bored," said Violante, thoughtfully. "I hope he is not. Here comes that absurd animal Leandro again. Did you ever see anything so outrageously ridiculous?"

Ludovico and the Contessa then rose from their seats, and Violante taking his arm drew him in the direction in which the Marchese Lamberto had led the white satin domino.

CHAPTER IX

Paolina's Return to the City

There remained now but one day more of that Carnival, which remained memorable for many years afterwards in Ravenna, for the terrible catastrophe that marked its conclusion.

All that these people, whose passions, and hopes, and fears have been laid open to the reader, were doing during those Carnival weeks was gradually leading up, after the manner of human acts, to the terrible event which rounded off the action with such fatal completeness. And the catastrophe was now at hand.

During the reception at the Castelmare palace on that night of the last day of Carnival but one, the white domino, whom Ludovico had rightly supposed to be Bianca—a guess which had been shared by many other persons in the room—had pretty exclusively occupied the attention of the Marchese Lamberto. And it must be supposed that the resolution was then taken between them which led to the summons of Signor Fortini, the family lawyer, to the palazzo on the first day of Lent, as was related in the first book of this narrative. It was on the morning of Ash Wednesday, it will be remembered, that the lawyer had received from the Marchese the formal communication of his intention to marry the Signorina Bianca Lalli.

The reader knows, also, that what took place in the interval between the night of the reception at the Palazzo Castelmare and the morning of the first day in Lent was not calculated, as might have been supposed, to assist in bringing the mind of the Marchese to a final determination to that effect. The terrible degree to which his jealousy and anger had been excited on the night of the ball at the Circolo by Ludovico and Bianca will also not have been forgotten. The conduct which had awakened that jealousy was, in a great measure, if not entirely, innocent on the part of both the offenders, as the reader will also, no doubt, remember. The similarity of the costume adopted by the Marchesino and Bianca was entirely accidental. And this, trifling as the circumstance may seem, had contributed very materially to arouse the Marchese's wrath and jealous agony. Bianca, perhaps, under the circumstances, ought not to have danced as frequently as she did with the Marchesino. She at least knew that the Marchese Lamberto had already conceived the most torturing jealousy of his nephew. Ludovico, on his part, was of course utterly unconscious that he was giving his uncle the remotest cause for umbrage by his attentions to the successful Diva.

Then came the little tete-a-tete supper—tete-a-tete by accident rather than by design, as the reader may remember; and the officious and spiteful eavesdropping and tell-tale denunciation by the angry poet.

Nevertheless, and despite of all these circumstances and of the temper of mind in which he quitted the ball-room that night, it is certain that the Marchese did, on the morning of the following Ash Wednesday, send for his lawyer and announce to him formally his intention to make the Signorina Bianca Lalli his wife.

We have seen all the agonies of irresolution and indecision—all the alternating swayings of his mind, as passion or prudence predominated at the moment. He seemed utterly unable to bring himself, save fitfully, to the final adoption of either line of conduct. And yet, at the moment when his jealousy most furiously boiled over, he decided on taking the first overt step towards the accomplishment of the deed.

Was it possibly that he was urged irresistibly forwards by the fear that if he did not at once make the prize he so eagerly coveted irrevocably his own, the power to make it so might pass away from him? that, after all, his nephew might have found the goddess as irresistible as he had found her himself; and that she might prefer the younger to the older Marchese di Castelmare?

Whatever the reflections might have been that at last drove him to take the definitive step of applying to his lawyer, we know that they were not of a pleasant kind—that the state of the Marchese's mind was anything but a happy or peaceful one during the hours that preceded his sending the message to Signor Fortini.

The manner in which the lawyer received the communication made to him, and his determination, on further consideration, to make the Marchese Ludovico at once aware of the step contemplated by his uncle, will not have been forgotten. The reader will, it is hoped, remember also how, sallying forth after his early dinner for this purpose, Signor Fortini encountered the Marchese Ludovico in the street; how the latter communicated to the old lawyer the state of anxiety he was in about the Signorina Bianca Lalli, whom he had lost in the Pineta; and finally how the lawyer and the Marchese together had gone to the Porta Nuova, by which the road leading to St. Apollinare and to the Pineta quits the city, in order there to make inquiries, and the terrible reply to their inquiries that there met him.

What that reply was had not been immediately clear to the lawyer. For, as far as the circumstances of the previous events were then known to him, there were two persons, Bianca Lalli, the singer, and Paolina Foscarelli, the Venetian artist—two young girls missing, who were both known to have been out of the city in that direction that morning; two young girls of whom he knew little more than this, that they had apparently reason to feel a deadly jealousy of each other. Which of these two was the one whose dead body lay there under the city gateway before him, he had no immediate means of knowing. For Ludovico, who had raised the sheet that covered the features of the dead, and had, of course, become on the instant aware of the truth, had fallen into unconsciousness, without uttering a word beyond the one agonized outcry that, for the moment, had left little doubt on the mind of the lawyer that the victim at their feet was the girl Paolina.

But, of course, the means of setting at rest the doubt on the lawyer's mind were very soon at hand; at hand even before Ludovico recovered from his short fainting fit. For the same man among the Octroi officers, who had recognized La Lalli when she had passed with Ludovico in the morning, was now able to say that the woman who now lay dead in the gateway was in truth no other than the poor Diva.

Paolina, in fact, was by that time safe at home, and had been well scolded by Signora Orsola for having given her such a fright by playing the truant for so long.

Of course her old friend called upon her for an account of the hours which had elapsed during her prolonged absence. And Paolina, in reply to this demand, gave a very intelligible account of the time. But unfortunately, most unfortunately, as the sequel showed it to be, this account rested solely on her own statement. Of course old Orsola saw not the smallest reason for doubting any part of it. And the explanations which she gave of her movements, and of the motives which led to them, embodied in the following statement of what happened from the time when she left the church to the time when she re-entered the city, are the result of her subsequent declarations, when called upon to account for her occupation of those hours.

The aged Capucine friar had, as we know, watched her take the path that led to the farmhouse on the border of the wood. And having looked after her as long as she was in his sight, he sighed heavily, and, turning away, went back to his prayers in the church. But had he been able to watch her on her way a few minutes longer, he would, if the girl's own account of her movements were correct, have seen her change the direction of her walk.

About half-way between the eastern end of the church, by which the path the friar had indicated to Paolina passed, and the farmhouse on the border of the forest, another path, skirting what had once apparently been the cemetery attached to the church, turned off at right angles to the left, so as, after some distance, to rejoin the road on its way towards the city. And this path, according to her own account, Paolina took; thus abandoning her intention of reaching the forest at the spot where the farmhouse stood. Why had she thus changed her purpose?

Various thoughts and feelings, which had presented themselves to her in the space of the minute or two she had occupied in walking round to the eastern end of the church, had contributed to produce this change in her purpose.

Unquestionably the first feeling which arose in her mind, on seeing what she had seen from the window of the church, was one of jealousy. But she combated it vigorously; and if she did not succeed in altogether conquering it, that fiend being, by the nature of not to be vanquished so by one single effort, however valorous—at least put it to the rout for the present. She had known all along that Ludovico frequently saw La Bianca. She knew that he would meet her at the ball; and, doubtless, the object of their expedition this morning was, as the friar had suggested, to show the stranger the celebrated Pineta. Having thus, in some measure, tranquillized her heart, she began to think how lovely the forest must be on that fine spring morning; how much she, too, should like to see it; how good an opportunity the present was of doing so. Perhaps, too, there was some little anticipation of the slight punishment to be inflicted on her lover, when he should be told that she had visited the Pineta alone at the very time when he had been in her immediate vicinity engaged in showing it to another.

And with these thoughts in her head, she made her inquiries, and started on her way. But before she had walked many steps, other thoughts began to present themselves to her mind. How did she know how far they had gone from the farmhouse? Might they not still be in the immediate neighbourhood of it? Might she not, very probably, fall in with them? And would not that be exceedingly disagreeable? Would not have all the appearance of having followed them purposely from motives of jealousy? Would not her presence be unwelcome? Would there not be something of indelicacy even in thus following one who evidently preferred being with another?

These considerations sufficed to produce the change in her purpose, and in the direction towards which she turned her steps, that has been mentioned. So she returned by the path, which has been described, into the road, and proceeded along it on her return to the city. She did not trip along as briskly and alertly as she had done in coming thither; but walked slowly and pensively with her eyes on the ground. She was thus a good deal longer in returning than in going. And when she had reached the immediate neighbourhood of the city, she turned aside before entering the gate, into a sort of promenade under some trees near the city wall, and sat down on one of the stone benches there to think a little.

And presently; as she was busy thinking, she was startled into much displeasure against herself by discovering that two large utterly unauthorised tears were running down her cheeks.

What was the meaning of that? Surely she was not jealous still, after all the good reasons for not being so, that she had so conclusively pointed out to herself?

No, she was not jealous. She would not be jealous. But it would have been so nice in the Pineta. The sun was now high in the heavens. The birds were singing on every tree; and Ludovico was enjoying it with that woman, whom, when she had seen her at the theatre, she had found it so impossible to like or to tolerate. Yet she would not, could not, doubt that Ludovico loved herself, and her only.

She dried her tears, and determined that she would not let doubts of what she really did not doubt torment her. But still she sat on and on upon the bench in the shade musing on many things—on the Contessa Violante, on the steps Ludovico had said that he would take this very first day of Lent towards the open breaking off of all engagement with that lady, and on the amount of scandal and difficulty that would thence arise.

Then her fancy, despite all her endeavours and determinations to the contrary, would go back to paint pictures of the beauty of La Bianca, as she sat by the side of Ludovico in the little carriage. How lovely she had looked, and how happy, so evidently pleased with herself, with her companion, and with all about her. And Ludovico had seemed in such good spirits—so happy, so thoroughly contented. He did not want any one else to be with him. He was far enough from thinking of the fond and faithful heart that would have been made so happy—oh, so happy—if it had been given to her to sit there by his side.

She sat thinking of all these things till she was roused from her reverie by the city clocks striking noon. It was three good hours later than she had supposed it to be; and she jumped up from her seat, intending to hasten home to Signora Orsola Steno.

All this Paolina stated partly to Signora Orsola on her return home, and partly in reply to inquiries subsequently made of her by inquirers far less easily satisfied.

But chance—or, what for want of a better designation, we are in the habit of so calling—had decreed that Signora Orsola should not be delivered from her suspense so quickly.

On turning into the shady promenade under the city walls, a little before reaching the Porta Nuova, Paolina had strolled onwards, before sitting down on one of the benches that tempted her after her walk, till she fancied that it would be shorter for her to reach the Via di Santa Eufemia by another gate, which gave admission to the city at the other end of the promenade, instead of by turning back to the Porta Nuova. And thus, though she had in truth returned to the city, the men at that gate were quite right in their statement that she had not returned by the way they guarded.

The road, however, by which Paolina proposed to return to her home led her past the residence of the Cardinal, and, as she passed, it occurred to her that it would be well, and save another walk, to look in at the chapel and put together the things she had left in it on finishing her task there, so that they might be ready for a porter to bring away when she should send for them.

For this purpose she ascended the great staircase of the Cardinal's palace, and was at once admitted to pass on into the chapel, as a matter of course, by the servants, who had become quite used to her visits there; and, from this point forwards, the accuracy of her statements was easily proved by other testimony besides her own.

It would not have taken her long, as she had said to herself, to get her things together and make them ready for being fetched away. But in the chapel she found the Lady Violante on her knees on the fald-stool before the altar. It was the first day in Lent, and, accordingly, a period of extra devotion. The sins, the excesses, the frivolities, of the Carnival had to be atoned for by extra prayers and religious exercises; and if Violante had herself been guilty of no sins, excesses, or frivolities, during the festive season, yet there was abundant need of her prayers for those who had.

On hearing a light footfall behind her she looked round; and, on seeing Paolina, rose from her knees, and advanced a step to meet her.

"You are come to take away your things, cara mia. The scaffolding has already been removed. I suppose you are very glad that your task here is done; and it would be selfish, therefore, to say that I am sorry. How often it happens, Paolina, that we are tempted to wish what we ought not to wish."

"I don't think, Signorina, that I often wish what my conscience tells me I ought not to desire; and I should have thought that such a thing had never occurred to you. I wished very much to do something this morning, and I began to do it; but then I thought that I ought not to do it, and I did not."

"Then, my child, you are all the happier. It is a happy day for you."

Paolina sighed a great sigh, and dropped her eyes to the ground.

"Then I suppose the evil wish was not wholly conquered," said Violante, looking into her companion's eyes with a grave smile.

"It was this, Signora: I walked out very early this morning to St. Apollinare in Classe, where I am to make some copies of the Mosaics, which I hope to begin to-morrow. A scaffolding has been prepared for me; and I went to see that all was ready."

And then poor little Paolina was tempted to pour out all her heart and its troubles to her gravely kind and gentle friend. And Violante spoke such words of comfort as her conscience would allow her to speak in the matter. And the talk between the two girls ran on; and the minutes ran on, too. And poor old Orsola Steno, at the end of her stock of patience at last, had taken the step that has been narrated.

And thus it had come to pass that Paolina had played the truant, and that her protracted absence had led to Signor Fortini's momentary doubt as to the identity of the corpse he had seen brought into the city.

BOOK V

Who Did the Deed?

CHAPTER I

At the City Gate

Bianca Lalli lay dead at the city gate. Fresh from her triumphs, her successes, her schemes, her hopes, her frolic, at the full tide of her fame, and her matchless beauty, the poor Diva was—dead!

How she came by such sudden death there was nothing whatever in her appearance to tell—scarcely anything to tell that she was dead. In a quiet composed attitude stretched on her back, she lay in the light white dress she had put on for her excursion with Ludovico. With the exception of a broad blue ribbon round the waist, and another which bound her wealth of auburn hair, her entire dress was white. It was now scarcely whiter than her face. But there was on the features neither disorder nor sign of pain.

From a feeling of natural respect for death, and perhaps, also, for the extreme beauty of the young face in death, the bearers of the body had covered it with a coarse linen sheet, such as they had chanced to find to hand. But the duty of the officers of the gate would have required them to uncover the face, even if Ludovico in the first agony of his doubt had not already done so. There, amid the pitying throng of rough men, she lay beneath the sombre old gateway vault. The extraordinary abundance of her hair fell in great loose tresses, some making rich contrast with the white dress that covered her shoulders, and some of it thrown back behind over the door on which the body lay.

A terrible and deadly sickness came over Ludovico, and his face became almost as white as that of the corpse. His head swam round; and, reeling back from the sight that met his eyes, he swooned, and would have fallen to the ground had the lawyer not caught him.

"I suppose," said Fortini, to the men who crowded round the body, while he paid attention to the Marchesino, "I suppose that there can be no doubt that she is dead?"

"She's as dead as the door she lies on," said one of the men who had helped to carry the body, shaking his head gravely, as he looked pitifully down on her; "as dead as the door she lies on, more's the pity, for she looks like one of them that find it good to live, more's the pity, more's the pity."

"Che bella donna! E proprio un viso d'angiolo," said another; "and so young too. There's some heart somewhere that'll be sore for this."

"Pretty creature; it is enough to break one's own heart to look at her as she lies there," said a third. While a fourth of the rough fellows stood and sobbed aloud, and let the tears run down his furrowed cheeks, without the smallest effort to control or hide his emotion. For an Italian, especially an Italian man of the people, unlike the men of the Teuton races, is never ashamed of emotion. He very often manifests a great deal which he does not genuinely feel; but he never seeks to hide any that he does feel.

All this while the officials at the gate, some six or eight of them, standing thus round the extemporized bier, were closely questioning the men, who had been the bearers; Ludovico and the old lawyer were thus shut out from the circle which had formed itself around the body, and were on the outside of it. A boy, belonging to one of the gate officials, brought, at the lawyer's bidding, a glass of cold water, by the help of which the young Marchese was quickly restored to consciousness. He was able to rise to his feet again before the officers had concluded their official questioning of those who had brought in the body. And the lawyer looked anxiously into his face to ascertain that he was capable of understanding what was said to him, as he stood, still apparently half-stunned by the shock of the event, against the doorway of the little dwelling of the gatekeepers.

"Stand where you are and say nothing; we will go away together presently," whispered the lawyer in his ear, griping him hard at the same time by the arm, and giving him a little shake, as if to rouse him to comprehension; a mode of speaking and acting on the part of Signor Fortini, which would have seemed very extraordinary to the young Marchese at any other time, but which he was now too much overpowered by what had happened to notice.

Signor Fortini had no official character or function, which in any way gave him the right, or made it his duty to meddle with the circumstances, that had occurred by chance in his presence. But he was so well known to all the city, was mixed in one way or another with so many matters of business, and was so much and so generally looked up to, that the people at the gate, hardly knowing what their own duty required of them under circumstances so unusual, turned to him for directions as to what they ought to do.

"What you have to do, my good friend, is simple enough," said the lawyer, addressing the superior official at the gate; "you must, in the first place, receive and take charge of the body. You must inquire of these good folks all they have to tell you, together with their names and addresses. You must draw up a processo verbale, embodying all such information; and then you must have the body conveyed to the mortuary at the hospital, at the same time making your report to the police, and delivering up the body into their custody. In such a case as this, it will be well, too, that these worthy men, who have brought the body here, should go with you to the police, the more so," he added, as his quick eye marked a certain blank look in the faces of the men, "the more so, as they must be recompensed for their trouble and labour, and it is by the police that the payment for it must be made."

"Un processo verbale! Yes, one knows that; but under circumstances so strange—grazie a Dio so unheard of—if your worship would have the kindness to put one in the way of it. Your worship is familiar with affairs of all sorts. Just an instant."

"We must hear first what these men have to say. First take down their names and addresses."

The men gave them, as the lawyer remarked to himself, with perfect willingness and alacrity.

They then related that having been at work in the forest, cutting up the branches and trunk of a tree, which had fallen from old age and natural decay, they were going to another part of the Pineta, a short distance off, where another fallen tree awaited their axes and saws, when they saw a lady asleep as they thought on a bank. They were about to pass on without interfering with her in any way, when one of their party remarked that it was odd that all the noise they had made had not wakened her, for they had come along laughing, singing, and talking loudly. This had led them to approach closely to her; and then, as they looked at her, a suspicion of the truth began to come to their minds. They touched her, and found that she was dead. She was not quite cold, they said, and were quite sure of that fact. They looked at her, and looked all around to see if they could perceive any sign of the cause of her death. But they could see nothing. There was, as far as they could see, no trace of blood, either on her dress or anywhere around the spot where she lay. And then they had borrowed a door from the farm near St. Apollinare, and had brought the body here, and that was all they knew about it.

"Had they seen any other person in the forest that morning?"

"Not a soul; and they had been in that part of the Pineta, or at least at no great distance, all the morning from sunrise."

"Would they be able to find again and to know the spot on which they had found the body?" the lawyer asked.

"Oh, yes," they said, "easily. It was not by the side of any of the ordinary tracks through the forest—but not very far from one of them; as if the lady had turned aside from the path, and sought out a quiet spot to enjoy a siesta without being disturbed."

"It is pretty clear," said the lawyer, "that it has been a case of sudden death during sleep—probably from disease of the heart. Now, my friend," he said, turning to the senior of the officials, "you have only simply to state what we have heard in writing and carry it to the police. Meantime, it will be as well to remove the body at once. Let a couple of your people accompany the men who brought it here—they may as well carry it to the mortuary."

So a sheet was obtained from a neighbouring house, the more perfectly and decently to cover the body, preparatory to its being carried through the streets. Ludovico stepped hurriedly forward from the doorpost, against which he had been leaning, and looked eagerly once again at the calmly-tranquil and still beautiful face before they covered it with the sheet. And then the six men took up their burden, and, with two of the gate-officers marching at their head, moved off towards the hospital.

Then the lawyer put his hand on Ludovico's shoulder in a manner that was strange, and that would at once have seemed so to the Marchese had he at the time had any attention to give to such a circumstance, and said in a peremptory and authoritative sort of voice, very unlike his usual manner when speaking to a person in the social position of the Marchese,

"Now, come with me, Signor Marchese. Let us go. We can do no more good here." And he put his arm within that of Ludovico, as if to lead him away, as he spoke.

The Marchese suffered the old man thus to lead him from the gate without speaking a word.

"Now, Signor Marchese," said the lawyer, as soon as they had turned the corner of a street, which took them out of sight of the city gate, "now, lose no time. Make for the Porta Adriana, and quit the city by that. There is an osteria in the borgo outside the gate, where you can get a bagarino with a quick horse for Faenza; thence cross the mountains into Tuscany. You may easily be over the frontier this night; you have plenty of time, only none to lose. It will be at least two hours before any steps can be taken; you may be beyond Faenza by that time. Have you money about you? If not I can supply you. I have a considerable sum about me—One word more: Do not venture to remain in Florence. The grand Ducal Government would not refuse the demand of the Nuncio in such a case; and the demand would surely be made. Better get on to Leghorn; and make for Marseilles."

"Good God, Signor Fortini! What are you talking of; and what are you dreaming of? What is it that you have got into your head?" said Ludovico, rousing himself, and stopping short in his walk to turn round and face the lawyer.

"Look here, Signor Marchese, your father was my friend and patron; your grandfather was my father's friend and patron; and, therefore, bad as this business is, I think, and will think, more of old times and old kindnesses than of what I suppose is my duty now. But don't lose time by trying to throw dust in my eyes. What is the use of it? What I have got in my head is what every man, woman and child in Ravenna will have in their head before this day is over. Have you sufficient money about you?"

"Signor Fortini, once again I don't know what you are driving at. I insist upon your speaking out your entire meaning. What is it you imagine?" said Ludovico, speaking angrily, but now very pale.

"Imagine! What can I imagine? The matter is, unhappily, but too clear. Why of course I imagine that you have by some means, which the medical people will find out fast enough, doubt it not, killed that unfortunate woman in the Pineta."

"Signor Fortini!" exclaimed Ludovico, in a voice in which horror, indignation and dismay had equal shares.

"Marchese, how can anybody have any doubt on the matter. Alas, that I should have to say so, it is too self-evident. You persuade this poor creature to go out alone with you into the Pineta at an extraordinary hour of the morning, knowing then, or according to your own showing, becoming aware soon after you started—that it was your uncle's intention by a marriage with this woman to destroy utterly every prospect you have in the world. What other human being can have had any ill-will against this woman, or any interest in destroying her? Your interest in doing so is of the very strongest possible kind. It was no case of robbery. The girl was put to death by some one, who had an interest in doing so. She is last seen alive with you; I find you with a singularly scared and troubled manner pretending to make inquiry respecting her, your real object evidently being to ascertain whether the fact of the murder were yet known, and to give rise to the impression that you knew nothing of the poor woman's fate. Then, when confronted with the corpse you are seen to be absolutely overcome by your emotion. Now, as I have simply stated the facts, do you imagine that a moment's doubt will be felt as to who has done this deed?"

Ludovico felt the cold sweat break out on his forehead, as he listened to the lawyer's words. The logic of the facts did most unquestionably seem to make out a fatally strong case against him. And it was difficult to judge—very difficult even for the shrewd and practised lawyer to judge—whether the consciousness of crime, or the horror of seeing by how terribly strong evidence the suspicion of crime was brought home to him, were the cause of the emotion he manifested.

Signor Fortini, again, with rapid and practised acuteness, ran over all the circumstances in his mind; and his conclusion, unavoidable, as he felt it, was that the Marchese must have done the deed. That the criminal authorities would come to the same conclusion he could not feel the smallest doubt.

"Good God! Signor Fortini, this is very dreadful! it is as new to my mind—it comes upon me now for the first time, as much as if I had not known the fact of her death. But I see it—I see it all; as you put the matter now before me. What am I to do?—gracious heaven, what am I to do?"

"I have already told you, what you have to do; the only thing that you can do. You have time enough to make it quite safe, that you may be across the frontier before any pursuit can overtake you. As for pursuing you across the frontier, that can only be done diplomatically, and of course by means which would leave you ample time to quit Tuscany."

"Signor Fortini, I am innocent of this crime. It is a crime which sickens me with horror to think of. What passed in the Pineta passed exactly as I told you. I left that unhappy girl sleeping, intending to be absent from her but a few minutes. And as there is a God in heaven I never again saw her till I saw her dead at the gate," said Ludovico, speaking with intense earnestness.

"But even if you should convince me, Signor Marchese, that such were in truth the case, whom else do you think you would be able to convince? Not one, not a single soul; above all, certainly not one of those who are used to the investigation of crime, or of those who would have to pronounce judgment on it. If I were perfectly and entirely persuaded of your innocence I should still urge you to fly. The facts of the case are too strong against you."

"But is that the advice you would give to an innocent man, Signor Fortini? Is that the course which an innocent man would take? Should I not by flying add such an additional damning circumstance to the other grounds of suspicion, as to render all possible hope of clearing myself vain?" remonstrated Ludovico.

"It is true, it would do so; and the argument is, I am bound to say, the argument of an innocent man. In any other case, in any other case, I should say face inquiry and prove your innocence. But, Signor

Marchese, I dare not recommend you to do so. The facts, as I said, are too strong for you. Remember, too, that you do not throw away any chance by flight. For the only possible circumstance that could exonerate you would be the discovery that the deed was done by some other; and should that ever be proved or provable, you would at once return, plainly stating that you fled, not from guilt, but from a due appreciation of the fatal weight of suspicion that the circumstances and the facts cast on you. In such a case, in such a very improbable case, I should not hesitate to testify that, being by accident made aware of the circumstances, I had recommended and urged you to fly. No innocent man is bound to suffer for the misfortune of lying under a false suspicion if he can help it. You cannot face the suspicion that will rest upon you; instant flight is the only course open to you."

"Did you not say yourself at the gate just now, Signor Fortini," said Ludovico, making a strong effort to recover the use of his almost stunned faculties"—did you not yourself say that it was evidently a case of sudden death, probably from heart disease?"

"Pshaw! to the people there; to those blockheads at the gate, I said so, of course I did; but the medical folks will soon find out all about that."

"But again, as you remarked very truly, the only possible motive that I could be suspected of having for wishing the death of this unfortunate woman must be supposed to arise from my knowledge of the fact that my uncle had proposed marriage to her."

"And is not that motive enough, per Dio?" interrupted the lawyer.

"Doubtless it might, at all events, seem so to some people. But you spoke of my persuading her to go on this unhappy excursion with a view, as your words imply, of committing the crime you suspect me of. Now I knew nothing of any such intention on the part of my uncle till she communicated it to me when we were in the forest."

"That is your statement—"

"And you must remember, Signor Fortini, that I made that statement to you before I knew anything of her death."

"Before you knew anything of her death. Pshaw! You are assuming your innocence of the deed. Yes, I remember what you said. I remember only too well. Had you not spoken to me, there might have been no proof that you knew anything at all of your uncle's purpose. I wish to heaven you had not said a word to me on the subject. I shall have to testify that you declared to me, that your uncle's offer to her had been communicated to you by her. It will be impossible to avoid that. And it will be impossible to persuade the magistrate that you had not previous knowledge of such a purpose from other sources."

"But why should any such intended offer on the part of my uncle be ever heard of at all?" urged Ludovico. "He will most assuredly never be willing to speak of it, and—"

"Che! As if that old man, her so-called father, will not be open-mouthed as to that—as if he would not proclaim it to the whole city. Ah—h—h! it is a bad business, Signor Marchese, a bad business.

"And is it possible, Signor Fortini, that you do really in your own heart believe me to be guilty of this deed?" said Ludovico, with a sigh that was almost a groan, and looking steadily and wistfully into the eyes of his companion.

"What is more to the purpose, unfortunately, is that it does not signify a straw whether I believe it or not. You will not be judged, Signor Marchese, by my belief; and I am very sure what those who have to judge you will believe. I have some experience of these matters. I know the courts. I see the exceeding difficulty of believing anything else as to this death than that it was done by your hands; by you, who had the opportunity and the motive, whereas, it is impossible to suggest any semblance of such motive on the part of any other human being; by you, in whose company she was last seen alive. She had valuable ornaments about her person. If you had removed them it would, at least, have left it open to the magistrates to attribute the deed to another motive, and to other hands. I see all this. I see the whole case before me; and, I tell you, that your only chance is to escape while it is yet time."

"My solemn assertion, then, produces no effect on your mind, Signor Fortini?" said Ludovico, looking at him steadily.

"Signor Marchese," said the lawyer, with an impatient shake of the head, "let us look at the matter from the opposite point of view. If you had killed this woman, let us say, what would your conduct be? Would you not, in that case, make exactly the assertions that you now make? That is the terrible consideration that makes all assertion valueless in the case of such suspicion. But, once again, why dwell on my belief in the matter, which is nothing to the purpose? I have put your position, whether you are guilty or not guilty, clearly before your eyes. I counsel you, and strongly urge you, while yet unaccused, to escape from the accusation, which will be made against you within an hour. I am ready to assist you with the means of escaping—"

"Signor Fortini, I cannot avail myself of them. I have made up my mind I will not add another such damning ground of suspicion against me. Here I will remain to answer, as best I can, all the accusations that may be brought against me. I will not fly."

The old lawyer shook his head and sighed deeply.

"A bad business," he said, "a very bad business. It will kill the Marchese Lamberto; and I won't say what I would not have given to have escaped seeing your father's son, Signor Marchese, in the position in which you stand."

"Will you carry your kindness yet one step further, Signor Fortini, and, despite my rejection of your first advice, tell me what you think I had better first do now immediately, I mean—on the supposition that I am determined to remain in the city?"

"I think," said the lawyer, after a pause for consideration, "that the best course for you to take in the case would be to go at once to the magistrates and make your statement to them of the circumstances according to your own version of the story, stating that you hastened to do so on seeing the dead body at the city gate; I think that is the best thing you can do. Observe, I cannot say that I think it likely that, if you do so, you will pass this night under the roof of the Palazzo Castelmare; but, if you are determined to remain in the city, I think that is the best thing you can do."

"That, then, I will do," returned the Marchese. "I thank you, Signor Fortini, for the advice which I can follow, and not less for that which I cannot follow. Good-evening."

"Good-evening, Signor Marchese. I hope it may be better with you than I fear. And, of course, if you need me, as you will, you will summon me, and I will not fail to be with you within a few minutes of your call."

"Thanks, Signor Fortini. Addio."

"One word more, Signor Marchese, before you go. When you uncovered the face of the woman lying dead yonder you exclaimed, 'Paolina!' What was the thought that led you to do so? You could not have mistaken the identity? Of course, you know that I question you only in your own interest?"

"Did I say 'Paolina?' replied the Marchese, with an apparent effort at recollecting himself.

"You did. On seeing the face you exclaimed, 'Paolina mia!'—so much so, that I felt no doubt that it was this Paolina who lay dead there. What was it moved you to that exclamation?"

"I don't know. I can't tell. I was very anxious about Paolina. The thought of her was uppermost in my mind, I suppose."

"Humph!" said the lawyer, thoughtfully and doubtingly.

All this conversation had passed hurriedly in the small deserted street into which Ludovico and the lawyer had turned on leaving the city gate; and, when they parted, the two men took different directions, the lawyer returning to the gate with the germ of an idea in his mind, which the last portion of his conversation with the Marchese had generated there, and which subsequent circumstances tended to develop, and the Marchese Ludovico going in the direction of the Palazzo del Governo.

CHAPTER II

Suspicion

The Marchese Ludovico told the lawyer that he would go immediately to the magistrates and make a voluntary statement of all that he knew of the circumstances connected with Bianca's death; and he fully purposed doing so. But he did not do it immediately. There was another visit which he was more anxious to pay; and which the hint that had dropped from the old lawyer to the effect that it was very probable he might not pass that night in his own home, determined him to pay first at all hazards.

This visit, as may readily be imagined, was to Paolina. And to the modest little home in the Strada di Santa Eufemia he hurried as fast as his legs would carry him, as soon as he quitted Signor Fortini. Paolina, on returning home after her conversation with the Contessa Violante in the Cardinal's chapel, had remained there busy with the preparation of her materials for beginning her work at Saint Apollinare on the following day.

She looked up as he entered the room with an arch smile on her lips and in her eyes which, perhaps, did not reflect altogether faithfully the feeling in her heart.

"Yes, I saw you, you naughty, inconstant boy, when you little thought my eye was upon you. I saw you with—Ludovico, there is something wrong," she said, suddenly changing her laughing tone for one of alarm as her eye marked the expression of his face. "I am sure from the way you look at me there is something amiss. What is it, Ludovico mio? What has happened to vex you?"

"A great and terrible misfortune has happened, my Paolina; and I have run to you in all haste that you might not hear it from any lips but my own. You were going to say just now that you saw me with Bianca Lalli, were you not? Where and when did you see us?"

"In a bagarino, driving towards the Pineta. I was up at a high window in the church on the scaffolding prepared for my work," said Paolina, deadly pale, and breathless with apprehension.

"Ah! you saw us from the window. I took her there at her request to see the Pineta. We started on leaving the ball-room. In the forest she became sleepy: I left her sleeping on a bank, and meaning to return to her in a few minutes. I could not find the spot again for some time; and when I did find it she was gone. After searching the wood in vain for hours I returned to the city, and—at the gate—not an hour ago—I saw her brought in—dead!"

"Dead! La Bianca dead!" cried Paolina, much shocked; and with every vestige of the half-formed suspicions which had been tormenting her suddenly erased from her mind by the terrible tidings and the sadness of the end of the unfortunate Diva.

"Dead, my Paolina; and I am suspected of having murdered her," he said slowly, and with an accent of profound despair.

"What—what! You suspected! By whom? What does it mean? La Bianca murdered—and by you. What does it mean, Ludovico mio? For pity's sake, tell me, what does it mean?"

And the pale features began to work, and the large deep eyes filled with tears, and the neat moment she fell back into a chair sobbing hysterically.

"I was the last person with whom she was seen alive; and—there was, it seems, strong reason why it may be supposed that I should wish her dead—God help me! I learned this morning—the poor girl told me herself, to my extreme surprise—that my uncle, the Marchese Lamberto, had proposed marriage to her. You can understand, my darling, that such a marriage would be a very dreadful misfortune to me: therefore, people think that I put the unhappy girl to death."

"Oh, my love, my love; come to me, come to me, and let me hold you!" said the poor girl, struggling to speak amid her convulsive sobbing, and holding out her hands towards him. "Oh, my Ludovico, this is very dreadful. But it is impossible—impossible! They will know that it is impossible that you could have done such a thing. Murder! You—murder a defenceless girl! Oh, it is nonsense. Nobody will believe anything so monstrous."

"Thanks, my Paolina—thanks, my own darling. At least there is one heart that knows me. And, my Paolina, it is an immense comfort to me—not that I doubted it for an instant—but it is an infinite comfort to me to know that you, at least in your heart of hearts, are certain that I did not—that it never could have entered into my mind to do this thing."

"I believe it! I could just as soon imagine that I myself had done it. But, Ludovico, my beloved, it will not be believed; it is too monstrous. You are known here; it cannot be believed."

"And yet, my Paolina, one who has known me all my life, who was my father's friend—one who knows me well, and who looks at things as the magistrates will look at them—he believes it; believes it so much, and is so certain that others will believe it, that he strongly urged me to escape from the city, and from the country. That, Paolina, knowing my innocence, I would not do. To save myself from the stake I would not have gone away without telling you, my own one, that I had not done this deed. I could not go, and so leave you—"

"My own—my own! How I love you, my Ludovico, now in the time of this great trouble better than ever I did before. There was no need to tell me, my love, that your hands are innocent of murder. But surely—surely you did well not to fly, leaving the hideous accusation behind you."

"So I thought, my own love—my own high-minded right-thinking darling—so I thought; and here I stay to answer my accusers. But the fatality of the circumstances is such that—in truth, I see little hope of clearing myself, save by the possible discovery of the causes that led to this terrible death."

"Was there anything to show how she—that is, I mean, whether she—died by violence?" asked Paolina.

"Nothing—nothing whatever. As we saw the body under the city gateway, when the men who found it brought it in, there was not the smallest trace of violence visible. She lay as if, save for the deadly pallor of her face, she might have been still sleeping. And I am most anxious for the medical examination of the body. It may be that they will be able to discover that death was produced by some natural cause."

"Surely that is the most likely. Had any robbery been committed?" asked Paolina thoughtfully.

"None—none whatever; and she had valuables exposed on her person which were untouched. This is one of the worst circumstances against me; as it excludes the idea of the dead having been done by common malefactors for the sake of plunder."

"And no marks of violence? It must have been a natural death; such things do happen. I remember hearing of a case-"

"I must go, darling; I must leave you. I must hasten to the Palazzo del Governo to make my statement of what has occurred. It is hard to leave you, my Paolina—very hard to leave you, not knowing when or under what circumstances I am likely to see you again."

"Ludovico, see me again!" shrieked the girl, as a new and dreadful idea presented itself for the first time to her mind; "why—you will come to me when you have spoken to the magistrates; you will tell me what they say."

"I fear me, Paolina, that it will not be in my power to do that," returned Ludovico, with a melancholy smile. "Should they leave me at liberty, of course I shall fly to you on the instant they dismiss me. But, you must not expect that, my love. I shall be detained doubtless, until—until the truth has been discovered respecting this horrible tragedy. One kiss my own, own darling before we part."

She sprang into his opened arms with a bound; almost before the words had quitted his lips, and clasped him to her heart with all the strength she could exert. Then drawing herself a little back, and placing her two little hands on the front of his shoulders; she said, speaking with breathless hurry, "See now, my love, my only love. You must remember all the time, that there is no hour of the day or night that I shall not be thinking of you, and loving you all the time, always, always. And remember, that if all the whole world says that you did this thing, I shall still know that it was as impossible as that I did it myself. Remember that always, my best beloved."

"Thanks, my Paolina; it will be very sweet to me to remember it. And dearest, one thing more. It will hardly be likely that in the present circumstances, under all this weight of misfortune, my poor uncle will be likely to have time or attention to give to you, But if you have need of anything—of advice, of assistance, of protection—speak to the Contessa Violante, and—stay, you shall take a message to her from me. Tell her that I begged you to say, as from me to her, that in the teeth of all appearances I am innocent in thought, word, and deed in this matter. I think she will believe it; I must go, my love, my own!"

"Pray God, it be not for long, tesoro mio. I shall pray to the Holy Virgin for you morning and night."

"Addio, Paolina mia. Yet one kiss, anima mia, addio,"

From the Strada di Santa Eufemia Ludovico hurried as quickly as he could to the Palazzo del Governo; but found that he was not in time to be the first bearer to the police magistrate of the tidings of what had happened. The report of the officials at the gate had already been given in, and the police had already taken possession of the body.

The magistrate received him with grave courtesy, saying that he was glad the Signor Marchese had presented himself in order to throw what light he could on this sad affair, as rumour had already reached his (the magistrate's) ears mixing the name of the Marchese Ludovico with the subject in a manner that would have made it his duty to call the Marchese, had he not of himself judged it right to anticipate the action of justice in the matter.

Then Ludovico related clearly and shortly how the excursion to the Pineta had been imagined and planned between him and Bianca at the ball; how they had put their plan into execution; how he had left her sleeping in the forest; and had been unable to find her again; how he had returned, after spending much time in fruitless seeking, and had shortly afterwards, being then in the company of Signor Giovacchino Fortini, seen the dead body of the unfortunate lady brought into the city by men who had discovered it in the forest.

The magistrate listened attentively to this history in silence, save that he once or twice interrupted Ludovico to ask at what o'clock it had been that the different incidents happened. Then he reduced the whole statement to writing, and read it over to the Marchesino.

"Your lordship parted then from Signor Fortini, after witnessing in his company the arrival of the corpse at the gate, nearly an hour ago. You did not come to make your report to us here at once? I must ask you how you have employed the interval?" said the magistrate shooting a sharp glance from under his black eyebrows at Ludovico, who was sitting opposite to him, with a little table between them, on which there were writing-materials.

"In visiting a lady, to whom I was very anxious to tell these unfortunate circumstances myself, instead of allowing them to come to her ears in any other manner," answered Ludovico simply.

"The lady's name? I ask in confidence, you know; unless of course the fact should turn out to have any bearing on the discovery of the truth as to this most unhappy business."

"The lady is the Signorina Paolina Foscarelli, a Venetian artist sent here to make copies of some of our mosaics, and recommended to my uncle the Marchese Lamberto."

"With whom you had no acquaintance previous to her bringing that recommendation?"

"None whatever."

"But since that time you have become intimate with her?"

"It is true."

"Signor Marchese, this is a most lamentable and unhappy affair. It is my duty to point out to you, what doubtless your own good sense has already suggested to you—that the mere facts, as you have related them to me, place you in a very unfortunate position. But most unhappily—it is exceedingly painful to me to have to say it—there is, if what has already reached my ears be true, worse, much worse behind. I am obliged to ask you what conversation, of a special nature, passed between you and Bianca Lalli during your excursion?"

"I will make no pretence at not understanding your question, Signor, nor any attempt to conceal the truth. I have already stated the facts; or that, which you have evidently heard, could not have reached your ears. The Signorina Bianca Lalli confided to me the fact, that my uncle the Marchese Lamberto had offered marriage to her."

"Most lamentable, and to be regretted in every way," said the magistrate, gravely shaking his head. "You perceive, Signor Marchese, the terrible, but inevitable suggestion, that arises from the fact of your having been made aware of a purpose so disastrous to your interests?"

"I call your attention, Signor, again to the fact, that nothing would have been known of any such communication having been made to me, had I not spontaneously mentioned the circumstance myself."

"It is true, Signor Marchese, and it will not be forgotten that this circumstance was spontaneously mentioned by you. But you must observe, that the fact of the proposal made by the Marchese Lamberto would have become known in more ways than one. And unhappily the fact that such a proposal had been made, would throw a very disagreeable light on the extraordinary circumstances of this death. To whom would the death of this unfortunate woman be profitable? That is the fatal question, Signor Marchese, which it is impossible to avoid asking."

"I am aware of the cruelty of the inference suggested by the circumstance, Signor Commissario," said Ludovico sadly.

"Have you any suggestion to offer yourself as to the possible means by which this woman may have met with her death?" asked the Commissary of Police.

"As far as I could see at the city gate, and according to the statement of the men who found the body, there was no indication of violence whatever to be found on it. My suggestion therefore, and my trust is, that the cause of her death was a natural one:"

"That will be a question for the medical authorities to decide," said the Commissary.

"I was about to ask you whether they had proceeded to any examination yet?" said Ludovico.

"Not yet; we shall have the report immediately; and it shall be at once communicated to you."

"At the Palazzo Castelmare?" said Ludovico, though he had but very little hope that he should be allowed to remain at large.

The Commissary shook his head very gravely.

"I need hardly tell you, Signor Marchese, how painful it is to me to be compelled to announce to you that we cannot find it consistent with our duty to allow you under the circumstances to quit this building. The utmost that can be done to make your detention as little uncomfortable to you as possible, shall be done. And I can only say that I trust it may be but for a short time."

"Permit me to observe, Signor Commissario, that after seeing the dead body at the gate, to say nothing of all the hours previously, if I had been guilty, I had abundance of time to escape, and to place myself beyond the reach of the Papal authorities, before I could have been overtaken. I might have done so, but did not. Might not that be held to justify you in allowing me to retain my liberty until the course of your inquiries may again require my presence?"

"I fear not, Signor Marchese, I fear not. The fact that such a crime has been committed throws a terrible responsibility upon us. As to your not having availed yourself of opportunity to escape, I may remark that you may have been detained, not so much by your desire of meeting inquiry, as of having the interview, of which you told me just now. You say that you came directly from the Signorina Foscarelli's dwelling hither. At that time it was too late for hope of escape. I fear, Signor Marchese, it will not be consistent with my duty to allow you to depart."

So Ludovico was conducted to a very sufficiently comfortable chamber reserved for similar occasions, and found himself a prisoner, waiting trial on suspicion of murder.

CHAPTER III

Guilty or Not Guilty?

Signor Fortini hurried home, when he quitted the Marchese Ludovico in the little quiet street, in which they had talked together after the terrible sight they had together witnessed at the city gate, and shut himself up in his private room to think. He was much moved and distressed, more moved than the practised calm of the manner natural to him, and the slow movements of old age, allowed to be visible.

What a dreadful, what a miserable misfortune was this. A tragedy, if ever there was one, which would for ever strike down from their place an ancient and noble family, whose merit and worth had from generation to generation been the pride and the admiration of the entire city—a tragedy which would come home as such to the heart of every human being in Ravenna. Great heaven, what a fall!

And this was the first outcome of the disastrous purpose of his old friend the Marchese. Truly he had felt that nought but evil—evils manifold and wide-spreading—could arise from so insane a line of conduct. But he had been far from anticipating so overwhelming a calamity as the first result of it.

Then, the deed itself! It would cause an outcry from one end of Italy to the other. It would be a disgrace, and an opprobrium to the city for many a year. What! Ravenna invites, entices this hapless girl, who had been the admiration of so many cities, to come within her walls; and in return for the delight which she had given them—murders her. Other cities vie with each other in doing honour to the gifted artist. She ventures to Ravenna, and—is murdered.

There was a bitterness in Signor Fortini's consideration of the matter from this point of view, which was more poignant than any other man than an Italian would quite understand. For nowhere else do municipal pride, jealousy, and patriotism run so high.

A foul and cruel murder had been done: so much was certain. Signor Fortini had not the smallest hope that the death would be found to have resulted from natural causes. And then came the consideration whether there could be any hope that, after all, the deed had been done by some other hand than that of the young Marchese di Castelmare.

After thinking deeply for several minutes, the lawyer shook his head. That such a deed might have been done in the forest on the person of one found sleeping there, whose appearance was such as to hold out the expectation of booty to a plunderer, was possible—not very likely, but possible. Possible enough to suppose that lawless and evil-disposed persons might have been wandering there-depredators on the forest, who exist in great numbers—smugglers making their way across the country by hidden paths, or what not? Possible enough that such a deed might have been done, and the perpetrators of it far away before the discovery of the body, away to the southward, and across the Apennine into Tuscany in the space of a few hours. But all such possibilities were conclusively negatived by the certain fact that no plunder had been attempted, that plunder could not have been the object of the murderer.

Alarmed before they could carry their object into execution by the approach of footsteps? Was this a plausible or a possible theory?

No; for the poor Diva had valuable ornaments visible on her person, an enamelled gold watch at her girdle, a diamond pin or brooch at the fastening of her dress on her chest, to possess themselves of which would have needed less time than was required for the perpetration of the murder. It was wholly impossible to suppose, on any hypothesis, that the murder could have been committed for the sake of plunder, and that these ornaments could have been left untouched.

It had been observed, and was noted—not in the report drawn up by the officials at the gate, but in the more exact and detailed report furnished by the police on their taking of the body into their charge—that the brooch, which has been mentioned, was unfastened, so as to be left hanging in the dress by its pin. But this circumstance did not seem to be of much moment, as it might well have been that Bianca herself had unfastened it before falling asleep.

No, it was but too clear, as the lawyer said to himself, that murder and not robbery had been the object of the perpetrator of the crime.

There was, it was true, nothing improbable in the story told by the Marchese Ludovico. That the girl should have been overpowered by sleep, after having passed the night at the ball, and then started on an expedition so foreign to her usual habits, was abundantly likely. That he might have become tired of sitting still while she slept, and might have strayed away from her, not intending to quit her for more than a few minutes and a few yards, was also perfectly probable. That having so strayed he might have been unable to find his way back again to the spot where he had left her, or to be certain whether he had found the same spot or not, would not seem at all unlikely to any one acquainted with the Pineta. All this story was likely and natural enough.

But—the motive—the inevitable inference from that terrible cui bono question. For whom was it profitable, that this poor girl should be put to death? According to the fatal information, which, by his own account, he had received but a short time previously from the victim herself, information, the truth and accuracy of which were well known to the lawyer from the Marchese Lamberto himself, the whole future prospects in life of the Marchese Ludovico depended on the life or death of this unhappy woman.

If the Marchese Lamberto carried out his insane intention of marrying La Bianca Lalli his nephew would become simply destitute. After having been accustomed, from the cradle to the age of four-and-twenty, to all that riches could procure—after having lived in the sure expectation of wealth up to an age when it was too late to think of making himself capable of earning a competence for himself in any conceivable manner, this marriage would take from him suddenly, and for ever, all such prospect; and the death of the woman who had bewitched his uncle thus fatally would make all safe, for the Marchese Lamberto was not a marrying man—was, as all the town knew, the last man in the world to have dreamed of taking a wife now at this time of his life.

No; it was the fatal fascination, the witchery, the lures of this one woman. Remove her, and all would be right.

Ah! The mischief, the woe, the scandal, the disgrace, the irretrievable calamity, and the misery, that this accursed folly of the Marchese Lamberto had caused. Ah! to think of all the sorrow and trouble this woman brought with her into the city when she was so triumphantly welcomed within the walls by these two unhappy men—the uncle and the nephew.

It was strongly and curiously characteristic of the Italian mind that Signor Fortini, in coming to the conclusion that this deed must, beyond the possibility of doubt, have been committed by the Marchese Ludovico and none other, was mainly and specially moved by compassion for the perpetrator of the crime. There is something in this Italian mode of viewing human events and human conduct curiously analogous to that conception of mortal destinies on which the pathos of the old Greek tragedy mainly rests.

How cruel was the fate which had thus compelled the young man to perceive that the life of this girl and his own welfare were incompatible!

How dreadful the pitiless working of the great, blind, automatic, destiny-machine!

To raise a murderous hand against the life of a sleeping girl—how dreadful! How great, therefore, must have been the suffering which impelled a man to do so!

He had evidently been driven to desperation by the prospect of the utter and tremendous ruin that threatened him; and "desperation;" the absence of all hope, is recognised, both by the popular mind of Italy and by its theoretic theology, as a sufficient cause for any course of action. It is especially taught by Roman Catholic theology that it is, above all things, wicked so to act towards a man as to drive him to desperation; and the popular ethics invariably visit with deeper reprobation any cause of conduct which had tempted another man to make himself guilty of a violent crime than it does the criminal himself.

Thus, lawyer and law-abiding man as he was, with all the habits of a long life between him and the possibility of his raising his own band against the life of any man, Signor Fortini, as he mused on the tragedy which had fallen out, felt more of compassion for the Marchese Ludovico, and more of anger against the folly of his uncle.

This thing, too, which the Marchese Lamberto had announced his intention of doing, sinned against all those virtues which, let the professions of the moral code say what they may, stand really highest in an Italian estimation. It was eminently unwise; it was imprudent; it was indecorous; it was calculated to produce scandal; it would bring disgrace upon a noble name; it was ridiculous; and, besides all this, it necessarily drove another to "desperation."

"A fool! An insane idiot! Worst of all fools—an old fool! To think that a man, who had stood so many years in the eyes of all men as he had stood, should come to such a downfall. It would serve him no more than right, if it were possible, that all the consequences of what had been done should fall on his own head."

Still, during all the musings which seemed to force him to the conclusion that the crime which had been committed was the deed of the Marchese Ludovico, the old lawyer did not lose sight of the idea which had been suggested to his mind by that exclamation of Ludovico on the first sight of the murdered woman. He did not, in truth, as yet think that it was worth much; but he kept it safe at the bottom of his mind, ready for being produced if subsequent circumstances should seem to give any value to it.

After musing an hour while these thoughts passed through his mind, the old lawyer thought he would go as far as the Palazzo del Governo to learn what steps had been taken, and whether—though he had very little doubt on that point—his unfortunate young friend had been detained in custody.

Signor Pietro Logarini, the head of the police, was an old acquaintance of Signor Fortini, as, indeed was pretty well everybody in any sort of position of authority in the city.

"A bad business this, Signor Pietro," said Fortini, shaking his head.

"The worst business, Signor Giovacchino, that has happened in Ravenna as long as I can remember. It is very terrible."

"Is the poor young fellow—?" Signor Fortini completed his question by a movement of his eyes, of one shoulder, and one thumb, quite as intelligible to the person he addressed as any words would have been.

"Yes, of course. There was no help for it, you know."

"Of course not. I suppose he came here as soon as he parted from me. It so happened that we were together at the gate when the body was brought there," said Signor Fortini.

"So I understand. You will be called on for your evidence as to his manner on being confronted with it."

"Of course; fortunately I have nothing to say on that point that can do any damage. He was much moved, naturally; we both were; but nothing more than any man in his place would have been."

"But the worst, the only fatal point in that confession of his, is that the girl told him of the Marchese Lamberto's intention of marrying her. Why in heaven's name did he let that slip out?"

"My notion is that it just did slip out, as you say. An old hand, a man accustomed to be at odds with the laws and the police, would have known better. Did he make the same statement here?" asked Fortini, rather surprised.

"On my asking him, as I felt compelled to do, what special conversation had passed between him and the girl that morning, he told me the fact," replied the Commissary.

"But what led you to ask him such a question?" said Fortini.

"Ah!—something that had reached my ears. We are forced, you know, Signor Giovacchino, to have very long ears in our business. His conversation with you to-day was held in the street, a bad place for such talk, Signor Giovacchino."

"And not chosen by me for such a purpose, as you may imagine. Little could I guess what sort of confidence I was about to hear."

"Not that it makes any difference. All that would have had to come out, you know, Signor Giovacchino."

"Oh, quite so, quite so; no, no difference in the world. Did he come to you immediately on leaving me?"

"No; it would have been better upon the whole if he had done so. He went first, it seems, to the residence of a lady, one Signorina Paolina Foscarelli, being very desirous, he said, of not leaving her to hear of the business from other lips than his own. It is a pity, because his abstaining from flight might have been something in his favour, if he had not made it appear, that his remaining in the city might have been caused by his desire to see again this Paolina. Do you know anything about her? I see by our books that she came here last autumn from Venice. What is she like?"

"It so happens that I never saw her. But I am told that she is pretty—very pretty—remarkably so."
"Ah—h—h! that's what kept the poor young fellow from running till it was too late to run. And yet," continued the Commissary, pausing on his words, and tapping his forehead with his finger as if a new idea had just occurred to him—"and yet the young Don Juan goes out tete-a-tete into the forest with this other girl."

"Che volete?" returned the lawyer with a shrug. "Boys will be boys, and women—are women."

"Yes; but the women sometimes don't quite like—" and the Commissary allowed the remainder of his sentence to remain unspoken, being apparently too much occupied with his thoughts to speak it.

"I suppose the medical report can hardly have been made yet?" asked the lawyer, on whom the suppressed meaning of the Police Commissary's broken sentence was not lost.

"No; there has not been time. It was too late in the afternoon. Professor Tomosarchi will make a post-mortem examination the first thing to-morrow morning; and I daresay we shall have his report in the course of the day, if, as is most likely, there is nothing to call for more than a superficial examination."

"I shall be very anxious to hear the result of his investigation—very. I will look in, if you will allow me, to-morrow morning. And now I think I will go to that unfortunate man, the Marchese Lamberto. I should not be at all surprised if I were to find that he had heard nothing about all this. Only think what it is I shall have to tell him—the woman about whom he has been so mad as to have determined on sacrificing to her everything, fame, position, friends, respect, everything—is dead! It is his monstrous proposal that has caused her death; and the same folly has made the representative of his house a murderer and a felon. Think, Signor Pietro, what that man's feelings must be when these tidings are told him."

"Depend upon it, the whole city knows all about it by this time," said the Commissary.

"But I think it exceedingly likely that he has not been out of his library, all day," returned the lawyer.

"But the servants will have heard the news. Ill news travels fast," said the Commissary, with a shrug.

"Yes; but the servants will hardly have ventured to repeat such tidings to him. Two to one it will fall to my lot to tell him. A pleasant office, isn't it, Signor Pietro?"

"Not one I should like to undertake. Good-evening, Signor Giovacchino. If I don't see you to-morrow morning I will send you a couple of lines with the result of the medical examination."

"Thanks, Signor Pietro; but I will look in about the beginning of your office hours to-morrow morning. I feel as if I should be able to think of nothing else but this terrible business for some time to come. Felice sera."

And so the old lawyer went off to call upon his client, the Marchese Lamberto, truly dreading the interview, and yet not without a certain degree of satisfaction, and a kind of I-told-you-so feeling in the prospect of announcing to the unhappy Marchese those terrible first-fruits of the disastrous purpose, in condemnation of which the lawyer had spoken so strongly a few hours ago.

CHAPTER IV

The Marchese Hears the Ill News

Signor Fortini judged rightly, when he said that he thought it probable that the Marchese Lamberto had not quitted his library, from the time when he had left him there, after the conversation, in which the Marchese had avowed his purpose with regard to La Bianca.

The shrewd lawyer had well understood, that the final decision with regard to such a purpose, and the definite announcement of it, which the Marchese had made to him, his lawyer, were not likely to dispose such a man to meet the eyes of his fellow-citizens. Had Fortini known that the Marchese had been made aware of the purposed excursion of his nephew with the singer—as the reader knows that he had been by the officious meddling of the Conte Leandro, it might have seemed strange that he should have chosen just that day and hour for the declaration of his intention. Was it that he hastened to acquire such an authority over Bianca, as might enable him to put an end to any such escapades for the future? Was it that he was infatuated to that degree, that he feared, that if he did not make haste to secure the prize, it might be taken from him by his nephew?

However this might have been, the overt step he had taken had certainly not had the effect of tranquillizing his mind. The hours of that day, since the lawyer left him, had been passed in the most miserable manner by him.

The servants had all learned, that there was something very decidedly wrong with their master. The man who usually attended on him personally, surprised at his master spending the day in a manner so unusual with him, had made various excuses to enter the library two or three times in the course of the day. Each time he had found the Marchese, instead of being busily employed, as was usual with him, when in his library, either sitting in his easy-chair with his hands before him, and his head hanging on his breast, doing absolutely nothing; or else pacing up and down the room.

As the afternoon went on, and the Marchese still did not go out, his valet, really uneasy about him, found the means of watching him without entering the room. Again and again he saw him rise from his chair and, after two or three turns across the room, return to it. Often he went to the window, and looked out, as if expecting something. Three or four times he observed him start violently at the sound of a door banging in some other part of the palace.

Once in the course of the afternoon the servant had had a genuine excuse for entering the room. The Conte Leandro had called, and asked if the Marchese was at home. He had not seen the Marchese Ludovico in the course of the day, and was curious to find out what had been the result of the eavesdropping that he had retailed to the Marchese Lamberto. That it had not availed to induce the Marchese to interfere in any way to put a stop to the excursion, the Conte Leandro had the means of knowing, as will presently appear. But his curiosity was doomed to remain unsatisfied. The Marchese had replied with a savage ill-humour, that the old servant had never seen in his master before, that he did not want to see the Conte, leaving the domestic to modify the harshness of the reply as he might.

When, however, some hours later, Signor Fortini came to the door, and despite what the servants told him of the state their master was in, and of his refusal to see the Conte Leandro, insisted on being announced, the Marchese admitted him.

The first thought that flashed through the lawyer's brain, when he came into the presence of his old friend and client, was a profound sense of self-congratulation at his own freedom from all connection with womankind.

His own experience of married life, essayed in early years and happily brought to a conclusion after a probation of a very short time, had, as has been hinted, not been a happy one. He had very deeply felt; some five-and-forty years ago, that nothing in the Signora Fortini's life had become her like the leaving of it. And during all those years of widowhood, the remembrance of that first burning of his fingers had sufficed to make the old gentleman a consistent misogynist.

"Ah, here is another specimen of women's work," he thought to himself, as he observed the utter wretchedness of the Marchese's appearance, and the traces in him of a day spent in misery. "And he, too, who had escaped for fifty years! If I had avoided the springes for fifty years, I don't think I should have been caught at last. Maybe, it is all the worse for coming to a man so late. Now here is this man, who had everything the world could give to make his happiness, wrecked, ruined, destroyed, blasted by the sight of a painted piece of woman's flesh, and the lure of a pair of devil-instructed eyes. And he knows that it is ruin. He knows which is the evil, and which the good, and yet is so besotted, that he has not the power to take the one and leave the other. Is not the sight of the unhappy wretch, as he sits cowering there, afraid, evidently afraid to meet my eye, a warning and a caution?"

And, in truth, the appearance of the Marchese might have been held, to justify these reflections of the lawyer, who was right in supposing that no tidings of what had happened had reached the Marchese since he had parted from him after their interview that morning. Attributing, therefore, the state of utter moral prostration, mixed with a kind of restless nervous agitation, in which he found him, to the consciousness of the terrible results he was about to bring upon himself by the folly he had decided on committing, the lawyer could not prevent the thought occurring to him that were it not for the dreadful circumstances that seemed to bring home the suspicion of murder to the Marchese Ludovico, the tidings he brought of the death of the unfortunate woman would be, if not a relief at the moment, yet the most fortunate exit for the Marchese from the position he had made for himself.

"Good-evening, Signor Giovacchino. You have come, of course, to ask whether the representations you made to me this morning have availed to induce me to waver in the purpose I announced to you," said the Marchese, scarcely looking up so as to meet the eye of the lawyer.

"Signor Marchese," returned Fortini, "it is my turn this time to communicate to you intelligence which will strike you, I fear, to the full as painfully as I was struck by what you told me this morning." The Marchese started; and the lawyer observed that the start seemed to continue and propagate itself, as it were, into a tremor, that ran through all his person, as he said, with chattering teeth: "What do you mean? Has anything happened?—anything—out of the common way, eh?—eh?—what—what is it?"

"That has happened, Signor Marchese, which makes all further consideration of the step you confided to me your intention of taking this morning unnecessary. The lady, whom you purposed to make your wife, is no more."

"No more—how no more?—what—what is it you mean?" said the Marchese, evidently terribly shocked, as was manifested by the tremor and shivering which seized him yet more violently than before; yet still without looking up so as to meet the lawyer's eye.

"She is dead, Signor Marchese," said the lawyer, looking at him curiously.

"Dead—La Bianca dead! I don't believe it. It is some scheme for frustrating the purpose you disapproved of—some plan managed between you and my nephew. You have sent her away, and want to persuade me that she is dead."

"Your mind is unhinged by the shock of my intelligence, Signor Marchese—naturally enough—or such an absurd notion would not have occurred to you. I have seen the dead body of Bianca Lalli. It is now in the custody of the police," said the lawyer, with slow gravity.

"The police!" cried the Marchese, shooting a momentary glance up into the lawyer's face.

"Necessarily so; for, Signor Marchese, the unhappy—the miserable truth is that a foul murder has been committed. The girl was murdered in the Pineta this morning."

"Murdered! Gracious heaven! Murdered—but why murdered? Why may she not have died by a natural death?—that is—I mean—of course I mean, if there were no evident marks of violence on the body."

The lawyer paused a minute, as if some cause of perplexity had been suggested to him by the words of the Marchese, before he replied, "There were, in truth, no marks of evident violence on the body, or, at least, none such as an unskilled eye would observe on a very superficial examination. But all that will be ascertained at the medical examination, which will take place to-morrow morning. But I think it can hardly be doubted that the death was not a natural one," said the lawyer, shaking his head gravely.

"And the Marchese Ludovico?" asked the Marchese, rather strangely, as it struck the lawyer, seeing that nothing had as yet been said to connect the young Marchese with the catastrophe, and he was not aware of the fact that the Marchese knew of his nephew's excursion to the Pineta.

"That, alas! is the worst part of the bad story—we, at least, here in Ravenna are perhaps excusable in thinking it the worst. The fact is, Signor Marchese, that this death took place under circumstances which seem to leave no doubt that the deed was done by the hand of the Marchese Ludovico."

"The hand of the Marchese Ludovico! Gracious heaven! But that is nonsense, Signor Fortini. No doubt? How can there be no doubt, merely because he was with her in the forest?"

There was something in the Marchese's manner which made it seem to the lawyer as if he must have already heard of the tragedy that had happened, and of the suspicion that had been thrown on his nephew. "Were you aware, then, Signor Marchese," he asked, "that the Marchese Ludovico had gone to the Pineta with this unhappy woman?"

The Marchese dropped his head upon his chest and paused a minute, passing his hand slowly across his brow and before his eyes, before he replied, "Yes, I knew that," he said, at length; "the Conte Leandro told me of it."

"Your people told me, just now, that you had refused to see the Conte Leandro, when he called," remarked the lawyer, again looking puzzled.

"Yes, I refused to see him because my mind was full of the conversation we had this morning. You know I promised you, Signor Fortini, that I would think over the matter again; and I was engaged in doing so. I have been thinking of it all day; I was thinking of it still when you came in."

"Thinking still of your purpose of making the woman, La Bianca, your wife. Then you could not have heard of her miserable end when I came in, as I supposed, indeed, you could not have heard," remarked the lawyer.

"Heard of it? Why of course not. That is clear—that proves that I could not have heard of it, you know," said the Marchese, with a strange sort of eagerness.

"When was it, then, that you heard from the Conte Leandro, that the Marchese Ludovico was in the Pineta with La Bianca?" asked the lawyer.

"At the ball," replied the Marchese, after a minute's thought, "at the ball. He came to me and told me that they had planned an excursion to the forest, as soon as they left the ball-room. The Conte Leandro told me of it, because, he said, he thought it an imprudent thing, and I should disapprove it. But why should I, you know? I said nothing to either of them about it. Why not let them have such an innocent enjoyment? Young people must be young, you know, Signor Fortini. For my part, I preferred making the best of my way to my bed, after being up all night." There was a strange kind of nervous eagerness and hurry in the Marchese's manner of saying this, which struck the lawyer as affording yet further evidence of the degree to which his mind had been utterly unhinged by the struggle which had been going on in it, doubtless for a longer time than he, the lawyer, was aware of, between the influence over him which the singer had acquired, and his sense of the terrible nature of the step she was inducing him to take. It seemed necessary to recall his attention to that view of the matter which was now of the most urgent interest, the suspicions which rested on the Marchese Ludovico.

"As you say, Signor Marchese," he resumed, "that Signor Ludovico should have been with La Bianca in the forest, affords no proof sufficient to convict him of being the author of this crime; although the fact of his being the last person in whose company she was ever seen alive, does suffice, in a certain degree, to throw on him the onus of showing that he is innocent of it. But the worst is—the damning feature of the matter is, that he had a very strong and intelligible reason for wishing this Bianca out of the way. Remember that your marriage with her would have the effect of reducing him to beggary. Put that fact side by side with the facts that he takes her to a solitary place in the Pineta, and that she is shortly afterwards found there murdered; and I am afraid—I am dreadfully afraid that the judges will not resist the conclusion that, in truth, seems forced upon them. It is a bad business, Signor Marchese; a very bad and ugly business."

"But I had not mentioned to the Marchese Ludovico my intention with regard to the girl. How could he have been led to do such an act by such a motive, when he knew nothing of it?" said the Marchese, after several minutes of consideration.

"Unfortunately he did know it, and has himself stated that he knew it. It seems that the girl herself took the opportunity of their drive together to tell him of the fact. Would to heaven that she had never done so," said Fortini, with a deep sigh.

"But anybody must see that it is a thousand times more probable that she should have been killed by robbers—vagabonds tramping through the country. The Pineta is always full of them. I am sure I would no more lie—I would no more wander there alone!—Of course the unfortunate girl must have been murdered by brigands."

"If any robbery had been committed, there might be reason to hope so, or at least ground for such theory. But, unfortunately, she had exposed on her person valuables exceedingly tempting to a thief; but they remained untouched."

At that moment there came a loud and hurried rapping at the door. The Marchese started violently in his chair, and turned deadly pale; another proof, if more were needed, of the degree in which his nervous system had been shaken by the intelligence he had received, coming, as it did, on the back of all that had previously contributed to unhinge his mind. In the next instant, a servant put his head into the room, saying that the Conte Leandro had returned, and was urgent to be admitted to see the Marchese, declaring that he had a very important communication to make to him.

"I cannot see him. I will not see him. I will see nobody. Signor Fortini, would you have the kindness to let him understand that I am not in a condition to see anybody?" said the Marchese, apparently much agitated.

The lawyer stepped rapidly to the door, and at the stair-head found the Conte Leandro, bursting with the news, which he had hoped to be the first to communicate to the Marchese, and which, of course, showed how wise and timely had been his own interference in telling the Marchese of the proposed excursion of Ludovico, and how disastrous had been the results of his not having paid due attention to it.

"My dear Conte," said Fortini, "I have just done the painful task which you, doubtless, have kindly come to undertake. You must excuse the Marchese if he declines, for the present, to see you. You will readily understand how terrible the shock has been to him. He is, as might be expected, quite broken down by it. In truth, I wish you had had the telling him instead of me. It was most painful."

"But, Signor Fortini," urged the poet, eagerly, as the lawyer was turning away to return to the Marchese, "are you aware—have you heard what is said in the town?—that the Marchese had offered marriage to La Bianca, and that this was the cause—of course I do not believe anything of the kind myself—but I assure you it is what people are saying. And I think the Marchese ought to be told, you know, for—"

"I will tell the Marchese of your kind intention, Signor Conte," said the lawyer; "I think it would be better for you not to attempt seeing him now. And, in the meantime, you cannot do better than to contradict, most emphatically, any such monstrously absurd reports, as those you have mentioned."

"You know, of course, that Ludovico is arrested; and I am shocked to say, that the general opinion in the city is very much against him. Of course I need not tell you that I am perfectly convinced of his entire innocence. But who, except a really attached friend, would you get to believe it, under the circumstances? Ah! I am afraid it will go hard with him," said the Conte; speaking with eager volubility, "I am sadly. afraid it will go hard with him."

"It seems to me, Signor Conte, that any such speculations are a little premature. The Marchese Ludovico has not been even officially accused as yet. At any rate you can console yourself, Signor Conte, with the consideration that you have a magnificent subject for a tragedy in your hands. To such a genuine poet as yourself, that is enough to counterbalance any misfortune that only touches our friends."

And with that the old lawyer turned away to go back to the library; while the poet, though not altogether without a somewhat annoying notion that he was laughed at, was nevertheless delighted with the excellent idea that had been suggested to him.

"I made him understand that you could not see him. All he wanted was to tell you just what I have already communicated to you," said the lawyer, as he came back into the room. "He said too, by-the-by, that all the town was talking of the offer of marriage made by the Marchese Lamberto to Signora Bianca Lalli—"

"Of course, of course," groaned the Marchese, tossing himself restlessly from one side to the other of his chair. "And to think that at the very time, at the hour when I was communicating to you the decision I had arrived at with regard to—to that unfortunate—to poor Bianca, she was even then, as it would seem, lying dead in the forest. It is very, very terrible."

"And I told the Signor Conte that he could not do better than contradict such a report wherever he heard it," added the lawyer, who began almost to fancy, from a something that seemed strange to him in the Marchese's manner, that the catastrophe which had come to relieve him in such a terrible manner from the scrape he had got himself into with the singer, was not altogether unwelcome to him.

"It is of no use, Fortini," returned the Marchese, with a groan; "it is of no use. That old man, her reputed father, knows it; their servant knows it; Ludovico knows it: and, of course, his knowledge of it will have to be made public."

"Nevertheless, the denial of it by such a tongue as that of the Conte Leandro Lombardoni can do no harm in the meantime," said the lawyer, quietly. "It may be," he added, "it may be that something may turn up to prevent any public accusation of the Marchese. It may be that he is not guilty. It may be that the deed may yet be brought home to some other hand."

"Do you think that, Fortini? do you think that likely?" said the Marchese, with a quickly withdrawn anxious look into the lawyer's face.

"No, frankly, I do not think it likely. I fear that it is very certain that his hand is the guilty one. Nevertheless, it may be—it is difficult to say—it may be. At all events, it is always time enough to abandon hope. I must leave you now, Signor Marchese; I will see you again to-morrow morning."

"Many, many thanks, my good Signor Giovacchino. Do not forget to come. Remember how dreadfully anxious I must be to hear what passes: above all, the result of the medical examination—specially the result of the medical examination."

"I will not fail to come. I miei saluti, Signor Marchese."

CHAPTER V

Doubts and Possibilities

In passing through the hall of the Palazzo the lawyer, who was well acquainted with every servant in the house, took an opportunity of speaking a few words to the Marchese's old valet, Nanni.

"The Marchese seems to have been a little overtired when he came back from the ball this morning, Nanni; and then this is a sad affair about the Marchese Ludovico."

"Ahi, misericordia! To think that I should live to hear of a Castelmare arrested in Ravenna. The world is coming to an end, I think, Signor Giovacchino."

"Vexing enough; but not so bad as all that, I hope. No doubt Signor Ludovico will be able to clear himself before long."

"Clear himself!" re-echoed the old servant, very indignantly; "that's just what they say when some poor devil of the popolaccio is at odds with the police. The Marchese di Castelmare clear himself! Well, I've lived to see a many things, but I never thought to see the day that such people should dare to meddle with a Castelmare."

"The Marchese Ludovico himself thought fit to go to them to give explanations."

"Ah! He'd have done better to take no notice of 'em, to my thinking," said the old man, shaking his head. "But is it true, Signor Giovacchino, what people say, that—?"

"There is mostly very little truth in what people say, Nanni," interrupted the lawyer. "But I'll tell you what: a good servant should hear all and repeat nothing. It's natural that such an old friend as you should want to know all about it, and to you I shan't mind telling the whole story as soon as I know the rights of it myself. But it vexes me to see the Marchese so put out about it; and then I don't think he has been quite well latterly."

"Nothing like well, these days past, Signor Giovacchino. The Marchese has not been like himself noways. I think he is far from well."

"Does he get his rest at night? That is a great thing at his time of life. He seems to me like a man who has not had his natural sleep. I suppose he went to bed when he came home from the ball?"

"Yes, directly. He seemed in a hurry like to get to bed. When he was about half undressed he said it was time I was in bed myself, and sent me away, and I heard him lock the door."

"Does he generally lock the door at night?" asked the lawyer.

"No; and I knew by that that he meant to have a good sleep, and not be disturbed this morning. So I never went near him till I heard his bell, between ten and eleven o'clock; and when I went he was just getting out of bed, so that he had a matter of six hours' sleep."

"It don't seem to have done him much good any way," rejoined the lawyer, thinking to himself that the hours during which Nanni supposed his master to have been sleeping, had more probably been spent in restless agitation, the result of bringing his mind to the determination which he had definitely announced to the lawyer, when he had summoned him about an hour after he had risen from his sleepless bed. "I shall come and see how he is to-morrow morning," the lawyer added; "and I hope I may bring some good news about Signor Ludovico."

Behind the Palazzo Castelmare there was an extensive range of stabling and coach-houses, with a large stable-yard opening on to a back street, which was the nearest way to the house of the Signor Professore Tomosarchi, on whom Signor Fortini thought he would call, just to ask whether he had yet seen the body, or at what hour in the morning he thought of making his post-mortem examination. Crossing the stable-yard for this purpose, the lawyer was accosted by Niccolo the groom, who was engaged in doing his office on a handsome bay mare at the stable-door.

Niccolo was the oldest servant in the establishment, having filled the same place he now held under the Marchese's father. He was an older man by several years than the Marchese Lamberto; and he it had been, who, when the present Marchese was a child of ten years old, had put him on his first pony, and been his riding-master. Old Niccolo, like every other old Italian servant of the old school, held, as the first and most important article of his creed, the unquestioning belief that the Castelmare family was the most noble, the most ancient, and in every respect the grandest in the world, and the Marchese Lamberto the greatest and most powerful man in it. He was a good sort of man in his way, was old Niccolo; went to confession regularly; and did his duty in that state of life to which it had pleased Providence to call him according to his lights; was honest in his dealings; knew in a rough sort of way that veracity was good, and unveracity bad, to such an extent as to understand that truth-telling should be the rule and lying the exception; and was faithful to the death to his employer.

Old Niccolo was also a very perfect specimen of the product of a peculiar way of thinking, which was a speciality of the rapidly disappearing class to which he belonged. He did not imagine for a moment, that the laws and rules of morality and duty, by which he had been taught, that he ought to regulate his own conduct, were at all applicable to his master. Even if he had ever troubled his mind by plunging so far into the depths of speculation, as to consider, that in truth the various matters forbidden in the commandments were in the sight of God, or, what was more within his ken, in the sight of the Church, equally forbidden to all men, still it would have been clear to him that there was no reason why such great people as the Marchese di Castelmare, with Cardinals for his friends, and wealth enough to pay for any quantity of indulgences and masses he might require, should not indulge in peccadilloes and vices which poorer folks cannot afford. Probably, however, he had never reached any such profundity of speculation. He saw that the Church and its ministers treated his superiors very differently from their treatment of him, and expected from him quite different conduct from that which they expected from them. And the result was an habitual and practical belief, that the great folks of the world, of whom he considered that his own master was unquestionably the greatest, were far above the laws in every sort which were binding on himself and the like of him.

Nor of all the many acts which honest Niccolo would have scrupled to do on his own account, would he have hesitated a moment to become guilty at the command, or on the behoof of, his master. As for his own soul's weal, it probably was sufficiently safeguarded by the paramount nature of the duty which required him to do the will of his employer; or, in any case, what was his soul that any care for it should come into competition with the will of the Marchese Lamberto di Castelmare? Niccolo would have been profoundly ashamed at admitting to any one of his own class that the family he served were not so great and so masterful as to render it a matter of course that their will must override all other considerations whatsoever.

To old Niccolo it was indeed as a symptom of the end of all things—as a rising of the powers of darkness against the established order of God's world that a Marchese di Castelmare should be arrested. It was incomprehensible to him. There was but one power great enough, as he understood matters, to accomplish so dread a catastrophe; and that was the power of the Marchese Lamberto himself. And he inclined accordingly to the belief, that if indeed the Marchese Ludovico were in prison, the truth was that for some inscrutable reason the Marchese Lamberto chose that so it should be.

"Is it really true, Signor Giovacchino," whispered the old man, coming close up to the lawyer, as the latter was crossing the stable-yard; "is it really true that the Marchese Ludovico has been put in prison?"

"Well, that much is true, I am afraid, Niccolo; but I hope it may not be for long," said Fortini, pausing in his walk, as though he were not unwilling to talk to the old man.

"Couldn't ye say a word to the Marchese, to take him out?" said the old groom coaxingly; "if so be as the woman is dead, what is the use of any more ado about it?"

"Well, I hope there may not be much more ado about it. She was probably killed, poor woman, by some strolling vagabonds. But I wish it had not happened to vex the Marchese just now. He is not well, the Marchese. Has he ridden much lately?"

"Hasn't backed a horse since the first week in Carnival," said the old groom emphatically.

"I hope he will take to his riding again, now Carnival is over. I think it helps to keep him in health," remarked the lawyer.

"I'm sure I wish he would, for my part," returned the groom; "and I wished it this morning, I can tell you. I was a-taking his own mare out this morning—it's a week since she has been out of the stable—and she was that fresh it was pretty well more than I could do to hold her. I brought her in all of a lather, and splashed with mud to her saddle-girths. People; must ha' thought I had been riding a race, that is, if any of them had seen me when I came into the yard; but there wasn't a soul of 'em stirring. Catch any of the lot up at that time the first morning in Lent."

"He is getting old, too. It would have been a mighty hard horse to ride that my friend Niccolo would not have been able to hold a year or two ago," thought the lawyer to himself, as he walked out of the stable-yard into the little back street that runs behind the palazzo, and pursued his way thoughtfully towards the residence of the celebrated anatomist.

And again, as he walked, the lawyer turned his mind, with all the analytical power of which he was master, to the question whether or no there were any possibility of hope that the Marchese Ludovico were innocent of the crime imputed to him, whether there were any other theory possible by virtue of which any other person might be suspected of the deed.

His anxiety to speak with Professor Tomosarchi indicated, indeed, that he had not wholly abandoned, despite what he had said on that point both to the Marchese Ludovico and his uncle, the hope that the death might be pronounced to have resulted from natural causes. Possibly, had the lawyer possessed more medical knowledge, this chance might have seemed to him a somewhat better one; but, to his thinking, it was altogether incredible that a healthy girl of Bianca's age should lie down to sleep, and, without any such change of position as would disorder her attire—without any evidence of a death-struggle—should simply never wake again. Again the lawyer's meditations told him that small hope was to be found in this direction.

Were there any persons in the city who might be supposed to feel enmity or ill-will towards the singer? Many a one of the young nobles had, doubtless, been kept at arms' length by Bianca in a manner that might easily be supposed to breed hatred in a vain and ill-conditioned heart. But murder—and such a murder! It was difficult to suppose that such a cause should be sufficient to produce such an effect; yet vanity is a very strong and a very evil-counselling passion.

Vanity? Ha! could it be? Surely there never was so absurdly, so grossly, vain a creature, as that Conte Leandro? And the poor murdered Diva had quizzed, and snubbed, and mortified him again and again. The lawyer had heard that much; and Leandro was aware of the fact that Bianca was to be in the Pineta at that time. So much was clear from what the Marchese had said. But she was to be there with Ludovico—how could the poet expect to find her alone? Could it be that he had followed them merely for the sake of making mischief and rendering himself disagreeable, and had chanced to come upon her asleep and alone? Could this be the clue?

But it would surely be easy to ascertain to a certainty whether the Conte Leandro had left the city that morning or not. If only it could be shown that he had done so? The amount of probability that he had really been the perpetrator of the crime, or the possibility of convicting him of it, would signify comparatively little. It would be sufficient if only a competing theory, based on a possibility, could be set up; if only such an alternative possibility could be presented to the minds of the judges as should justify them in feeling that the matter was too doubtful to warrant a conviction.

Then, suddenly, as he thought on all the causes of hatred that Bianca might be supposed to have inspired, his mind reverted to those words which Signor Pietro Logarini, the head of the police, had let drop when speaking of the Signorina Paolina Foscarelli:—"Women, who are fond of a man, don't like to see him with another woman, and a beautiful one, under the circumstances in which the Marchese might have been seen with Bianca."

That was the sense of the remark to which the Commissary had partially given utterance; and now the lawyer thought of it. He was tempted to believe that Logarini had been struck by the same idea that had before flashed into his mind almost with the force of a revelation.

Might it not have been the hand of the Venetian girl, maddened by jealousy, which had taken the life of her rival, while she slept?

Such a story would by no means be now told for the first time. Very far from it. Men had not now to learn furens quid foemina possit.

Paolina was known to have left the city at that suspiciously strange hour of the morning. She was known to have been, at all events, at no very great distance from the spot where the crime was committed.

And was it not possible that, on the theory of Ludovico's innocence, the true explanation of the exclamation, which had escaped from him at the city gate, was to be found in supposing that he, too, had been struck by a similar thought? Might not that outcry on Paolina, uttered when the speaker knew well that it was Bianca and not Paolina that lay dead before him, have been forced from him by the sudden thought that she had done the deed then revealed to him?

For the first time the shrewd lawyer began to feel a real doubt as to the author of the crime, It might be that the Marchesino was innocent after all, that his account of the events of that morning, as far as he was concerned, was simply true. As his mind dwelt on the matter the case against Paolina seemed to acquire additional force. It could be proved that this girl had been deeply and seriously attached to the Marchese Ludovico. It could be proved that she had seen her lover tete-a-tete with so dangerous a rival as the singer in circumstances that she had every right to consider very suspicious. It could be proved that she had been not far from the spot where the murder was committed much about the time when the deed must have been done.

It is an essentially and curiously Italian characteristic that the lawyer's rapidly growing conviction that Paolina had indeed been the criminal was strengthened and made easier of acceptance to his mind by the fact that the suspected criminal was not; a townswoman but a Venetian. It would have seemed less possible to him that a young Ravenna girl should have done such a deed. But one of those terrible Venetian women of whom so many blood-stained tale of passion and crime were on record!

Signor Fortini really began to think that his mind had strayed into the true path towards the solution of the mystery at last. And he was very much inclined to think that the germ of such a notion had already been deposited in the mind of the Police Commissioner.

In any case here was wherewithal to establish such a case of suspicion as should make it difficult for the tribunal to condemn the Marchesino on such evidence as could be brought against him, supposing no new circumstances to be brought to light.

Not for that reason, however, was the lawyer disposed to relinquish the idea which had occurred to him as to the possibility of incriminating the Conte Leandro. The more circumstances of doubt it was possible to accumulate around the facts, so much the better.

Signor Fortini thought that he saw his way clearly enough to the means to showing that it was very presumable that the Conte Leandro had conceived a violent and bitter hatred of the murdered woman, It was enough to base a case for suspicion on. The lawyer had no idea that the poet had been the murderer. He did not dream of the possibility that he should be convicted of the crime. He had, doubtless, been quietly in bed in Ravenna at the hour it had been committed. But he might find it difficult to prove that he had not quitted the city on that Wednesday morning. And the suggestion of the possibility of his guilt would, at all events, be an element of doubt and difficulty the more.

With these thoughts in his mind Signor Fortini suddenly changed his immediate purpose of going to the Professore Tomosarchi; and determined to walk as far as the Porta Nuova and make inquiry himself of the people at the gate as to the testimony they might be able to give respecting Paolina's exit from the city at a very early hour on that morning. At the same time, it might be possible to lead them into imagining that they had seen some other passenger, who might have been the Conte Leandro. It was very desirable that this inquiry should be made without delay. For it was no part of the duty of the gate officers to make any written note of such a circumstance; and it would entirely depend on their recollection to say whether such or such a person had passed the gate. At the same time, that such a person as this Paolina Foscarelli should pass out of the city at such an hour in the morning, was sufficiently out of the ordinary course of things to make it very unlikely that it should not be remembered by the officials.

As the lawyer pursued his way towards the gate in deep thought he was comforted as to the complexion of his client's case by the consideration of his own state of mind. He found it impossible to come to any definitive conclusion as to the balance of the probabilities. At one moment his mind swung back to his original conviction that the Marchese Ludovico had yielded to the temptation of making himself safe from the destitution that awaited him if his uncle's purpose were carried out. The persuasion that it was so seemed to come like a flash of light upon him. Then, again, thinking of all the stories of what women have done under the influence of a maddening jealousy, he reverted to the superior probability of the other hypothesis.

Arrived at the gate the lawyer's success was greater than he had ventured to anticipate. Both the persons respecting whom he made inquiry had been seen to pass out of the city at a very early hour that morning.

To his great surprise he heard that the Conte Leandro had passed the gate before it was daylight; and the officer had been struck by the strangeness of the circumstance. He was much muffled up in a large cloak, with a broad-brimmed hat drawn down over his eyes and face. But his person was perfectly well known to the official; and he had recognized him without difficulty.

He also perfectly well remembered seeing the girl—a remarkably pretty girl—pass through about an hour or a little more afterwards. And, imagining that the one circumstance explained the other—that it was an affair of some assignation outside the city in the interest of some amourette that was attended by difficulties within the walls—he had thought no more about it.

But Signor Fortini knew enough to feel very sure, that the exceedingly singular facts, as they seemed to him, of both these persons having gone out of the city in the direction of the Pineta at such an unusual hour, was not to be accounted for by any such explanation. But neither did it seem in any degree likely or credible, that these two facts, the passing out of the Conte Leandro, and the passing out of Paolina, should have had any connection with each other in reference to the murder in the Pineta.

It was strange, very strange!

It was so strange and unaccountable that Signor Fortini felt that, unless some fresh circumstances should be brought to light beyond those which had as yet become known either to him, or to the police, it was safe to predict that the tribunal would not have the means of coming to any conclusion concerning the author of the murder.

The lawyer turned away from the gate, and strolled through the streets without any intention as to the direction in which he walked, so deeply was he pondering upon the possibilities that were brought within his mental vision by the extraordinary facts he had ascertained.

He would almost have preferred, he thought, as he pursued his way profoundly musing, that it should have been shown that one only, instead of both the persons towards whom the possibilities he had imagined, pointed, had gone at that strange hour towards the locality of the crime.

Nevertheless, as he said to himself, the more doubt, the more elements of difficulty, the better. In truth the chance seemed to be a very good one, that it might never be known who gave that wretched girl her death.

CHAPTER VI

At the Circolo Again

At the Circolo that evening there was no lack of subject for conversation, as may be easily imagined. The rooms were very full, and every tongue was busy with the same topic.

"For my part I don't believe that La Bianca is dead at all. What proof have we of the fact? Somebody has been told that somebody else heard some other pumpkin-head say so. Report, signori miei, is an habitual liar, and I for one never believe a word she says without evidence of the truth of it," said the Conte Luigi Spadoni, a man who was known to make a practice of reading French novels, and was therefore held to be an esprit fort and a philosopher, in accordance with which character he always professed indiscriminate disbelief in everything.

"Oh come, Spadoni, that won't do this time. Bah, you are the only living soul in the town that don't believe it then. Evidence, per Dio! Go and ask the men at the Porta Nuova, who received the body, when the contadini brought it in," cried a dozen voices at once.

"But Spadoni has the weakness of being so excessively credulous," said a bald young man with gold spectacles, looking up from a game of chess he was playing in a corner.

"Who, I? I credulous? That is a good one! Why I said, man alive, that I disbelieved it," cried Spadoni, eagerly.

"I know it, and very credulous indeed it seems to me, to believe that all the people, who say they have seen the prima donna's dead body, should be mistaken in such a fact, or conspiring without motive to declare it falsely. I call that very credulous," said the chess-player, quietly.

"Did you ever see such an addle-pate. He can't understand the difference between believing and disbelieving," rejoined Spadoni triumphantly, and carrying the great bulk of the bystanders with him.

"But as to the poor girl being dead, there is unhappily no shadow of doubt at all," said the Baron Manutoli; "I saw old Signor Fortini the lawyer just now, who told me that he was at the Porta Nuova when the body was brought in."

"And is it true that the Marchese Ludovico was with him, and fainted dead away at the sight of the body?" said a very young man.

"It is true that Ludovico was there with Fortini at the gate, but I heard nothing about his fainting; and should not think it very likely."

"Well, I don't know about that, I should have thought it likely enough by all accounts," said the Conte Leandro Lombardoni, whose face was looking more pasty and his eyes more fishy than usual.

"Much you know about it. Why, in the name of all the saints, should it be likely? What should Ludovico faint for?" rejoined Manutoli, fiercely.

"What for? Well, one has heard of such things. And as for what I know about it, Signor Barone, maybe I have the means of knowing more about it than anybody here," said the poet.

"Here is Lombardoni confesses he knows all about it," cried one.

"That ought to be told to the Commissary of Police" said another

"I say, my notion is that Lombardoni did it himself," exclaimed a third.

"Ah, to be sure. What is more likely? We all know how the poor Diva snubbed him. Remember the fate of his verses. If that is not enough to drive a man and a poet to do murder I don't know what is. To be sure, 'twas Leandro did it," rejoined the first.

"I can believe that, if I never believe anything else," said Spadoni.

"Let's send to the Commissary and tell him that the Conte Leandro confesses that it was he that murdered La Bianca, cried one of the previous speakers.

"What on earth are you dreaming of," cried the persecuted poet, turning ghastly livid with affright; "I know nothing about the matter, nothing! How in the world should I know anything about it?"

"Oh, I thought you knew more about it than anybody else just now," sneered one of his persecutors.

"He looks to me very much as if he did know something about it in sober earnest," said the bald-headed chess-player; who had been looking hard at the evidences of terror on the poet's face.

"But where is the Marchese Ludovico?" asked the same young man, who had heard that the Marchese had fainted at the sight of the body.

A general silence fell on the chattering group at this question: till Manutoli answered with a very grave face "Ah, you must ask the Commissary of Police that question, Signor Marco."

"You don't mean that he is arrested," returned the youngster thus addressed.

Manutoli nodded his head two or three times gravely, as he said, "That is the worst of the bad business; and a very bad business it is in every way."

"You don't mean that you think Ludovico can have done it, Manutoli?" said one of the others.

"No, I don't say I think so. I don't know what to think. I should have said, that I was just as likely to do such a thing myself, as Ludovico di Castelmare. But if there is any truth in what is said, that the Marchese Lamberto was going to marry the girl, it looks very ugly. God knows what a man might be driven to do in such a case."

"I suppose if the old Marchese were to marry and have children, Ludovico would have about the same fortune as the old blind man that sits at the door of the Cathedral?" asked the previous speaker.

"Just about as much. He would be absolutely a beggar," said the Conte Leandro, who appeared to find considerable pleasure in the announcement.

"I think, that if that was the case, and Ludovico had put the unlucky girl out of the way, it would be the Marchese Lamberto who ought to bear the blame of it. An old fellow has no right to behave in that sort of way," said one of the group.

"Of course he has not. To bring a fellow up to the age of Ludovico in the expectation that he is to have the family property; and then to take it into his head to marry when he is past fifty. If Ludovico had put a knife into him instead of into the girl, I should have said that it served him right," said another.

"And what was the good of murdering the girl? If the old fellow wants to be married, he will marry some other girl if not this one. Girls are plenty enough," said a third.

"Ay, but not such girls as La Bianca—what a lovely creature she was! I don't wonder at the Marchese being caught by her, for my part, seeing her every day as he did," remarked a fourth.

"Bah, girls are plenty enough, as Gino said, and pretty girls too. And if the Marchese was minded to marry, it wasn't the murder of this poor girl that would stop him," said one of the others.

"And that is a strong reason, as it strikes me, for thinking that Ludovico had nothing to do with it. He must have known, as well as we, that it was likely enough his uncle would find somebody else," remarked Manutoli.

"Well, we shall see. But I would wager a good round sum that Ludovico did it," said the Conte Leandro; who had by that time recovered his tranquillity.

"Oh, now here's Leandro, who begins to think again that he does know something about it," said the Barone Manutoli.

"I said nothing of the sort, Signor Barone. How should I know? But everybody may have his opinion, and that is mine. We shall see by-and-by," returned Leandro, waspishly.

"I'll tell you what, signori miei," said Manutoli; "let it turn out as it may, it is the saddest and worst affair that has been seen in Ravenna for many a day. I won't admit the thought, for my part, that the Marchese Ludovico has really committed this murder. I should prefer to suppose, that some vagabonds had done it for the sake of robbery, and had been disturbed before they could carry out their purpose, or anything. But it is a very sad affair. I would have done I don't know what, rather than that it should have happened. Think what will be said. That's what an artist gets by venturing to Ravenna. You will see the noise that will be made all over Italy."

"But why does it follow that anybody is to blame, at all? Why may she not have put herself to death?" said one of the previous speakers.

"A suicide! that is a new idea. But it does not seem a very promising one. Why should she kill herself? She was in the full tide of success, and had just received an offer of marriage, if what we hear is true, from the richest man in Ravenna. Is it likely that she should choose just that moment to make away with herself?" replied another.

"In any case the doctors will know what to tell us about that. They can always tell whether anybody has killed themselves or been murdered by somebody else."

"By the way, Signor Barone, have you heard whether the medical report has been made yet? But I suppose the police would not let us know what the doctor's opinion was, if it had been made. Who knows who has been employed to examine the body?"

"I know!" answered the Baron Manutoli, "the Professore Tomosarchi. And whatever can be found out by examining the body, he will find out, depend upon it. I was asking about it just now. The examination will take place to-morrow morning."

"But who ever heard of such a thing as going off to the Pineta at that time in the morning, and after being up all night at a ball too?" said Lombardoni, spitefully. "Why, it looks as if a man must have had some scheme, some out-of-the-way motive of some kind to do such a thing."

"Not at all," returned Manutoli angrily, "I don't see that at all. A charmingly imagined frolic, I should say, a capital wind-up for a last night of carnival. I should have liked it myself."

"And then," said one of the others, "one can't refuse such a girl as La Bianca. And it's two to one that she asked Ludovico to take her, for a lark."

"But I happen to know," said Leandro, quickly, "that it was he who proposed it to her. He persuaded her to go."

"And how in the world do you know that, pray?" asked Manutoli, turning sharply upon him.

"I—I heard it said. I was told so. I am sure I don't know who it was said so. Nobody has been talking about anything else. Some fellow or other said that Ludovico had proposed the trip to her."

"The fact is, in short, that you know just nothing at all about it. You happen to know, forsooth! It seems to me, Signor Conte, that you are strangely ready to fancy you know anything that might seem to go against Ludovico," rejoined Manutoli.

"And what would be the result if it should turn out that he was guilty—if he were condemned?" asked one of the younger men, looking afraid of his words, as he spoke them.

"God knows, the galleys, I suppose. But one must not imagine such a thing. It is too frightful," said Manutoli.

"Horrible! Shocking! Impossible!" cried a chorus of voices.

"Good God! Result! The disgrace and destruction of the noblest family in the province. The ending of a fine old name in infamy. Gracious heaven, it is too horrible to think of," exclaimed Manutoli, with much emotion.

"It would kill the old Marchese as dead as a door-nail, for one thing," said another of the group of young men.

"And serve him right too. If it is really true that he has contemplated being guilty of such a monstrous piece of injustice and folly," said the same man, who had before expressed a similar opinion.

Just then a servant of the Circolo came into the room and put a note into the hands of the Baron Manutoli.

"It is from Ludovico, asking me to go to him. So there's an end to our game of billiards, Signor Conte," said Manutoli to one of the group; "I must go at once."

"But you'll come back here after you've seen him, won't you? You'll come back and tell us all about it, Manutoli?" said two or three of the group which had been discussing the topic.

"I don't know, I shall see. I will, if I can—if it's not too late. It may be that I shall be detained with him. I suppose that he has had no means of communicating with any of his people since the police folk clapped their hands on him."

"Do look in here for a moment, Manutoli. We shall all be anxious to hear about him, poor fellow,", said another of the young men, who had pressed around Signor Manutoli as soon as it was known from whom his note had come.

"If I can I will. It is likely enough he may want me to go somewhere else for him. We shall see. A rivederci, Signori."

CHAPTER VII

A Prison Visit

The note which had been given to the Baron Manutoli begged him to come with as little delay as possible to the Palazzo del Governo.

Adolfo Manutoli was a somewhat older man than the majority of those who had formed the group which had been discussing the all-absorbing topic of the day at the Circolo; and he was Ludovico di Castelmare's most intimate friend among the younger members of the society in which he lived. It was a friendship strongly approved by the Marchese Lamberto, as might have been perceived by his selection of Manutoli to accompany him on the occasion of meeting La Lalli on her first arrival in Ravenna, as the reader may possibly remember. And the special ground of this approval was Manutoli's strong advocacy of the projected marriage between Ludovico and the Contessa Violante, and his consequent disapproval and discouragement of his friend's friendship and admiration for Paolina. He was not a man who would have counselled or desired his friend to behave badly or unworthily to Paolina or to any woman; for he was a man of honour and a gentleman. But, short of any conduct which could be so characterized, he would have been very glad to see the Marchese quit of an entanglement which alone stood in the way, as he conceived, of his forming an alliance so desirable in every point of view as the marriage with the great-niece of the Cardinal Legate.

"Can I be permitted to see the Marchese Ludovico, Signor Commissario? He has requested me to come to him," said the Baron, on arriving at the police-office.

"Certainly, Signor Barone. I myself sent his note to you. Though, on his own statement of the very unfortunate circumstances connected with this unhappy affair, I was compelled to detain him, still there is at present no definite accusation against him which should justify me in preventing him from having free communication with his friends. You shall be taken to his room immediately. You will see, Signor Barone, that we have endeavoured to make him as comfortable as the circumstances would allow."

"Manutoli," said Ludovico, after the first expressions of astonishment and condolence had been spoken between the young men, "of course I knew I should see you here before long; and my note was to call you at once, instead of waiting to see you in the morning; because I want you to do something for me before you sleep this night—something that I don't want to wait for till to-morrow morning."

"To be sure, my dear fellow, anything; I am ready for anything, if it takes all night."

"Thanks. Well, now, look here: I am innocent of this deed—"

"S' intende; of course you are."

"S' intende, of course; that's just the worst of it. It is so much a matter of course that I should say I had not done it if I had, that my saying so is of no use at all. Nevertheless, to you I must say that I neither did it nor have I the slightest conception or suspicion who did. And you may guess that the fact itself is a horror and a grief to me that I shall never get over, putting this dreadful suspicion of my own guilt out of the question. A horror and a grief, and a remorse, too; for if I had not moved away from her the tragedy could not have happened."

"I really do not see that you need blame yourself for—"

"I ought not to have left her side. Yet, God knows, it never entered my head to dream of the possibility of any harm; all seemed so still, so peaceful, so utterly quiet; yet, at that moment, the hand that did the deed could not have been far off."

"Let the circumstances have been what they might," resumed Manutoli, after a moment's pause, "nobody would have dreamed of connecting you with the deed had it not been for the strong motive which seems so clear and intelligible to every fool who sets his brains to work on the matter. I suppose it is true that you had been informed of your uncle's intention to offer the poor girl marriage?"

"True that I had been told of it, for the first time, by herself during our drive, poor girl."

"Ah—h—h! To think of such a man being guilty of such insane folly—and of all the misery that is likely to grow out of it. How on earth did she ever contrive to get such a fatal influence over him?"

"She schemed for it from her first arrival here—aimed avowedly to herself at nothing less than inducing the Marchese di Castelmare to marry her—and succeeded. For all that, I'll tell you what, Adolfo—there was a great deal more good in that poor girl than you would have thought."

"Bah! Good in her—Well, she's gone. She has had her reward, poor soul; and I pity her with all my heart. But as for the good in her—"

"There was good in her, and not a little. I tell you that if you or any one else could have heard all that passed between us, I should hardly be suspected of having murdered her, poor girl."

"That is likely enough; but—"

"Do you know, Manutoli, I have a very strong idea that if this had not happened, the marriage with the Marchese would never have come off?"

"You think that, between us all, we should have induced him to listen to reason?"

"I don't know about that; I was not thinking of that; I think that Bianca would have been induced to listen to reason; I think that the scheme would have come to nothing through her renunciation of it."

"When, according to your own account, she had been scheming all the time she has been here to bring it about?" said Manutoli, with arched eyebrows.

"Yes, even so. She had never known—how should she?—that such a marriage would turn me out on the world a beggar; she had never known what sort and what degree of misery and ruin it would bring about to all parties."

"And you told her this?"

"Yes, in some degree I told her. As to the effect of such a marriage on myself, I told her simply the entire truth."

"And you are disposed to think that the Diva—No, poor girl! I didn't mean to speak sneeringly of her. She has paid for her fault a heavier penalty than it deserved, any way. You are disposed to think, then, that she would have given up the prize of all her scheming—this marriage, which was to have given her everything in the world that she could desire, and more than she could have ever dreamed of attaining; she would have voluntarily relinquished all this, you think, for your sake?"

"I'll tell you what it is, Manutoli. A man can never appreciate, can never fathom, the depth of woman's generosity till he has tried it."

"But, caro mio, after all I don't want to be hard upon her, poor soul, God knows!—but to expect generosity on such a point from such a woman—"

"You may say what you will, Manutoli, I know what she was, poor girl, as well as you do—better, a great deal; for, I tell you, that there was a real generosity in her nature. Look here," continued Ludovico; after a pause of a minute or two, "I would not say it to anybody else than you, or to you either, except under circumstances that make one wish to state the whole truth exactly as it was. It seems so coxcomblike, so like what our friend Leandro would say; but I may say it to you. The fact is, I have a kind of idea that that poor Bianca was inclined to like me. She cried when I told her—"

"Aha, j'y suis! Now I begin to be able to fathom the depth of a woman's generosity. Given the fact of becoming Marchesa di Castelmare, the lady was not disinclined to become so by catching the nephew instead of the uncle; and small blame to her."

"You do not do the poor woman justice, Manutoli."

"Any way, I do you justice; and I know you well enough, Ludovico mio, to understand that the generosity of such a girl as this poor Lalli was, taking that special form, must have been very touching to you."

"You forget, Manutoli, how little accessible I was to the flattery of any such preference, with my whole heart full of a very different person."

"And I was just thinking, to tell you the truth, how the little scene in the bagarino would have struck that other person if she could have seen La Bianca giving you to understand, amid her tears, upon what terms she would consent not to come between you and your natural inheritance."

"That other person did see us in the bagarino; and that brings me to the motive which led me to beg you to come to me this evening. Somehow or other, it has become known to these people here that Paolina went out of the Porta Nuova at a very early hour this morning. The fact is, that she simply went out to see whether the scaffolding, which I had had prepared for her copying work there, was all right, and ready for her to begin her task there; and all that can be proved, of course. But the same idea that occurred to you just now, that Paolina might not have liked to see me driving with La Bianca, has suggested itself to some other wiseacre, I beg your pardon, Manutoli, and it seems that an absurd notion—a notion the monstrous absurdity of which is a matter of amazement to me—has been engendered that my poor Paolina may have been the perpetrator of the crime. The idea! If they only knew her! But the Commissary here has been cross-questioning me in a way that shows that is the notion he has in his head. Whether they know that Paolina really did see us in the bagarino together—she did so from the window in the Church of St. Apollinare—or whether they only know that she left the city by that gate early in the morning, I can't tell; but it is sure to be found out that she did really see us, the more so, that she will say so to the first person who asks her" the poor innocent darling. And what I want you do is to see her, and prepare her, poor child, for the possibility of being arrested, and make her understand that no harm can possibly come to her. Try to save her from being frightened. She knows well enough, just as well as I know myself, that I have not done this thing. Try to make her understand that a little time only is necessary for the finding out of the real culprit; that it is sure to be discovered, and that, as far as we are concerned, it is all sure to come right."

"You wish me to go to her at once?"

"Yes, if you would be so kind. What I am anxious for is that you should see her before any order for her arrest shall have been issued. But that is not all. I want you to see Fortini also. I want you to ascertain from him how far it is possible or probable that any suspicion may rest on Paolina in consequence of the facts which are known; how far it is likely that any attempt may be made to set up a case against her. And I want you to tell him that it will be wholly and utterly vain to make any such attempt, that the result would only be entirely to cripple my own defence. For you must understand once for all, and make him understand once for all, that rather than allow her to be convicted of a deed of which she is as innocent as you are, I would confess myself to be the guilty party. It shall not be, Manutoli, mark what I say, it shall not be, that she shall be dragged to ruin and destruction by my misfortune, or imprudence, call it what you will. Of this, of course, you will say no word to her. But I beg you to leave no shade of a doubt as to my settled purpose in this matter on the mind of Signor Fortini. It is he, of course, who will have the duty of preparing and conducting my defence; and it is essential that he should understand this rightly. Will you do this for me?"

"Of course I will—this or anything else that I can do for you. But I can't undertake to say what Signor Giovacchino Fortini may think, or say, or do in the matter, you know. I will take your message, and then, of course, you will see him yourself in the course of to-morrow morning. Of course, old fellow,

I need not tell you that I am sure you did not murder the girl; but it is altogether one of the most mysterious things I ever heard of. Nevertheless my notion is that we shall find out the culprit yet. And you may depend on it that two-thirds of the whole population of the town will be moving heaven and earth to get some clue to the mystery for your sake."

"It seems to me, too, that such a deed cannot but be found out. I should be more uneasy than I am, did I not console myself with thinking so. Now go to Paolina, there is a dear good fellow."

"One word more—shall I see the Marchese?"

"I think, perhaps, it is best not to do so. Of course Fortini has been with him, and told him everything. I almost thought that I should have seen him here this evening; but, under the circumstances, I am better pleased that he should stay away. Better leave him to Fortini."

"Good-night, then."

"Good-night. You will let me see you to-morrow?"

"I won't fail. Good-night."

CHAPTER VIII

Signor Giovacchino Fortini at Home

The Baron Manutoli was Ludovico di Castelmare's very good friend. But there are two sorts of friends—friends who show their friendship by wishing, and endeavouring to obtain for us, what we wish for ourselves; and friends, whose friendship consists in wishing for us things analogous to what they wish for themselves;—who endeavour to procure for us, not what we wish, but what they consider to be good for us.

Now the Baron Manutoli belonged to the latter of these two categories. He was some years older than Ludovico; had been a married man, and was now a widower with one little boy, the future Baron Manutoli; and considered himself as having been blessed with a supreme and exceptional degree of good fortune, with regard to all that appertained to that difficult and often disastrous chapter of human destinies which concerns the relations of mankind with the other sex. Happiness and advantages, ordinarily incompatible and exclusive of each other, had in his case by a kind destiny been made compatible. For the representative of an old noble family to remain single, was bad in many points of view. But on the other hand—when one's ancestral acres are not so extensive as they once were, and in nowise more productive—when one likes a quiet life enlivened by a moderate degree of bachelor's liberty, when one sees the interiors of divers of one's contemporaries and friends, when one thinks of mothers-in-law, and sisters-in-law, and a whole ramified family-in-law!—the Baron Manutoli, though he had grieved over the loss of his young wife when the loss was recent, was now, after some ten years of widower's life, inclined to think that of the man, who had a legitimately born son to inherit his name and estate, who had done his duty towards society by taking a wife, and who was yet enabled to enjoy all the ease and freedom from care of a bachelor's life, it might be said, "Omne tulit punctum."

Far as he was from undervaluing the importance of the social duties of a man and a nobleman in respect to these matters, he had always been an earnest advocate of the marriage which Ludovico was expected to make with the Contessa Violante; and had regarded poor Paolina, from the first, as an intruder and disastrous mischief-maker; and Ludovico's love for her as the unlucky caprice of a boy, respecting which, the evident duty of all friends was to do all they could to discourage it, put it down, and get rid of it.

So that in the matter of the commission which Ludovico had entrusted to him, the Baron was likely enough to have somewhat different views from those of his friend.

What a happy turning of misfortune into a blessing it would be, if this shocking affair should be the means of getting rid of this unlucky Paolina altogether! Not, of course, that the Baron was capable of wishing that such getting rid of should be accomplished by the unjust condemnation of the poor girl for such a crime. God forbid! But, if there should be found to be a sufficient degree of suspicion—of unexplainable mystery—to cause the exoneration of Ludovico, and at the same time, an intimation to the Venetian stranger that she would do well to remove herself from the happy territory of the Holy Father, what a Godsend it would be!

Then, again, as to the real fact of Paolina's innocence, Manutoli was seriously disposed to think that there might be grounds for considerable doubt. Ludovico's assertions to that effect were of course unworthy of the slightest attention; the mere ravings of a man in love. Of course, also, the menace he held out, that if any attempt were made to throw the onus of the crime on Paolina, he would meet it by avowing himself guilty, was as entirely to be disregarded. The paramount business in hand was to clear his friend of this untoward complication in the matter of the crime which had so mysteriously been committed. The next consideration was to set him equally free from his entanglement with Paolina. And with these thoughts in his mind, the Baron decided that, upon the whole, it would be better that he should have an interview with lawyer Fortini, before making his visit to the lady.

He knew that it was too late to look for the lawyer at his "studio;" and therefore went directly to his residence, where he found the old gentleman just concluding his solitary supper. Being the evening of Ash Wednesday, the meal had consisted of a couple of eggs, and a morsel of tunny fish preserved in oil, very far from a bad relish for a flask of good wine. And the lawyer was, when Manutoli came in, aiding his meditations by discussing the remaining half of a small cobwebbed bottle of the very choicest growth of the Piedmontese hills.

"I owe you a thousand apologies, Signor Fortini, for coming to trouble you with business, and very disagreeable business too, here and at such an hour," began the Baron; "but the interest we all feel—"

"Not a word of apology is needed, Signor Barone. About this shocking affair in the Pineta, of course, of course? Pur troppo, we are all interested, as you say. Will you honour my poor house, Signor Barone, by tasting what there is in the cellar? I ought to be ashamed to offer this wine, my ordinary drink at supper, to the Barone Manutoli"—(the old fellow knew right well that there was not such another glass of wine in all the city, and that it was rarely enough that his noble guest drank such)—"but it is drinkable." And so saying, he called to his old housekeeper to bring another bottle and a fresh glass before he would allow Manutoli to say a word on the business that brought him there.

"And now, Signor Barone," said the old lawyer, as soon as the wine and the praise it merited, had been both duly savoured, "about this bad business? Do you bring me any information? Information is all we want. I hope and trust information is all we want," he repeated, looking hard at the Baron.

"Of course, that is all we want; information which should put us on some clue to the real perpetrator of this crime."

"That is what we want; that is the one thing needful; and it is absolutely needful," said the lawyer, again looking meaningly in his companion's face.

"Of course that is what we want. But even supposing no light upon the matter can be got at all, it is not to be supposed that—that any judge would consider there was sufficient ground for assuming our friend to be guilty?"

"Ah, that's just the point; just the point of the difficulty. We must not expect, Signor Barone, that the judges will look at the question quite with the same eyes that we do. They will have none of the strong persuasion that we—ahem!—that the Marchese Ludovico's friends have—that he is wholly incapable of committing such a crime. On the other hand, they are men used to suspicion, and to the habit of considering a certain amount of suspicion as equivalent to moral certainty. And I confess—I must confess, my dear sir, that I am very far from easy as to the result, if we should be unable to find at least some counterbalancing possibilities, you understand?"

"But it seems to me, Signor, that such are already found; and it was just upon this point that I was anxious to speak with you to-night. I have just seen Ludovico. He sent for me to the Circolo. And what he mainly wanted was to bid me go to the Signorina Paolina Foscarelli, in order to prepare her for the probability of her own arrest, and to comfort her with the assurance that no evil could come to her. Also I was directed by him to tell you, that any attempt to fix the guilt of this deed on the girl, would be met by an avowal—a false avowal, of course—that he is himself the guilty person."

"Ta, ta, ta, ta! Mere stuff, chatter, the talk of a boy in love with a pretty girl," said the lawyer.

"Just so, just so. Of course we pay no attention to all that. I promised to go to the girl as he told me; and I shall do so presently. But I thought it best to see you first. The fact is, Signor Fortini, that I do not feel any one bit of the certainty that he professes to feel, that this Venetian girl may not have been the real assassin."

The lawyer looked shrewdly into Manutoli's face, and nodded his head slowly three or four times. "What would there be so unlikely in it," pursued Manutoli; "girls, and Venetian girls too, have done as much and more before now? We know that she is in love with him. She sees him going on such an expedition as that with such a girl as La Bianca. She has already, no doubt, had cause to be jealous of her. Ludovico used to see the Lalli frequently. What is more likely?"

"Stay, Signor Barone, one minute. This is an important point; you say that this Paolina saw her lover with La Bianca. How do you know that? and how did it come about?"

"Ludovico just told me so; and the girl, it seems, herself told him. Her story is that she went out to St. Apollinare at an early hour this morning to look after a scaffolding or some preparation of some kind that had been made for her to copy some of the mosaics in the church; and that from a window of the church, being on the scaffolding, she saw Ludovico and La Bianca driving by in a bagarino. Now all this probably is true enough. The question is, What did she do then, when she saw what was so well calculated to throw her into a frenzy of jealousy? My theory is, that she followed them into the forest, dogged their steps, and finding her opportunity at the unlucky moment when Ludovico left Bianca sleeping, did the murder there and then."

The old lawyer started up from his seat, and thrusting his hands into the pockets of his trousers took a hasty turn across the room; and then resuming his seat, tossed off a glass of wine before making any reply.

"And a very good theory too, Signor Barone. I make you my compliment on it," he said at last. "I was not aware of all the facts, the very, important facts, you mention. I had ascertained that this Venetian girl left the city by the Porta Nuova at a strangely early hour this morning; and that was enough already, to fix my eye upon her. But what you now tell me is much more important; advances the case against her to a far more serious point. Upon my word," continued the lawyer, after a pause for further meditation; "upon my word I begin to think that it is the most likely view of the case that this Signorina Paolina Foscarelli has been the assassin. At all events it seems quite as likely a theory as that the Marchese should have done it. Fully as likely," added the lawyer, rubbing his hands cheerily; "the motive, as motives to such deeds go, is quite as great in her case as in his. Greater, or at least more probable! Jealousy has moved to such acts more frequently than mere considerations of interest."

"To be sure it has," cried Manutoli; "I think that the circumstances bear more conclusively against her than against him; I do, upon my life."

"If only something do not turn up to show that it could not have been done by her, I think—I do think that we have got all that is absolutely necessary for us. For observe, Signor Barone, it is not necessary that she should be convicted. If there is such a probability that she may have been the criminal as to make it impossible to say that it is far more likely that one of the parties suspected should be guilty than the other, there can be no conviction, and our friend is safe."

"But I say that all the probabilities are in favour of the hypothesis that she did the deed," cried Manutoli, warmly.

"Much will depend on the report of Tomosarchi," said the lawyer. "The inquiry arises, how far it was possible for a young girl to do that which was done."

"It is evident that she was murdered in her sleep," observed the Baron.

"It looks like it; it seems clear that there could have been no struggle of any sort. Still, we must hear how the murder was done; we must know whether the means were such as might have been in the power of this girl," rejoined Fortini.

"Well, we shall know all that to-morrow. God grant that the Professor's report may be a favourable one," said Manutoli, thinking little of the savageness of his wish as regarded the poor artist. But, to the mind of the Baron, it was a question between one who was a fellow-creature of his own, and one who could hardly be considered such. How was it possible to put in comparison for a moment the consideration of a fellow-noble of his own city and that of a poor unknown foreign artist?

"I trust it may; I build much on the fact that there was no struggle. She was put to death by some means which scarcely allowed her time to wake from the sleep," returned the lawyer. "You are going, then, now, Signor Barone, to see this Paolina?"

"Yes; if I find her still up, which I suppose I shall, for it is not late," said Manutoli, looking at his watch.

"Better be a little cautious in speaking to her, you know; best to avoid alarming her," said Fortini.

"The express object of my visit to her is to prevent her from being alarmed," rejoined the Baron.

"Yes; but—what I mean is that—it would be desirable, you see, to lead her to speak. What we want now is to know exactly what she did and where she went after seeing the Marchesino and La Bianca in the bagarino together. Also to ascertain whether she was seen by anybody to do whatever she did or to go wherever it was she went. And, I think, that you might very probably learn this from her more effectually than I should. She would be more likely to be on her guard with me, you see."

"I'll try what I can do; my real belief is that she is the guilty person," said Manutoli.

"To-morrow I will see what I can do at St. Apollinare. She cannot have been in the church without seeing and speaking to somebody. There are a Capucin and a lay-brother always there, I take it; we shall see what they can tell us. But I can't go out there till after the medical examination. I have arranged with my old friend Tomosarchi to be present at it," said the lawyer.

"I shall be most anxious to hear the result," said the Baron.

"If you will be here about ten o'clock—my breakfast hour—I shall be able to tell you."

"Thanks. A rivederci dunque—"

"Stay; one more word before you go, Signor Barone. As we are both engaged in this inquiry, and both interested on the same side, I may as well tell you, perhaps, that there is one other person to whom my attention has been drawn as being open to suspicion in this matter—the Conte Leandro Lombardoni."

"The Conte Leandro! You don't say so! Impossible!"

"Just listen one moment, Signor Barone. It is certain that the Conte Leandro passed out of the city by the Porta Nuova at a very early hour this morning—at an earlier hour than either the girl Paolina or the Marchesino and La Bianca."

"The Conte Leandro—out of the Porta Nuova—at such an hour in the morning. For what possible purpose?"

"Ay, that is the question. For what possible purpose? But the fact is certain. Though endeavouring to conceal himself by means of his cloak, he was perfectly well recognized by the men at the gate. For what possible purpose? No doubt you know, Signor Barone, much better than I, who am not much in the way of hearing of such things—unless in cases where I make it my business to hear of them, you understand, Signor Barone, you, no doubt, know that the Signor Conte has been besieging, as I may say, this poor Lalli woman with his attentions and verses ever since she came here; also, that the lady would have nothing to say to him or to his verses—that she has, in short, snubbed him and mortified his vanity in the sight of all the town during the whole of the past Carnival."

"That is true—it is all true," cried Manutoli, eagerly, and looking almost scared by the ideas the lawyer was presenting to his mind. "It is even truer, than you, perhaps, are aware of. She said sneering and cutting things of him in his hearing both at the Marchese Lamberto's ball and at the Circolo ball; I happen to know it."

"Hey—y—y—y?" said the lawyer, uttering a sound like a long sigh, with a question stop at the end of it; and then thrusting out his lips and nodding his head up and down slowly while he plunged his hands into the pockets of his trowsers. "I'll tell you what it is Signor Barone," the old man added, after a pause of deep thought, "I was anxious to find such plausible grounds of suspicion against other parties, such element of doubt, such possibilities as might make it difficult for the judges to condemn our friend. I wanted to puzzle the court; but, per Bacco! I have puzzled myself. This afternoon, I confess to you, I had little doubt but that the Marchesino had, in a fatal moment of anger and desperation, committed the crime. But, upon my word now, I know not what to think. Here we have three parties, each of whom we know to have been acted on by one of three strong passions. We have jealousy, and wounded vanity. Which of the three has done the deed?"

"It is an extraordinary circumstance," said the Baron Manutoli, "that they were jeering at the Conte Leandro at the Circolo just now, about the way the Diva had snubbed him and his verses, and accusing him in joke of having been her murderer. And, as sure as I am now speaking to you, Signor Fortini, he looked in a way then that I—a—a—in short that I thought very odd—turned all sorts of colours. But then, you know, he is always such an unwholesome-looking animal."

"One of the vainest men I ever met with," said the lawyer, musing.

"Oh—for vanity—I believe you. Leandro has not his equal for vanity."

"And strong vanity, deeply wounded, by a woman too, will breed a hate as violent and vicious, perhaps, as any passion that ever prompted a crime," rejoined the lawyer, still meditating deeply. "Per Dio Santo!" he exclaimed, after a pause of silence, striking his open palm strongly on the table, as he spoke, and speaking with a sort of solemn earnestness, "I am inclined to think, after all, that he is the man. The Marchesino," he went on again, thoughtfully, "went out for a frolic—intelligible enough; The girl went out to look after the preparations for her work—again quite plausible. But in the name of all the saints what took the Conte Leandro out of the Porta Nuova at that hour of the morning, after passing the night at a ball?"

"I still think that the Venetian girl has done the deed," said Manutoli, whose opinion was no doubt in some degree warped by his desire that the criminal should turn out to be a foreign plebeian rather than a Ravenna noble. "After all Leandro is not the man to do such a deed. He is such a poor creature. Besides, it seems to me that the girl's motive for hate was the stronger. I don't know that wounded vanity has had many such crimes to answer for, whereas jealousy—and such a jealousy—why, it is an old story you know."

"Well, we shall see. Any way, I am very much more easy as to the result. Short of such evidence as it seems very highly unlikely should be forthcoming, I do not think that there can be any conviction at all. It is most extraordinary that in the case of such deed, done in such a place, at such a time, there should be so many persons so fairly liable to strong suspicion."

"Of course, to produce the result we wish, a case must be set up against Leandro?" said the Baron.

"Of course. Leave that to me, or rather to the police. No doubt their inquiries have already put them on his track. The fact of his having gone out of the city by that gate, at that hour, is quite enough."

"And now I must be off to see this Signorina Foscarelli. I don't half like the job."

"I daresay you will find her easy enough," said the lawyer, not quite understanding the nature of Manutoli's distaste for his errand. "Good-night, Signor Barone."

CHAPTER IX

The Post-Mortem Examination

The Baron Manutoli found Paolina quite as "easy" as the lawyer had imagined that he would find her; but his task was not altogether an easy one in the sense he had himself intended. She made not the slightest difficulty of telling him, that when she had seen Ludovico and Bianca drive past the church towards the forest she had felt a strong temptation to follow them thither; she told him all about the conversation she had had with the old monk, and repeated the directions she had received from him as to the path by which she might reach the Pineta, and return that way towards the city, without coming back into the high-road, till she got near the walls. She confessed that, when she had followed the path behind the church leading to the Pineta, for some little distance, she had changed her mind, and had turned off by another path, which had brought her back into the high-road not far from the church; and she said that she had then walked on till she came near the walls, where she turned aside to sit down on one of the benches under the trees of the little promenade; that she had sat there for some time—she did not know how long; had then gone in to the Cardinal Legate's chapel, where she had conversed with the Contessa Violante, whom she knew from having often met her there before; and had at last returned home at a very much later hour than she had expected, and had found her friend Signora Orsola Steno uneasy at her prolonged absence.

"And did you mention to the Contessa the shocking fact of the prima donna's death?" asked Manutoli, suddenly, thinking that he was doing a very sharp bit of lawyerly business in laying this trap for Paolina.

"How was it possible that I should do so, when I knew nothing about it till Ludovico told me several hours later?" answered the girl, with an unembarrassed easiness and readiness that almost changed Manutoli's opinion as to the probability of her guilt.

He reminded himself, however, that the same woman, who could be capable of such a deed might also be expected to have the presence of mind and readiness necessary for avoiding any such trap as that which he had laid for her.

He was, at the same time, strongly, but perhaps not altogether consistently, impressed with the fact; that during the whole of his interview with her, she did not once distinctly and directly deny that she had had anything to do with the crime. When warning her, as he had been charged by Ludovico to do, of the probability that she might be arrested, he had allowed her to understand that the circumstances of this case were such, that the question of who was the guilty person became nearly an alternative one between herself and the Marchese. On which, instead of protesting her own innocence, she had strongly insisted on that of Ludovico, which seemed a very suspicious circumstance to the Baron Manutoli.

He had tried to lead her to express some feeling, or, rather, some remembrance of what had been her feeling when she saw Ludovico and La Bianca in the bagarino together; but there she became reticent, and would say little or nothing—another suspicious circumstance in the eyes of the Baron, so that, when he quitted her, he was, upon the whole, rather confirmed than otherwise in his previous opinion as to her guilt.

"Well, Signorina," he had said, in rising to leave her, "I came here, in compliance with my friend's request, to re-assure you on the subject of the warrant which will, in all probability, be issued to-morrow morning for your arrest. You best know whether you have any reason for alarm. My own opinion is, that if you have nothing to reproach yourself with, you have nothing to fear. I trust it may be so."

"I am grateful to you for coming, Signor," Paolina said. "You will see Ludovico again. Tell him that I am as sure of his innocence of this horrid thing as if he had never quitted my side."

How Paolina passed that miserable night it is useless to attempt to tell. How happy all, ay, even all, the days of her previous life seemed to her in comparison with the misery of the minutes that were then so slowly passing.

Early the next morning Signor Fortini called at the house of his friend Dr. Buonaventura Tomosarchi, the great anatomist, for the purpose of accompanying the Professor to the room at the hospital, where the body of Bianca was awaiting the post-mortem examination which had been ordered by the police.

"I suppose," said Fortini, as they walked together, "that there is no possibility, in such a case as this, that the death may have been a natural one?"

"Oh, I would not say that at all. Such things occur at all ages. I do not think it is likely, specially in the case of such a magnificent organization as that of yonder poor girl; but there is no saying, and, above all, no use in attempting to guess when we shall so soon know all about it," said the Professor, a man some ten or fifteen years younger than the old lawyer.

"Is it possible that death may have been caused by foul means, yet by such as may elude your investigation?" asked Fortini.

"I think not—I should say almost certainly not in such a case as the present. There are poisons that act subtly and instantaneously, but there is the odour in most cases, in almost all some indication of their operation on the organization."

Arrived at the hospital they found a couple of assistants, pupils of the Professor, awaiting his arrival. There was also an official on the part of the police, and there were two or three persons waiting in the hope of being allowed to be present at the examination. The police officer, however, very summarily declared that this could not be permitted. Fortini was so well known, and held such a kind of half-official position and character in the city, that he passed on unquestioned on the arm of the Professor.

The body lay exactly as it had been brought in by the labouring-men who had found it in the Pineta. The beautiful face was perfectly calm, and in the lineaments of it the difference that there is between death and sleep was scarcely perceptible. The white dress was almost as unruffled and as spotless as when she had put it on. It had been fastened about midway between the neck and the waist by a diamond pin or brooch; but this fastening was now undone, and the brooch was hanging loosely on one side of the bosom of the dress. It was impossible to suppose that this jewel should have been so left by anybody who had had the opportunity and the desire of plunder. It might have been unfastened by the wearer before she slept for the sake of more full enjoyment of the balmy breezes of the pine-forest: and the result of this loosening of the dress was that the light folds of it opened freely as far down as the waist, so that the slightest drawing aside of them, such as even the breeze might effect, was sufficient to leave bare the entire bosom.

On either shoulder and on the bosom lay the large heavy waves of the rich auburn hair. In death, as she had been in life, she was still a wonder of beauty; and the two men, the old lawyer and the Professor, little as, from years, character, and habits of mind, their imaginations were susceptible of being deeply touched by such a sight, stood for awhile by the side of the table on which the body had been laid, and gazed in sad silence on the sight before them.

"One might think she was still sleeping, poor creature," said the lawyer, after a silence of a few minutes.

"Ay, almost. It is a wonderfully lovely face. Seems difficult to believe, doesn't it, that any man—. Much less such a man as the Marchese—should have stood over that figure, and so looking down on it, have decided on destroying it?" said the Professor.

"Perhaps no man did so," said the lawyer.

"Case of death from natural causes, you mean? I am afraid not, I am afraid not. Can't say for certain yet; but, judging from appearances, I fear there is no likelihood that such was the case," rejoined the Professor.

"I was not thinking of that," replied Fortini. "I meant that what a man could hardly have had the heart to do might, perhaps, have been done by a woman. Beauty is not, I fancy, always found to produce quite the same sort of effect on another female as it is wont to produce on the other sex."

"Might have been done by a woman? That seems hardly likely, I think, caro mio. In the Pineta at that hour of the morning? Che! What woman is likely to have been there?"

"Well, we happen to know that there was a woman very near the spot where the crime was committed at the time that it was committed."

"You don't say so?" interrupted the anatomist. "Good heavens! This is quite new to me, and, of course, most important. I am delighted to hear what seems to cast so strong a doubt on the guilt of the Marchesino."

"And that is not all. We know further," continued the lawyer, eagerly, "that the woman in question had the strongest of all the possible motives that ever influence a female mind to hate—to desire the death of this poor girl that now lies here. The question is, whether this death was caused by any means which a woman—a young girl—may be supposed to have used," said the lawyer.

"Ha! a case of jealousy, I suppose? You don't mean it. God knows, I should be more glad than I will say if there were any means of showing that the Marchese Ludovico had no hand in the matter. If it were brought home to him it would kill my old friend the Marchese Lamberto outright; I do believe it would kill him."

"I thought at first, to tell you the truth, Signor Professore, that it must have been the Marchesino who did the deed; the circumstances seemed so terribly strong against him. But—certain facts have come to my knowledge—in short, I begin to have very great hopes that he was in reality wholly innocent of it; and still greater hopes that if we cannot succeed in bringing the crime home to any other party, yet that the difficulty and doubt hanging about the case will be so great that all conviction will be impossible."

"A woman, you tell me? A young woman, I suppose, from what you say?" said the Professor, inquiringly.

"Yes; a young woman, and, as I am told, a very pretty one—a certain young girl—a Venetian artist, of the name of Foscarelli—Paolina Foscarelli, with whom it seems the Marchesino was foolish enough to fall in love. Well, this girl sees the Marchese and Bianca driving out alone together at that time in the morning to the Pineta—that much we know—sees them cheek by jowl together in a little bagarino, doing heaven only knows what—billing and cooing. Now it seems to me that she would, under these circumstances, be likely to feel not altogether kindly towards the lady in possession, eh, Signor Professore? You know the nature of the creatures better than I do; what do you think about it?"

"Similar little accidents have produced as terrible results before now—ay, many a time, there is no denying that. If we can ascertain how the deed was done it will be likely enough to throw some light on the probabilities of the case," returned the Professor, proceeding to scrutinize carefully the body as it lay before in any way disturbing the position or the garments.

"Ha! what have we here?" he cried, as he perceived, and, at the same time, pointed out the existence of a very small red spot upon the white dress just above the waistband. In an instant, as he spoke, he whipped out a powerful magnifying-glass, and carefully examined the tell-tale spot by its aid.

"Yes, that is a spot of blood—blood sure enough! but it is very singular that there should be such a minute spot, and no more; no, I can find no further trace," he added, after a careful and minute examination of every part of the dress.

"Might not any trifling accident—the most insignificant thing in the world—produce such a mere spot as that—a scratched finger—either her own or another person's?" asked the lawyer.

"Well, hardly so; a slight stain might easily be so caused; but hardly a round spot like that. That spot must have been caused by a small drop falling on that place—not by the muslin having been brought into contact with any portion of blood, however small. How could that one little round drop of blood have come there?" said the anatomist, thoughtfully. "It is singular enough."

Then, when the dress had been removed preparatory to the examination of the body, the Professor himself and his assistants minutely searched every part of it—in vain. There was no other, even the smallest, mark of blood to be found.

"Are you sure that that spot is blood?" asked the lawyer.

"Are you sure whether a deed is signed or is not signed when you see it?" retorted the anatomist. "Yes; that spot has been caused by a drop of blood falling there—a very minute drop. Of that there can be no doubt. And now we must proceed to examine the body externally. If there should be nothing to be learned from that, we must see what revelations the knife may bring to light."

And then the Professor, aided by his pupils, proceeded to institute a minute and careful examination of the body.

At the first sight it appeared to be as unblemished in every part of it as Nature's choicest and most perfect handiwork could be. So little did a mere cursory view suggest the possibility that life would have been destroyed by any external violence, that the Professor was about to take the necessary steps for ascertaining what light could be thrown on the manner of her death by the internal condition of the different portions of the organism, when the sharper eyes of one of the young assistants were drawn to a very slight indication, which he immediately pointed out to his superior.

The appearance in question consisted of a very small round white spot, around which there was a slight equally circular redness. It was situated nearly in the middle of the body, just below the meeting of the ribs on the chest, about a broad hand's breadth above the waistband—in such a position, in short, as to be very nearly at the point where the neck-opening of the dress ceased.

No second glance was needed, as soon as the Professor's attention had been called to this appearance, to ensure the riveting of his attention on it. Nor was much examination necessary to convince him that he had now, in truth, discovered the cause and the means of death.

The slight mark in question was, in fact, the trace of a wound inflicted by a very fine needle, which had pierced the heart, and, having caused immediate death, had been left in the wound, ingeniously hidden by means which it needed a second look to discover. The effect of this discovery on the Professor was singular. He seemed taken aback by it, and, one would have said, alarmed at it, in a manner which it seemed difficult for Signor Fortini to account for. "What is it astonishes you so, Signor Professore," said he; "surely you were prepared to find that a murder had been done? I never had any doubt of it; and why not in that way as well as another? And a very ingenious mode of inflicting death in a quiet way it seems to be."

"Yes, indeed. The fact is that I was struck by—"

The Professor broke off speaking suddenly with a start; and darted a quick alarmed glance at the face of Signor Fortini, who did not fail to remark it, and to be much puzzled by the Professor's manner.

The latter, while he had been speaking, had stooped to examine the minute trace of the wound closely, and had put his finger on the spot; and it was on doing so that he had interrupted himself, and shown renewed symptoms of surprise and dismay. What this closer examination had shown him was the fact that an infinitesimally small portion of white wax had been very neatly and carefully introduced into the orifice of the wound, in such a manner as to prevent all effusion of blood, and almost to escape the observation of the naked eye.

"Why, one would say you were a novice at this sort of thing, Tomosarchi, you seem so much affected by it," said the lawyer; "what is it that moves you so? Why, you are as pale, man, as if you were bringing to light a crime of your own instead of somebody else's."

"Ah! not that exactly. No, but it is a very singular thing. One would say that this death must have been caused by some one who had some little knowledge of anatomy, or, at least, had been put up to the trick by some one else who possessed such knowledge," said the Professor, recovering himself with an effort.

"And that is what our friend the Marchesino Ludovico is most assuredly innocent of. I take note of your remark, Signor Professore," said the lawyer.

"But one would think, that all the other persons on whom it is possible that suspicion might rest, must be equally void of any such knowledge," returned Tomosarchi.

"How do we know that? How can I tell what strange odds and ends of knowledge this Venetian artist may have picked up. Artists, they have constantly more or less acquaintance with medical students, and such like. Some knowledge of anatomy is needful to them in their business. For my part, it seems to me very likely that this girl might have such knowledge as would teach her so easy a way of getting rid of her rival. Then you will observe that very little physical strength was needed for the infliction of such a wound. It might have been done perfectly easily by the hand of a young girl. I declare it seems to me that the result of your examinations tends to make it more probable than ever that the Venetian is the criminal."

"Well, it may be so. Certain it is, that no degree of strength beyond what she, or any other such person could have exerted, was needed for giving that death to a sleepy person. But it is equally clear that a certain amount of special knowledge was required for the purpose," rejoined the anatomist. "And now," added he; "I must draw up my report. A rivederci, Signor Fortini! A rivederci, Signori!"

"One word more, Signor Professore, before I leave you," said the lawyer; "is the special knowledge you speak of, such as—any member of your profession we will say—would be possessed of."

"Well, I should not say that it was likely such a method of concealing a crime would have suggested itself to such a one, more than to another. It is the clever invention of one who meditated murder. But, I may say at once to you, what I shall have to say in due season to the magistrates, that the trick is not a new one. I have heard of such a thing before now."

"But not as a common thing," pursued the lawyer.

"Quite the reverse—as a very strange and peculiar thing," replied the Professor.

"And when did you hear of a case of murder committed in this strange and peculiar manner?" persisted the lawyer.

The Professor shot a sharp quick glance at the lawyer's face; and his own flushed red as he replied, "Ay—if I could remember that—but it is a reported case; anybody may have read it. A murder was committed by similar means in the Island of Sardinia, not very long ago!"

"Not very long ago," reiterated the lawyer, musingly.

"No, not very long ago; but the case has been reported, I tell you. Anybody may have read it."

"Humph," said the lawyer, as he turned to go, with his mind evidently busily at work both on the strange sort of confusion that had been visible in the Professor's manner, and on the circumstances he had elicited from him.

"I'll tell you what," said one of the young students to the other, while they were engaged in preparing to consign the body of the murdered woman to the police. "I'll tell you what: I'll be blessed if I don't think the governor knows, or has a shrewd guess, who it is has done this job. Did you mark the way he looked, and went as pale as death, when I showed him the place?"

"Bah, nonsense! He was vexed that he had not seen it himself. How should he know anything about it?"

"I don't know how; but I know him, and his ways," said the first speaker.

"But if he thinks he has any guess at the murderer, why don't he say it at once?" asked the younger lad.

"Ah, yes, I think so; I should like to see him at it. That's not his business, that's the lawyer's business. You may depend on his keeping his own secret, if he has got one. The governor likes quiet sailing in still water, he does. But if he did not see something more in this little bit of steel and atom of wax, that have stopped a life so cleverly, than the mere things themselves and the effect of them, why, then, I know nothing about old Buonaventura Tomosarchi, that's all."

"How see something more?" said the younger lad, open-eyed.

"Saw who put 'em there, Ninny. It is not everybody who could be up to such a dodge; and I feel sure the governor could make a shrewd guess who did that clever trick."

CHAPTER X

Public Opinion

The post-mortem examination had taken place at an early hour, before the members of the idler portion of the society of the city had come forth from their homes. An Italian idler—one of the class who, in common Italian phrase, are able to "fare vita beata," to lead a happy life, i. e. to do nothing whatever from morning till night—an Italian of that favoured class never passes his hours in his own house, or dwelling of whatever kind it may be. As soon as he is up and dressed he goes out into the city to enjoy the air and sunshine if it be fine weather, to saunter in cafes or at the Circolo, if it rain.

Professor Tomosarchi and lawyer Fortini had been earlier afoot, and the scene described in the last chapter had passed, and the general results of the examination were beginning to be known in the city, when the jeunesse doree of Ravenna began to assemble at the Circolo. It was known also by that time that the young Venetian artist, with whom Ludovico was well known to be on intimate terms of some kind or other, had been arrested at her lodging at an early hour that morning, on suspicion of having been concerned in the murder of La Bianca.

Of course that terrible event continued more than ever to occupy the attention of all Ravenna, almost to the exclusion of every other topic of conversation. It was very easy to understand the nature of the motive, which might be supposed to have led Paolina to do the deed. And when it became known farther, that the means by which the death of the victim had been brought about were such as might easily have been accomplished by the weakest woman's hand; and that it had been discovered that Paolina had been in the Pineta—for such was the not quite accurate form which the report assumed just about the time when the crime must have been committed, the general opinion inclined very much to the notion that she, the stranger from Venice, was, indeed, the assassin.

Precedents were hunted up, and many a story told of women who had done equally desperate deeds under similar provocation.

"I feel very little doubt of it, myself," said Manutoli; "there is nothing improbable in such a solution, while it is in the highest degree improbable that Ludovico should have raised his hand against a sleeping woman, enticed by him in the forest for the purpose. Bah! It is monstrous."

"He would have been more to be pitied than blamed if he had done it," said another of the young men, who did not bear himself a reputation of the most brilliant sort; "if I had a rich uncle I swear by all the saints, that I would not let the prettiest woman that ever made a fool of a man, come between me and my inheritance."

"Ludovico was not the man to have done it any way. Besides, the mischief had not been done; it was only a project talked of. There might have been a hundred ways of breaking off so absurd a match. It would have been time to have recourse to les grands moyens, when the thing had been done, and all else had failed. To my notion jealousy has done it."

"So say I. Two to one I bet that it turns out that the Venetian girl has done the trick."

"But have you heard, all of you, that there is a third horse in the field?" said the Marchese Faraoni whose palazzo was close to the house in which the Conte Leandro lived; "there is another candidate for the galleys. Has nobody heard that our poet was arrested before he was out of bed this morning?"

"What! Leandro?"

"The Conte Lombardoni?"

"No!"

"You don't mean that?"

"What, arrested for this murder of La Bianca?"

"Impossible!"

"But quite true, nevertheless. Anybody can easily assure themselves of the fact by walking as far as the Palazzo del Governo."

"Leandro arrested on suspicion of murder? Well, I think the tragedy is passing into a farce."

"It will be fatal to Leandro. He will die of fright, if no other evil happens to him."

"Think of the cantos of verse he will make on it."

"He will die singing, like a swan."

"But do you know anything about it, Faraoni? Have you any idea how he has come to be implicated in the matter?"

"I learnt at his own lodging that he did not come home to bed the night of the ball, but was absent from home at the time the murder must have been committed. And then I was told that the men at the Porta Nuova had declared that they had seen him pass out of the city going in the direction of the Pineta at a very early hour that morning."

"Per Bacco! it is very strange. What, in the name of all the saints, could he be doing out there at that time, when all honest folks were in their beds?"

"Remember all the snubbing he has had from the poor Diva all through carnival. By Jove! it looks very queer."

"Do you remember how he turned all sorts of colours here last night, when we were talking of it?"

"And how anxious he seemed to say everything that appeared to make it bear hard upon Ludovico?"

"Yes, and contradicted himself. First, he knew about it, and then he knew nothing."

"Per Dio! I don't know what to think of it."

"So, then, there are now three persons suspected—Ludovico; and the Venetian girl, and the Conte Leandro?"

"And all three were not far from the spot where the deed was done, and all three had motives, more or less credible, for doing it."

"Ludovico, because his uncle was going to marry the woman, which would have cut him out of his inheritance; the Venetian girl, because she loved Ludovico, and saw him making love to the poor Diva; and Leandro, because she snubbed him, and laughed at him, and would have nothing to say to either him or his verses."

"And the one certain thing is, that the unlucky Diva lies dead, and was murdered by somebody. Upon my life, it is the queerest thing I ever heard of."

"What do you think of it, Manutoli?" said one of the speakers in the foregoing dialogue to the Baron, who was an older man than most of the others there.

"My notion is that the girl is the guilty party," said Manutoli. "As for Leandro, it seems too absurd. I don't think he has courage enough to kill a cat: Besides, I daresay he hated La Bianca quite enough to slander her, and backbite, and that sort of thing; but murder—"

"She made fun of him. Leandro don't like to be laughed at, specially by the women, and, more specially still, when other fellows are by to hear it and then those poets are always such desperate fellows I should not wonder—" said one of the young men.

In the meantime, while talk of this sort was going on at the Circolo, Signor Fortini was on his way out to St. Apollinare in Classe, according to the intention he had expressed on the preceding evening; but he was not making the expedition alone. Signor Pietro Logarini, the Papal Commissioner of Police, was bound on the same errand. The old lawyer, as he passed under the gateway of the Porta Nuova in his comfortable caleche, overtook Signor Logarini, who was about to proceed to St. Apollinare on foot, and who had paused at the gate for the purpose of making some inquiries of the officials there.

"Good morning, Signor Pietro. I suppose we are bound for the same place; will you permit me to offer you a seat in my carriage?" said the lawyer.

"Thanks, Signor Giovacchino, I shall be glad of the lift. Yes, I suppose we are about the same business, and a bad one it is. I was making a few inquiries at the gate; but I don't see that there is much to be gleaned there," said the Commissary, as he got into the lawyer's carriage.

"Well, it seems to me that we have reaped a pretty good harvest there already," returned the lawyer.

"Enough to make the matter one of the most puzzling I ever had to do with," returned the Commissary. "You have heard, I suppose, that we have arrested the girl Paolina Foscarelli, and the Conte Leandro Lombardoni?"

"No; but it was a matter of course that you would do so—specially the girl," said the lawyer.

"We could not avoid arresting the Conte also; it is so unaccountable that he should have been going out of the city, and so near the place of the crime."

"What account does he give of the matter himself?" asked the lawyer.

"No very clear one; and he seems to be frightened out of his senses; but that proves nothing. One man takes a thing coolly, another is so flushed that you would think he was guilty only to look at him; but there is little to be judged from such appearances. I don't much think the Conte had anything to do with it, for my part."

"What were you asking about at the gate?"

"Well, I thought I would just ascertain if any other parties had passed the gate that same morning," said the Commissary.

"Others! Have we not enough to make a sufficient puzzle already?" said Fortini.

"Yes, indeed; but information is always useful. The men say that they are quite sure that no other person of any kind whatever passed the gate either outwards or inwards, during the night till the Conte Leandro passed in the morning; and then the girl not long afterwards; and then the Marchesino with the prima donna."

The lawyer remained plunged in thought for some minutes, as the carriage rolled over the flat dismal-looking road towards the old church; and then he said, shaking his head, and pouting out his lips, "I think we shall find, Signor Pietro, that that girl has done it. There's nothing a jealous woman will not do. We shall find, I think, that to have been the case; that is, if we succeed in finding out anything at all. Perhaps the most likely thing is that we may never know what hand did the deed."

"Oh, come, I hope better things than that. That would not suit our book at all. We must find it out if we can; and it is early days yet to talk of being beat. We are not half at the end of our means of investigation yet, Signor Giovacchino," said the Commissary.

"It may be that something may be to be picked up at the church here."

"And then I must go on to the farm-house, where the Marchesino and the prima donna left their carriage."

"We'll have a talk with the friars first."

As Fortini spoke the carriage drew up at the west front of the desolate old basilica. It was a fine spring morning, and by the time the lawyer and the Commissary reached the church, the sun had dissipated the mist, and it was warm and pleasant.

The great doors of the church stood yawningly open as usual, and the gate of iron rail was ajar. And at the south-western corner of the building, just where the sun-ray from the south-west made a sharp line against the black shadow cast by the western front of the building, an old Franciscan was sitting; not Father Fabiano, but his sole companion, Friar Simone, the lay-brother.

Neither Signor Fortini nor the police Commissary had ever seen the old guardian of the Basilica; but they were sufficiently instructed in the details of Franciscan costume to perceive at once that the figure before them was not a priest, but only a lay-brother.

"Is there any place, frate, where I can put my horse and carriage under shelter for half an hour or so?" said the lawyer, as the old friar, having risen from his seat in the sunshine, came forward towards the carriage.

"There is place enough and to spare, Signori," said the old man, pointing with a languid and wearylike gesture to the huge pile of half-dilapidated conventual buildings on the southern side of the church; "you can put horse and carriage as they stand into the old barn there, without undoing a buckle. I will open the door for your lordships, if it will hang together so that it can be opened."

The lawyer and the Commissary dismounted from the carriage, and the former proceeded to lead his horse into the huge barn of the convent; while the latter employed himself in observing every detail of the surrounding localities with those rapid all-seeing and all-remembering glances that the habits and education of his profession had rendered a part of his nature, preparatory to the investigations they had both come to make.

CHAPTER XI

In Father Fabiano's Cell

"You can enter the Basilica at your pleasure, Signori; the gate is unlocked," said the lay-brother, indicating the entrance to the church with a half-formed gesture of his hand, which fell to his side again when he had half raised it, as if the effort of extending his arm horizontally had been too much for him. It was a matter of course to him that any human beings who came to St. Apollinare could have no business there but to see the old walls, which he, the friar, would have given so much never to see again.

"We will do so presently," said Signor Logarini, in reply; "but, in the first place, we wish to speak with Father Fabiano—he is the custode of the church, is he not?"

"Father Fabiano is ill a-bed, Signor; I am only out of my bed since yesterday, and it is as much as I can do to crawl. There's not many days in the year, I think, that we are both well; and if we should be both down together, God help us. It is not just the healthiest place in the world, this."

"What is the matter with the padre? Has he been ill long?" asked the lawyer, with a glance at the Commissary.

"Since yesterday afternoon. Why, I tell you I was in bed yesterday; he down, I must turn out. Ah—h—h! it 'll all be over one of these days."

"But what ails the custode?" asked Signor Logarini again.

"Fever and ague, I suppose; that is what is always killing both of us more or less. Pity it is so slow about it!" muttered the lay-brother, returning to his seat in the sunshine.

"But I suppose that Father Fabiano is not so ill but that we can speak with him? It is important that we should do so," said the Commissary, eyeing the friar with a suspicious glance.

"There is nothing to prevent you or anybody else going to him that choose to do so—nothing to prevent any one of those cattle doing so, for that matter. There is neither bolt nor latch; you can go into his chamber, if you are so minded," returned the lay-brother, rather surlily.

"Will you go and tell him that—Signor Fortini from Ravenna wishes to speak with him, and would be obliged by his permission to come into his room for a few minutes. We don't wish to disturb him more than is necessary."

"I'll tell him—though you might as well go to him yourselves at once for that matter; it is weary work going up the stairs so often—and I can hardly crawl."

And, so saying, the poor old lay-brother tottered off to one of the numerous doorless entrances of the half-ruined mass of building, and set himself wearily to climb a small stair, the foot of which was just within it.

The lawyer and the Commissary looked at each other; and the latter said, with a wink at his companion, "I thought it better, you see, to say nothing about the Commissary of Police; it would have frightened the old fellow out of his wits; and it is always time enough to let him know who we are if he won't speak without. But I know these animals of friars, Signor Giovacchino, I know them well; and there isn't a man or woman, townsman or countryman, noble or peasant that I wouldn't rather have to deal with than a monk or a friar. Let 'em so much as smell the scent of layman in any position of authority, and it makes 'em as obstinate and contradictious and contrary as mules, and worse. If this old fellow here has got anything to hide, you'll see that we shall not be able to get it out of him."

"But I don't see what interest or wish he can have to hide anything from us," said Fortini.

"N—n—no; one don't see that he should have but one can't be too suspicious, mio buono Signor Giovacchino," said the police authority; "and then, what does he mean by being ill?" he added, after a little thought; "he was well yesterday. It looks me very much as if he did not want to be questioned."

"I should not think that he can have much to tell. We shall see whether his account confirms the story of the girl as to what took place in the church. But the probability is that that part of her tale is all true enough. The question is what did she do with herself during all those hours that elapsed between the time she quitted the church and the time when she reached her home? And I have little hope that the friar should be able to throw any light upon that," said the lawyer.

"We shall see; here comes the lay-brother. Ugh! what a life it must be to live in such a place as this from one year's end to the other; nothing but a frate could stand it," said the Commissary, looking upon the desolation around him with infinite disgust.

"Father Fabiano is not much fit to speak to anybody; the cold fit of the ague is very strong upon him. But if you choose to go up to him you can—specially as there is nothing to stop you. He is in the right-hand cell on the first landing-place up that staircase," said the lay-brother, feebly pointing to the entrance, from which he had come out.

The lawyer and the police official followed the indications thus given them, and found, as old Simone had said, that there was neither bolt, lock, nor latch to prevent any creature that could push a door on its hinges, from entering the little bare-walled room in which the friar lay beneath a heavy quilted coverlet on a little narrow pallet.

There was not so much as a single chair in the room. The walls were clean, and freshly whitewashed; and the brick floor was also clean. There were a few pegs of deal in the wall on the side of the cell opposite to the doorway, on which some garments were hanging; and on the wall facing the bed there was a large, rudely carved, and yet more rudely painted crucifix. By the side of the bed nearest the door there hung, on a nail driven into the wall, a copper receptacle for holy water, the upper part of which was ornamented with a figure of St. Francis in the act of receiving the "Stigmata," in repousse work, by no means badly executed. And pasted on the bare wall, immediately above the pillow of the little bed, was a coloured print of the cheapest and vilest description, representing the Madonna with the seven legendary poignards sticking in her bosom, and St. Francis, supported on either side by a friar of his order, kneeling at her feet.

These objects formed absolutely the entire furniture of the cell. There was nothing else whatsoever in the room; neither the smallest fragment of a looking-glass, nor any means or preparation for ablution whatsoever.

The old monk lay on his back in the bed, wit his head propped rather highly on a hard straw bolster; and the extreme attenuation of his body was indicated by the very slight degree in which the clothes that covered him were raised above the level of the bedstead. On the coverlet upon his chest, there was a rosary of large beads turned out of box-wood. The parts of each bead nearest to the string and in contact with each other were black with the undisturbed dirt and dust of many years. But the protuberant circumference of each wooden ball was polished to a rich shining orange-colour by the constant handling of the fingers.

It seemed both to Signor Fortini and to the Commissary, that there could be no doubt about it, that the old man was really ill. He was lying in his frock of thick brown woollen, and the cowl of it was drawn over his head. He seemed to be suffering from cold, and his teeth were audibly chattering in his head; and his thin, thin claw-like hands shook as they clutched his crucifix. His face was lividly pale, and his eyes gleamed out from under the cowl with a restless feverish brightness.

That he was ill could hardly be doubted. And it seemed to the lawyer and the Commissary as well as to the old lay-brother, natural enough to suppose that a man who fell ill at St. Apollinare was ill with fever and ague. But whether that were really the nature of his malady, his visitors had not sufficient medical knowledge to judge; but it was probable enough that the aged monk had had quite sufficient experience of fever and ague, to know pretty well himself, whether he were suffering from that cause or not.

"We are sorry to find you ill, father," said Fortini; "and though we have come from Ravenna on purpose to speak with you, we would not have disturbed you if our business had not been important. Are you suffering much now?"

"Not much more than usual," said the sick man, shutting his eyes, while his pallid lips continued to move, as he muttered to himself an "Ave Maria."

"And can you give us your attention for a few minutes?" rejoined the lawyer.

"I will answer to your asking as far as I can; but my head is confused, and I don't remember much clearly about anything. It seems to me as if I had been lying on this bed for months and months," replied the old friar.

"And yet, you know, you were up and well yesterday morning, when you were with the young girl who came to copy the mosaics, you know, on the scaffolding in the church?" said the lawyer.

"Yes; I was with the girl—Paolina Foscarelli, a Venetian—on the scaffolding. Was it yesterday?"

"Yesterday it was that she was here. Yesterday morning. And it is hardly necessary to ask you if you know what happened here in the Pineta much about that time, or shortly afterwards. You have heard of the murder, of course?"

So violent a trembling seized on the aged man as the lawyer spoke thus, that he was unable to answer a word. His old hands shook so that he could hardly hold the beads in his fingers, while his chattering teeth and trembling lips tried to formulate the words of a prayer.

"Did you, or did you not hear that a dreadful murder was committed yesterday morning in the Pineta not far from this place?" said the Commissary, speaking for the first time, and in a less kindly manner than the old lawyer had used.

A redoubled access of teeth-chattering and shivering was for some time the only result elicited by this question. The old friar shook in every limb; and the beads of the rosary rattled in his trembling fingers, as he attempted to pass them on their string in mechanically habitual accompaniment to the invocations his lips essayed to mutter.

"It is a terrible thing to speak of truly, father; and we are sorry to be obliged to distress you by forcing such a subject on your thoughts; but it is our duty to make these inquiries; and you can tell us the few facts—they cannot be many or of much importance—which have come to your knowledge on the subject," said the lawyer, speaking in more gentle accents.

"I heard nothing; but I saw," said the aged man, closing his eyes, as if to shut out the vision which was forced back upon his imagination; and fumbling nervously with his beads, while his pale blue lips trembled with mutterings of mechanically repeated ejaculations.

"Take your time, padre mio," said the lawyer gently, making a gesture with his raised band, at the same time, to repress the less patient eagerness of the Commissary of Police; "we do not want to hurry you. Tell us what it was that you saw."

CHAPTER XII

The old friar opened his haggard eyes, which gleamed out with a feverish light from the bottom of their sockets, and from under the shadow of his cowl, and looked piteously up into the lawyer's face. "A little time—a moment to collect my thoughts," he said, passing his parched tongue over the still dryer parchment-like skin of his drawn lips, and painfully swaying his cowled head from one side of the hard pillow to the other, while large drops of perspiration gathered on his brow.

The Commissary shot a meaning glance across the pallet on which the old man lay, to the lawyer, in evident anticipation of the importance of the revelation, heralded by so much of painful emotion.

"By all means, padre mio; collect your thoughts. We are sorry for the necessity which obliges us to force your mind back on such painful ones," said the lawyer, laying his hand on that of the friar, which was still fumbling with the shining bog-wood beads, scarcely more yellow than the claw-like fingers which held them. "You saw—?"

Still no reply came from the old friar's lips. He writhed his body in the bed, and the manifestation of his agony became more and more intense. The eager impatient air of the Commissary changed itself into one of persistent dogged determination; and he quietly drew from his pocket a note-book and the means of writing in it.

"Now, father, you will be able to tell us what you saw?" said the lawyer in a soothing coaxing voice.

"I saw," said the old friar at length, speaking with his eyes again closed—"I saw the dead body of the woman who had passed the church towards the Pineta in the morning, brought back by six men from the forest. They passed by the western front of the church, and I saw that the body was the body of the woman I speak of."

The Commissary shut up his note-book with a gesture of provoked disappointment, and shrugged his shoulders impatiently.

"If that is all you have to tell us, frate, you need not have made so much difficulty about it," he said; "we knew all that before, and need not have come here to be told it. Plenty of people saw the bringing in from the forest of the body of the murdered woman, and would give evidence to the fact without making so much ado about it. Is that all you saw?"

"Did you not see," said the lawyer, again motioning his companion to be patient; "did you not see another young woman in the forest yesterday morning?"

"Not in the forest," replied the friar without any difficulty. "Not in the forest; I saw another young woman here yesterday, but it was in the church. She came here to make copies of some of the mosaics. I had been previously told to expect such an one."

"Did she come to the church before the time when you saw the other lady pass towards the forest?" asked the lawyer.

"Yes; about half an hour or more before," answered the friar.

"And where was she when the second lady passed, going towards the Pineta?" asked the lawyer again.

"She was on the scaffolding in the church, which had been prepared for her to make her copies of the mosaics."

"Do you know whether she saw, or was aware that the second lady had passed the church to go towards the Pineta?"

"I know that she was aware of it; I was with her on the scaffolding. We both together saw the woman who was afterwards brought back dead pass in a bagarino with the Marchese Ludovico di Castelmare, towards the Pineta."

The lawyer looked hard at the Commissary; and the latter in obedience, as it seemed, to the look, took out his note-book again, and made a note of the declaration.

"And what did the young lady who came to copy the mosaics do afterwards? Where did you part with her?" resumed the lawyer.

"She left the church, and walked in the direction of the forest. I parted from her at the door of the church."

"And did you see her any more in the course of that morning?" asked the lawyer again.

"I did not: I saw her no more from that time to this," replied the friar. During the whole of this interrogation, he had appeared far less distressed and disturbed than he had been before speaking of his having seen the body of La Bianca carried past the church towards the city. He had answered all the questions concerning Paolina readily and without hesitation.

"I don't think we need trouble you any further, frate," said the Commissary. "I hope that you will soon get over your touch of fever; and then, if we need you, there will be no difficulty in your attending, when wanted, in the city. I don't see, that there is anything more to be got at present," he added, addressing the lawyer.

So the two visitors bade the friar adieu, and went down the stairs on to the open piazza in front of the church.

"Does that fellow know anything more than he tells us?" said the Commissary, as they stepped out of the narrow entry on to the green sward of the piazza.

"I fancy not; I don't see much what he is at all likely to know," replied the lawyer.

"Nor I; but his manner was so remarkable. One would have said that he was conscious of having committed the murder himself. In all my experience I never saw a man so hard put to it to tell a plain and simple fact."

"Well, the poor old fellow is ill, you see. And then, no doubt, the sight of the body brought back out of the forest made a terrible impression on him. The extreme seclusion, tranquillity, and monotony of his life here, the absence from year's end to year's end of any sort of emotion of any kind, would naturally have the result of increasing the painful effect which such an event and such a sight would have upon him. My own notion is that there is nothing further to be got out of him."

"There is our friend the lay-brother sitting in the sunshine just where we left him. We might as well just see what he can tell us before going back to the city."

"He seems very ill, the padre," pursued the Commissary, addressing himself to brother Simone, as he and the lawyer lounged up to the spot where he was sitting; "the fever must have laid hold of him very suddenly; for it seems he was well enough yesterday morning."

"That is the way with the maledetto morbo," returned the lay-brother; "one hour you are well—as well, that is to say, as one can ever be in such a place as this—and the next you are down on your back shivering and burning like—like the poor souls in purgatory. Doubtless the more of it one has had, the less there is to come. That's the only comfort."

"The padre's mind seems to have been very painfully affected by the sight of the body of the woman, who was murdered in the forest, as it was being carried back to the city. Did you see it too?" asked the lawyer, observing the friar narrowly, as he spoke.

"Si, Signor, I saw it too, and a piteous sight it was. Father Fabiano and I were both out here on the piazza when the body was carried past. For I was just coming from the belfry yonder, where I had been to ring Compline; and the padre was at the same time coming out of the church, where he had been as usual with him at that hour, at his devotions before the altar of the Saint."

"Then at the hour of Compline the father had not yet been taken ill?" observed the Commissary. "Scusi, Signor; I think he had been struck by the fever at that time. He fell a-shivering and a-shaking so that he could hardly stand, when the body was carried past. But that is the way the mischief always begins. Ah, there's never a doctor knows it better than I do, and no wonder."

"You don't think then," said the lawyer, "that it was the sight of the dead body that moved him so?"

"Why should it?" said the lay-brother, in the true spirit of monastic philosophy; "why should it? all flesh is grass; there is nothing so strange in death. He sighed and groaned a deal, but that is often Father Fabiano's way when he comes out from his exercises in the church. He seemed as if he could hardly stand on his legs: but, bless you, that was the fever. He took to his bed as soon as ever the men carrying the body were out of sight. He's an old man is Father Fabiano."

"Where had he been all the time between the time when the painter lady left the church, and the hour of Compline?" asked the Commissary, who had been busily thinking during the lay-brother's moralizings.

"Ever since a little after the Angelus he had been on his knees at the altar of St. Apollinare, according to his custom. He told me so, when he came to give me my potion; for I was down with the fever yesterday morning."

"Do you know where he was before the Angelus?" returned the Commissary.

"He had to ring the Angelus himself, seeing that I was down with the fever. And he came back to the convent in a hurry, fearing that he was too late. There's very little doubt that it was heating himself that way that made the fever take hold of him."

"Where was he hurrying back from, then? Where had he been?" asked the Commissary, endeavouring to hide his eagerness for the reply to this question under a semblance of carelessness.

"He told me, when he came to my cell, that he had been into the forest; and it was plain to see that the walk had been too much for him; he's too old for moving much now, is Father Fabiano."

"He had been into the forest; and when he came back at the hour of the Angelus, he seemed quite overcome by his walk?" said the Commissary, recapitulating, and taking out his note-book as he spoke.

"Yes, he did; so much so, that as I lay on my bed and listened to the Angelus bell a-going, I thought to myself that the old man had hardly the strength to pull the rope," said the lay-brother.

"Hardly strength to pull the rope," repeated the Commissary, as he completed the note he was scribbling in his note-book. "Well, I hope he will soon get over his attack of fever. I think we need not trouble you any further at present, frate—what is your name, my friend?"

"Simone, by the mercy of God, lay-brother of the terz' ordine—"

"That will do, frate Simone," interrupted the Commissary, adding a word to the entry in his note-book. "Now, Signor Giovacchino, if you are ready, I think we may get your carriage out of the barn and go back to Ravenna."

"We have not got much for our pains, I am afraid," said the lawyer to the Commissary of police as they began to leave the Basilica behind them on their way back to the city.

"Humph!" said the Commissary, who was apparently too much absorbed in his own meditations to be in a mood for conversation.

"Signor Giovacchino," he said, suddenly, after they had traversed nearly half their short journey in silence, "my belief is that your young friend the Marchese has no hand in this matter."

"I am convinced he had not," said the lawyer, who was, however, very far from having reached any conviction of the kind; "but what we want is some such probable theory on the subject as shall compete successfully with the theory of his guilt in the matter."

"That theory—shall I give it you? It is not only a theory; it is my firm belief as to the facts of the case."

"You suspect—"

"I more than suspect—I am very strongly persuaded that this murder has been committed by the girl Paolina Foscarelli."

"My own notion—"

"Look here, this is how it has been. The Marchese Ludovico has made love to this girl—has made her in love with him—taking the matter au grand serieux, in the way girls will—specially, I am told, it is the way, with those Venetian women. Well, by ill chance, as the devil would have it, she sees her lover starting on a tete-a-tete expedition into the Pineta with this other girl—just the woman of all others in the world, as I am given to understand, to be a dangerous rival, and to excite a deadly jealousy. This much we have in evidence. Further, we know that the girl Paolina was expected to return from her expedition to St. Apollinare early in the morning—say at nine o'clock, or thereabouts—whereas she did not return till several hours afterwards. In addition to all this, we have now ascertained that when she left the church she did not set out on her return towards the city, as she might naturally be expected to have done; but, on the contrary, went in the direction of the Pineta. Then, assuming the story, told by the Marchese to be true, we know that, about the very time that this Paolina was entering the forest, her rival was lying asleep and alone there in the immediate neighbourhood. We know that the means adopted for the perpetration of the crime were such as to be quite within a woman's physical power, and that the weapon used for the purpose such as a woman may much more readily be supposed to have about her than a man; what do you say to that as a theory of the facts? Is not the evidence overpoweringly strong against this Venetian?"

"Of course my own attention had been called to the case of suspicion against her. But I confess I had not been struck by the last circumstance you mention; and it seems to me a very strong one. How can it be supposed that a man—a man like the Marchese Ludovico—should chance to have a needle about him? The case of suspicion against him, mark, altogether excludes the notion that he went out prepared to take the life of this unfortunate woman. It is suggested that he put her to death in order to escape from the ruin that would have ensued from his uncle's marriage with her. No other possible motive for such a deed can be conceived. But he knew nothing of any such purpose on the part of the Marchese till the girl herself told him of it as they were driving together to the forest. Therefore, he had not come out prepared with a needle for the purpose of committing murder. Neither, it is true, does the theory we are considering suppose that Paolina came out prepared to do such a deed. But the weapon used is a needle. Is it more likely that a man or that a woman should have by chance such an article about them? I confess it seems to me that this circumstance alone is sufficient to turn the scale of the probabilities unmistakably."

"But that is not all," said the Commissary, laying his finger impressively on the lawyer's sleeve; "my belief is that that old friar, padre Fabiano, is aware of the fact that the murder was committed by Paolina Foscarelli. I am not disposed to think that he had any hand in the doing of the deed; but I think the he has a knowledge of her guilt. He is ill now, doubtless; but I do not believe that he is suffering from fever and ague. He is suffering from the emotions of horror and terror. We know that he was in the Pineta much about the time at which the murder must have been committed, and very near the spot where it must have been committed. And he comes back in a state of terrible emotion and consternation. His manner in speaking to us to-day you must have observed. I have no belief in an old friar being so terribly impressed by the mere sight of a dead body."

"That is all true," said the lawyer, nodding his head up and down several times; "and the circumstances do seem to point to the probability of your conclusion; but—"

"But why, you will say, should the old man, if he has a merely innocent knowledge of that which I suspect him to know, refuse to tell the whole truth simply as he knows it? I will tell you why not. In the first place, if you had had as much experience of monks, and friars, and nuns, as I have, you would know that it is next to impossible to induce them ever to give information to justice of any facts which it is possible for them to conceal. It seems to them, I fancy, like recognizing a lay authority in a manner they don't like. They will communicate nothing to you if they can help it."

"Yes, that's true. I know that is the nature of them," assented the lawyer.

"Then, observe, this Father Fabiano is a Venetian, a fellow-citizen of the girl. You know how the Venetians hold together. You may feel quite sure that if he did know her to be guilty of a crime, he would screen her to the utmost of his power. Of course I have not done with him yet. Tutt' altro. We must have an account of that morning stroll in the Pineta from the old gentleman's own lips.

Meantime, I do not think that we need consider our trip to-day to have been altogether thrown away."

"Very far from it. Very far from it, indeed. Honestly, I think that you have hit the nail on the head, Signor Pietro. There is nothing like the practical experience of you gentlemen of the police, who pass your lives in playing at who-is-the-sharpest with the most astute of human beings."

"And beating them at their own game," said the Commissary, self-complacently. "If that murder was not committed by Paolina Foscarelli, I will give you or anybody else leave to call me a blockhead."

And therewith Signor Fortini and his companion drove under the old archway of the Porta Nuova and entered the city.

BOOK VI

Poena Pede Claudo

CHAPTER I

Signor Fortini Receives the Signora Steno in His Studio

It was the end of the first week in Lent; and all Ravenna was still busily engaged in talking, thinking, and speculating on the mysterious crime that had been committed on Ash Wednesday morning in the Pineta. The excitement on the subject, indeed, was greater now than it had been immediately after the event. For, by this time, everybody in Ravenna knew all that anybody knew on the subject; the manner, time, and place of the murder, and the different competing theories which had been started to account for it, and with the conflicting probabilities of which the judicial authorities were known to be occupying themselves.

These, as the reader knows, were three; based, in each case, on the fact that the suspected person was known, or was supposed to be known, to have been at, or near, to the spot where the crime was committed at the time when it had been committed.

The Marchese Ludovico was indisputably known; on his own confession, to have been in the immediate neighbourhood of the spot at the time when the murder must have been done.

Paolina Foscarelli was equally indubitably, and by her own confession, not far off from the neighbourhood of the spot at the same time.

Of the Conte Leandro Lombardoni it was known only that he had passed out of the city gate leading in the same direction, at a time which might have enabled him to be present where the deed was done, at the hour when it must have been done. The evidence as to propinquity to the place was less strong in his case than in that of either of the others; but it was supplemented by the unaccountable strangeness of his passing out of the Porta Nuova towards the Pineta at such an hour, and on that particular morning.

The Marchese Ludovico stated that he went thither for the purpose of showing the Pineta to the prima donna, who had never seen it. And there was nothing incredible or greatly improbable in the statement.

Paolina declared that she had gone to St. Apollinare in pursuit of her professional business. And the declaration was not only very probable in itself, but could be shown by evidence to be true. Only, while it accounted for her presence in the church of St. Apollinare, it left her departure from the church with her face turned, not towards the city, but towards the Pineta, unaccounted for.

In the case of the Conte Leandro, it was difficult to imagine the motive that could have induced him to leave the city at that hour, in the manner in which he was proved, by the testimony of the men at the gate, to have done. And he gave no assistance himself towards arriving at any satisfactory explanation of so strange a circumstance. He was unable, or unwilling, to account in any way for his conduct on that Ash Wednesday morning.

"He had thought it pleasanter to take a walk that fine morning, than to go to bed after the ball."

Nothing could be more unlike the usual known habits and tastes of the Conte Leandro, than such a freak. But supposing such a whim to have occurred to him, would he have set out on his walk evidently intending to be disguised—with a cloak wrapped round the fantastic costume in which he had been at the ball? Was such a supposition in any wise credible, or admissible?

In each of the three cases there seemed also to be a motive for the deed that might be deemed sufficient to have led to it; and from which neither of the parties suspected could show that they were free.

In the case of the Marchese Ludovico, it was the terrible temptation of delivering his family name from ridicule and disgrace, and himself from the prospect of absolute beggary.

In the case of Paolina, it was the madness of woman's jealousy, wrought to a pitch of desperation by circumstances similar to such as had ere now produced many a similar tragedy.

In the case of the Conte Leandro, it was the cruel mortification of a man whose monstrous vanity was notorious to the whole city.

These were the three hypotheses between which the possibilities of the case seemed to lie to those whose position or means of information gave them any real knowledge of the facts. But there was a section of the outside public which had set up for itself and preferred yet a fourth theory—namely, that the prima donna had committed suicide. The holders of this opinion were mainly women; and at the head of them; was the Signora Orsola Steno. In an agony of grief, indignation, and despair at the accusation brought against her adopted child, and the arrest by which it had been followed up, she loudly maintained her own conviction that the evil and wicked woman had brought her career to a fitting close by putting herself to death.

"Likely enough she may have endeavoured to entrap the Marchese Lamberto; but not very likely," old Orsola thought, "that that exemplary nobleman should have been caught by her wiles. Likely enough she may have plotted to play her last card, by giving the Marchese Ludovico to understand, that the only way to avoid the ruin which would fall upon him by her becoming his uncle's wife, was to take her himself. How any such overtures would be received by the noble Marchese Ludovico, all Ravenna ought to know; and at all events she, Orsola Steno, knew surely enough. And upon that rebuff, and utter failure of her last hope despair had come upon the wretched creature, as well it might, and she had put an end to herself."

To her, Orsola Steno, the case was clear: and she only wondered that anybody could be so blind as not to see it.

But what if such a supposition were simply inconsistent with the known facts? What if it were simply impossible that any person should inflict on themselves such an injury as that which it was evident the murdered woman had sustained; and more impossible still that they should have been able to adopt the means for concealing the wound which the assassin had adopted? What if such was the perfectly unhesitating judgment and declaration of the medical authorities? Such people as Orsola Steno, and those who shared her opinion, are ordinarily impervious to any such reasoning. It is remarkable that, in any case of doubt or circumstances of suspicion, the popular mind—or, at all events, the Italian popular mind—is specially disposed to mistrust the medical profession. They suspect error exactly where scientific certainty is the most perfect, and deception precisely in those who have the least possible imaginable motive for deceiving. Probably it may be because the grounds and means of the knowledge they mistrust are more wholly, than in any other case, beyond the sphere of their own conceptions.

When old Orsola Steno was told that the doctors declared that it was not within the bounds of possibility that La Bianca should have put herself to death in the manner in which she had been put to death, nothing could exceed the profundity of the contempt with which she sneered in reply:

"Ah! they'll say anything to make out that they know more than other folks, and, maybe, they often know a deal less. Don't tell me. How should they know what a woman will do when she is driven? I know what women are, and I know what them doctors are; and you may believe that an old woman, who has been a young one, knows more what such an one as that Bianca can do, when she has no hope before her, than all the doctors."

"But it is impossible—physically impossible that she could have done it."

"Ta, ta, ta, ta! Physic, indeed; what's physic got to do with it? I should like to physic them that try to throw suspicion on a poor innocent girl all to make out their own cleverness."

So Signora Orsola victoriously, and to the great increase of her confidence in her own powers of insight, continued to hold her own opinion, and it was shared by many other similarly-constituted minds.

The old Venetian woman had lived a very quiet life in the strange city to which fate had brought her, making but few acquaintances, and holding but little intercourse with those few; but now, under the terrible misfortune which had happened, she was stirred up to activity in every way in which activity was possible to her. She went to the Palazzo Castelmare and endeavoured to see the Marchese Lamberto in vain. She was told that the Marchese was ill, and could not see any one.

She went to the Contessa Violante, of whose acquaintanceship with Paolina she was aware, though she had never before seen her, and, oddly enough, the Contessa Violante was disposed to share, or to become a convert to, her own opinion respecting the mode of Bianca's death. The young Contessa was, doubtless as ignorant of all such matters as old Orsola could be. Her education had been entirely conventual, and those who dwell in the inner sanctums and fortresses of the Church have a curiously instinctive aversion to the certainties and investigations of medical—especially of surgical—science; and the Contessa Violante was, perhaps, hence prepared to vilipend and set at naught the dicta of the scientific authorities.

It was likely that her mind was also warped by the conceptions of what were probable, likely to be providential, and even suitable, in the case of such a person as the deceased singer. Of course, the whole life of such an one was, to the Contessa Violante, a thing abominable and accursed in the eyes of Heaven. It was more strange that all others, who led similar lives, and were engaged in such a profession, should not make an evil end of themselves than that one such should do so.

The Contessa Violante, therefore, was disposed to share the conviction of her visitor, as she most sincerely and cordially sympathised with her in her affliction. To her, also, it was wholly impossible to believe that Paolina had done this thing; nor was it credible to her that Ludovico should be guilty of such a deed. Of the three persons accused she would have found it more possible to believe in the guilt of the Conte Leandro; but, on the whole, she preferred to avoid the necessity of assuming that either of the accused were guilty by admitting the hypothesis of Signora Orsola.

"And if you will take my advice, Signora, I think that the best thing you could do would be to go to Signor Fortini, the lawyer, who is interested in the matter on account of being the lawyer of the Castelmare family. I have always heard him spoken of as an upright and respectable man. I have heard my uncle speak well of him. If I were you I would go and talk to him; you will very easily find out where his studio is. Go and tell him who you are, and what your interest in the matter is, and I have no doubt but that he will receive you kindly and listen to what you have to say."

And Signora Orsola took the Contessa Violante's advice, and went directly to the lawyer's studio in the little cloister under the walls of the cathedral, on leaving her adviser. As Violante had said, she had no difficulty whatever in finding it.

The lawyer was at home, and Signora Orsola was at once ushered into the inner studio, which has been described in a former chapter.

Signor Fortini was, to all appearances, entirely unoccupied; but it is probable that his mind was fully employed in striving to see his way through some portion of the difficulties that hedged about on all sides the subject on which, more or less, all Ravenna was intent. He was sitting before his table, thickly covered with papers; but had thrown himself back in his leather-covered arm-chair, and was grasping his stubbly chin with one hand, the elbow belonging to which rested on the arm of his chair, while the dark eyes, shining out beneath his contracted forehead, were fixed on the ceiling of the little room.

"Signora Orsola Steno," he said, as he half rose, and courteously offered his visitor a seat by the side of the table, so placed as to be fronting his own, while the sitter in it was exactly in a line between him and the window.

"Sua Signoria mi conosce. Your lordship knows me, then," said the old woman, whose surprise at finding herself thus recognized sufficed to put altogether out of her head all the carefully arranged opening of her interview with the lawyer which she had taken much pains to prepare.

Signor Fortini had, in truth, never seen the old woman, and had scarcely ever heard of her before the terrible event, which was now bringing her into his presence. But her name, the nature of her connection with Paolina, and very many other particulars concerning her had become known to the lawyer in the course of the investigations which that event had imposed upon him.

"Sufficiently, Signora, though I never had the pleasure of speaking to you before, to be aware of the nature of the business which has induced you to favour me with this visit," replied the lawyer, with grave courtesy.

"Well, then, Signor Dottore, I hope you will excuse—"

"There is not the smallest need for any apology, Signora. Anzi—I am very glad that you should have thought it well to call on me; I shall be most happy to hear anything that you may wish to say to me."

"You are very polite, Signor Dottore, I am sure," said the old woman, hesitatingly; for she was alarmed at the idea, which the lawyer's courtesy had suggested to her cautious mind, that she might be supposed to be engaging his professional services, and might thus find herself, before she was aware of it, involved in expenses which she had no means of meeting, and no intention of incurring; "you are extremely polite, but—you see, Signor, it is best to speak plainly—I am a very poor woman; and I have not the means—and I am sure—perhaps I ought not to have troubled sua Signoria; but it was the Contessa Violante who advised me to come to you."

"Indeed; I am beholden to the Signora Contessa Violante. As you say most judiciously, Signora, it is best to speak quite plainly. With regard to any professional services, which it might be otherwise in my power to render you, it is necessary to say at once that I am engaged in this most unhappy business on the behalf of my old client and friend the Marchese Ludovico di Castelmare. There can be no question, therefore, of any professional remuneration to me in the matter from any other quarter. Anything that may pass between us," he continued, perceiving that his visitor had not fully comprehended what he sought to convey to her, "must be of the nature of private conversation, and will not entail on you," he added, yet more plainly with a good-humoured smile, and putting his hand on her sleeve as he spoke, "any possible expense whatever."

"Thank you kindly, sir; and, truth to say, it is not so much that I wanted to ask you to say or to do anything, as only just not to say what a many people in this city are wicked enough to say and to think," said old Orsola, much re-assured, and persuaded that she was approaching the business in hand in the most cautious and clever manner imaginable.

"I hope, Signora, that I shall not say anything which it is wicked to say; but what is it that people are wicked enough to say?" rejoined the lawyer, who knew now perfectly well what the wicked saying was.

"Why they say, Signor Dottore—some of them—some of them are wicked enough to say that that dear blessed child has—it is enough to blister one's tongue to say it—has done that dreadful thing; Santa Maria abbia misericordia—that murder in the forest. O Dio mio! Why—"

"Is she any relative of yours, Signora, the Signorina Paolina Foscarelli?" asked the lawyer, quietly.

"No relative by blood, Signor; but she is the same to me as a daughter. I took her when she was left an orphan—"

"And she has lived with you ever since?"

"Ever since she has lived with me as if she was my own, Signor; and if anybody in the world ever knew another, I know her; and, bless your heart, she isn't capable of lifting her hand against a fly, let alone a Christian. There never was such wicked nonsense talked in this world since world it was; and I'm told, Signor Dottore, that you have said that she had been the one as did this deed; and—"

"Stop, stop, my good Signora Orsola! Are you aware that you are accusing me of being guilty of punishable defamation and slander? I say that the Signorina Paolina Foscarelli committed murder?

Who on earth could ever have told you so monstrous an untruth? Allow me to assure you that I never said anything of the kind."

"Oh, Signor Dottore, I am so glad to hear you say so. What lies people do tell, to be sure; I am sure it was a very good thought of the Contessa Violante to tell me to come to you; and since you say that the poor child is innocent, as innocent she is, as the child unborn—"

"Stay, Signora, stay; you go too fast—somewhat too fast. Unhappily, I am by no means in a condition to say that your young friend is innocent of this crime; appearances, it must be admitted, are very much against her; we must hope that they can be explained. I accuse no one; it is not my province to do so."

"But you don't think the judges will believe that my child could have done such a thing? If they only knew her! You don't think that, do you, Signor Dottore?" said the poor woman, with a voice and manner of piteous appeal.

"They will judge according to the evidence and the probabilities of the case. It is impossible to say as yet to what conclusion these may seem to point. The Marchese Ludovico is an acquaintance of yours and of the Signorina Paolina, is he not?"

"An acquaintance? why they are engaged to be married," almost shrieked poor Signora Orsola; "has not your lordship heard that they are engaged to be married?"

"Indeed! and you are acquainted with the Contessa Violante too. Do you know whether her ladyship is aware of the engagement you speak of? I ask, because she is an old friend of the Marchese Ludovico."

"To be sure she is aware of it. She and Paolina have often talked it over together. Altro che, aware of it."

"Humph," said the lawyer thoughtfully; and then remained silent for a minute or two, while old Orsola looked at him wistfully.

"It must be very terrible to you then, Signora, to think that the Marchese should be suspected of this shocking crime, since you have such reason to feel an interest in him," said he at last, looking up suddenly at his companion.

"Lord bless your heart," exclaimed the old woman in reply; "the Marchese never did nothing of the sort, no more than my poor innocent lamb did it. Nothing of the kind."

"Perhaps, then, you would not mind saying who did do it," said the lawyer; "since you seem to know all about it."

"Why she did it herself to be sure. It is a wonder anybody should doubt it. And a like enough end for such a baggage to come to," said Signora Orsola, with much bitterness.

"You do not seem to have been among the admirers of the Signora Bianca," said the lawyer, with a furtively shrewd look at the old woman.

"Admirers, indeed! She had too many admirers, I am thinking. A good-for-nothing, impudent, brazen—well, she has gone to her account, so I won't be the one to speak ill of her."

"You seem to have had considerable opportunities of becoming acquainted with her character, Signora Orsola. Had you much acquaintance with her?"

"I never saw her but once in my life, and that was at the theatre on the last Sunday night of Carnival. The Marchese had given us a box."

"And it was upon that occasion then, that she impressed you so unfavourably. The Signorina Paolina I suppose was with you at the theatre?"

"Of course she was. Would it be likely, I ask you, Signor Dottore, that the Marchese took the box for me?"

"And no doubt the Signorina Foscarelli was impressed by the actress in the same manner that you yourself were."

"Of course she was, as any other decent young woman would have been; let alone being, as Paolina is, engaged to be married to the Marchese."

"I have no doubt, Signora, that your remarks are perfectly just. If the manners and conduct of the young women now-a-days were regulated a little more in conformity with the ideas of such persons of discretion as yourself, the world would be all the better for it. But I don't quite see how the behaviour of the prima donna on the stage could have had anything to do with the circumstance of the Marchese Ludovico's engagement to the Signorina Foscarelli," said the lawyer, with the most demure innocence of manner.

"You don't see it, Signor Dottore. Perhaps you were not in the theatre that night. If you had been you would have seen it fast enough. The way she went on, when the Marchese Ludovico was a-giving her a lovely nosegay of flowers—hothouse flowers, if you please—as big pretty near as this table; not just a-throwing them on to the stage the way I've seen 'em do it many a time at the Fenice; but putting them into her hand; and she, the minx a coming up to the box to take 'em before all the people as bold as brass."

"Ah, I see? The Signorina Foscarelli naturally did not quite like that," said the lawyer, encouragingly.

"Like it! Who would have liked it in her place, I ask you? And that painted hussy a-going on they way she did; making such eyes at him, and smiling and a-pressing her hand to her bosom, that was just as naked as my face; and looking for all the world if she could have jumped right into the box, and eaten him up. Like it, indeed!"

"No doubt it was provoking enough. And your adopted daughter, Signora Steno, would not be the right-minded and well-brought-up girl I take her to be, if she did not express to you her disgust at such goings on," said the sympathizing lawyer.

"You may say that. She expressed it plain enough and not to me only, but to the Marchese himself well, when she saw him afterwards. She let him know what she thought of the painted huzzy. And she told him, too, some more of the truth. She told him that the creature knew well enough what she was doing, or trying to do. The way she looked straight up at my poor child in the box, where we were, was enough to make the blood curdle in your veins. If ever I saw a face look hatred, it was the face of that woman when she looked up at our box. She looked at the poor child as if she could have taken her heart's blood. She did. Ah! bless your heart, she knew all about it. Talk of the old

Marchese, indeed. Yes; the creature had set her mind upon being Marchesa di Castelmare. Not a doubt of it; but it was the nephew she wanted, not the uncle; and she knew that my Paolina stood in the way of her scheming; and Paolina knew that she knew it."

Old Orsola paused, out of breath with the length and vehemence of the tirade, which her feelings had prompted her to utter with crescendo violence. She was verbose; but the lawyer had listened with the most perfect patience and unflagging attention to every word she had uttered.

"It is, indeed, clear enough," he said, shaking his head, "that between two women so situated with reference to each other, there could have been no very kindly feeling. And it must be confessed that this unfortunate Bianca Lalli was, by all accounts, just the sort of woman that was likely to be a very dangerous rival."

"She; a common, impudent, low-lived, brazen-faced, worn-out Jezebel. No; not where my Paolina stood on the other side. She couldn't take the Marchese away from her with all her arts. And that's why she went and put an end to herself. But she's gone—she's gone, where her painted face and her lures won't be of any more service to her. And so I won't say any evil of her. Not I. It's a good rule that tells us to speak well of the dead. Ave, Maria gratia plena, ora pro nobis, nunc et in hora mortis nostrae," said the old woman, crossing herself and casting up her eyes in attestation of the Christian nature of her sentiments.

"Amen!" said the lawyer, piously, while he waited to see if the exuberance of his visitor's feelings would lead her to throw any further light on the state of feeling that had existed between Paolina Foscarelli and the murdered woman.

"I always say and think, for my part," continued the old woman, perceiving that her companion sat silent, as if expecting her to continue the conversation; "I always think that the blessed Virgin knows what's best for us. Maybe it's just as well that that poor miserable creature did as she did. For we all know what men are, Signore Dottore; and there's no saying what hold she might have got upon the Marchese."

"And no doubt that is the feeling of our young friend Signorina Foscarelli?" said the sympathetic lawyer.

"To be sure, to be sure it is," said the old woman, meaning to credit Paolina with the piety she had understood herself to have expressed; "she did take a mortal aversion and dislike to the woman, and small blame to her. But now she is gone, Paolina is no more likely to say anything against her than I am myself."

"Quite so, quite so. And I hope the magistrates may take the same view of the circumstances, that you have so judiciously expressed, Signora," said the lawyer, who was abundantly contented with the result of his interview with the Signora Steno, as it stood, and did not see any further necessity for prolonging it. "You may tell the Contessa Violante, if you should see her, that I am much obliged to her for having sent you to me," he added, as he rose to open the door of his sanctum for the old lady; "Beppo, open the door for the Signora Steno. Farewell, Signora, we shall meet again."

CHAPTER II

Was it Paolina After All?

Orsola Steno quitted the lawyer's studio as entirely contented with the result of her interview as she left him. She doubted not that she had fully impressed him with her own conviction as to the explanation of the mysterious circumstances of the singer's death; that Paolina's innocence would be readily recognized; and that her adopted daughter would shortly be restored to her in the Via di Sta. Eufemia.

The lawyer remained for some time seated in his chair in deep thought after his visitor had left him.

Suddenly he let his open hand fall heavily with a loud clap on the table before him, disturbing the papers on it from their places, and causing the fine blue sand, which stood in an open wooden basin for the purpose of doing the office of blotting-paper, to be spilled in all directions by the concussion, and said aloud, "By God! That girl has done it!"

"Ah, talk of the passions of men," he went on, in a lower muttering voice, after some further moments of meditation; "they are nothing—they are child's play compared to the blind animal-like impulses that force a woman's will into their service when any of the master passions of the sex are touched. A woman's jealousy; it is as plain as the sun at noonday. And we are puzzling our brains looking on this side and on that, to find a possible explanation of the facts. Talk of a tigress and her whelps! There's a young girl who looks as innocent as a St. Agnes, and speaks as if butter would not melt in her mouth. Take—threaten to take—her lover from her, and she turns upon you like a scorpion at bay. Furens quid foemina possit. Ay indeed. And they are all alike. That old woman there; why she was ready, with all her 'Ave Marias' and 'Ora pro nobis,' to kill the woman again if she were not killed already, out of pure sympathy with the wrong done to her adopted daughter. I don't think there is a doubt about it. I should like to wager a hundred to one that the Venetian girl put her rival to death. The story is neither a new nor a strange one."

"Whether the commission of the deed can be brought home to her," he continued, after another period of musing, "that is another question; and one with which, however interesting it may be to my good friend Pietro Logarini, we need not trouble ourselves. And after all, what a good thing it is that things should have fallen out as they have. That old fool of a Marchese! It is a lesson to believe in nothing and no man, when one thinks of it. The death of that woman is the saving of the name. But, per Bacco! I must not say so too loudly," thought the old lawyer to himself, with a grim smile, "or I shall be doing just what the old fool of a woman has been doing. Yes, that was the last link in the chain of the evidence we wanted. She was on the spot at the time—the death-dealing weapon was essentially a woman's weapon, and the murdered woman was her feared and hated rival—and now we have direct evidence that she felt her to be such. If the judges can find any other hypothesis supported by stronger circumstantial evidence than this—why, I think that I had better go to school again."

With these thoughts in his mind, Signor Fortini determined to go and see his crony, Signor Pietro Logarini, at the Palazzo del Governo. He found that active and able official just returned from another visit to St. Apollinare in Classe, which appeared not to have been very fruitful of result.

"I can make nothing out of that old friar," said the Police Commissary to his friend, as they sat in the private cabinet of the former; "and I am very much afraid that we shall make nothing out of him. For quiet, aggravating obstinacy and passive resistance, recommend me to a monk."

"What induced you to go out there to-day?" asked the lawyer.

"Why, I am very strongly persuaded—I feel sure almost—that that old fellow could tell something to the purpose if he would speak. And I am more convinced of it from his manner to-day than ever. The other animal—the lay-brother—I am pretty sure knows nothing about it."

"Is the friar about again, or still in bed?" Fortini.

"Oh, he's in bed safe enough; at least I found him there, shivering and shaking, and counting his beads, and answering a plain question with 'Ave Maria' and 'Ora pro nobis,' and the rest of it. I don't believe he has the fever a bit. I believe that he has been scared out of his wits by something he has seen. But the devil wouldn't get out of him what it was if he don't choose to tell you. Oh, I know them!" said the Commissary, provoked by his fruitless excursion.

"I suppose," said the lawyer, looking doubtfully into the Commissary's face, "I suppose it is not on the cards that the old fellow was the murderer himself?"

"Ha!" said the Commissary, with a start, "that is a new idea. But no," he added, after a little consideration, "no, that's not it; it would be very difficult even to imagine any motive. An old man, eighty years old. No, it's not that. But, if I am not very much mistaken, he knows something."

"In that case, I should have thought that means might have been found to make him speak," said the lawyer, drily.

"What means? I profess I don't know any. The devil of it is, you see, Signor Giovacchino, that it will not do to treat those fellows roughly. There would be the deuce and all to pay. There he lies, shivering, and trembling, and muttering, and going on as if he was imbecile; and swearing he is too ill to leave his bed. I don't see how we are to get him here into court."

"Well, I've had better luck this morning; and had not to go out to seek it. My witness came to me; and I think I have got some important evidence," said the lawyer, with much of the exultation of a successful sportsman over a less fortunate rival.

"The deuce you have. There is a luck in those things. But if your evidence came to you—Who the devil would ever think of coming to a Commissary of Police as long as they could stay away, if they pleased."

"Well, my witness was not altogether a willing one; or at least she came to me for the purpose of saying something very different from what she did say."

"But you did not come here merely to boast, I am sure, Signor Giovacchino. You are going to tell me what you have been able to learn, eh?" said the Commissary.

"Boast, no, not I! There's nothing to boast of. Besides, you know my interest in the matter is of a different nature from yours, Signor Pietro. All I want is to clear my friend and client, the Marchese Ludovico. You, of course, are anxious to bring the crime home to somebody."

"True," said the Commissary, nodding his head.

"And of course, therefore, any light I can throw upon the matter, I am ready enough to bring to you, unless it were of a nature to incriminate the Marchese," returned the lawyer.

"Of course, just so. And what you have learned this morning—"

"Tell's all t'other way; I have no difficulty in allowing that, on the first blush of the matter, I felt no doubt that the Marchese was the guilty party. It only shows that one ought always to have doubts of everything. It looked so very bad. The Marchese takes the girl into the wood, comes back without her, and very shortly afterwards she is found where he left her, murdered. And he is known to have had the greatest possible interest in getting rid of her. Would it not have seemed a clear case to any one?"

"So one would have said indeed," assented the Commissary.

"Well, the Marchese had nothing to do with it. At the present moment I feel—well, hardly any doubt at all that the deed was done by the girl Paolina Foscarelli."

"That's my notion too," said the Commissary, taking a pinch of snuff, and proferring his box to his visitor; "but what is the new evidence."

"Well, the girl lives, it seems, with an old woman, a country-woman of hers, a certain Orsola Steno. And this morning the old lady comes to my studio for the avowed purpose of begging me not to countenance in any way the very mistaken notion that her adopted daughter had murdered the prima donna; the truth being, as she was good enough to inform me, that the latter had committed suicide."

"Bah, what senseless nonsense!" interrupted the Commissary, indignantly.

"Of course. I pointed out to the old lady that her theory was, according to the medical testimony, simply impossible; but that naturally made not the slightest difference in her opinion of the matter. And then, aided by a little gentle assistance, she prattled on, an old fool, admitting, or insisting rather, that there had been bitter hatred and animosity between Paolina and the murdered woman; that Paolina had conceived the bitterest jealousy of the singer; that she was persuaded that the latter was scheming with a set purpose to lure her acknowledged lover, the Marchese, away from her; that she was further persuaded that the singer nourished the bitterest hatred of her, Paolina. What do you say to that, Signor Commissary? How does the land lie now, eh?" said the lawyer, triumphantly, in conclusion.

Signor Pietro nodded his head with most emphatic approbation and confirmation of his friend's opinion.

"Is not it the more likely story in every way?" pursued the lawyer; "just look at it. The Marchese is known to every man, woman, and child in Ravenna; and being known for what he is, it would be difficult to persuade anybody that he had lifted his hand to murder a defenceless and sleeping woman. But we can all of us easily understand that it is exceedingly likely that he may have so behaved as to make these two women furiously jealous of each other; at least to have made this girl Paolina, to whom, it seems, he had promised marriage, desperately furious against the other, whom she had but too good reason to suspect of having attracted the preference of the Marchese. Then look at the instrument with which the murder was accomplished, a needle. Is it in any way likely that the Marchese Ludovico should habitually carry such a thing about with him? Is there any unlikelihood that the girl may have had such a thing about her; Amico mio Pietro," said the lawyer, in conclusion, tapping his fingers on the Commissary's coat-sleeve as he spoke, "that Venetian girl is the murderess! The deed was done under the influence of maddening jealousy."

"How on earth could that old woman come to you with a budget of such damning facts against her friend? Do you think she—the old woman—has any guilty knowledge of the crime?"

"Lord bless you, no! If she had, she would not have been so simple. No, she firmly believes her own theory of the matter, that the poor Diva killed herself. She is too firmly persuaded of it to perceive the bearing of her admissions of the hatred that existed between the two girls."

"I learned something yesterday," said the Commissary, "which all looks the same way, not much, but in such a case every little helps. This old friar—this Padre Fabiano—is, we know, a Venetian; and now I have ascertained that, years ago, before he came here, there was some connection of some sort—acquaintance, friendship of whatever kind you like—between him and the parents of the girl Paolina. I think it likely enough that the frate's friendship was more particularly with the girl's mother rather than with her father, we know what friars' ways are, and, maybe, we should not go far wrong if we imagined that the Father had reason to feel a fatherly interest of a quite special kind in the young lady. Now all this is worth only just this. Why did the frate return from the Pineta in such a state of terror, agitation, and horror? Why, supposing him to have seen, or in any way become acquainted with facts calculated to produce such an effect upon him, does he obstinately refuse to give us any information upon the subject? How will this answer fit? In the course of that walk to the Pineta, undertaken, no doubt, because the old man felt anxiety as to what was likely to follow from the probable meeting of the two girls after the scene witnessed in his presence by Paolina from the window of the church—in the course of that walk, let us suppose, the friar became acquainted with the fact that this girl—his daughter, we will say, for, in all probability, she is such—had murdered her rival. The knowledge of the fact sends him back to his cell half dead with horror and fright. His interest in Paolina ties his tongue, and frustrates all our efforts to get any explanation from him. How will that do, eh, Signor Giovacchino?"

"Admirably well. Clearly helps to give consistency and probability to our theory of the facts. I begin to think that all danger to my client is at an end, and, upon my word, I am more glad of it than I can tell you; it would have been a shocking thing. I am an old Ravenna man, you know, and should have felt it differently from what you would, you know."

"True; but I am glad enough that the Marchese should be cleared in the matter, and so will the Government be—very glad."

"I suppose there is no objection to my seeing the Marchesino?"

"Oh, certainly not the least in the world. It is a pity that he should be detained here any longer; but I am almost afraid to take the responsibility of discharging him before some formal inquiry has been made."

"Naturally, naturally. When do you suppose you will be ready to bring the affair to a trial?"

"Oh, very soon. If there were any chance of getting that old frate into court it would be worth while to wait for him; but I am afraid that the longer we wait the worse his fever and ague will get. But I shall have another try at him out there first."

And with that Signor Fortini passed to the chamber in which the Marchese Ludovico was confined.

CHAPTER III

"Signor Marchese," said the old man, stretching out his hand with, for him, a very unusual degree of impulsive cordiality, "I have come to make amende honorable—I need hardly say how delighted I am to do so. It is not only that I think I may say there is now very little chance of any mischief falling on you in consequence of that unlucky excursion to the Pineta, but that I am able, thank God, to say that I have myself no longer the smallest suspicion that you had any hand in the crime that has been committed there."

"Has anything been discovered, then?" asked Ludovico, eagerly. "Ah—h—h! that would be good news indeed," added the young man, drawing a long breath of relief, the evident strength of which feeling afforded a measure of the suffering he had endured more indicative of the real state of his mind than any amount of depression which he had before allowed to be apparent.

"Well; enough, I think, has been discovered to relieve you of all suspicion—enough, as I said, to convince my own mind very satisfactorily that you are innocent of all complicity in the matter."

"I confess that I should have preferred, Signor Fortini, that my own assertion should have sufficed to produce that conviction," replied the young man, somewhat drily.

"My dear Signor Marchese, permit me to say that such preference would have been ill founded. Is not my conviction, based upon the probabilities of the known facts, of much greater value than any mere acquiescence with your assertions? These are matters, my dear sir, which must be looked at reasonably, and not merely sentimentally. If you had committed murder—if I had committed murder, should we not either of us, have denied it as resolutely as you denied this? If the circumstances are such as to cause a man—any man—to be suspected at all, no words of his can be worth anything whatsoever on the subject; and you must admit that, the circumstances being as they were, it was impossible that the first suspicion should not have fallen on you. You may believe that no efforts or activity have been wanting on my part for the discovery of the means of removing this suspicion. Let us be thankful that they have, to a very great degree, been successful."

"And what has been found out? For God's sake tell me all about it! I declare, for my own part, I could almost believe that I had done it myself in my sleep, or in a fit of madness without knowing it, so utterly impossible does it seem to me to imagine what hand it could have been that did the deed."

"Signor Marchese, the hand that did that deed was no other than the hand of the Venetian girl, Paolina Foscarelli," said the lawyer, with deliberate and impressive slowness, emphasizing his words with extended forefinger as he uttered them.

"Pshaw! Is that all you have to tell me?" cried the Marchese, jumping up from his chair, and pacing the room with impatient strides. "It is an absurdity upon the face of it; I should have hoped that nobody in Ravenna would have believed it possible that I could have been guilty of such a deed; but, by Heaven, the whole city will see that it is more likely that I should have done it than Paolina! It is simply absurd."

"Signor Marchese, prepossessions, and previous notions of what might have been expected to be possible, are of no value in such a case as this against the logic of facts and circumstances. Other young women, who seemed as little likely to be capable of such a deed as this Signorina Foscarelli, have committed such—and have done it under the pressure of motives exactly similar to those which we know with certainty to have been vehemently operative in the heart of the Venetian."

"Motives! What conceivable motive could have existed to—"

"What motive? The most powerful of all the passions that ever drove a woman to become guilty of crime—jealousy; jealousy, Signor Marchese, has been the motive of this murder. Look at the facts as they stand: we know that this Paolina Foscarelli was in the immediate neighbourhood of the spot where the deed was done, and as nearly as possible at the time when it was done; we know—excuse me, Signor Marchese, for speaking very plainly; it is absolutely necessary to be plain—we know that this girl had great reason to feel jealous of La Bianca. Remember that she saw you and the singer driving tete-a-tete together in that solitary place at that unusual hour. I leave it to your own feeling to estimate the degree of jealousy which such a sight, together with other previous circumstances, was calculated to produce in this girl's mind; but, if that be not enough, we know, as a matter of fact, that she had, even previously to seeing what was, so calculated to drive her jealousy to a pitch of fury, expressed jealousy, animosity and hatred against the woman whom she considered as her rival. We have this in evidence—the perfectly unimpeachable evidence of the Signora Orsola Steno. Add to that, again, that the method of the murder was just such as a woman was likely to adopt, and that a man was very little likely to think of, or to have the means of, in his possession. Put all these certain facts together, Signor Marchese; and I think it will be impossible for even your mind to resist the conviction that must force itself upon every one who considers the circumstances."

The Marchese stopped in his agitated walk to and fro across the floor of the chamber, and gazed into the lawyer's face with an expression of bewilderment and pain, which the old man met with a keen and steady glance, and a grave shake of the head. The Marchese, after encountering his eye for a few moments, struck his open hand on his forehead, and threw himself on the chair he had left without uttering a word.

"And to you, Signor Marchese, it assuredly cannot appear strange that the circumstances I have enumerated should carry with them the conviction to other minds that Paolina Foscarelli is guilty of the murder of the singer," continued the lawyer, speaking very slowly and fixing the keen glance of his dark bright eyes on the working face of his companion; "to you, above all others, this cannot appear strange, since—to your own mind this suspicion first occurred."

"What do you mean? I! Signor Fortini. What strange notion is misleading you? I don't know what you mean!" cried the Marchese, while a look of horror gradually crept over his face.

"When the body of the murdered woman was brought into the city, when we two stood in the gateway, and when your hand raised the sheet that covered the face of the dead, you exclaimed aloud 'Paolina!' What was then the thought that was in your mind? I imagined, at the time, that you recognized her in the dead woman before you. A very few minutes, however, sufficed to show that it was not Paolina, but Bianca who lay there murdered. And then, amid the horror of the first idea of your guilt, which the nature of the circumstances rendered inevitable, I thought no more of the exclamation you had uttered. But I have not forgotten the fact. You did, on seeing Bianca dead before you, exclaim, 'Good God! Paolina!' What was the thought in your mind, Signor Marchese, that prompted that exclamation? What but the sudden spontaneous rush of the conviction that it was she who had done the deed on which you were looking?"

For a few moments the Marchese seemed too much stunned by the inference, and the appeal of the lawyer, and by the vision of the consequences, which he purposed drawing from it, to utter any reply to the demand which had been made on him.

"You mistake, Signor Fortini," he gasped out at last; "you are in error. I cannot have made any such exclamation. I have no consciousness of anything of the kind. In any case no such monstrous idea, as you would infer from it, ever entered into my mind. You know how anxious I was about Paolina's prolonged absence. I was thinking of her; at least, I suppose so, if, indeed, I uttered her name. I have no recollection. I don't know why I should have done so. All I know is that no such horrible and impossible suggestion ever presented itself to my mind for an instant. If it were otherwise," continued the young man, after a few moments of painfully concentrated thought, "if it were otherwise, why did I not suggest such a solution of the mystery when I found myself accused of the crime?"

"That, Signor Marchese, those who know you best will be least at a loss to understand," replied the lawyer. "The motive that ruled your conduct then, is the same that rules it now. You were then unwilling, as you are now unwilling, to exculpate yourself at the cost of inculpating one who is dear to you. Your objection, I am bound to tell you, carries no weight with it. I cannot abandon that part of my case that rests upon the striking fact that your own first impression was that Paolina was guilty."

"I utterly deny, and will continue to deny, that any such impression was ever present to my mind. I wholly refuse to avail myself of any defence based on any such supposition; on any idea at all, that Paolina Foscarelli is guilty. I know that she is as innocent of this deed as the angels in heaven. I will proclaim her innocence with my last breath. I will not accept any acquittal on the hypothesis of her guilt. I will rather avow that I did the deed myself. In one sense I did so. In one sense I am guilty of her death. For it was I who took her to the place, and into the circumstance that led to her death."

"Signor Marchese, in this matter the truth of the facts is what is wanted. It is that, and that alone that the magistrates will endeavour to discover. A great many facts, as I have pointed out to you, will be before them. Mere statements, one way or the other, will have little avail. Quietly and seriously now, supposing we reject the theory of Paolina's guilt, are you able yourself to conceive any other possible explanations of the facts? Can you yourself suggest any other theory whatsoever?" said the lawyer, throwing his head on one side, and interlacing the fingers of his clasped hands in front of his person, in calm expectation of the Marchese's answer.

"There was another theory. I heard that the Conte Leandro had been arrested on suspicion of being the assassin. It would be very dreadful. God forbid that I should say that I suspected the Conte Lombardoni of having done this foul deed. But I cannot avoid seeing that it is a great deal more likely that he should have done it than Paolina," returned the Marchese.

"The accusation against the Conte Lombardoni has been abandoned, and he has been set at liberty," replied the lawyer; "there was, in fact, nothing against him, except the singular circumstance of his having gone out of the city towards the Pineta, at a very unusual hour on the morning of that same unlucky Ash Wednesday; and that he has at last thought fit to explain."

"At last?" said Ludovico.

"Yes; for a long time he utterly refused to give any explanation of the fact whatsoever; and his manner was altogether such as to strengthen the notion that it was possible that he might have been the criminal. He has told the truth at last. And it is no wonder that he was loth to tell it, for it is not much calculated to increase his popularity in the city."

"Why, what is it? I never used to think anything worse of him than that he was a fool," rejoined the Marchese.

"A fool, and a very mischievous and malicious one, as fools mostly are. What do you think took him out of the city that morning of the first day in Lent? Simply the desire to play the spy on you and the poor woman who has been killed."

"No, you don't mean it? the noxious animal!" exclaimed Ludovico, with intense disgust.

"It seems that he overheard you and the singer make your appointment for the excursion, and that, moved by curiosity and the hope of making mischief, he determined to be beforehand with you on the road, and picking up, if he could, the means of paying off both the lady and yourself for some of the mortification your ridicule had caused him," said the lawyer.

"I could not have believed it possible; the mean-spirited spiteful wretch! I did not think he had it in him!" said Ludovico.

"A man is apt to be spiteful towards those who cause him to suffer greatly. And there is no suffering greater to a man as vain as the Conte Leandro than the mortification of his vanity. But his spitefulness has been punished: first, by a couple of days' imprisonment, and a fright which half killed him; and secondly, by the sort of reception which you may suppose awaited him when he was released as the result of his explanation. I think he has had his due," added the lawyer, grimly.

"But how does his explanation exclude the possibility that he may have been the assassin after all? Why may not the same mortified vanity that incited him to play the spy, have moved him to take deadly vengeance on the woman he hated so bitterly? The man who was capable of the one is likely enough to be capable of the other. He is the man who may fairly be suspected of being capable of stabbing a woman as she slept!" argued the Marchese, with intense indignation.

"No," said the lawyer, shaking his head; "depend upon it we did not let him go till it was made clear that he could have had no hand in the crime. He was able to prove beyond the possibility of a doubt, that he had returned to the city, entering it by the Porta Sisi, before the earliest time when the murder could have been committed. No; that notion has to be abandoned."

"And no other idea has been started?—no suspicion? Have the investigations of the police led to nothing?" asked Ludovico, with profound discouragement.

The lawyer shook his head. "I have told you," he said, "how the case stands, Signor Marchese. An idea was started at one moment that the old friar at St. Apollinare might have been the man. Strangely enough he also was in or near the Pineta much about the same time. But the total absence of all assignable motive—an infirm octogenarian; no, that is not it. But the truth is, Signor Marchese, that our inquiries with reference to this Padre Fabiano have brought to light facts which tend to make the case stronger against the girl Paolina Foscarelli."

"I tell you, Signor Fortini, that the notion of her guilt is more entirely preposterous than any other possible imagination. I have told you that I would, rather than accept it, avow myself the murderer;—ay, and think that I had done it too, and forgotten it," said the Marchese, with extreme vehemence.

"But, Signor Marchese," returned the lawyer, with imperturbable calmness, "it matters nothing to the result, whether you will accept the idea of the Venetian girl's guilt or not, seeing that you will not be called upon to pronounce judgment in the case. The fact is, that every reasonable consideration points to that conclusion. I wish with all my heart, that the criminal was one in whom you were less interested." The meaning of which phrase in Signor Fortini's mouth, probably was, that he wished the Marchese felt less interest in her who was the criminal. "But I was about to tell you that the police have become acquainted with the fact, that this Padre Fabiano, who is a Venetian, was formerly very closely connected in some way with the family of Paolina Foscarelli. It seems very probable that he was, in fact, her father. Now he followed her to the forest, and returned thence in a state of great and painful agitation, which all mention of the subject renews and increases; and. further, the old man obstinately refuses to give any account or explanation of his walk to the forest. The conclusion which has suggested itself to the police authorities—not at all an unnatural or unreasonable one—is that the old man has been cognizant of the deed done by the girl."

The Marchese seemed struck by this statement, and remained in silent thought for a few minutes. "Paolina," he said, at length, "had motives of hatred against the woman who has been killed, the friar had motives for feeling strong interest in Paolina. Why may it not be conceivable that he may have adopted her cause to the extent of committing a crime with the view of righting what may have seemed to him to be her wrongs? The explanation may seem a not very probable one; but no possible or conceivable explanation of the terrible fact is a probable one, and, certainly, it is more likely that the old friar should have done the deed than the young girl."

"Humph!" said the lawyer, after spending some minutes of deep thought on the idea the Marchese had put forward; "I am not quite so sure that it is more likely. However, the theory is a plausible one, and deserves attention. Depend upon it, we shall not lose sight of the old gentleman, let him shiver and shake as much as he may; and now, Signor Marchese, I must go to your uncle," said the lawyer, rising.

"How does he bear up under all this misery?"

"Not well, not well. I cannot say that it has fared well with him during these days; but I have some comfort in store for him. I think I may venture to assure him that there is no need to imagine that his name has been disgraced by the commission of a crime, or that there is any danger that such should continue to be believed to be the case, either by the magistrates or by anybody else. You will come out of this dreadful business scatheless, Signor Marchese, I thank God for it?"

"I will not come out scatheless at the cost of Paolina's condemnation," said the Marchese, doggedly.

"But the Marchese Lamberto, you see," continued the lawyer, without taking any notice of his companion's interruption, "the Marchese Lamberto has been hit from more sides than one. The most unfortunate and lamentable fascination that this woman seems to have exercised over him—the deplorable fact that he should have proposed marriage to her, and that this fact should be universally known, it is impossible that he should not have suffered, and still suffer terribly. Honestly, I cannot say that I think he will ever altogether get over it—he will never be the same man again. Would to God that fatal woman had never come near Ravenna!"

"Many thanks for your visit, Signor Fortini, and for all the kindness you have shown me since this sad misfortune befell. Tell my uncle how much I have felt and feel for him. Addio, Signor Fortini. If anything new should turn up you will not fail to let me know it? Think of what I said about the friar; and mind, once more, and once for all, I will not come scatheless, as you say, out of this business and leave Paolina to be held guilty."

"Addio, Signor Marchese."

Signor Fortini had rather mitigated than exaggerated the truth in speaking to the Marchese Ludovico of his uncle's state of mind. During all these days his condition was truly deplorable. He had never, in all this time, left the Palazzo, and had scarcely left his own chamber. He absolutely refused to see anybody save Signor Fortini. He could not sleep by night, or remain at rest in the same place for half-an-hour together during the day.

Of course he could attend to none of the numerous duties—mostly labours of benevolence—that usually occupied his time. His servants thought that he was losing his reason; yet, in the midst of all the terrible distress that was weighing him down, the usual kindness and considerate benevolence of his nature and habitual conduct had shone out. The only one thing that he had given any attention to was the gratification of the wishes, and the promotion of the welfare, of an old servant.

Niccolo, the old groom who was mentioned, as the reader may, perhaps, remember, on the occasion of a certain conversation which Lawyer Fortini had with him, as having been all his life in the service of the Marchese, and of his father before him, was getting, as he had himself remarked to the lawyer, almost too old for his work. He had always hitherto absolutely refused, with the masterful obstinacy of an old favourite, all proposals of retirement; but, on the next morning but one after the fatal Ash Wednesday, while the Marchese had been in such a state of painful agitation that he could hardly bear to be addressed by his own servant, he had, to the great surprise of all the household, sent for old Niccolo, who had remained with him more than an hour.

On coming out from the interview the old groom said that he had himself asked for the audience his master had given him; but it did not seem at all clear to the other servants when or how he could have done so. He said that he had spoken to his master on the subject long before; and how kind and good it was of the Marchese to think of his old servant's affairs in all his trouble. His master had arranged for him, he said, what he had long wished for, though it seemed to all the household that old Niccolo had always rejected any proposal of the sort. He was to have a pension, and go to live with a niece of his who was married in Rome.

It was odd that none of his fellow-servants had ever heard anything of any such niece. But old Niccolo was not a man of a communicative turn; and perhaps nothing had ever chanced to lead him to speak of her. Now he was to join her at once; he was to start for Faenza that very afternoon, so as to catch there the diligence from Bologna to Rome.

But why such a sudden start? Why should he go off and leave them all, at a few hours' notice.

Well, the fact was, that the day after the morrow was his niece's birthday. And he thought he should like to give her the joyful surprise of seeing her old uncle and learning the new arrangements on that day. And his dear thoughtful master, who was always so kind to everybody, had entered into his scheme, and so arranged it.

And so it was; old Niccolo was gone to Rome as he had said. But he had given nobody any address by which to find him in the Eternal City. And a little jealousy, perhaps, was felt at the good fortune which had thus befallen one out of several who would have liked the same. But all admitted that it was a remarkable proof of the thoughtful kindness of the Marchese in the midst of his own troubles.

And how terribly those troubles pressed on him was evident to the whole household; and, by means of their reports, to the entire city. Everybody in Ravenna knew with how heavy a hand affliction had fallen upon the Marchese Lamberto. And everybody talked of it. Sympathizing pity and blame were mingled in the judgments which were being passed on the Marchese every hour, and in every place where men or women met; and the proportions in which they were mingled differed greatly. None, however, could fail to see and to admit that the fall from the high pinnacle, on which the Marchese had stood, had been a very terrible one. It was felt that it was a fall from which he could never, under any circumstances, entirely recover.

The women were, for the most part, more indulgent to him than the men. As for the unfortunate Bianca, they held that a righteous and deserved judgment had fallen upon her, in which the operation of the finger of Providence was distinctly visible. To be sure it was a signal warning to all men, as to the evils which might be expected to flow from any sipping of the Circean cup which such creatures proffered to their lips. But what fate could be too bad for the Siren herself? To think of the audacity, the shameless effrontery of such an one in daring to spread her lures, and wind her enchantments around such a man as the Marchese di Castelmare. Of course he, poor man, could not but feel her death as a terrible shock. What he had set his heart on had been violently and awfully taken away from him. And how true it is that the blessed Saints know what is most truly for our good! But what is all that to the dreadful accusation hanging over the Marchese Ludovico? A Castelmare in the prison of Ravenna under accusation of murder! And if it really were the case, that the unfortunate young man, driven by the prospect of being hurled down from his position and robbed of his inheritance, had done this deed, how great, how terrible, must be the remorse of the Marchese Lamberto!

It was curiously characteristic of the moral nature and habits of thought of the people, that the Marchese Ludovico, even on the hypothesis that he had committed the murder, was very leniently judged for his share in the tragedy.

The men were more inclined to bear hard on the Marchese Lamberto. An old fool! at his time of life, to offer marriage to such a woman as La Bianca. To disgrace his name; to cover himself with ridicule; and above all, and worst of all, to behave with such infamous injustice to his nephew. Nevertheless the tragedy was so shocking and so complete, that even those who were disposed to condemn his conduct the most severely, could not but feel compassion for so crushing a weight of misfortune.

As the opinion, however, began to gain ground in the city, that the Marchesino Ludovico had, after all, not been the author of the murder; that the first impression, however clearly the circumstances seemed, at the first blush of the thing, to point to it, was a mistaken one; and that the far more probable opinion was that the Venetian girl, Paolina Foscarelli, was the murderess, and jealousy the incentive to her crime, the compassion for the Marchese Lamberto became proportionably less. The feeling was rather, that as far as he was concerned he had got nothing worse than what he richly deserved. And who should say that all was not upon the whole for the best as it had pleased heaven to cause it to fall out? The Marchese Lamberto was saved, despite his own folly, from a disgraceful and degrading marriage; and Ludovico was saved from the ruin which threatened him.

Nor, muttered the more cynical, was that all the good that was involved in what, at first sight, seemed so great a misfortune. Ludovico, too, was prevented from doing a foolish thing. It was a very different matter in his case from that of his uncle: he would be doing no wrong to any heir; and he was at that time of life when men do fall in love, and are excusable if they are led by it into doing foolish things; not to mention that, after all, the marriage he had proposed to make was a very different one from such a monstrous alliance as the Marchese Lamberto had meditated.

But still was it not a great blessing that the Marchesino should be prevented from throwing himself away in that manner? The first match in Ravenna to be carried off by an obscure and plebeian Venetian artist. Truly it was all for the best as it was.

In their different degree these two stranger women were both noxious, dangerous, and had done more mischief in Ravenna than the lives of either of them were worth. And if Providence had in its wisdom decreed that they should mutually counteract and abolish each other—why it would behove them to see in it a signal instance of the overruling wisdom of Heaven.

In the meantime, however, while every imaginable variety and modification of the above ideas and opinions were forming the staple of every conversation in every street, house, cafe, and piazza of Ravenna, the two men, whose conduct was thus canvassed, were assuredly suffering no light measure of retribution for aught that they had done amiss.

To Ludovico the tidings which reached him of the favourable turn matters were taking as to the probability of his having himself to answer for the murder of the singer, were neutralized in any effect they might otherwise have had of bringing him happiness, by the fact that he was exculpated only in exact proportion to the increasing probability that Paolina might be held guilty of the crime.

If, in truth, he carried in his own bosom the consciousness of his own guilt, it may easily be imagined how horrible to him would appear the prospect of escaping from the consequences of it by such means. And if that were, indeed, the dreadful truth, the repeated declarations which he had made to Signor Fortini to the effect that, rather than see Paolina condemned as guilty, he would confess himself to be the murderer, would in no wise appear as mere ebullitions of his determination to save at all price the girl he loved.

But, during those days Ludovico suffered, he either bore his sufferings with much more of manly self-command than did his uncle, or else his agony was (as Signor Fortini, who saw them both, could testify) much less severe than that which seemed to be slowly dragging down the Marchese Lamberto to the grave.

The lawyer had told Ludovico that he was then going to his uncle; and, in fact, he did so. But the old man dreaded doing so more than he could have himself believed that he could have feared any similar duty.

In truth, the condition of the Marchese Lamberto was pitiable

He would see no one, save Fortini; but he was most anxious for his visits—very naturally anxious to hear from day to day, and almost from hour to hour, how matters were going—whether any new circumstances had been discovered; what change there was in the probabilities as to the final judgment respecting the crime; and there was a restless feverishness in his anxiety, a shattered condition of the nervous system that made the lawyer seriously fear that the Marchese's reason would sink under the strain.

He had again and again urged him to allow a medical man to see him; and had once mentioned the Marchese's old friend Professor Tomosarchi. But the irritated violence with which the suffering man had rejected the proposal, had been such as to lead the lawyer to think that he should be doing more harm than good by reiterating it.

It was not surprising, indeed, that the Marchese should be utterly beaten down and vanquished by the misfortunes that had fallen upon him; they attacked him from such various and opposite sides.

His love for Bianca—or, let me say (in order to satisfy readers who are wont to weigh the real meaning of words as well as those who are in the habit of taking them unexamined at their current value), his longing to possess her—was genuine and intense. The step he had determined to take gives the measure of his eagerness in the pursuit of her—of his conviction that he could not live without her; and the object of this great, this intense, this all-mastering passion had been snatched away from him; the unappeasable agony of such a bereavement can, perhaps, only be adequately measured by those who have felt it.

Then all the evils which, despite his shrinking from them, he had faced for the sake of gratifying this imperious passion, had fallen upon him as fatally of though the price of his facing them had been paid to him. All the loss of credit, of respect, of social station, which he had found it so dreadful to contemplate, had been incurred—and for nothing. How long and terrible had been the struggle, which of those two incompatible objects of his intense desire—Bianca, or the social position he held in the eyes of his fellow-citizens—he should sacrifice to the other; it had seemed to him so impossible to give up either that the necessity of choosing between them had almost unhinged his reason. And now he was doomed to forego them both.

Then, again, Ludovico, and the dreadful position in which he stood! and, if he were condemned, on whose head would fall the blame of the disgrace which would thus overwhelm the family name? If his nephew were held to be guilty of this crime, would not all the odium of having driven him to it fall on him?

Truly there was wherewithal to bow down a stronger heart and head than those of the Marchese Lamberto.

According to Fortini's view of the matter, the tidings which he had to bring the Marchese that morning ought to have gone far to tranquillize and comfort him. Let it be shown that the heir to the Castelmare name and honours had not committed a terrible crime, and was not in danger of being convicted of it, and, in his opinion, all the worst of the evils which had fallen on the Marchese were at an end. That was the only really irreparable mischief; the city would have its laugh at the Marchese for his sensibility to the charms of such a charmer as the singer. But even that would be quenched by the startling change of the comedy into a tragedy. The Marchese had shown that he was no wiser than many another man; and it would be but a nine days' wonder; and as to the mere loss of the woman who had done all the mischief, the lawyer had no patience with the mention of it as a loss at all.

Pshaw! The one really important matter was to clear the heir of the house of all complicity in the crime of murder; and yet the lawyer had a strong feeling, from what he had already seen of the Marchese, that the good news of which he was the bearer in that respect would not give the Marchese all the comfort that it ought to give him.

And the result of the visit to the Palazzo Castelmare, which he paid immediately after leaving the Marchesino Ludovico in his prison, perfectly responded to his anticipations in this respect.

CHAPTER V

"Miserrimus"

He found the Marchese in a state which really seemed to threaten his life or his reason. It would scarcely be correct to say of him that he was depressed, for that phrase is hardly consistent with the feverish condition of excitement in which he was. There was evidence enough in his appearance of the presence of deep-seated and torturing misery, especially devastating in the case of men of his race, constituted as they are with nervous systems of great delicacy, and unendowed with that robustness of fibre which enables the more strongly-fashioned scions of the northern peoples to stand up against misfortune, and present a bold front to adversity.

There is no connection in the minds of this race between the repression and control of emotion and their ideal of virile dignity. Reticence is impossible to them. The Italian man, it is true, has been often described as eminently reticent; and the northern popular conception represents him as apt to seek the attainment of his object by the concealment of it. Nor is that representation an erroneous one. But the two statements are in no wise inconsistent. The Italian man is by nature, habit, and training an adept at concealing his thoughts; he rarely or never seeks to conceal his emotions.

Whether there were thoughts in the Marchese's mind, which he had no wish or intention to disclose to his visitor, might be a matter of speculation to the latter. But he certainly made no attempt to hide the misery which was consuming him. The outward appearance of the man was eloquent enough of the disorder within. He had always been wont to be especially neat and precise in his dress; clean shaven, and with that look of bright freshness on his clear-complexioned and well-rounded cheeks, which is specially suggestive of health, happiness, and well-to-do prosperity. Now his cheeks were hollow and yellow, and grisly stubble of uncared-for beard, covered his deeply-lined jaws. He was dressed, if dressed it could be called, in a large loose chamber wrapper, the open neck of which, and of the shirt beneath it, allowed the visitor's eye to mark that the emaciation which a few days of misery and anxiety had availed to cause, was not confined to his face only.

But yet more remarkable was the terrible state of nervous restlessness from which he was evidently suffering. He was unable to remain quiet in his easy chair even while his visitor remained with him. He would every now and then rise from it without reason, and pace the room for two or three turns with the uneasy objectless manner of a wild animal confined to a cage. Again and again he would go to the window, and gaze from it, as though looking for some expected thing or person. He spoke and behaved as if he had been most anxious for the coming of the lawyer, and yet, now he was there, he seemed scarcely able to command his attention sufficiently to take interest in the tidings Signor Fortini brought him.

"Thank God, Signor Marchese, the news I bring is good. Thank God, I am able to express to you my conscientious opinion that the Marchese Ludovico had no more to do with the murder of this unfortunate woman than I had. And such is now the general opinion throughout the city."

"Is there anything new? Has any—any—discovery been made?" said the Marchese, and his teeth chattered in his head as he spoke.

"Nothing that I can quite call a discovery," returned the lawyer; "but small circumstances in such a case as this, when carefully put together, form a clue, which rarely fails, when one has enough of them, to lead up to the desired truth."

"Ah!—small circumstances, as you say—yes—but circumstances—eh?—do they not often—must we not be very careful—eh?" and the Marchese shook as he spoke, till the lawyer really began to think that he must be labouring under an attack of the same illness that had seized on father Fabiano.

"Fortunately, Signor Marchese, the circumstances all point, in the present instance, in the direction we would wish. That is," added the lawyer, hastily, "God forbid that I should wish such a crime to be brought home to any human being, but in the interests of truth and justice; and of course our first object is that the Marchese Ludovico should be cleared."

"Of course, of course. Why naturally, you know—But—in what direction—eh?—do the suspicions—that is, the opinions—you, yourself, Signor Giovacchino—who do you think now could have done the deed?" said the Marchese, finishing his sentence with an apparent effort.

"My notion is," said the lawyer, speaking strongly and distinctly, "that the murder was committed by the Venetian girl, Paolina Foscarelli. You are aware of the circumstances that first directed suspicion towards her. Alone they are very strong; but some other little matters have come out. She has now been examined several times; and the account she gives of the hours that passed between the time she left the church of St. Apollinare, and the time when she was first seen afterwards is a very lame and unsatisfactory one. Then, my friend, Signor Logarini, of the police, who has been most praiseworthily active in the matter, has discovered that the old friar, who has the charge of the Basilica, and who is a Venetian, was connected with the parents of this girl, which renders it extremely probable that he may wish to screen her; and that fact, taken in conjunction with the very strong reasons we have to think that the friar has some knowledge of the deed, and his very manifest reluctance to tell what he knows, seems to point in the same direction."

"The friar at St. Apollinare," said the Marchese, with blue trembling lips, as he looked keenly into the lawyer's face; "why it is impossible that he could know anything about it. The friar—"

"Impossible? why impossible, Signor Marchese? We know that he was in the Pineta much about the time the deed must have been done."

The Marchese threw himself back in his deep easy chair, and covered his face with his hand. The lawyer paused, and shook his head as he looked at him.

"The friar in the Pineta!" he exclaimed, getting up from his chair after a minute or two, and taking a few disorderly steps across the room.

"You see; Signor Giovacchino," he continued, returning to his seat, "I have been so shaken by all the misery I have gone through, and all the sleepless nights I have passed, that—that—that I am hardly in a fit state to appreciate the value of the—the facts you lay before me. I have been trying to think—I am afraid—very much afraid for my own part that no weight is to be attributed to any testimony which may be got from the friar of St. Apollinare."

"Why so, Signor Marchese?" asked the lawyer, shortly.

"I know the old man very well. I have often talked with him. He is not in his right mind: certainly not in such a state of mind as would justify the magistrates in paying any attention to his statements," said the Marchese, in a more decided manner than he had before spoken.

"I spoke with the old man at some length the other day, and I cannot say that that was my impression at all. In my opinion he was quite enough in his senses to know how to withhold the information which, I suspect, he could give us if he would. May I ask, Signor Marchese, how long it is since you have spoken with him?"

"Oh! a long time. How could I speak to him, you know. I do not suppose he often comes into the city. And it is ever so long—a year or more—since I was out at St. Apollinare; as far as I can remember," said the Marchese, with a rapid sidelong glance at the lawyer; "but I am convinced the old man is not in his right mind," he added, not without some vehemence; "and it is dangerous to put any faith, or to build at all upon anything that such a person may say. Why, he is always seeing visions; and what is such an one's account worth of anything he may fancy himself to have seen."

"Well, Signor Marchese, the tribunal will form its own opinion upon that point. For my own part, I cannot help feeling glad of any scrap of evidence which tends to corroborate the opinion that the Marchese Ludovico has been erroneously and precipitately accused."

"Of course, Signor Giovacchino, of course. A chi lo dite! And I am truly obliged to you for coming to me with the news you have given me. But you can understand, perhaps—in part, Signor Giovacchino, in part—not altogether—what I have gone through in these days. My mind has been shaken—sadly shaken, amico mio. I shall never recover it—never," said the Marchese, letting his head fall on his bosom.

"Nay, Signor Marchese. I would fain hope it is not so bad as all that. Let this business of the trial be over, and the Marchese Ludovico, as I doubt not, entirely cleared and absolved, and all will yet go well. The rest is matter of sorrow which time may be trusted to heal."

"The trial! Ay, the trial. When—eh?—when is it likely to come off, Signor Giovacchino. Yes, as you say, it would be a good thing if that were over," said the Marchese, with a manner that indicated a high state of nervous irritability.

"It won't be long; there is little or no hope of any further light being thrown on the matter; some day next week, I should say; I don't think they will be longer than that; and the sooner the better—only, that I am afraid you may find the ordeal a disagreeable one."

"Who? I? Why should I—? That is, of course, on Ludovico's account—"

"Excuse me, Signor Marchese; but you must feel, surely, that it will be absolutely necessary for you to be present in court."

"I? I be present? Why, don't you see that I am unable to leave my chamber—shall probably never leave it again; how can I be present in court? It is out of the question."

"Your lordship will pardon me, Signor Marchese, if I point out to you that it is quite indispensable that you should appear in court on the occasion of the trial," returned the lawyer, firmly. "Your own excellent judgment, and sense of what is fitting and due to your own position, will, I am sure, put this matter in an unmistakeable light before you. Think a little what the inferences, the remarks, the suggestions would be to which your absence on such an occasion would give rise; not to mention that it can hardly be doubted that the tribunal will think it necessary to examine your lordship respecting certain points—"

"Me? What can I tell? What can it be necessary to examine me for? I know absolutely nothing; it is impossible that I should know anything of the matter; besides, I am too ill to leave my chamber."

"Of course, if Tomosarchi were, after visiting you by direction of the tribunal, to certify that you were not in a fit state—"

"I won't see Tomosarchi; no testimony can be needed to the fact that I am in no condition to leave the house; I tell you, Signor Fortini, I will not see him; I cannot see anybody."

"I fear, Signor Marchese, that it would be impossible in any other way to avoid complying with the request of the tribunal for your presence. Besides that, it would be far better, in every point of view, that you should show yourself in the court. The fact of your absence on such an occasion could not but be unpleasantly remarked on," urged the lawyer.

"Why? What can I be wanted for? What can I tell them? It is very evident that I am, and must needs be, utterly ignorant of the whole matter," returned the Marchese.

"There are various points on which the magistrates will, doubtless, wish for the information which your lordship can give them, although you may have no means of throwing any light on the main facts of the assassination. They will wish, for instance, to ask respecting the circumstances of the Marchese Ludovico's expedition to the Pineta. The police, you must remember, Signor Marchese, are already aware that you were cognizant of the Marchese Ludovico's intention of taking La Lalli to the Pineta. That has been ascertained from the admission of the Conte Leandro—"

"A thousand curses on the Conte Leandro," exclaimed the Marchese.

"His figure in the matter is a deplorable one, truly; but you can understand, Signor Marchese, that the court will desire to ask some questions of you on this head—nothing that you can have any difficulty in answering or any objection to answer; but I am sure you will see, on consideration, that it would have a very bad effect for your lordship to show the least desire to avoid being present."

"It will be most distasteful to me—very painful, indeed—I don't think it ought to be required of me under all the circumstances," pleaded the unhappy man.

"Unpleasant it will be, doubtless; the whole affair has not been a pleasant one for anybody concerned in it, Signor Marchese—for any one in Ravenna, I may say. But you may depend upon it that it will be the wish of the court and of everybody present to make it as little painful to you as possible. And it is my very serious and very urgent advice to you to make the necessary exertion, and not to express to any one either the intention or the wish to absent yourself."

And then the lawyer took his leave—not surprised that the Marchese, broken down and in the state in which he saw him, should feel it very disagreeable to face his fellow citizens on the occasion of the trial; but, perhaps, having some other thoughts in his mind besides those he expressed as to the ill effect likely to be produced by any refusal of the Marchese to make his appearance in the court.

CHAPTER VI

The Trial

The police authorities were longer in preparing their case than Signor Fortini had anticipated they would be; but at length it was known throughout the city that the day for the trial had been fixed. It was to take place on a Monday morning towards the latter part of Lent.

It had been rumoured in the city that the delay had been occasioned by hopes which the authorities had conceived that the female prisoner would be induced to make confession of the crime. The imprisonment and the repeated interrogatories she had undergone had produced a great effect upon her. She had become downcast to a very much greater degree than she had been in the days immediately following her arrest. She was very silent, refraining even from the earnest and frequent protestations of her innocence, which, during the early days of her imprisonment, she had seized every opportunity of making. She passed many hours apparently plunged in deep introspective thought; she wept much, and passed much of her time in prayer.

And the judgment of the experienced people about her led them to interpret these manifestations as signs of an approaching confession. When at length the day for the trial was fixed, it was reported that Paolina Foscarelli had confessed. But the criminal authorities keep the secrets of their prison house in such matters; and nothing certain was known upon the subject.

The very general impression, however, throughout the city was that, whether she confessed or not, she was the real criminal, and that such would be declared by the tribunal to be the case. And such a solution of the mystery was readily accepted by the Ravenna world as the most satisfactory that under the unhappy circumstances could be arrived at.

The disgrace that rested on the city in consequence of the perpetration of so foul a crime, and on such a victim, had been felt throughout the city to a degree, that can be duly appreciated only by those, who are acquainted with the strength and the exclusiveness of Italian municipal patriotism. And it was a matter of general congratulation that the perpetrator of it should turn out to be no Ravennata citizen, but an unknown stranger from Venice. It would have been dreadful indeed if such a deed should have been brought home to the door of a scion of the oldest and most distinguished noble family in Ravenna. Of course everybody had all along known, and had said from the beginning, that whatever might turn out to be the truth, this at least was impossible and altogether out of the question.

To many minds the guilt of the Venetian girl seemed so clear that it appeared altogether superfluous to spend time and trouble in bringing her to confess it. Her hatred of the victim she had confessed; and the confession of it was in evidence. The motive for that hatred was perfectly well known and understood. It was a motive that many a time ere now had led to similar deeds. She was close at hand when the crime must have been committed. She could give no satisfactory account of her reasons for going thither, or of the occupation of her time during the hours, which must have comprised the moment of the assassination. And the manner of the murder rendered it infinitely probable that it must have been the deed of a female. What more could be wanted? It was rarely that a murder had ever been brought home to the murderer by circumstantial evidence of a more conclusive and irresistible character.

Signor Fortini was among those who thought and reasoned thus. But in the several interviews which he had had with the Marchese Ludovico, he had not judged it judicious to enlarge to him on this part of the subject. While assuring him that he might make himself perfectly easy, and that his innocence in the matter would beyond all doubt be fully recognised, he had preferred to lead him to imagine that the result of the trial would be altogether negative; that it would be found that no case that would warrant a conviction should be made out against any party.

Signor Logarini had meanwhile made one or two more excursions to the Basilica of St. Apollinare. But he had gained nothing by his pains. The padre Fabiano was on each occasion found in bed, no whit better to all appearance than he had been on that day when the police Commissary and Signor Fortini visited him together. Nor had Signor Logarini's persevering cross-examinations availed to obtain anything more from the aged friar than repetitions of his first statements. Nevertheless the Commissary was confirmed more than ever in his opinion that the friar knew something; if he could only be made to speak. Still it had been determined not to attempt to bring the old man by force before the tribunal. There was every reason to think that nothing would be obtained from him in addition to what he had already said. In all probability he was really ill, more or less, as Signor Logarini said, and living under the government of the Holy Father, it was necessary to treat ecclesiastical personages with a greater degree of consideration than might have been accorded to such under similar circumstances on the other side of the frontier between the territory of the church and Austria.

Despite the friar's illness, however, Fra Simone, the lay-brother, had once or twice been observed lately in Ravenna. He was seen sauntering through the streets with his long linen wallet over his shoulder, stopping at a corner for a little gossip here, and receiving a contribution to the store in his bag from some friar-loving devout old woman there. There was nothing remarkable in such a sight in the streets of Ravenna in any way. Only Fra Simone was very rarely seen there. And when Signor Pietro Logarini, without whose knowledge scarcely a cat stirred abroad in Ravenna, was told of the circumstance, he said to himself that the Padre Fabiano was interested in knowing what people said and thought of the coming trial.

Signor Fortini had in the meantime, not without infinite difficulty succeeded in persuading the Marchese that he must bring himself to submit to the ordeal of being present in the court on the occasion of the trial. The Marchese's extreme dislike to appearing thus publicly had been in no degree overcome or diminished. And it was only the lawyer's positive and repeated declaration, that he would assuredly be sent for, if he did not spontaneously present himself, that had availed to induce him to say at length that he would go. Every possible attention, the lawyer had assured him, would be paid to him, and everything done to make his attendance as little disagreeable to him as possible. Of course, as Fortini urged, it was well known, through the city how dreadfully he must have been affected by the sad circumstances that had happened—people would be prepared to see him looking ill and changed. Curious? Yes, of course people were curious—it was impossible to prevent them from being so; but he, Fortini, would take care that their curiosity should not be manifested in any way that could be offensive to the Marchese.

Thus, an unwilling consent to attend the sitting of the court on the morning of the trial had been forced from the unhappy Marchese, from him who, so few weeks ago before the fatal coming of the fascinating singer to Ravenna, had been the happiest, the most prosperous, and the most secure of men; and it had been arranged that Signor Fortini should, on that morning; call for him at the Palazzo and accompany him to the tribunal.

When the morning came it seemed to Signor Fortini as if he should have to do all his work over again. He found the Marchese up and dressed. He had not shaved himself, however, declaring, with abundant appearance of truth, that, in the state he then was, it was utterly beyond his power to do so, and he absolutely refused to allow it to be done for him; and the effect of the stubbly grisled beard of a week's growth or so on the hollow lantern jaws, which all the city had been accustomed to see clean shaved, and plump, and florid with health, was such as to render him barely recognizable as the same man by the eyes that had known him all his life. It seemed, too, to the lawyer that the shocking change which had taken place in him was even more painfully marked by his attempt to dress himself in his usual manner than it had been in his chamber wrapper. His clothes, which were wont to fit so well, and set off to advantage his well-made and stalwart figure, hung about him in bags and pantaloon-like folds, a world too wide for his shrunken form.

On the first entrance of the lawyer he protested that the effort was altogether beyond his strength, that it was impossible for him to go through the ordeal. Did they want him to die before their eyes on the benches of the court?

A renewed suggestion by Fortini to the effect that the only means by which the necessity could be avoided would be by a certificate from the medical authority trusted in such matters by the court—his own old friend the Professor Tomosarchi, produced only a reiterated and violent declaration that he would not receive any visit from the Professor.

Eventually, the strong representations made by the lawyer of the much greater unpleasantness, and the very much to be deprecated effect, of entering the court as an unwilling witness in forced obedience to a mandate from the tribunal, decided the wretched Marchese to allow himself to be led down to the carriage.

Even as he came, bent and shaking, down the great staircase of the Palazzo leaning on Fortini's arm, and had to pass, in crossing the hall to the carriage, all the servants of his household, most of whom had not seen him since the evening of the last day of Carnival, and who were urged by curiosity to take this opportunity of looking at their terribly-changed master, it seemed to him that his martyrdom had commenced.

He passed through the streets of the city with the blinds of the carriage drawn down, and with his eyes closed as he lay thrown back into the corner of it: but, as he felt it draw up at the entrance to the "prefettura," he suddenly grasped the lawyer's hand, and Fortini felt, with a shudder, that his hand was as cold as that of a corpse. He was altogether in such a state that Signor Fortini began to fear that there really would be some catastrophe in the court before the business of the day could be concluded.

With the aid of a servant on one side and of the lawyer on the other, however, he was got out of the carriage, and, almost supporting him, the lawyer, who had made all his arrangements previously, led him into the building by a private door and to the chamber in which the tribunal was sitting by a private passage used only by the magistrates, and opening into the court in the immediate vicinity of the seats occupied by them, by the side of which a chair had been assigned to the Marchese.

Nor had Signor Fortini's cares and preparations ended there. He had spoken with each one of the magistrates who were to try the case, in no wise telling them of the Marchese's unwillingness to appear, but representing the terrible state of mental and bodily prostration to which the dreadful nature of the late events had very naturally reduced him, and which would have rendered it utterly impossible for him to appear in court, but for his indomitable will, and the high sense of duty, which had led him to think it, under the circumstances his duty to do so.

To no soul had he whispered a word of the Marchese's very marked reluctance to attend at the trial, save to his old and intimate friend of many years standing, the Professor Tomosarchi, whom he had thought it advisable to consult as to the desirability of his seeing the Marchese before he was called on to make the effort. To his surprise he had found Tomosarchi almost as unwilling to see the Marchese, as the Marchese had been to see him. He did not say at once, as the latter had done, that he would not see him, but while admitting the strong desirability that the Marchese should be present at the trial, he yet manifested a strong reluctance, which the lawyer could not understand, to taking any share in the task of persuading and preparing him to do so.

The magistrates, who were all of them old friends of Signor Fortini, and to each of whom he had spoken, separately on the subject, had seemed to find no difficulty in understanding, that it was very natural under all the circumstances, that the Marchese should have been terribly affected, both in body and mind, by the late events. It had been suggested to them by the lawyer, that it would be well to avoid, as far as possible, anything that should make it necessary for the Marchese to speak at all, even in saluting him on his entrance. When therefore, just after the court had assembled, the Marchese, trembling and shivering in every limb, was led in by the little door that opened close behind the seat he was to occupy, the magistrates contented themselves with rising and bowing to him in silence. The court, as might have been expected, was very full; and it was impossible to prevent a very marked and audible manifestation of the shock produced upon the spectators by the changed appearance of one so well known to them from running through the crowd.

Even in the territories of the Pope, a criminal court is in these days an open and public one. There is no jury, and the criminal, or suspected person, may be subjected to any amount of examination on oath. But, in other respects, the method of procedure is not very dissimilar from our own. The prosecution is conducted by an officer analogous to our attorney-general, or by his substitute; and is defended by any advocate of the court whom he may employ for the purpose. The appreciation of the credibility of testimony, the greater or lesser value of circumstantial evidence, the application and interpretation of the law, and the award of sentence, remain with the judges, subject to appeal to a higher court. Moreover, in the present case, the inquiry assumed more of the form of a general attempt to ascertain the solution of an unexplained mystery, than would have been compatible with the forms of our criminal courts, inasmuch as there were two prisoners to be tried for the crime, whom no theory of the circumstances had suggested to be accomplices, and the conviction of either of whom, according to the hypothesis which had been started, involved the absolution of the other.

The judicial oath is administered not as with us, but by requiring the accused person, or the witness, to assert that he is speaking the truth, while placing the extended hand on a carved representation of the crucified Redeemer. And there can be no doubt that this ceremony has a very strong effect on the imagination and nervous system among the easily moved races of the south. Many a crime has been avowed, because the paralyzed lips of the criminal were absolutely incapable of pronouncing the lie he fully purposed to speak, while he thus openly appealed to the material figure which had the power of enabling the sluggish southern imagination to realize the presence of the Creator.

There would be little interest in detailing at length the proceedings of the trial; since nothing was elicited that would be in any way new to the reader, or that was calculated to throw any fresh light on the circumstances to be inquired into, until the business in hand was nearly concluded.

Every tenderness had been shown to the misfortunes and to the terrible state of suffering of the Marchese. A full statement of his own conduct at the ball, and on the following morning, had been extracted, with very little indulgence in the process, from the Conte Leandro, from whose white and pasty face the perspiration had rained beyond the power of any handkerchief to control it, while he described himself as an eavesdropper, an informer, and a spy. And all that had been required from the Marchese Lamberto was the admission that the Conte Leandro's statements, as far as regarded what had taken place at the ball, were correct.

But the fact was that the case was well-nigh prejudged before the professed trial began. All Ravenna, including the police authorities, who had investigated the matter, and the judges who came into court well instructed in all that had been done, and all that could be known upon the subject, had made up their minds that the stranger girl was and must have been the criminal. It was infinitely more agreeable to everybody concerned to suppose that such should be the case rather than that such a damning blot should fall on the noblest house in the city, and that in the person of one of the most popular men in it; and, at the same time, it must be owned that the case was so strong against Paolina that a prejudice against her could hardly be called a corrupt one.

Her own conduct during the trial had tended yet farther to impress the minds of all present against her. Not that there was anything in her appearance and manner that was otherwise than calculated to conciliate pity and favourable opinion. Her entrance into the court had excited the greatest interest. She had on a black silk dress made in the simplest and plainest possible fashion; and the colour of it, where the neckband encircled her slender throat, made an absolutely startling contrast with the utterly colourless whiteness of her skin. Her manner was very subdued, very quiet; nor did she exhibit any signs of fear; or much of emotion, save to those who were near enough to her to perceive a quiet, silent, and undemonstrative tear steal occasionally down her dead-white cheek.

But when examined as to her disposal of herself after leaving the church of Apollinare—as to her motives for changing her purpose, if it were true, as she stated, that she did change her purpose of entering the Pineta—she became embarrassed and failed to give any satisfactory reply.

Ludovico had, at an early stage of the proceedings, been removed from the court, after having been in vain again and again requested by the judges to abstain from interfering with the progress of the case against Paolina.

At last, when almost everybody in the court had made up their minds that there could, in truth, be no doubt that the young Venetian, goaded to frenzy by her jealousy, had been the author of the murder, and quite everybody was convinced that such would be the decision of the judges, the latter were on the point of retiring from the court to confer, and consider their sentence, more as a matter of form, probably, than anything else, when an incident occurred that made a change in the aspect of matters.

CHAPTER VII

The Friar's Testimony

In a criminal trial in the states of His Holiness the Pope, there is none of that absolute and inflexible adherence to certain rigid forms and rules which gives to many of the proceedings of our courts that character of an inevitable destiny-like march which is so dramatic in its operations—that sense of the presence there of a power greater than that of the greatest of the men concerned in the administration of it, which constitutes on large element in an Englishman's respect for the law. At times this automatic power, which has been thus created Faust-like, by reason of the impossibility of pre-adapting its mechanism to the exigences of every case, works to unforseen and undesired ends—sometimes even to absurd ones. And, with thinkers of a certain phase of modern thought, it has been a favourite taunt against the average British mind, that it rather delights in the contemplation of such abnormal workings of the great automatic law in which it has created. Some manifest mistake or error has occurred. The man supposed to be murdered walks into court; but it is a minute too late; the verdict has been given—the sentence pronounced. All the court judges, witnesses, counsel—look at each other in dismay; the great law automaton cannot be made to swerve in its path by any power there. And the average Englishman likes the contemplation of such a case, it is sneered; and the sneer may be joined in by those who, under other systems, have the immediate power of setting any such mistakes right by a word. But the sneer, let the Englishman be assured, would by no means be joined in by the population, who are subject to the action of courts and judges thus able by superior word to direct the course of justice.

The new incident which suddenly arose to change all the aspects of the trial and its results would, as far as the analogy of the Roman mode of proceeding and our own holds good, have been too late in one of our courts to produce the results which it did produce. The judges were on the point of retiring to consider their decision and sentence when they were met at the little private door, by which they were about to leave the court, by one of the ushers. And the consequence of the few words he spoke to them was that they gave an order—turned back, and resumed their places.

It might well have been that the new incident might have been prevented from bringing about the result it was calculated to bring about in the Ravenna Court; but the miscarriage would have been caused in an altogether different way from that which has been spoken as sometimes characterising our own courts.

It was very clear to everybody present that the judges would pronounce Paolina to be guilty of the crime they were investigating; and to everybody present, with one or two exceptions, this was a very agreeable and satisfactory winding-up of the unhappy affair. Ravenna would be able to wash her hands of the matter. It was wholly, both in conception and execution, the work of a stranger. Since so great a misfortune had happened, it could not be more satisfactorily accounted for.

It is probable enough, therefore, that any Tom, Jack, or Harry, who, at that conjuncture, had presented himself at the prefettura for the avowed purpose of bringing a new light to the solution of the mystery which had been already so satisfactorily solved, might have experienced considerable difficulty in obtaining for himself any access to, or hearing from, the judges.

But the person who had now thus presented himself at the prefettura of Ravenna belonged to a body, the very lowest and poorest members of which, in that country, can always find, somehow or other, some means of compassing almost any object which is not disapproved by some superior member of their own corporation. The new-comer was a friar—old Father Fabiano, the priest of St. Apollinare, as the reader may have conjectured.

The police agents had been anxious to produce him there, as the reader knows, and he had baffled their wishes. Now the result which it had been desired that he should contribute to had been brought about, or as good as brought about, without him. What did he want there now?

There was an old usher about the court, however, whose advancing years were beginning to make him disagreeably conscious that the time was at hand when a sentence to a long term of purgatory—to say nothing of any severer doom—might make it exceedingly desirable to him to stand well with all those who are understood to have influence with the government in the world beyond the grave; and, if there had been no such person, the friar would have known somebody—some old or young woman, probably—or he would have known some other friar who knew some such, who would have been able to influence some brother, lover, or husband, in the way he wished. As it was, Father Fabiano had no difficulty at all in conveying the message he wished to communicate to the judges.

They turned back to their places in the court, to the surprise and sudden awakening of new interest in the audience, and ordered that the new witness who had presented himself should be admitted and heard.

And Father Fabiano, bowed with age, and his hoary head bent down on his breast, but neither shivering nor shaking, advanced to the witness-table. The crucifix was lying on it, and the friar, with the manner of a man recognizing in a new employment tools which he is well used to, at once stretched out his emaciated and claw-like hand, and made oath that he was about to speak the truth.

The Procuratore of the court then began to examine the old man with reference to his knowledge of the circumstances connected with the visit of Paolina Foscarelli to the church of St. Apollinare, and her disposal of herself after leaving it; but the friar replied that it would be uselessly occupying the time of the court to enter into any such particulars, inasmuch as he had come thither to prove that Paolina had nothing whatever to do with the crime.

"But," remarked the Procuratore, "if it is in your power to do that, why did you not give the necessary information to the Commissary of Police when you were, on several occasions, examined at St. Apollinare?"

"Signori miei," said the old man, addressing himself to the court in general, "it is no affair of mine to meddle with the administration of human justice. No words that I could say could undo the deed, or bring the murdered woman back to life. Evil enough had been done. Why should I cause further trouble, and sorrow, and shame, to others? It was more fitting to one of my order to leave retribution in the hands of Him who can best award it, and whose mercy may touch the heart of the sinner with repentance."

"But if so, frate mio," rejoined the Procuratore, "what, pray, is the motive that now brings you here?"

"Surely, the determination that the innocent shall not suffer for the guilty. It seemed to me that it would never be known, save to Him who knows the secrets of all hearts, what hand had done that terrible deed; but now I know that the fallibility of all human judgment has led questi Signori to the conclusion that the girl Paolina is guilty, and her condemnation would be a misfortune greater than the first—I knowing the hand which did that deed."

"Ha, you know the murderer; you suppose you know him? You come to offer us your guess, your suggestion?"

"I come, Signori miei, with pain and sorrow and great reluctance, to save you from condemning an innocent person by naming him who is guilty."

A sort of buzz and almost shiver of interest, anxiety, and expectation ran through the court, as the old friar spoke the above words in a stronger voice than that in which he had yet spoken.

"Friar," said the Procuratore solemnly and severely; "it is my duty, before you speak, to warn you to take heed to what you say. You are about, you say, to make an accusation the most tremendous that one man can bring against another. Bethink you whether you are able to substantiate what you are about to utter. Remember that, if you cannot substantiate it, it would be a hundred-fold better that your suspicion should remain unuttered."

The Procuratore, as well as every one else in the court, had little or no doubt that the friar was about to accuse the Marchese Ludovico as the perpetrator of the murder. And some, among whom were Signor Fortini, and Signor Logarini the Commissary of Police, were persuaded that the old man was going to trump up some story in the hope of saving his countrywoman, Paolina.

"Were it not for the necessity of protecting the innocent, Signori, God knows how much I should prefer to carry my terrible secret with me to the grave. Signori miei, these eyes SAW the deed done, that put the sleeping woman to death. Only God and I, the lowest of his servants! God and I saw the Marchese Lamberto di Castelmare do that deed!"

A loud indignant murmur of incredulity was beginning to rise throughout the crowded court, like the first getting up of a storm wind.

But it was suddenly hushed, and turned into a spasm of horror and intense shock, that made every man hold his breath, when the sound of a sudden heavy fall was heard; and it was seen that the Marchese Lamberto had fallen insensible to the ground.

CHAPTER VIII

The Truth!

The Professor Tomosarchi was in the court, and had been, as it happened, though unseen by the Marchese, fixing his eyes on him at the moment when the catastrophe narrated in the last chapter occurred. Springing forwards, therefore, the medical man was in a moment by the side of his old friend.

If, according to the strict letter of the requirements of their duty, the magistrates or the police authorities present ought, under the circumstances, to have prevented the free departure of the accused man to his own home, it did not occur to any one to do so. Professor Tomosarchi and Fortini between them, got him, still insensible, to his carriage, and took him to his home.

"Is it more than a mere fainting fit?" said the lawyer, as they both were supporting the person of the insensible Marchese. "Could you not do some thing to restore consciousness? Can that old friar have spoken the truth?"

"Apoplexy," said the Professor, with a serious and almost scared look into the other's eyes. "Apoplexy, and no mistake about it. Don't you hear the stertorous breathing. No, nothing can be attempted till we get him home. We shall be at the palazzo in a minute. We shall see; but I doubt—I doubt!"

"You mean that his life is in danger?" asked the lawyer.

"In danger! I have hardly any hope that he will ever return to consciousness or speak another word again."

"Good God! you don't mean that," cried the lawyer, much shocked.

"Indeed I do; it is possible, but very improbable that he should rally sufficiently to survive the attack," replied the Professor.

"Perhaps," rejoined the lawyer, gravely and sadly after a few moments of silence; "perhaps it would be best so. I fear me—I much fear me, that this can hardly be looked on but as the confirmation of that old man's declaration."

The Professor looked hard into the lawyer's eyes, as he nodded his head, without speaking, in grave assent.

They arrived in another minute at the door of the Palazzo Castelmare. The servants ran out, and they carried him up into the chamber where, ever since that fatal Ash Wednesday morning, he had, as Fortini now well understood, been suffering a long agony of remorse, apprehension, despair, all the intensity of which it was difficult to appreciate.

Life was not yet extinct when they laid him upon his bed; and the Professor proceeded to do what the rules of his science prescribed in the all but hopeless effort to combat the attack. But the miserable man had suffered his last in this life, and every effort to bring him back to further torture was unavailing. Within half-an-hour after he had been brought back to his palace he breathed his last.

"It is all over with him," said the Professor, looking up across the bed to the lawyer standing on the other side of it; "there was no possibility of prolonging his life—happily for him, and happily for everybody connected with him, and for all of us. Who would have thought a short month ago that such a life could have so ended?"

"The 24th of March, Signor Professore, is the anniversary on which, more fervently than on any other day of the year, I thank God for all his mercies," said the lawyer, with grim solemnity.

"I don't understand you, Signor Dottore; what has the 24th of March to do with this?" said Tomosarchi, staring at him.

"On the 24th of March, four-and-forty years ago, the Signora Fortini departed this life, Signor Professore. But for that gracious disposition of Providence, who knows that his lot, or worse, might not have been mine? From Eve downwards, Signor Professore, from Eve downwards, it is the same story—always the same story, in one shape or another—in one shape or another."

The Professor, who was the lawyer's junior by some thirty years, turned away with a shrug of the shoulders, and stepped across the room to the small escritoire near the window. There opening, without hesitation, and with the manner of a man familiar with the place, a small concealed drawer, he called the lawyer to him.

"Just come here and look at the contents of this drawer, Signor Fortini. There is a curious meaning in them."

Fortini went across from the bed to the escritoire, and the Professor took from the drawer and showed to him a small coloured drawing of a human form, with just such a mark on it as had been visible on the spot of the wound which had destroyed La Bianca's life. He showed him also, in the same secret receptacle, a long very finely tempered needle, and a small quantity of perfectly white wax.

"Good God, Professor! Were you aware of the existence of these things here?" cried the lawyer, aghast.

"I knew that they were where I have now found them some four or five months ago—towards the end of last year. You do not remember, probably, some curious details of a crime that was perpetrated a year ago or more in the island of Sardinia. I don't know that the details were published save in the medical journals. You know how great an interest our unfortunate friend used to take in all such matters. We talked over that curious case. He doubted the possibility of causing death with so little violence, and by means which should leave so little trace behind them. I showed him how readily and easily it might be done. You may judge then, Signore Dottore, of the misgivings that assailed me when I discovered how that unhappy singer had been put to death. You will understand, too, why he so absolutely refused to see me, and how little desirous I was to see him."

"But, Signor Professore—what should you have done if—?"

"If that girl had been condemned. You may guess that my state of mind has not been a pleasant one. I did not know what to do: I hoped that no conviction would have been arrived at. Of course it would have been impossible to keep silence while that poor girl suffered the penalty of the crime I had such strong reason to think was the work of another. Truly it is in all ways best as it is."

"You are taking it for granted that the tribunal will give credit to the friar's testimony; but that is not certain; nay, it is not certain—at least, we do not yet know—we have only his assertion that he saw the Marchese do the deed. With these evidences before us," continued the lawyer, "we can hardly doubt that the fact was so. But stay—what is this?—a letter addressed to me—'Al Chiarmo Signor Dottore Giovacchino Fortini. To be opened only after my death, and in case my death shall happen within one year from the present time!' Perhaps this may render any further doubts as to the conduct we ought to pursue unnecessary. Let us see."

And Signor Fortini sat down to open and read the packet; while the Professor returned to the bed on which the dead man was lying, and occupied himself with paying the last duties to his friend's remains.

The letter was a very long one, consisting of several sheets of closely-written paper. It is unnecessary to add to these pages by giving a transcript of it, because the facts which it detailed at length are either such as the reader is already acquainted with or such as he can readily imagine for himself.

When the narrative reached the events which had occurred at the ball in the early hours of the Ash Wednesday morning, after mentioning the circumstance of the information which had been conveyed to the writer by the Conte Leandro Lombardoni as to the projected expedition to the Pineta, the Marchese went on to describe the state of mind in which he had left the Circolo. He protested that, although every smallest detail of what he did had remained stamped on his memory with a vivid clearness that would never more be obliterated, it would be unjust to judge his conduct as that of a man in the possession of his senses. He was, he said, mad—MAD!—and carried away by a hurricane of passions altogether beyond his power to control. He had not formed any distinct intention of following his nephew and La Bianca to the Pineta till he reached his own house. He had happened to approach the Palazzo from the back, through the stable-yard; and had there found old Niccolo, the groom, up. Then the idea of waylaying the pair in the forest had occurred to him. He had ordered a horse to be saddled; and had told the groom to let no one know that he had left the palace. He then went up to his room, dismissed his valet, and locked the door, as the servant had related to Signor Fortini. Then descending to the stables, by one of those private doors and stairs so frequently to be found in old Italian palaces, and generally contrived to communicate with the principal sleeping chamber of the dwelling, he mounted his horse, and rode furiously to the Pineta, quitting the city, not by the Porta Nueva, but by the next gate towards the south. He must have reached the forest before Ludovico and Bianca had left the city. He put his steaming horse into the abandoned hovel of a watcher of the cattle on the marshes; and then skulked about the edge of the wood in the vicinity of the road which enters it from the city. All this time he had, as he again and again declared in the long and repetitive document in the lawyer's hands, no formed intention of any sort in his mind. All he knew was that he was mad, and suffering torments worse than any imagination had ever depicted the tortures of the damned; the pulses were beating, and the blood was rushing in his ears and in his eyes, he wrote, in such sort that all sounds seem to him one universal buzzing, and all objects vague and uncertain, and tinged with the colour of blood.

And, in this condition, he waited and waited till almost a wild hope began to creep upon him that the Conte Leandro had lied to him.

Suddenly he saw them coming towards the edge of the wood.

With difficulty, he stood upright, resting the front of his shoulder and his forehead against the trunk of a tree, from behind which he glared out, while his eyes were blasted by what he saw.

Judging more sanely than the poor Marchese was able to judge, and putting together all the circumstances and conduct and declarations of the other parties, we may probably conclude, that though he saw enough to madden the heart and brain of a man whose mind had already been warped and distorted by jealousy, he did not see aught that could have been deemed to menace the future happiness of Paolina. No doubt La Bianca, despite her declared intention to make the Marchese Lamberto a good and true wife, had he married her, would have preferred to become Marchese di Castelmare by a marriage with his nephew. No doubt she had a liking for Ludovico of a different kind from that which she had professed to feel for his uncle. No doubt her imagination had been fired, and her heart awakened to long for such love as she had seen given to each other by Ludovico and Paolina, which she too well understood to be of a kind which, despite her good resolutions, would not be found in her union with the Marchese Lamberto. And no doubt these feelings manifested themselves in her visible manner during the conversation which followed her confession to him of the engagement between her and his uncle.

It may also be suggested to those who have never been called upon to act as Ludovico was called upon to act, under the circumstances of receiving such a communication, so communicated from such a woman, that they would do well not to judge too severely any such parts of his behaviour under the ordeal, as may have been of a nature to produce a very deplorable effect on the jaundiced mind of his uncle, though, in reality, there was little real meaning and less serious harm in them.

Of course the unfortunate Marchese could not be expected to see or reason on what he saw in any such mood or tone. As he said in the writing he had left, what he saw as Ludovico and Bianca entered the forest, side by side, in deep and close talk, made a furious madman of him. He dodged, and watched them, as they sat down together—as they continued to talk in close confidence—till he saw her lay herself down on the bank to sleep, and saw him after a while quit her side.

Then the devil entered into him, and ruled his hand with a whirlwind power which he could no more withstand than the chaff can withstand the tempest blast.

He came and stood over her as she lay on the turf—the beautiful, noxious creature. She had destroyed him; body, soul, and mind, she had destroyed him. And now—and now—ahi, ahi! After all he had suffered, after paying all the price he had paid! Ah, how lovely as she lay there sleeping—placidly sleeping, she! And he was to be cheated! Her beauty, her love was to be given to another.

No, no, no, poisonous, baneful, sorceress; no, be what might, that hell should never be!

He put his hand to the breast-pocket of his coat, and took from it a small pocket-book.

If man will find evil passions, the devil will always find means. Surely there must be some shadow of truth in the old legends that tell how the fiend aids those who give themselves to him.

The Marchese had, on leaving his chamber, quickly changed the coat he had worn at the ball for a morning one. And it so happened that in that was a pocket-book which contained the articles needed for the perpetration of the murder, placed there by him one day—in times that seemed now ages ago—when he was going to ask some explanation of the facts that had interested him from Professor Tomosarchi.

Like a balefully illumining lightning gleam, the clear memory that those things were there at his hand flashed across his mind.

In another minute the deed was done.

And, in a few minutes more, the Marchese, looking the madman he felt himself to be, got off his panting horse in his own stable-yard, threw the rein to the scared old groom, and regained his room as he had left it. Then the letter went on to speak of the terrible, the dreadful days and hours which had elapsed since that time. It was during the hours of that first morning, while it seemed to the excited mind of the Marchese that every sound that was audible in the Palazzo must herald the coming of those who had discovered the deed, that it had occurred to him to send for his lawyer and give him instructions for the preparation of his marriage contract. He would lose nothing by doing so, for the fact of his offer of marriage to the murdered woman would assuredly not be kept secret by the old man, her reputed father, and the maid-servant. And the fact of his declaring such an intention, and giving such instructions at that date, would very powerfully contribute to prevent any mind from conceiving the idea that he could have been cognizant of the death of La Bianca at the moment when he was so acting.

And in truth, as the lawyer, examining his own mind, said to himself, it had been this fact which had mainly prevented two or three little circumstances from pointing his suspicions in the direction of the truth.

CHAPTER IX

Conclusion

Little more need be added to complete this story of a great singer's Carnival engagement, and the consequences that arose out of it.

The consternation, the talk, the moralizings, of the little city may be readily imagined.

Of course the written statement left by the unhappy Marchese made all further judicial inquiry unnecessary. When the hand of a mightier power than that of any earthly judge struck him down before the eyes of all that world whose good opinion he had valued so highly, in the manner that has been related, the tribunal, of course, declared the business before it to be suspended. The result made it needless ever to resume the sitting. No retarded evidence against the Marchese had been given in court—no record of any accusation against him remained in the archives of it: and this was deemed to be a great point among a people who do not, by any means, hold that the law is the same "de non apparentibus et de non existentibus."

Of course there was no further obstacle to the marriage, in due time, of Ludovico and Paolina. A proper interval had, of course, to be allowed to elapse before the knot was definitively tied; but it was settled, and known to be settled by all Ravenna, and the strange and moving circumstances which had attended the young Marchese's fortunes had the effect of causing his marriage with the Venetian artist to be accepted by the "Society" more tolerantly than, perhaps, might otherwise have been the case. There was a sort of feeling that the whole affair was exceptional; that the higher powers had visibly taken the management of it into their own hands; that it was destined so to be, and must be, as such, accepted. Too much of pity, of wonder, of congratulation, and of condolence, were due from all his world to leave any space for censure on account of his marriage.

Doubtless there were explanations between them as to that hapless expedition to the Pineta; and doubtless they were satisfactory. Assuredly Ludovico never in his moments of most severe self-examination, sharpened, as such self-examination was, by the terrible nature of the result which had seemed to grow out of his conduct on that Ash Wednesday morning, could accuse himself of having done aught that could reasonably be held to leave at his door the responsibility of the events that had followed from it. Italian men are not apt to bring into any prominence the idea that where evil or misfortune is found their fault of some kind must exist also. They are content, for the most part, to accept the notion that all such matters are sufficiently accounted for by attributing them to "disgrazia"—the absence of favour, that is to say—the want of that favour at the Heavenly Court which it is on every occasion of life seen to be so necessary to successful well-being to possess at the Courts of Heaven's ecclesiastical, or lay vice-gerents.

Paolina insisted on employing a part of the time which necessarily elapsed before her marriage in completing the engagement she had undertaken, and the promise she had made to her English patron. But she found herself compelled to beg that some other specimen, chosen from among the wonderful wealth of early Christian art that remains at Ravenna, might be substituted for that in the choir of St. Apollinare. She made the attempt to return to the scaffolding by the side of the window, but she found that her strength was unequal to the task. She could not bear to look on the prospect from that window. By agreement with her employer, some further figures from the mosaics in San Vitale were substituted for those which had originally been selected in St. Apollinare. Her associations with the former church were of a more pleasant character; and Paolina never visited the desolate old building "in Classe" again. When the specimens selected in lieu of those in the latter building had been completed, Paolina and her friend and protectress returned with them to Venice, where it had been arranged that they were to be delivered to the Director of the Gallery.

In the ensuing Carnival Ludovico came hither, and the marriage was there solemnized. It is not intended to insinuate that he had not often made the journey from Ravenna to Venice in the interval. More of his time was probably passed there than in his native city. From Venice the newly married couple proceeded to Rome, and it was not till three or four years later, that the Marchese and Marchesa di Castelmare, bringing with them their two boys Lamberto and Ludovico, and their little Violante, the most exquisite little fairy that ever was seen, returned to make the Marchese's ancestral palace, ancestral city, their home.

There was one other stranger in Ravenna whose lamentations over the fate that had ever brought him thither were as loud as they were sincere. The poor old singing-master, Quinto Lalli, was left, by the death of his adopted daughter, as destitute of the means of support as desolate in his home and heart. He was not worth much; but it would be unjust to suppose of him that his violent outcry on her murderer was wholly or mainly prompted by the former consideration. There had been a real and strong affection between him and his adopted daughter, and her death in truth left him utterly desolate.

Yet he never again quitted the city he so much regretted having ever seen. His comfortable support was adequately provided for by the Marchese Ludovico. And often in after years—on summer evenings on a stone bench beneath a fig-tree in the garden of the cottage provided for him, and in winter at the chimney corner of its tiny parlour—might be seen the tall spare nun-like figure of a grave and gentle lady, earnestly labouring at the somewhat up-hill task of consoling the old man, and striving to shape the teachings of his Bohemian life to a better lesson than he was apt to draw from them. It was the Contessa Violante; and it may be concluded from her occupation both that she succeeded in escaping the pursuit of the Duca di San Sisto, and that her great-uncle the Cardinal did not succeed in becoming Pope at the most recent vacancy.

After the return of the Marchese and Marchesa di Castelmare to Ravenna, however, the greater number of the hours of the Contessa Violante were spent in the home of her little god-daughter Violante di Castelmare, and of her friend Paolina.

Thomas Adolphus Trollope – A Concise Bibliography

A Summer in Brittany. London. 1840, 2 volumes.
A Summer in Western France. 1841, 2 volumes.
Impressions of a Wanderer in Italy, Switzerland, France, and Spain. 1850.
The Girlhood of Catherine de Medici. 1856.
A Decade of Italian Women. 1859. 2 volumes.
Tuscany in 1849 and 1859. London. 1859.
Filippo Strozzi: A History of the Last Days of the Old Italian Liberty. 1860.
Paul V the Pope and Paul the Friar: A Story of an Interdict. 1860.
La Beata: A Novel. 1861. 2 volumes.
Marietta: A Novel. 1862.
A Lenten Journey in Umbria and the Marches of Ancona. 1862.
Giulio Malatesta: A Novel. 1863.
Beppo the Conscript. 1864.
Lindisfarn Chase. 1864.
A History of the Commonwealth of Florence From the Earliest Independence of the Commune to the Fall of the Republic in 1531. 1865. 4 volumes.
Gemma: A Novel. 1866.
Artingale Castle. 1867. 3 volumes.
Dream Numbers. 1868.
Leonora Casaloni: or The Marriage-Secret. 1869. 2 volumes.
The Garstangs of Garstang Grange. 1869. 3 volumes.
A Siren. 1870. 3 volumes.
Durnton Abbey: A Novel. 1871. 3 volumes.
The Stilwinches of Combe Mavis: A Novel. 1872. 3 volumes.
Diamond Cut Diamond. 1875. 2 volumes.
The Papal Conclaves, As They Were and As They Are. 1876.
A Peep Behind the Scenes at Rome. 1877.
The Story of the Life of Pius the Ninth. 1877. 2 volumes.
Sketches from French History. 1878.
What I Remember, 1887. 2 volumes.
The Further Reminiscences of Mr. T. A. Trollope. 1889 A third volume to the above.